Philomath, Oregon

How Do I Love Thee

How Do I Love Thee

by Lucille Iremonger

William Morrow and Company, Inc.
New York   1976

Printed in the United States of America.

1 2 3 4 5   80 79 78 77 76

Library of Congress Cataloging in Publication Data

Iremonger, Lucille.
    How do I love thee.

    1. Browning, Robert, 1812-1889, in fiction, drama, poetry, etc.
2. Browning, Elizabeth Barrett, 1806-1861, in fiction, drama, poetry, etc.
I. Title.
PZ3.I6405Ho3   [PR6017.R45]   823′.9′14   75-34315
ISBN 0-688-03013-0

Design: H. Roberts

How do I love thee? Let me count the ways.
I love thee to the depth and breadth and height
My soul can reach, when feeling out of sight
For the ends of Being and ideal Grace.
I love thee to the level of everyday's
Most quiet need, by sun and candle light.
I love thee freely, as men strive for Right;
I love thee purely, as they turn from Praise.
I love thee with the passion put to use
In my old griefs, and with my childhood's faith.
I love thee with a love I seemed to lose
With my lost saints—I love thee with the breath,
Smiles, tears, of all my life!—and if God choose,
I shall but love thee better after death.

—*Sonnets from the Portuguese* by Elizabeth Barrett Browning

INTRODUCTION

EVER SINCE MY CHILDHOOD ROBERT AND ELIZABETH
Browning have been part of my life.

When the mere handful of my maternal ancestors who escaped the guillotine fled France after the Revolution, they took
refuge in San Domingo in the West Indies. After another revolution there they made the short sea journey to Jamaica. That was
how I came to be born in the island from which the families of
both Robert and Elizabeth sprang and to share much of the same
background. I was a passionate reader of their poems, and at an
unusually early age I chose Robert's collected works for my first
school prize. The two poets seemed to belong to me in a very
special way, and when my father, whose roots were in England,
sent me "home" I took every opportunity of visiting their beloved
Florence and the Casa Guidi. Over the years I read everything
I could find about them.

There were many splendid books to be had, biographies and
works of scholarship, and many articles in academic periodicals—
literally thousands of them—and wonderful collections of their
letters to friends and relations. If one devoted years of study and
much effort to reading them, an almost unbelievable story unfolded itself. Yet the general public, to whom it surely belonged,
was largely ignorant of it. That the world was fascinated by the
legend of the Brownings had been made clear by the resounding
and long-lasting success of *The Barretts of Wimpole Street*. Yet
that play had hardly touched on the riches available, and its sug-

gestion of an incestuous relationship between Elizabeth and her father seemed crude and uninteresting compared with the truth. Who would write the book, for people like me, which brought together the known facts about these poets and said the things about them which had not yet been said?

Then my American publisher asked me to write a book about Robert and Elizabeth Browning.

I was, and am, a historical biographer. Facts are sacrosanct to me, and it is a pain to tamper with them. Yet it is a novel that I have written, since I decided that only in that form could I have the freedom to tell the story as I saw it, though building it on a framework of jealously guarded facts. There has, I believe, been no distortion or falsification of the characters of Robert and Elizabeth or of the events and phases of their lives. Only in the interest of clarity, simplicity and momentum of the narrative have I tinkered with the strict truth, and then but slightly—where life has been, as it so often is, untidy, repetitive, inexplicit, enigmatic, confused or tedious. Accuracy has been preserved in matters as large as the events of the Italian War of Liberation and as small as the courses and cost of a particular meal for four in Florence in 1847. I hope that readers will be interested enough to go themselves to the excellent biographies which already exist and above all to the collections of letters. There they will find, perhaps to their surprise, how little in this book is fictional and how almost incredible was the real truth. A short list of selected books at the end of this volume may be of use.

I would like here to thank Messrs. William Collins, Sons and Company, Limited, publishers, and especially Mr. Philip Ziegler, for their generosity in allowing me to interrupt work on my biography of the fourth Earl of Aberdeen, Britain's Prime Minister in the Crimean War, in order to write this book; the late Marquess of Aberdeen and Temair, his widow the Marchioness, and the present Marquess, for their patience and understanding in the same situation; Mr. Bruce Hunter of David Higham Associates, Limited, for his sensitive, imaginative and unflagging support and encouragement; and Mr. Hillel Black of William Morrow and Company, Incorporated, for the warmth, enthusiasm and artistry in human relations which have made our association an unfailing pleasure.

For expert help in various fields, grateful thanks are also due to Sir Alec Douglas-Home, for information about the diplomatic situation in Florence during Robert and Elizabeth's stay there; to Dr. J. C. Macaulay, F.R.C.P., M.D., who put me on the right road to research about opium addiction; to Miss Susan Mayor (Mrs. J. Mordaunt Crook), head of the Costume Department at Christie's, for her knowledge of period dress; to Mr. John Somerville of the Old Masters Department at Sotheby's, for information about pictures; to the Hon. Christopher Lennox-Boyd, for sharing his antiquarian knowledge; to Mrs. Anna Sanna, for answering my queries about the Italian language and the customs of Florence; to the Principal of the Archive Section of the Bank of England, for details of the careers of Robert Browning's father and grandfather; to the Director of the Post Office, for supplying facts about the postal services of the period; to the Directeur General of the Archives de France, for replying in detail and at length to my historical queries; to the Special Collections Librarian of the Wellesley College Library, for her kind response to my enquiries; and to the Librarian and staff of Chelsea Library, for allowing me extended facilities for my research, and for their helpfulness and courtesy.

I acknowledge also with gratitude the permission to quote from copyright material most generously given by John Murray, Limited, publishers.

LUCILLE IREMONGER
34 Cheyne Row
Chelsea, London
(Five doors up from Thomas Carlyle's house)

1

HIS HAIR WAS SO BLACK AND HIS SKIN SO DARK that his vivid blue eyes came as a surprise. He seemed not to be a part of the City, with his horseman's gait and his carefree air. He smiled at the passersby as if he wanted to share his happiness. They froze, of course, into affronted English blankness.

It was Tuesday, May 20, 1845, and Robert Browning had looked forward to that day for three years. He could think of nothing but the woman he was going to meet when the clocks chimed their three slow strokes. The bells of London too should ring out. What was fated to be was about to be. All his life his instincts had guided him to the path he must take, and he had taken it.

At three o'clock he would be bowing before the most wonderful woman in the world. That Miss Elizabeth Barrett was so ill—dying, she had seemed to say in that letter—made the thought of her the more achingly sweet. Could a caged nightingale live? Perhaps the loveliness of her songs could only be born of pain. He would enter that frowning house which had barred him until now, see her face and kiss her hand, and she would allow him to love her. That was all he asked.

Meanwhile, in a back bedroom up two flights of stairs in the solid brick mansion towards which the dark young man was briskly walking a frail middle-aged woman was going through a nervous crisis. The room was dark and stuffy and full of heavy furniture. The woman was small and plain and very unhappy.

Miss Elizabeth Barrett was on the verge of panic, cold with terror simply because a young man called Robert Browning was coming to see her and talk about poetry. She had forgotten that she had been the idol of literary London since the publication of her last two volumes of poetry nine months before, in the autumn of 1844, and that she was already famous in America. She could only think that she was a wretched invalid who had been sealed up in that room for six years. Almost literally sealed up, for the edges of its three large windows had been pasted over with brown paper during the cold months, and her father had had a double door lined with green baize put up to shut out the air more effectively and soundproof her from footsteps and voices on the stairs.

She was used to her prison now. She liked its silence. The breathing of her little dog Flush was its loudest sound, then the gentle ticking of her clock, then the beating of her own over-excitable heart. She liked the dark, too. She didn't want to be disturbed.

Hardly anyone, no matter how distinguished, had been allowed to see her. She had refused Wordsworth twice, though he had descended from his pedestal to ask. She had made excuses to the young Tennyson, whom she admired to distraction. It was better so. She did not want a man's eyes on her as she now was. No man came into that room unless he was a member of her family or so old a friend that he might as well be one. Outside the family the only man who still saw in her the bright flower of a girl she had been was George Hunter, the battered old clergy-man who had pursued her for twelve years. Strange that he, so spiteful to her in all other ways, should be blind to the cruel changes of the years.

Now she was facing just what she had been avoiding for six years. She did not know who to blame, herself for weakness, or the young man for having forced himself upon her. He was coming only on condition that the visit was not to be mentioned. At least the gates would not be opened to other lioness hunters. In the meanwhile there he was, almost at the door, his eyes already on her.

She looked up at the wall, where an engraving of him hung beside those of Tennyson and Wordsworth and Carlyle, all uniform and all framed to match. How young he looked. How much a part of the world she had left.

It was hard to believe that this tiny, dark, brittle woman sitting despairingly on the edge of her sofa, with an Indian shawl clutched round her childish shoulders although the May afternoon was warm, was only thirty-nine. Her small oval face was drawn and sickly. She could never have been a beauty, but she must once have been seductive. There was something engaging about the nose so much too small for the wide full-lipped mouth with up-curling corners. The black velvet eyes under sweeping brows would have been huge in any face; in that fine, thin one they were enormous. Only the thick mahogany-coloured hair, with its shower of heavy curls on her shoulders, and the languid white hands, held any memory of youth. Her body was painfully thin. She moved with caution, as if she was afraid that those bird bones might easily break.

Now, perched on the edge of her large sofa, she was trying to see her room through the eyes of a young man-about-town unused to invalid spinsters. It had not yet had its May spring cleaning. Next week she would be carried into her father's bedroom next door, and all three windows would be thrown open. The months of dust would be swept up and out, the spiders and their webs would vanish, and her golden cocker spaniel would walk under the bed once more. Now it was at its worst.

At the thought of the poet's sensitive nostrils she seized a phial from the plush-covered table beside her. Immediately violent sneezes came from the little dog on the hearthrug.

"Flush, you fraud, it's not eau-de-cologne, and I haven't taken the cork out!"

She sprinkled vigorously, and the nose-tingling fumes of West Indian bay rum filled the room. The little dog sneezed even more dramatically and pawed his nose.

Mr. Browning could not fail to realize that the great sofa was a bed for all its scrolled head, fringed covers and rugs; nor that the smaller one pushed near the window was another. They might as well have been four-posters. Then, who could mistake that massive wardrobe for anything but a wardrobe, marble busts or no? She remembered Papa coming into the room with his arms full of those five fine heads, his lavish surprise gift to lift her out

13

of her depression at moving to this house which she hated, in this London wreathed in yellow mists, where not a leaf nor a sparrow but had soot on it. Three of them had gone on top of the wardrobe, and two on the bookshelves lined with red merino which dear Septimus and Octavius, Papa's seventh and eighth sons, had put up over the washstand and the chest of drawers. No one, she had thought then, would notice their lower halves for admiring Chaucer and Homer.

Mr. Browning would not be fooled for a moment. The famous poetess would be seen to be living side by side with her chest of drawers and her washstand and her wardrobe, and receiving gentlemen in her musty bedroom-sickroom.

Only that transparent blind which she had hung at the window last autumn, with its hand-painted scenes of castles and arched gateways and groves and strolling peasants, still seemed charming. Yet Papa had said, "It looks like the back window in a confectioner's shop." Perhaps Mr. Browning would think so too.

At least the ivy root her cousin Mr. Kenyon had given her for a window box had thrived, and its coarse leaves obscured the panes in a satisfactory black tangle. They blotted out the chimney pots and the grimy walls outside and made the room darker. Darkness was kind to her. It could not be too dark, that afternoon, to protect her from Mr. Browning's seeking young man's eyes, in which she would read a sick disappointment.

Mr. Browning was only thirty-three, and he was a man with an eye for fine fleshy women. His poems breathed passion and sensuality. Everywhere he exclaimed at laughing blue eyes and red mouths and long golden hair, at bare white shoulders and full breasts and plump round arms. The splendid young bodies were kissed all over till they burned, and even their souls were kissed out in a burning mist. His lovers did not stop short at burning kisses either, and his husbands were to the last man racked by precise imaginings of their wives' infidelities.

In the very midst of that enchanting poem where the little girl Pippa passed through the world on New Year's Day, inspiring everyone with her innocent childish songs, had suddenly come those carnal lovers. Straight from the murder of Ottima's husband, they lay remembering the first transports of their adulterous love.

OTTIMA: So lay we till the storm came.
SEBALD: How it came!

14

OTTIMA: Buried in woods we lay, you recollect;
      Swift ran the searching tempest overhead;
      And ever and anon some bright white shaft
      Burned through the pine-tree roof, here burned
        and there,
      As if God's messenger through the close wood screen
      Plunged and replunged his weapon at a venture,
      Feeling for guilty thee and me: then broke
      The thunder like a whole sea overhead,
      While I stretched myself upon you, hands
      To hands, my mouth to your hot mouth, and shook
      All my locks loose, and covered you with them . . .
                    Sebald, as we lay . . .
      Who said, "Let death come now! 'Tis right to die!"?

This hot-blooded, lascivious Mr. Browning was handsome, though her dear friend Miss Mitford wouldn't admit it. Elizabeth was the most fervent admirer of his poetry, so full of nobility as well as genius. Nothing in it shocked her—in private. She would always defend him. But it would be better to leave it at that.

If he thought that he was coming to sweep a silly and pathetic woman off her feet with his practiced charm, he was mistaken. If he was set on one of those heated affairs with his sinning Junos he would repent as soon as he saw her. She wished she did not mind the thought of his eyes so much.

Suddenly a shaft of sunshine broke through the light clouds of May and lit the geraniums and nasturtiums in the window box to glowing scarlet and orange against the black ivy. It lit the transparent blind, too, and the whole room came alive.

The door opened and Arabel Barrett came in. She had curls and a wide mouth like her sister, but her hair was fair, and where Elizabeth's chin was small and rounded hers was square. Arabel was at peace with herself, a kindly woman of thirty-two who had abandoned youth and now found fulfillment in serving her God and others.

"Oh, Arabel, I can't see him," Elizabeth's light voice climbed high in her distress. "I should never have given him permission to call."

"You surprised me, I must say, Ba," Arabel said imperturbably.

"He simply wouldn't take no for an answer. He's been writing to me every other day for five months."

They both glanced up at his picture. Arabel knew that the poets and authors on Ba's wall were among those nominated for eternal fame by Richard Hengist Horne, Elizabeth's peculiar editor friend, in his book, *The New Spirit of the Age*. Elizabeth had helped that raffish pursuer of heiresses to assess living pretenders to genius. Luckily only Mr. Horne's name had appeared on the book, and she had escaped the storm of fury which met it from those who were included and those who were left out. It had been a foolish undertaking—who could ever praise authors enough?—and Horne had fled to Germany to lick his wounds, leaving Ba her set of illustrations. She had framed her four favourites, and there they hung on her wall.

"He doesn't *look* very obstinate," Arabel smiled at the profile of a girlish young man with soft side whiskers, an oversweet little mouth under a large nose, and a rather weak chin.

"Well, he is. I'd like to meet him and talk about poetry. Only—I cannot. It's too much for me."

"Are you sure it wouldn't do you good, Ba?"

"No, no. He frightens me. Do you know how he began his first letter to me, a complete stranger? 'I love your verses with all my heart, dear Miss Barrett, and I love you too!' "

Arabel laughed. She could not take the young man on the wall seriously. "You should be used to such exaggerations from your hectic admirers—it's poetic license!"

"Oh, I took it for that. But nothing would do but I must see him at once. It was hard enough to say no in the first place, with Mr. Kenyon so anxious for us to meet."

Mr. Kenyon had begged her to receive "poor Browning." "And why poor Browning?" she had asked. "Because nobody reads him." She had fired up at that. "Better, then, say poor readers."

"Mr. Kenyon won't take umbrage," Arabel was saying comfortably as she opened a cupboard on the wall and took from it a bottle, a glass and a spoon. The cupboard's shelves were full of bottles and pillboxes. She poured a spoonful of the liquid into the glass. "He'll understand."

"Mr. Browning won't understand."

"If he's pressed you—?"

"Oh, he has. I told him again and again that I spent the winters sealed up here and never saw anyone. In the end he harassed me till I said, to put him off, politely, 'In the spring we shall see.' "

"Take this draught. It will settle your nerves."

Elizabeth drank, still talking.

"Before February was out he decided that spring had come. Do just look at his letter, Arabel."

Arabel opened a drawer and scattered the letters on her sister's lap. Elizabeth found the one she wanted and spread it out.

"Look how he heads it, 'Wednesday morning—Spring.' "

Arabel looked over her shoulder, waiting for the sedative to take effect. Ba really was more nervous than usual, if possible.

"Read the rest of it, Arabel."

Dutifully Arabel took the letter and read on. Ba had such a large correspondence with literary men and women. The whole family welcomed this proxy life, which was all she had; but they could not share it deeply. Arabel herself enjoyed the snippets of gossip Ba passed on, and her adored Miss Mitford, the famous novelist, had become quite a friend of the family. Last summer they had all gone out for a picnic to Three Mile Cross near Reading in Berkshire, where she lived, thirty miles out of London, and Papa had never found out!

But as to reading Ba's letters, there was too much talk of iambics and hexameters and accents and assonances and Latin and Greek poets in them. She was out of her depth. She had not shared lessons with the boys' tutor, Mr. MacSwiney, like Ba, nor wanted to. She and her pretty red-haired younger sister Henrietta had been happy to hem and sew, to learn to paint in water colours and to play the pianoforte. Granny Moulton had loved Ba best, but she had not approved of her tomboy ways or her desire to learn like a man. Papa had never refused Ba anything.

"Read it aloud," Elizabeth commanded.

" 'Real warm spring, dear Miss Barrett, and the birds know it; and in spring I shall surely see you. When did I ever fail to get what I set my heart on?' "

"You see? He must see me because he must. Not because I wish it. I put him off again, saying that for me spring came when the east wind had gone. I told him that last winter nearly killed me. He only answered, 'You shall laugh at east winds yet, like me.' We haven't even met, and already Mr. Browning is taking control of my life."

Elizabeth looked searchingly at her sister, then burst out, "The truth is, Arabel, I'm afraid of what he wants of me and of what he expects to find in me. My heart is beating like a sledgehammer and I feel dreadfully ill. Mr. Browning is handsome and brilliant. He's a dandy, Miss Mitford says. He goes to dinners and breakfasts. He dances the quadrille and the polka all night. He rides a great deal. He fences. They say women like him—find him charming. He's *young*." Suddenly her cry rang through the quiet room, "And, oh, Arabel, I'm old and sick and ugly!"

Arabel swung round at the pain which had given that small voice surprising strength.

"Ba, be quiet."

Arabel pressed her sister backwards onto the cushions, then crossed the room decisively to the bellpull. As she put her hand on it they heard the muffled sound of voices and footsteps coming up the well of the stairs. Arabel dropped her hand.

"Shall I turn him away? Quickly, Ba, decide. I can hear Wilson coming."

Elizabeth struggled to her feet, throwing aside the rugs. "No. That would be uncivil."

"Then lie down again."

"First, take down his picture. Quick, Arabel. Mr. Tennyson's too. Hide them under the sofa."

They were both still standing, flushed and flustered, when a stern-looking young maid opened the door and announced Mr. Browning.

He stood before them bowing beautifully.

His eyes. His eyes. She must see the look in them before she lowered hers to the carpet like Arabel, as was proper. For a second she looked full into those bright clear blue eyes steadily on hers. Her reaction was so strong that she swayed. With one of those fanciful images which always rushed into her mind she thought, It is as if an executioner's sword had glanced past my head and a golden crown had been put on it instead.

She could no longer see the black, black hair and the warm smile, the blue tailcoat with its sweeping lapels of a darker velvet, the black silk cravat covering the shirt front, the white slip outlining the smooth, flat apricot-coloured waistcoat or the lemon-coloured gloves of soft kid. She could only see the white nankeen trousers, which tapered to shoes of thin leather. They were so close-fitting that she could see the play of muscle in his thighs and calves.

Mr. Browning seemed to know her for Elizabeth Barrett. His bow completed, he took her hand and kissed it.

"Miss Barrett, I will not forget this moment as long as I live."

Elizabeth's eyes remained lowered but Arabel stole another glance at him, and was startled. Mr. Browning was looking at Ba, poor Ba, as if she were the most beautiful woman in the world. What did Mr. Browning see in this sad little famous sister of hers to make his own eyes shine with worship? Arabel looked at her again.

No, there was only Ba, poor Ba, in her black silk dress. She had only two gowns, a black silk one for the summer, and a black velvet one for the winter, fully lined against the cold.

Arabel pressed her sister once again to lie back against the cushions. She raised her feet and covered them with a rug. Mr. Browning pushed up his armchair to a nicely calculated distance, achieving the maximum of intimacy compatible with propriety. He had a big voice, and he had not stopped talking for a moment since he had entered the room.

Elizabeth watched him through her lashes as he sat beside her, leaning forward, his square sun-browned hands clasped loosely between his knees. This Mr. Browning was not at all what she had expected. He was certainly nothing like Mr. Horne's picture of him, now safely out of sight under the sofa—it was a hideous, vulgar caricature.

She would never have taken this Mr. Browning for a poet. There was nothing even studious-looking about him—he was certainly not effeminate, as Miss Mitford insisted. She liked his exuberance, his vitality. She liked his black hair, smoothly waving over his brow and curling crisply over his ears and his velvet collar. She liked his calm, happy blue eyes, his frank smile, his boyish demands for her attention. She liked his wide shoulders and the blocklike chest on his wiry body. He was vibrant—alive. He made everything in the room seem dead and dusty, stale and musty, but not in the way she had feared. He did not seem to notice anything in it except her. Because he was there she wanted to jump up from her sofa and begin to live and enjoy the world

19

again. He was like drinking champagne—Papa's best champagne, which he had sent aboard for her brothers Stormy and Henry when they had sailed for Egypt in his barque *Statira*.

Then he was so kind, so exquisitely considerate, Mr. Browning. Every word was a caress.

"I'll leave you to talk," Arabel said. "Shall I take Flush? You know how silly he is about gentlemen, and he won't go downstairs with anyone but me."

The cocker spaniel had retreated as far as he could get from Mr. Browning and was glaring at him and growling.

"Let him stay!" Elizabeth ordered absently.

They hardly saw her go, Arabel thought. Perhaps the visit would be a success after all. The sedative seemed to be doing its work. Thank the good Lord for morphine, without which Ba's life would have been even worse than it was.

2

ELIZABETH SCARCELY SPOKE, FOR MR. BROWNING had taken command. He seemed to take it for granted that everything to do with him must be of interest to her. It would be hard to absolve him from the sin of pride; yet he had a certain modesty. He spoke of his shortcomings with agony. Suddenly she realized that he was more nervous than she was. He wanted so terribly to please her. Like Flush. It was she who really held the power in that room.

"Why did you keep me waiting so long, Miss Barrett?"

"It was only five months."

"A lifetime between you and me. But it was much longer, really. Once I was not very far from seeing you. It was thanks to Mr. Kenyon."

"My kindest of friends."

"And mine. Well, one morning he said to me, 'Would you like to meet Miss Barrett?' Just like that. We were here in Wimpole Street, just passing your front door."

"Then why didn't we meet?"

"He rang the bell and we waited in the hall. Then the message came back. You were too unwell to receive visitors." His face fell as if the blow had just been dealt him. "It was years ago."

"I am truly sorry. But now you are here."

"To think we might have known each other all this time," he persisted stubbornly, "and now all those years have been lost forever." Then his face lightened, and he went on. "Still, you wrote your *Poems,* and when I came back from my travels in Italy last November there they were, left by Mr. Kenyon. Did you wonder why I took so long to thank you for the kind things you said about me?"

"There was no need for thanks," she began, but he was rushing on.

"I knew I must write to you, but I couldn't write a letter which you might take for a formal thank you with some compliments about your genius thrown in—not when I felt as deeply as I did."

(He had spoken, she remembered, of the fresh strange music of her poems, their rich language, and her true brave new thought. "So into me it has gone," he had declared, "and part of me it has become, this great living poetry of yours, not a flower of which but took root and grew.")

"On January the tenth—five months ago—I picked up my pen and wrote to you. At that moment the whole world changed for me forever." His blue eyes sought hers and she tried to wrest the conversation back to normality.

"Will you answer a question for me about your work, Mr. Browning?"

"You've only to ask."

"Will you please tell me why you entitled that wonderful series of yours *Bells and Pomegranates?* I'm sure it's very stupid of me, but I've never been able to discover the reason."

He was obviously bewildered that the question should be asked, but eager to oblige her.

"It's strange how no one understands, not even you. I only meant by that title to indicate an endeavour towards something like an alternation, or mixture, of music with discoursing, sound with sense, poetry with thought; which looks too ambitious, thus expressed, so the symbol was preferred."

He did not notice the blankness on Elizabeth's face or the little smile that took its place.

Now he was pouring out his whole history, telling her of his unshakable belief in his talent, his certainty that glory would be his, his furious impatience that his career had come to a grinding, ignominious halt.

"After my *Paracelsus* was published the immortals accepted

22

me as one of them," he boasted, waving a hand at the two literary celebrities still hanging on the wall.

He had met Dickens and Tennyson and that other brilliant poet, Landor, and Thomas Carlyle, the Scottish peasant of genius, and Macready the great actor-manager. His health had been proposed as "the youngest poet in England," and seconded by the crusty Wordsworth himself. He had been peppered with invitations to afternoon dinners and late suppers. He had, he believed, arrived.

"So you had."

"But that was ten years ago. Now I am thirty-three and nothing has gone right since then." He was bending forward and clenching his hands to impress the horror of it on her.

All his efforts to become a popular playwright with Macready's help had foundered, and in ugly quarrels. Then *Sordello*, which after seven years' work was to be more startling than *Paracelsus* and set him permanently among the stars, had done for him. With his saga of a medieval troubadour's soul he had committed literary suicide. Hardly any copies had been sold to the public. The literati had tried to read it, and had damned him. He had become a byword for unintelligibility. Ribald laughter rang round tables where he had been flattered. A poet could survive anything but ridicule.

Thomas Carlyle's clever wife Jane had read "the gibberish" through without discovering whether Sordello was a man, a city or a book. Tennyson had said the only lines he understood were the first: "Who will, may hear Sordello's story told," and the last: "Who would, has heard Sordello's story told"—and both were lies.

In his bitterness he had sworn never again to speak as Robert Browning but only in the voices of other men and women.

"So I brought out the first volume of my *Bells and Pomegranates* four years ago."

The little paper-covered booklets had been issued cheaply, so as to tempt the general public, but still they did not sell.

"I know all six volumes well. Your *Pippa Passes* is the poem of yours I most wish I'd written," Elizabeth cried, and then remembered the lascivious passage about Ottima and Sebald which she had been thinking of before he came.

The next volume had come out the next year, the one with

Porphyria's Lover in it. She felt the man's hot passion in Mr. Browning's description of how Porphyria bared her shoulder and loosened her hair. But why did her lover strangle her with it?

> I found
> A thing to do, and all her hair
> In one long yellow string I wound
> Three times her little throat around,
> And strangled her.

And why did he sit with his dead mistress clasped to him, waiting?

> And thus we sit together now,
> And all night long we have not stirred,
> And yet God has not said a word!

For some reason that poem always brought back to her mind the nightmares she had had as she approached her own thirtieth birthday, and one in particular, with its three gigantic serpents covered with evil-smelling, poisonous slime writhing before her while her beloved brother tried desperately to destroy them with vitriol. The serpents shrieked in pain but grew larger and larger. She had been in the last extremes of fear and agony. What could it all mean? What had she to do with serpents? Were Mr. Browning's fancies any weirder than her dreams? She could not speak to him of such things, of course.

"It's hard to believe that the author of *Porphyria's Lover* also wrote *The Pied Piper of Hamelin*," she said now.

"That was a joke, written to amuse poor little Willy Macready, who was ill."

"It will be loved forever, and not only by children. Can you recite from it? They tell me you recite verse exceedingly well."

Mr. Browning obliged with vigour.

> "Rats!
> They fought the dogs, and killed the cats,
> And bit the babies in the cradles,
> And ate the cheeses out of the vats,
> And licked the soup from the cooks' own ladles,
> Split open the kegs of salted sprats,
> Made nests inside men's Sunday hats,
> And even spoiled the women's chats,
> By drowning their speaking

With shrieking and squeaking
In fifty different sharps and flats."

To his surprise Miss Barrett's silvery voice joined his deep
one.

"Great rats, small rats, lean rats, brawny rats,
Brown rats, black rats, grey rats, tawny rats,
Grave old plodders, gay young friskers,
Fathers, mothers, uncles, cousins,
Cocking tails and pricking whiskers,
Families by tens and dozens,
Brothers, sisters, husbands, wives,
Followed the Piper for their lives."

Elizabeth was sitting up. They were laughing like children.
He was beating time on his knee with a silver matchbox like a
chunky, scaly little fish. He finished with a great noisy climax in
that loud voice of his.

"So Willy, let you and me be wipers
Of scores out with all men—especially pipers:
And, whether they pipe us free from rats or from mice,
If we've promised them aught let us keep our promise!"

"Prom-ice!" she cried breathlessly. "What a rhyme!" And I
nearly didn't keep my promise to see you this afternoon, she
thought.

After the laughter, the gravity returned. There was no con-
soling him for the fact that the world had ignored his poems, and
would probably do so again shortly when his next volume came
out.

"But I will succeed, I will be famous, I will not spare myself
—my talent demands release! Haven't I sacrificed everything to it
already? Haven't I dined and danced and jogged about for over
ten years?" His voice was fierce with resentment.

"Is that a sacrifice, then?" she asked wistfully. "To have
drunk of the full cup of life, with the sun shining on it? I have
lived only inside myself or in sorrow. There are few young women
in the world who have not seen more and known more than I
have, and I can scarcely be called young now."

He grimaced.

"I loathe society. But my parents have polished me up with
music masters and dancing masters and singing masters and riding

masters and boxing masters and fencing masters—to say nothing of masters to teach me Latin and Greek and Hebrew. It would break their hearts if I didn't put it all to use. So I do, and at what cost to me only God knows."

Suddenly Mr. Browning gave a jump. "Good Lord, what's this?"

His hand, flung wide in one of his expansive gestures, had struck Flush's cold nose, and his heavy signet ring had made it a painful blow.

His mistress tried to soothe the yelping dog. "It's only Mr. Browning come to call. Come and shake hands with him and forgive him. Flush!"

Flush leapt whimpering into her arms.

"Let him be," Robert Browning commanded, leaning down to look closely at him.

He was a jolly little dog for all his ridiculous dramatics. Miss Barrett was making a lap dog of a good gun dog—there was breeding there. Perky, and as vain as a cat, he would say. How the little fellow hated him!

"Flush is vainglorious and likes to rule here unchallenged," his mistress excused him. "He even resents the Aeolian harp in the window there that Papa gave me. He thinks it's speaking to me."

"He's jealous. I can understand that. I'm a friend of all dumb creatures. One of my best friends is a toad. And I've a spider friend who lives in the jaws of a great skull on my writing table."

"I don't care for toads."

"When I was a child I had a zoo, with efts and frogs and owls and monkeys—and an eagle, once—and a couple of large snakes."

"Spiders and toads. Monkeys and snakes. I prefer my golden Flushy with all his faults—jealousy and vainglory and cowardice, too, I'm afraid. Flushy is the prince of cowards. He runs away from the tiniest dogs and faints at the sight of water. My six brothers all sneer at him. He was a present from Miss Mitford. You know Miss Mitford, I think you said?"

Yes, he knew Miss Mary Russell Mitford, of the clacking tongue and the bobbing silver curls over the massive brow. She hadn't a shilling to bless herself with, but she went everywhere, gabbing and rending the skies with complaints at the drudgery of her life. She had struck worldwide fame with her sketches of village life in *The Lady's Magazine,* and now novels, plays and annuals poured out from the workingman's cottage outside London, where she lived among horses, dogs and geraniums.

Dr. Mitford, her disreputable father, had been the cause of all her troubles. He wondered whether Miss Barrett knew that as a handsome young doctor Mitford had been a sort of acolyte in Graham's notorious Temple of Health, and had, they said, lain naked with Nelson's love Emma Hamilton on public display in a bath of mud. Old men had come flocking to see the "Goddess of Health," and buy the quack's pills for potency. Mitford had wasted his wife's fortune as well as his own, and, to crown it all, had run through the twenty thousand pounds his ten-year-old daughter had won in a lottery. She had supported him to the end, while he pilfered the shillings she hoarded in a cracked teapot and went in and out of Newgate jail for debt.

Well, he was dead now, and the pug-faced old girl was lonely for him, always baying out her misery to all and sundry. So she was Miss Barrett's close friend. Surely a great deal too old for her? Sixty, if she was a day.

"Mr. Kenyon introduced us nine years ago, and we've been fast friends ever since. The kindest of all her many kindnesses was giving me Flush."

Flush growled at mention of his name.

"He came to me at a very bad time, and I really don't know how I would live without him now. He loves me, Mr. Browning, more than dog ever loved man or woman."

"Then Flush must love me too, whether he wants to or not."

He spread his knees, and placed both hands on them, bending again to stare at him. Flush's protuberant golden eyes stared back with implacable hostility.

"He's too fat," he said. "He needs exercise." I believe, thought Elizabeth suddenly, that even Flush will find himself doing what Mr. Browning wants.

There was a tap on the door, and the unbending Wilson came in.

"Miss Henrietta asks, ma'am, whether Mr. Browning doesn't intend to take a cup of tea before he goes."

At that moment the little gilt French clock on the mantel piece chimed the half hour.

Mr. Browning leapt to his feet.

"Oh, Miss Barrett! I've stayed for an hour and a half—and it has seemed like five minutes. *Will* you ever forgive me? Will you *ever* allow me to come again?"

Suddenly he was gone. She could hear Flush's breathing again. She could hear the clock's ticking. Soon she would hear her heart's beating.

Elizabeth lay with her eyes on the communicating door between his bedroom and hers. Her father would come. He never failed. He would not knock, merely give a tap of his fingernail and slip in.

From where she lay she could see his picture on the wall with Miss Mitford's under it. Her sister Arabel was already asleep near the window.

She heard her father's footsteps on the stair, then going into his room. In the dim light of the oil lamp she saw the brass ring of the door handle turn noiselessly, and then he stood looking down at her. The shadows made black caverns under his thick brows.

She raised her white hand in the darkness to greet him and whispered, "Papa."

"How are you, Ba?"

"Well, Papa."

She gazed happily up at his strong face, with the fine eyes and the full lips, thinking that without him her life would be empty.

"Did you eat all your supper?"

"Yes."

"And drink your claret?"

"Yes, Papa."

In fact, Flush had had less than usual of her supper. He had been prepared to gobble up her roast duckling despite its peppering of cayenne, but she had found herself eating quite heartily for once.

It was fortunate that Flush had so many undoglike tastes— even ginger cake with real hot Jamaican ginger. Papa would never realize how impossible it was for her to choke down all the concoctions he ordered Mrs. Tuckem the cook to send up.

"Did you have any visitors today?"

"Mr. Robert Browning, the author of *Paracelsus* and *Bells and Pomegranates*. He'll be another Tennyson, I think. He lacks his music, but he has a more powerful mind, and I find him a true soul-piercing poet. He loves Latin and Greek, as I do, and reads Hebrew too."

Mr. Barrett grunted. Another of Elizabeth's decrepit old classical scholars. She seemed addicted to them. That blind fellow, Hugh Boyd, had been the first, and doubtless Mr. Browning would not be the last.

"Mr. Kenyon has been pressing me to meet Mr. Browning for years. He's the son of an old friend."

Mr. Barrett lost all interest. His cousin, great fat John Kenyon, might have grown into a different world since they had been boys together in Jamaica, but he was reliable, and proud of the Barrett connection. He would not introduce anyone undesirable into the Barrett household. Miss Mitford and that other literary friend brought by him, Mrs. Jameson, had both proved acceptable. There was no need to worry about this man of the pomegranates.

Mr. Barrett was lowering himself, a little carefully, to his knees. He was nearly sixty, after all, Elizabeth thought, and his rheumatism troubled him increasingly, though he was still so remarkably young-looking and light of step. His hair was strong and thick, hardly touched with grey. His dark whiskers made him seem young too, but his mouth was set. The days when his boisterous laughter had rung through their lives had gone, but now and then the boy broke through the man of iron.

Now he was taking her hand. Kneeling, he clasped both his own over it.

"Our Father," he began, and she joined him, thrilling to his deep bass voice. She loved him more than anybody in the world.

His faith had never deserted him, not even when Mama had died suddenly sixteen years before at Cheltenham, the nearest spa, where she had been sent to take the waters. He had scratched a note to Elizabeth before leaving by coach. "She is now in the presence of Him to Whom she belongs, redeemed by the pouring out of His precious blood. I would say, Lord, not my will but Thine be done, Thou knowest best, teach us to submit patiently to all Thy inflictions."

Then he had added a pathetic, bewildered two lines. "I cannot say what I feel, for I scarcely can define my sensations, the blow is too recent."

No one had ever known what he felt, certainly not any of his children. They were like each other in that, he and she. They could not put their feelings into words, face to face with another human being. *He* could speak to his God, and *she* could write out her heart in poetry and in letters—never to each other.

His faith had supported him even through those horrible days when his creditors had forced him to put up his beloved Hope End, set in the beautiful Malvern Hills in Herefordshire, for sale, and prospective buyers had trampled all over the home they had loved for twenty-three years—even into Mama's room, which Papa had shut up the day he came home from burying her. Then the fat gentleman with the rings had come. Papa had seemed to go a little mad when, with the house actually sold over his head, he had refused to allow the buyer to set foot in the grounds. Mr. Thomas Heywood could only view his property with a spyglass from the nearest hilltop.

Elizabeth remembered when the letter had come informing Papa that he had lost all his money and was reduced from vast wealth to—what?—pauperism, if not ruin!

She had watched him open it and seen the spasm on his face. It had lasted only a second, then he had thrown himself back into the jokes and laughter of the boys. That was all he had ever revealed.

Then one day he had said, "Pack!" She would never forget that terrible silent game of cricket which he had played with the boys on their last evening. Next day they had left. Only his eldest son Edward had stayed behind, standing beside him to see them and her Aunt Bummy Graham-Clarke go off. Suddenly Papa had snatched little Septimus back from the carriage steps as he was climbing up after Octavius, the eighth and youngest boy.

Setty, his seventh son, had been ten then. He had been six when Mama had died, and Papa had taken him to sleep with him. Setty was a lively little fellow, with a shock of yellow hair, and he could make Papa smile when no one else could. Papa crouched down before his son. Setty had been looking forward to donkey rides on the Sidmouth sands with his brother Occy, and Papa knew it.

"Would you rather go with Occy?" he asked, his face strained. "Or stay with me?"

"I would far rather stay with you," Setty said and flung his arms around his neck.

Papa had taken Setty's hand and gone into the house with him with the nearest thing to a look of happiness she had seen on his face since her mother's death.

They all loved their father, for he loved them. Setty had meant it. They still called him by that baby name "Papa." He had said, "If they leave off calling me Papa I shall think they have stopped loving me!"

They had driven off in tears with Aunt Bummy Graham-Clarke to arrive at that dreary house in Sidmouth in Devon without a rushlight burning. That had been twelve years ago.

They had stayed in Sidmouth for three years. How the figure three recurred in her life! She had been three when she had left Granny Moulton's home, where she had been born, for Hope End. They had lived in Sidmouth for three years, before going for three years to that horrible furnished place in Gloucester Place in London. Then she had had another three years in Devonshire, in that place whose name she never could speak or write. Was three a magic number, or was three the limit of Papa's endurance? In any case, Papa's will was fate, inexorable and inscrutable.

Now Papa came to her room late every night to support her with the faith which upheld him. As a mere child, doubting, she had prayed, "Oh God, if there be a God, save my soul, if I have a soul." But she had shrunk from the horror of annihilation of the pulsating creature that was little Ba Barrett, and had clutched at God once more, as for life.

Now she longed for death. Only in work was there peace, and, while it lasted, pleasure. Yet for once, that day, she had been happy. She had felt a surge towards the life beyond the four walls of her cramped room where the windows did not even look out on the street. She had, for a moment, meant what she had said to Mr. Browning about envying him his life in the bright world of people. She had actually laughed over his child's poem about the rats. How much he loved life, Mr. Browning. While her father prayed she dreamed again of his visit.

She came to herself to hear her father embarking on his

closing prayer. "Dear God," he was intoning fervently, "bless this Thy child. Bring her peace. Make her strong to bear the afflictions which Thou hast laid upon her. Let her learn to say, Thy will be done."

"Thy will be done."

"Keep her above all things pure and unsullied. Let her be like the Blessed Virgin Mary, who was without sin. Look upon Thy white lamb, washed with Thy blood, and keep her unstained by the evil and lusts of the world. Amen."

"Amen."

He released her hand. Her thoughts had been straying during almost the whole of her father's visit. With a need for atonement she said urgently, "Don't go, Papa."

He rose but remained standing.

"It's most extraordinary," she said in a little rush, "how the idea of Mr. Browning besets me. I suppose it's because I'm not used to seeing strangers—but he haunts me. It's a persecution."

Her father smiled down at her. She could see the curve of his full lips widening to meet the cheek, and the cheek fold into the pucker she loved so well.

"It's ungrateful to your friend to use such a word," he said reproachfully.

It was as if he had given her permission to enjoy the company of the young man whose presence had stayed with her in the room during all those hours since he had left it and then had made her deaf to her father's prayers.

She was so touched that she kissed her father twice instead of once, as usual. Yet as she did so she felt a pang of guilt. She did not know why she had deceived him about how she really felt towards Mr. Browning.

3

AFTER THAT MR. BROWNING CAME ONCE A WEEK. He was still sworn to secrecy. Elizabeth said nothing about his visits either, even to Miss Mitford, her closest friend for the past twelve years despite their twenty years difference in age. Elizabeth had always needed a passionate friendship based on books, and Miss Mitford brought her London's literary gossip in letters and visits, published her poems and articles in her annuals, and loved her to distraction.

Once Miss Mitford had said to her, "When I am away from you I sit and think of you and the poems you are going to write, and of the brief rainbow crown called fame you are going to wear, until I seem to see you before my eyes. I am entirely absorbed by you, my dearest, with all my pride in you, and all my hopes for you, and all my love for you."

Elizabeth loved her too. They might yet share a home. Miss Mitford would nurse her devotedly and would never die in the poorhouse while *she* was alive.

After Mr. Browning's visit Elizabeth wrote to the brave old woman alone in her leaking cottage.

"My beloved friend, my dearest, dearest friend. Do you realize that I have not set eyes on your dear face for two whole months? I have no news to send you from my dungeon except that Flush has been washed and is a mass of golden curls. I think and think of you. How unworthy I am of even half your love, except that I love you! Love me, my beloved friend. And write and say if I can do anything, supply you with anything, such as gowns or collars etc.—now *do*. I shall send you a salmon, or some oysters perhaps, soon. Tell me how you are, and whether your rheumatism is troubling you. I kiss you in prospect. Am I not your own affectionate Ba?"

Only her closest friends were allowed to call her by that pet name, her brother Edward's first spoken word—Ba for Baby.

Should she mention Mr. Browning's visit after all? Perhaps it might be better just to refer to it, quite frankly, but not make too much of it. "And oh!—did I tell you in my last letter that I had seen Mr. Browning? He begged so hard I let him come, and I liked him very much. You and I differ about his genius, I know, but a poet is something after all. I beseech you to keep his visit to me a secret, or Mr. Horne and all the world will be knocking at my door."

Miss Trepsack came as usual from her lodgings to sit with Elizabeth after Sunday dinner with the family. She was seventy-six, but still slim and spry. Treppy was their living link with their Jamaican past.

She had been an orphan, a poor white planter's child, left to the care of the brother of that great figure of the past, Papa's grandfather, old "Patches" Barrett. Patches had had fifty thousand pounds a year, thousands of slaves, and tens of thousands of acres, yet he had worn patches on his knees and elbows to show he was not proud. His brother had taken Treppy to live with him and his slave concubine Madgikan and her four quadroon children, but soon he had died of yellow fever. In his will he besought his brother to free Madgikan and her children and see that Mary Trepsack was "cloathed, maintained and educated at the charge of my Estate until she attains the age of 14 years, then put out and Bound apprentice in Great Britain either to a Milliner or Mantua Maker, until she arrives at the age of 18 years or day of Marriage."

Treppy had never married. She had become a daughter to Patches and his wife at the Barrett mansion, Cinnamon Hill Great House, and a sister to their daughter, Papa's mother, and then had come over to England with her and her boys, Papa and his brother Matthew, in the winter of 1795, fifty years ago. Treppy had been loved by four generations of Barretts. She had held all Papa's twelve children in her dear sticklike arms—Elizabeth, Edward, Henrietta, Mary, Sam, Arabel, Stormy, George, Henry, Alfred, Septimus and Octavius. She had cried bitterly over the deaths of three of them, first Mary as an infant, then Sam, and then Edward, as grown men. Papa's mother had begged Papa in a letter from her deathbed, "Be a steady friendd to her, let her never feel want," and had left her two thousand pounds.

Treppy's lavender-coloured printed alpaca was new, and her bustle rode out proudly from a ramrod-straight figure.

"How smart you are, Treppy," Elizabeth sighed.

"You should buy yourself a new dress, Ba."

"Perhaps. How many petticoats are you wearing?"

"Four, sweetheart." Treppy had removed her bonnet, and was putting on a little house cap. She tied an apron of shot silk round her waist and shook out her embroidery.

"Tell me about Jamaica, Treppy."

Treppy missed Jamaica with a ceaseless ache, and after fifty years still lived in the cold damp of England like an unwilling visitor.

"*Well!*" she said now, and launched into her memories, a kind of magic incantation celebrating love and loss and praise and pain. Elizabeth lay in a half-dream while once again she heard Treppy yearning for Cinnamon Hill Great House, its casements open to the sea breezes, its flocks of barefooted house slaves, its feastings and weddings and christenings. Through Treppy's eyes she saw again the wains laden with bundled canes, drawn by long-horned white oxen, to be crushed in the sugarworks and heard the names of the old Barrett estates drop from her lips like music—Cinnamon Hill, Pleasant Valley, Spring, Blue Hole, Rose Hall, Crawley, Palmetto Point, Content, Retreat Pen. Through it all there flowed the sound of fiddles and fifes and the melodious and continual singing of the slaves. To hear Treppy talk one would think the slaves had sung all day long every day in one great deep-throated paean of joy.

Yet Elizabeth knew enough to make her hate the island. Papa's brother Uncle Matt had been in danger of his life again and again. In the eighteen thirties Papa had had to give up going to chapel because he could not bear to listen to what was said about slave owners from the pulpit. He had stopped seeing the neighbours, too, and stayed at home. Then, by bad luck, just when the bill to free the slaves was going through the English Parliament, there had been a lawsuit in the Court of Chancery between two branches of the Barrett family about the ownership of a parcel of slaves and steers. Everyone had looked at them as if they were criminals.

"That dreadful Jamaica!"

"What did you say, Ba?" Treppy had been interrupted in full flight.

"Oh, nothing. Tell me about Grandfather Moulton."

"Your grandfather?" Treppy was guarded.

"Yes, Papa's father. I don't know anything about him. Just that he died before I was born."

Elizabeth watched Treppy and saw her grow uneasy.

"That's right." Treppy examined her sewing.

"What's right?"

"Charles Moulton. Well, he died."

"When did he die? You didn't disagree when I said he died before I was born, yet something Papa once said made me think that wasn't so. And if it wasn't, why did Granny come over to England alone with her little boys? Why didn't Grandpa Moulton live with us, if Granny wasn't a widow?"

Treppy still did not answer. She would never, Elizabeth thought, tell the lie direct.

"Was there trouble, Treppy? Why don't I know anything about my grandfather?"

"He was the most beautiful man I ever saw in a short wig and knee breeches. And your Papa was the spitting image of him as a little boy. He worshipped the ground his father walked on— he used to follow him about everywhere."

"Then why doesn't Papa ever speak of him?"

"Does your Papa ever speak of anything, Ba? To his own children, above all?"

"Children!" Elizabeth spoke almost sharply. "Do you realize that I shall be forty on my next birthday? Octavius is twenty, and he's the youngest. There are no children in this house, Treppy."

"How time flies!" Treppy sighed. "I'm seventy-six, and it's all a long time ago."

36

"Did something go wrong, Treppy? Tell me. I've a right to know."

"I don't know what your Papa would say to me if I let my tongue run away with me. Let the dead past bury its dead!"

Elizabeth could see her searching for one of the Jamaican slave proverbs with which she fought her way out of awkward situations. Sure enough, she found one to cast into her frowning face.

"Marriage hab teeth and teeth hab toothache."

Treppy would not say another word; but, Elizabeth thought, in a way she had answered her question.

Elizabeth did not abandon hope of discovering more about her father's father. That night after her brothers and sisters had paid their mass Sunday visit to her room her father came to see her. He was in a good mood, pulling Flush's ears.

"Flush, will you go downstairs with me?" he teased, and Flush darted from between his hands and threw himself into Elizabeth's arms, licking her face.

"What a fool that dog is," her father exclaimed, straightening up.

Elizabeth had had Wilson, her own lady's maid, lay out a decanter and glasses. She set Flush down and poured out a glass of wine.

"Taste this, Papa, and tell me what you think of it."

He passed the glass to and fro under his nostrils distrustfully, sipped and gave a shudder.

"Why, what's this beastly, nauseous thing? Is it one of your medicines? Oh, I shall never, never get this horrible taste out of my mouth!"

"Papa! It's Cyprus wine and very good. Mr. Boyd sent me a phial as a very special present. It tastes of orange blossom and the honey of Mount Hymettus."

"There you are. Any wine must be positively vile which tastes as sweet as honey. On your own showing, it's beastly."

"Papa, as a drinker of port you can't be a judge of nectar."

She took the glass from him and offered it to the little cocker spaniel. He rushed forward to lick it, then fell back and ran away. Mr. Barrett roared with laughter and slapped his thigh.

Elizabeth laughed with him. Then she said: "Papa, I've been thinking. I know nothing at all about my Grandfather Moulton. It's a great yawning gap in my knowledge . . ."

Before she had finished she saw his face darken. His brows came down over his eyes, and his mouth snapped shut.

"Won't you tell me something about him?" she faltered, wondering why her heart should flutter and she should feel guilty when he was denying her something which was her birthright.

"We will read in the Scriptures now," he said. "It is time."

Obediently she lay back on the sofa, and he read to her and then prayed. There was anger in his prayers that night.

Robert Browning came to possess her past and she his. He learnt what an adored little tyrant she had been, the tiny cropped-haired, firstborn daughter of Edward Barrett Moulton-Barrett, sugar-wealthy Jamaican owner of the mansion of Hope End in Herefordshire, Justice of the Peace, High Sheriff of the County, pillar of the nonconformist chapel, dispenser of charity and father of twelve.

Both Robert and she had had violent tempers; both had been spoiled.

"You and I might have been brother and sister—so dark, and loving poetry, and with our West Indian backgrounds," she said.

But Elizabeth had longed to go out into the world, while Robert had only wanted to stay at home and had made his father take him away, first from school, and then from London University, despite the crippling hundred pounds he had donated to get him admitted there.

"I preferred my sweet, independent way of life. I was meant to be a poet and nothing else."

Robert thought of all the quarrels there had been in his happy home. His parents had wanted him to be a barrister. Old Basil Montagu, the Queen's Counsel, had offered to give him a pupillage free of charge and take him into chambers. The very thought of such an opportunity lost still made his poor father groan. He seemed to have forgotten his own youthful agonies at not being allowed to be a painter. Now he resented it that after nearly fifty years as a bank clerk his salary was still a pittance and wanted his only son to have a profession.

Well, it had been hard; but Robert had fought his battles and had won. He was doing what he had to do.

His father had made it possible for him to live at home and work, and plunged his hand into his shabby, half-empty pocket to pay for the publication of every one of his works after *Pauline* except the play Macready had commissioned. He had sent him abroad for months when he had been nearly out of his mind with depression after *Pauline,* and again after the failure of the play. Oh, he had been good to him! But he would repay him a thousandfold. There was no need to tell Miss Barrett about all that yet. The happy things first.

"You were lucky in your parents," she was saying.

"Most wonderfully so. My father is a saint. My mother and I are like one person. When she's ill I'm ill too."

Elizabeth looked a little sceptical. "My father has been everything to me, too," she said softly.

He listened carefully while Mr. Barrett's daughter sang her father's praises. "From the beginning he loved me best of all his children," she boasted, and it still seemed very important to her that it should be so.

As soon as she could stagger she had found her way to her father's bed every morning, struggling up the steep white cliff of his great four-poster until she reached him where he sat laughing and holding open his arms. She had snuggled down with him in the bedclothes, hiding her face in the pillows and whispering, *"Embrasse-moi!"*

Her father had told her that since Havannah, the family's pet dog, was a French poodle she could only understand French. Solemnly Elizabeth had learned to command her with a *"Venez"* or a *"Couchez."* Soon French had become their early morning language of love. She twined her arms about her handsome young father's neck, and stroked his hair and called him Sweet Puppy. She begged for kisses. She could never have enough kisses.

"And he loved me as much as I loved him."

As soon as Elizabeth was old enough he had taken her for walks and gallops over the hills and had petted her when she made up rhymes to please him. A little shyly, she produced an envelope from the drawer of her sofa-table.

"He gave me this when I was six, for writing a poem on Virtue."

For a moment Robert took the large, rather ill-formed writing for the child's, then realized that it must be her father's.

"'To the Poet Laureate of Hope End,'" he read out. "And that was you, of course!"

"There was a golden sovereign in it," she said, and put it away again carefully.

When she had been eleven she had discovered the poems of Alexander Pope, and had written a great derivative epic. "It was very bad. But when I was fifteen Papa had fifty copies of it privately printed at his expense. I dedicated it to him. He couldn't eat his supper when the package of books came from the printer's. He had to find his papercutter and cut the pages at once, and he read them between mouthfuls. Mrs. Tuckem the cook was not pleased at her dishes being treated like that!

"He was the most wonderful of fathers," she went on. "He never struck any of us, not even the boys. My rages were a by-word, but he only held me in his arms till I grew calm. I would sob and sob till I exhausted myself. Then he would explain that I must submit, and so I did, of course."

"You didn't fly to your mother to weep in *her* arms?"

"My mother was sweet and gentle—too much so. I loved her dearly. Bummy too—my Aunt Arabella Graham-Clarke, her sister. She lived with us for a long time, you know. But *he* was my god. The boys loved him too. He was like their brother, being so young-looking and so high-spirited. But *I* loved him best, and he loved *me* most of all."

There it was again. Was it so important then, to be loved best of all by a parent?

"Those were the happy days before troubles rained down on him, and we lost our home, and had to come to this horrible London. First my mother died and left him with the children— there were only eleven of us by then. Then dreadful troubles came in Jamaica, family legal troubles, and all that business about the slaves cost him a great deal of money."

"You mean, emancipation?"

She nodded. "I'm glad the slaves were freed, of course. But Papa suffered from it in many, many ways. It was a curse on us."

He knew what freeing the slaves eleven years before, in 1834, had meant to those who made their money from sugar and rum.

It had finished off what abolition of the slave trade with Africa had begun a quarter of a century before.

"Papa said we might as well hang weights to the island of Jamaica and send it to the bottom of the ocean at once. He said no one in their senses would dream of trying to cultivate sugar anymore."

Still, he had gone on trying. His brother Matthew, the Member of Parliament for Richmond in Yorkshire, had given up the seat he had held for seven years and gone out to Jamaica. It had been a terrible sacrifice for the brilliant, witty man, her favourite uncle.

"But Papa had a large family to support and provide careers for. My Uncle Matt had no children."

Mr. Barrett had bought ships with what capital was left after the sale of Hope End. First the slow old *David Lyon*, and then the *Statira*, had gone out to Jamaica to collect the sugar and rum, and bring them back for sale. The *Statira* made trips to Egypt with coal and returned with wool from Alexandria. Papa had fought the world for a living for them all.

"He has always been so strong and so loving, to me above all. I owe him everything in the world, even your presence here today, Mr. Browning."

Robert took his leave thoughtfully. He had a mind to have a word with dear old John Kenyon about his cousin Mr. Barrett. They had been boys together in Jamaica, he had said, and at Cambridge University at the same time.

John Kenyon's two hundred and fifty pounds of flesh was lapped in a green surtout of finest saxony edged with narrow silk braid. His satin stock was buckled round his fat neck like a dandy's, his doeskin trousers fitted like his skin. He was glittering with gold, too, with his massive gold chain, heavy gold ring and great round gold-rimmed spectacles.

There was nobody as lovable as John Kenyon, twice-married but childless Jamaican sugar baron, patron of poets and a poet himself. So Robert thought, walking with him before Sunday supper in his mother's garden.

"I've had the pleasure of meeting Miss Barrett at last," Robert began cautiously. Mr. Kenyon was supposed to think they had met only once. "Didn't you tell me you knew her father as a boy in Jamaica?"

"We were cousins, and boys together." Mr. Kenyon's intelligent eyes looked penetratingly at Robert—almost through him. "You've already heard something, eh? And it doesn't jibe with the delicious Miss Barrett's picture of her adored Papa, is that it?"

"She loves him devotedly and he her," Robert replied.

"Love comes in all shapes and forms. Edward Barrett keeps his family like spoiled slaves, with sleeping quarters and plenty of provender. But what he wants, that they must do or take the consequences."

"Why, his daughters are freer than any other young women in England! In what other household can three pretty unmarried women receive male guests without chaperones at any hour of the day? I'm told Miss Henrietta has three suitors call on her every morning."

"Edward Barrett regards his children as children. They're allowed their playmates. His sons go to him for every penny, and do as they're bid."

"I've met George. A barrister and manly, I thought."

"George slips the chain to go on circuit because his father wishes it, but he comes home again and toes the line as if he were nine years old. All six sons, and all three daughters, are slaves, and no less so because he loves them dearly and they love him—more so for that, indeed."

Mr. Kenyon mused a little, pushing at the gravel with a thin black cane with a gold head and a tassel.

"Still, I shouldn't judge him too harshly. One should be sorry for Edward Barrett."

"I don't understand, sir."

"No, you don't, Robert. You can't. You've Jamaican blood in your veins, I know that. Your grandmother was a Tittle, and the Tittles hailed from Port Royal, Jamaica, before ever they went to Saint Kitts. But you've never been to Jamaica yourself. You should go there. Then you'd feel the sun that heats the blood, that still heats Edward Barrett's, and mine, and yours, and Elizabeth Barrett's, and makes us all poets and passionate."

He laughed gustily.

"The Barretts have lived in Jamaica for over two hundred

years, Robert. That's a long time for blood to be on the boil in that wicked island!"

He continued to push at the gravel, his lips pursed.

"Well, I'll tell you what made Edward Barrett into the man he is, if you like."

In the sweet peace of his mother's garden Robert listened while the twilight came softly down. The scents of roses and sweet peas, lavender and honeysuckle, jasmine and wallflowers seemed to give way to the overpowering perfume of lilies, and the gentle evening air to change to the hot-fingered, searching breeze of a sultry island.

That evening in Jamaica there had been a great round golden moon calling to two boys not tired enough to sleep.

Already motherless, John Kenyon had just lost his father, and his cousin Edward's father and mother had taken him for a visit while his future was decided. The eight-year-old boys had spent the day ranging about the estate, had eaten hugely and were being put to bed by Treppy.

"Tell us a riddle, Treppy!" they squeaked. "Riddle-me-ree! Tell-me-a-riddle-and-perhaps-not!"

"I'll riddle you two and no more. Riddle-me-riddle, John-me-riddle, guess-me-this-riddle-and-perhaps-not!

As I was going to St. George's Hall
I heard the voice of someone call,
His beard was flesh, his mouth was horn,
And such a man was never born.

Guess me that riddle."

"A cock!" Edward squealed.

"Now the second. Deep it is, damp it is, fit for any man. What is that?"

They could not tell.

"A grave," Treppy said matter-of-factly, and rose. "Sleep well."

She stood for a moment at the open window with its jalousies flung wide, and gazed at the flat shining moon. The boys could feel its power drawing them outside. They heard her sigh as she turned and left the room.

When she had gone they sat up in bed. At that moment the

sound of drums and singing rose from the slave quarters. They looked at each other, slid out of bed and pulled on the clean clothes Treppy had laid out ready for them. Soon they were creeping into the banana clumps which stood about the slave lines.

Two men and two girls were dancing by the shifting light of flares. Half a dozen musicians, wearing necklaces of red seeds looped over their bare hairy chests, were beating drums, banging metal on metal, shrilling through whistles and blowing conch horns. One dancer after another dropped out as the pace quickened until only a tall, insolent-looking girl was left, brown arms gleaming with oil stretched above her head, skirts twirling about her thighs. The music came to a screaming climax, and she stamped her bare heels on the hard earth, dropped her arms, stepped over her partner's panting body and flung out of the circle of torchlight.

"That's Chloe," Edward whispered. "She scrubs the clothes."

Chloe stared rudely at him, he told John Kenyon. One day he would have her beaten.

They saw Chloe go over to an old woman and take a baby from her. There in the moonlight, unashamed, she bared her dark nipple and began to suckle it. The baby's face was brightly lit. It was fair-skinned. A mulatto.

As the boys tiptoed back into the hall old Job the butler emerged from the dining room carrying an oil lamp. They backed quickly onto the verandah. Treppy's voice came out to them, and her heels clicked sharply on polished floors. She came out onto the verandah.

"Put the rocking chair here, Job."

She sat rocking, staring at the moon and listening to the slave music. They were trapped. Edward beckoned John to the far end of the verandah where one of the windows was open. Silently, eyes on Treppy, they crept to it and slid over the sill.

It was then that they heard Edward's mother and father quarrelling violently in the unlit room about Chloe and her mulatto baby.

"First Beulah, and then Venus, and now Chloe, and all of them our own slave women. I haven't a child of yours without a mulatto half-brother or sister of the same age. How many para-

44

mours have you had already, Charles? How many more are there to come?"

Charles Moulton's charming, rather affected voice sneered out of the darkness. "It's the custom of the country."

"Does that make it right, Charles?"

"The Barretts seem to think so. It must be getting on for a hundred years since Hersey Barrett freed Katy and Nod and Nanny, his mulatto children by his slave woman Jane."

"Those were the bad old days, when there were no white women in Jamaica."

"Would you call your father's days the bad old days, too? Patches' own brother Richard bought freedom for his Negro wench Sibella and all her brats. And what about his other brother and his slave woman Madgikan and her four quadroons? Ask Treppy! She lived like a sister to Madgikan's piccaninnies."

There was no reply.

"And if *those* were the bad old days, too," the cruel voice went on, "what of your own brothers? Isn't your precious brother Sam living in sin with his own cousin, the lawful wife of another man, who has borne him four bastards? Hasn't your brother George got six children by the slave Elissa Peters? And doesn't he swear that he's going to free them all, and send them to England to be turned into ladies and gentlemen? Your friend John Graham-Clarke is to arrange for their schooling and careers in Newcastle—he's a great merchant there these days. And what of your third and last brother, Henry?"

"Henry, too?" Her voice was small. "I didn't know."

"Henry is living with a Negro mistress and has two mulatto boys already—Barrett boys! Are you daring to criticize me, Elizabeth? It's your family that has supplied your sons with twelve bastard first cousins, six of them black!"

"I don't have to like it, Charles. I won't bear it."

"Women have to bear it."

"Most do, because there's nowhere in Jamaica for a woman to go if she's left her husband and has no money."

"I'm glad you recognize that."

"But I can go back to Cinnamon Hill and be sure of a home for me and my children. I'll give you one more chance, Charles, for their sake. If you don't take it, I'll leave you. Do you hear me?"

Then the obscenities followed, deliberately hurled in that cold cruel voice at the woman in the dark room, an endless string of salacious details of what Charles Moulton did with his black wenches, and what he would continue to do, since black women were better than white women in bed.

The footsteps of Edward's mother fled from the room and the door banged. Charles Moulton laughed loudly. Then he too went to the door which led into the hall, and out onto the verandah. Pebbles crunched as he walked openly in the direction of the slave lines.

"Good night, Treppy!" they heard him call, almost gaily. "I should go to Elizabeth if I were you."

The noise of rocking stopped.

"Of course she didn't leave him then," John Kenyon said to Robert. "Women will endure almost anything to save a marriage, and rightly so. By the time she did he was keeping three native households."

It had taken years for Elizabeth Moulton to break; but Edward Barrett's happy childhood was destroyed that night while he stood in the dark listening to his mother weeping and learned to look on the father he adored as an enemy.

He had been too young for such a shock—for all the shocks. His contemporaries would have decades in which to adjust to a situation he had had to meet in minutes. His whole world was in ruins, with countless loving uncles, great-uncles, even far-distant ancestors, all joining in a kind of mowing dance of sin with despised partners to produce shameful half-sisters, half-brothers, and cousins innumerable. In the forefront was the figure of his father with his love of women which made his mother weep.

They had gone in silence to their bed, but John Kenyon had heard his cousin sobbing far into the night. Once he had touched his hand, trying to comfort him but had found a hard cold fist which would not unclench.

"He hated his father from that night," said this cousin and childhood friend of Elizabeth's father to Robert Browning over half a century later. "*I* didn't like it when I discovered that I have two coloured half-sisters by a slave called Ann Cooper. But the knowledge didn't come like that, so it didn't crush me. That night changed him completely."

In 1795 Elizabeth Moulton had left Jamaica for England with

46

her children and Treppy, and the family friend John Graham-Clarke had found them a house. When her father, old Patches, had died her son Edward had inherited all his wealth as his only legitimate grandson, and had changed his name by royal license to Barrett.

Charles Moulton continued to be an embarrassment. Wherever he settled, whether it was in New York buying slaves at the sales, or in England, or in Jamaica, he bred families and gave his bastards Barrett and Moulton names.

"When Ba was thirteen he died, at last. I don't suppose she knows anything about it all. Edward wouldn't think it fit for a pure woman's ears."

I don't suppose, either, Mr. Kenyon thought, gazing piercingly at young Robert Browning, that you know much about the Tittles in Jamaica, come to that! And you won't be hearing it from me. Jamaicans in England usually know little of their family history in the island; they've been sent over to forget it.

The keen eyes in the affable countenance met Robert's. "At any rate, it all goes to explain why Edward Barrett is such a strange father."

What was Mr. Kenyon trying to tell him? Robert asked himself. He was far too discreet to speak bluntly except of the dead. Was he saying that Edward Barrett was cruel to Elizabeth? That was ridiculous! Elizabeth's tiny silver bell of a voice rang happily when she talked of her "Papa."

"In Jamaica there's a flower," Mr. Kenyon was saying, staring fixedly at the delicate petals of the sweet peas, which were losing colour in the dusk. "Its petals are thick and fleshy and highly coloured. It opens them wide. Little insects find it irresistible—sometimes little animals too. When they venture onto them to taste the thick honey with which they're spread it snaps shut. It doesn't open again until there's nothing left but a few dry shards to be blown away in the breeze. It's called Venus's Fly Catcher. I've often wondered why such a thing should be called by the name of the goddess of love."

Robert remembered that Mr. Kenyon was a poet. Before he could speak the voice of his father came to them across the garden, calling them indoors to supper. John Kenyon turned, beaming, to join his old friend.

"Now there's a man who knows how to love!" he said.

4

ROBERT WAS HOPELESSLY IN LOVE WITH ELIZABETH, happily infatuated with the miraculous little creature whose charm and passionate desire to please had made her the favourite from birth of anyone close to her—her father, her grandmother, her uncle Matthew Barrett, all her brothers and her two admiring sisters so different from each other, Treppy, Mr. Kenyon and Miss Mitford. She seemed to draw everyone about her with her warmth, and now Robert too sunned himself in it.

When they had known each other for three weeks, meeting once a week, Robert brought her an armful of red roses and a small basket of his mother's strawberries. "When will you come and gather them for yourself?" he asked.

"Oh, no!" she answered him quickly. "Don't think of such a thing! There's no hope for me."

Outside June sunshine glittered on water, green leaves danced in the breeze, children skipped and shouted. Inside number 50 Wimpole Street Elizabeth lay on her sofa, still in her old black silk dress, and not a ray of sunshine crept into her room.

She was more a prisoner than those children she had freed, Robert thought. Two years ago she had read Mr. Horne's report of the commission set up to investigate child labour in the mines and factories. Then she had written a poem—simply written a poem, a gentle poem, in words everyone could understand.

> Do ye hear the children weeping, O my brothers,
>   Ere the sorrow comes with years?

They are leaning their young heads against their mothers,
    And *that* cannot stop their tears.
The young lambs are bleating in the meadows,
    The young birds are chirping in the nest,
The young fawns are playing with the shadows,
    The young flowers are blowing toward the west—
But the young, young children, O my brothers,
    They are weeping bitterly!
They are weeping in the playtime of the others,
    In the country of the free.

It hadn't perhaps been the most glorious of all her poems, but Miss Barrett had known what she was about. Lord Shaftesbury's magnificent speech of horror at the conditions which had been exposed had just been delivered in Parliament when *Cry of the Children* had come out in the August issue of *Blackwood's Magazine.*

The whole nation had gone up in flames. Men cried as they read it, clergymen declaimed it from their pulpits, mothers and schoolteachers taught it to children. Public feeling had been roused to such a pitch that Parliament had passed the first Act which took steps to improve the appalling conditions. Shelley had been right when he had called poets the unacknowledged legislators of mankind.

"Miss Barrett, I *know* that you can get well. Won't you simply try a little?"

She looked astonished.

"Try to do what?"

"Only come from that sofa to this armchair, then sit in it for just five minutes."

"It will exhaust me. After I'm dressed in the morning I have to lie quiet for an hour just to still the palpitations of my heart and pulse."

Only to please him, and with no belief in his extraordinary assertion that he could make her well—he, a young man who had only listened to a few medical lectures at the famous Guy's teaching hospital more than ten years before—she agreed. It really was quite amazing how dogmatic, and yet how considerate, Mr. Browning was.

He took both her hands in his, holding them firmly in his warm steady ones, while she got shakily to her feet. He led her very slowly to the big armchair and arranged her shawls and cushions. There was something comforting in the tender movements of this bluff, rather clumsy man. The five minutes went quickly, and she promised to try again in three days.

He brought her a novel by George Sand as a reward. She loved novels—good ones, indifferent ones, even bad ones, French ones in particular, and best of all those of the Frenchwoman who had left her husband, the Baron Dudevant, to scandalize the world as "George Sand," defying convention by her liaisons with geniuses like Alfred de Musset the poet, Chopin the composer, and Prosper Mérimée the novelist, and by dressing and smoking like a man.

He had commented on that, and she had been surprisingly frank.

"She's shameless, I know, in the disgusting way she dwells on the passion of love under its physical aspect, and Papa would be horrified if he found out! He'd as soon give me prussic acid if I were thirsty as let me read the canto of *Don Juan* he's got locked in a drawer!"

"Still, you read George Sand, and enjoy her?"

"She's as eloquent as a fallen angel. I'd give anything in the world to meet her—or to have a letter from her, even if it smelled of cigars. And it would, of course."

A week later, at Robert's urging, Elizabeth was carried downstairs to the drawing room by her brother Charles John—the eldest living son, the heir, the one with the terrible stammer, nicknamed Stormy because he had been born in a storm.

A week after that Elizabeth walked downstairs by herself and joined the family, though Stormy had to carry her up again. It was only five weeks since she had met Robert.

Always Robert led her in imagination outside the house, with Italy at the end of the road. Soon she had fallen in love with this country she had never seen. Whenever her courage failed her he could rouse it again with lyrical descriptions of his two journeys. How, he asked her, could an invalid ever hope to see Italy?

Before the end of the month Elizabeth actually went out for a short carriage drive with Arabel to the gates of Regent's Park. She was carried away with excitement, and wanted to drive into the park, then to Harley Place and leave a visiting card at Mr. Kenyon's house.

"It would be vainglorious, Arabel."

"Not on your first drive, Ba. You'll be so tired."

George came upstairs to ask how she was after the great expedition, grave as always, his face handsome in its bony, equine way.

"I walk as well as most children of two years old now," Elizabeth said. "I might get well after all, George."

"Don't hope for too much, Ba. You will take things quietly, won't you?"

As her smile faded he added hastily, "I don't mean to discourage you, Ba. It's just that false hopes—"

"I know, George. But I *am* better; and I may get better still."

"No one wishes that more than I do, Ba."

"Except Papa!"

More quickly than Robert dared hope came the letter which told him that she had got out of the carriage and walked in the park. That had been on the fourth of July.

"Never, pray, *pray*, never lose one sunny day," he exulted, "but go out and walk about." Boldly, he rushed on, "But don't surprise *me* one of those mornings by walking up to me, or in spite of all the begging pardon I shall have to do afterwards I shall . . ." He smiled as he finished the sentence. Then he thought again of the possible consequences of such rashness, and scratched out the words he had written. She couldn't be in any doubt as to how such a sentence must have ended. Yet how could she rebuke him? He had said nothing at all.

Everyone wondered aloud at the change in her. Her physician, the famous Dr. Chambers who attended the Queen, was surprised and pleased. In the mirror her cheeks were red and her eyes sparkled. She left it for her writing table, and wrote, slowly, a smile on her lips, on a small sheet of paper.

> I saw, in gradual vision through my tears,
> The sweet, sad years, the melancholy years,
> Those of my own life, who by turns had flung
> A shadow across me. Straightway I was 'ware,
> So weeping, how a mystic shape did move
> Behind me, and drew me backward by the hair;

And a voice said in mastery, while I strove—
"Guess who now holds thee?"—"Death," I said. But there,
The silver answer rang,—"Not Death, but Love."

Then Elizabeth had a relapse. When Robert called he was
sent away by a blank-faced Proudfoot, the butler. "Miss Barrett
is indisposed today, sir."

That was all he was entitled to. He could not even mount
the stairs to see her. He must go away and wait for a letter.

The days passed, and still no letter came. Robert called
again and again, to be told that she was in bed and could see no
one. Proudfoot either could not or would not tell him more. He
stayed at New Cross, not going out, meeting the postman in the
drive at every delivery.

At last her letter came, in a shaky hand which he hardly
recognized.

Dr. Chambers had been sent for. He had brought out the
dreaded stethoscope, had shaken his august head and turned down
the corners of his mouth. It would never do for her to spend the
winter in London. That would dissipate all the summer's benefits.
She must get away from the heavy fogs and the cold, the soot and
the dirt, and regain what she had already lost by this unfortunate
relapse. She must go south, out of England if at all possible, and
preferably to the Mediterranean. He had suggested Italy.

Italy! The bells rang for her and Robert. He could hardly
wait for her next letter.

Dr. Chambers's words had been reported to Mr. Barrett.
They waited for his reaction. Day after day went by. Nothing was
said.

The days grew into a week, and then into a fortnight. The
silence was oppressive. Elizabeth became more and more anxious,
then feverish with anxiety. Her brothers and sisters, too, waited
nervously, listening tensely throughout every evening meal. Elizabeth's unhappiness infected them, and they snapped at each other.
The whole household was restless.

It was Arabel who, in her quiet way, decided it was time for
action. She spoke to Henrietta. Henrietta spoke to George. George
listened sagely, pulling his moustache, and summoned a confer-
ence. The eight brothers and sisters sat round the great mahogany
dining table, which had been made from wood grown on the

Cinnamon Hill Estate in Jamaica. George sat at its head, and when they had all had their say he called for a vote. A deputation, it was decided, should visit Mr. Barrett and ask him what was to be done about Ba.

That night George, Henrietta and Arabel stood outside Mr. Barrett's study door. They had elected to wait until after dinner in case he broke the silence, but he had said nothing. Once inside the room, George spoke for them all.

"I'd rather," he told them afterwards, "go through my public examination at the University all over again."

He mopped his brow as if he had been through some terrible experience. Papa had that effect on his children, Arabel said. Henrietta said nothing at all and her little face looked even more stubborn and hopeless than before under the flame of her red hair.

Mr. Barrett had simply sat, his hands folded across his stomach, his mouth pursed into a plump little bud, staring into the empty fireplace. He had said nothing to George, or to Henrietta and Arabel, as now and then they tremulously echoed their brother's words. In the end their voices had died away, and even George had come to a stop. They stood there for endless minutes. Then they looked at each other, and crept to the door and out of it.

They were used to their father's silences, and his roars of anger. This was so important that they would have expected him to thunder at them if he disliked it. Perhaps, they said to each other, his silence meant consent. Growing more and more optimistic as the chill of that unbroken silence wore off, they decided that they would tell Elizabeth that her father had implied consent although he had not actually given it in so many words.

"I think you may take it that Papa is agreeable to your going away," George said to her when they had trudged up to her room, and stood before her. "Probably to Malta."

"Oh, George," she said joyfully. "You came in so solemnly, all of you, that I was sure you were bringing bad news."

"He didn't positively say it, mind you," Arabel clutched at the disappearing truth, "but he didn't forbid it."

"I think you may make your plans with confidence," George said. "He'll speak in his own good time, I've no doubt. We've told him what's been decided, and he has accepted it without protest."

"I don't know how to thank you," Elizabeth said.

Next day Robert was allowed to see her when he called— their first meeting for a fortnight. The sunshine and blue skies outside were as bright as their hopes.

"I wonder," he asked in his joy for her, "whether I mightn't be allowed to go to Malta and meet you there?"

She did not forbid it.

Elizabeth quickly regained her old vitality, looked in her mirror again with pleasure and went out for carriage drives once more.

"Order Wilson to pack," George said. "I've enquired about the tickets."

Wilson ran to and fro, her stolid face flushed, pulling out basket trunks, mending petticoats and ironing. It was nearing the end of July and Elizabeth must go in August, it was decided. George and Arabel would be going with her, for of course she could not travel alone. But they could not leave the country before definite permission came from Mr. Barrett. Nothing, not the smallest reference to a journey abroad, had been said by him. No date was fixed. Yet the winds of autumn were not far off.

Then, without warning, the blow fell. Aunt Arabella Graham-Clarke appeared in Elizabeth's room. Elizabeth saw her mother's timid eyes looking sorrowfully at her from under the mouse-brown braided hair.

"Your Papa's decided you're not to go abroad, Ba."

"Oh, Bummy! Why not?"

"He asked me to tell you what he has decided, that's all."

So, Elizabeth thought bitterly, he won't even tell me himself.

That night her father came to her room as usual. He knelt by her bed and prayed.

"Give this child of Thine fortitude and wisdom. Let her not strive after the things of this world, but submit herself to Thy will."

He kissed her on her forehead, a kiss that was like a reproof, and went straight to the door. He had not said a word about it. She knew that if she spoke she would be greeted with his deadening silence. She said nothing.

"Good night, Ba." At least he called her Ba. She looked up and gazed at him as he stood there looking at her. His dark blue eyes looked black as night.

"Good night, Papa."

He went through the door, and she watched it close.

Next afternoon Elizabeth's letter giving the news of her father's refusal reached Robert. He sat in his room for over an hour, his hands clenched before him on the table, telling himself over and over that only harm would come of his giving way to anger. Eventually his rage subsided, leaving him with a sick, choking feeling.

The edict must be accepted, George had told Elizabeth. There was nothing more to be done. Well, *he* would do something. The question was how?

He flung on his green riding coat, ran to the stables and saddled York, his cousin Reuben Browning's bay, to which his father gave stable room. There was nothing like a furious gallop over the fields for quenching anger—and for thinking things out. Tomorrow he would see her.

In her room at last, Robert stood looking down at Elizabeth, speechless with pity. Her face was as pale as a wax candle, with a transparency about it. Her white hands lay still on the soft plaid rug. Her body hardly swelled it. Only her feverish eyes, looking larger than her face, and that shower of dark curls, dressed by Wilson as carefully as ever, seemed to belong to a living woman. Yet she smiled at him. He never ceased to wonder at her courage— her joyousness, even—under the blows of life.

Now, however, as he looked at her he knew that the disappointment had been so cruel that even her brave spirit might not restore her. Mr. Barrett was a danger to her. He could end by killing her. "Wouldn't you like to be lifted to the chair?" he asked Elizabeth.

"No," she said listlessly. "What's the use?"

"To get well. To walk in the park with me. Am I never to know how far your lips are from mine when we walk?"

It was so hot that July that Flush was moving restlessly about, trying to find a cool place. Even the flowers he had brought drooped in his hand.

"Foolish dreams, Mr. Browning. I must return to reality and be content once more with my dungeon."

"Even to walk about your room is better than it was," he pleaded.

"I can write here as well as sitting up at a table."

He could not shake her out of her apathy. She was too full of lassitude even to resist his pleas that he might increase his visits. So he came again twice, at short intervals, and each time she lay as still as before.

There was only one thing to be done. Yet something warned him not to move too clumsily or too soon. He must be sure of what he was doing. Had he the right to urge her to disobedience, ill and dependent as she was? Was it for him to incite anger between her and her father?

Robert knew only too well the bitterness of family quarrels. Every day his father sighed over the rift between him and his own father, Robert's grandfather, the first of the three Robert Brownings. Yet Robert's father had been the victim.

A gruesome story it was, too. His father's mother, Maggie Tittle, the West Indian grandmother he had never known, had died when her boy was seven. It was the Tittles who had brought in the hot Jamaican blood John Kenyon was so conscious of. Five years after her death the boy had a stepmother, a tartar.

"You've no need of two wives, Mr. Browning," she had snapped, sweeping poor Maggie's portrait up to the garret.

She had grudged Robert's father the little income one of his mother's brothers had left him. It gave him advantages over her own brood. She and her husband had stopped him becoming a painter, or going to the University—at his own expense! Instead they had sent him out to manage the Tittle sugar plantation in Saint Kitts, where his Jamaican ancestor had finally settled.

Never was man less suited to the task of slave driver than Robert's father had been. He had broken the law, trying to teach a slave to read. Then, one beautiful morning, walking out to the canefields, he had stumbled over the body of his uncle murdered on his own plantation, head and hands severed, the private parts mutilated. Sickened, he had left the island at once.

Before he left the magistrate had handed him his uncle's cufflinks, taken from the body. When Robert had asked to see them, his father had replied with a shudder, "Do you want them? Then take them."

Robert's father had sailed home without permission from his

stepmother and his father. In their fury they seemed to have taken leave of their senses. Could it really be that a man in his middle fifties and his wife could have presented the poor young man with an account for all the expenses his father had been put to since he had been born, including the midwife's bill? It had been done.

Neither Maggie's money nor the property in Saint Kitts had been left to her little son when she died, though he had been meant to have them. His father and stepmother saw to it that he would never receive either. His private income from his uncle could not be touched. He would have that small raft against misfortune forever. But he must earn his living.

So Robert's grandfather had asked a favour of the great ones in the august Bank of England, where he was Principal of the Bank Stock Office, no less. Robert's father had climbed wretchedly up onto his clerk's stool in his corner, and had sat there ever since, rising no higher, living only for the old books and engravings to which he fled at the end of each dreadful day. A wasted life.

Well, what was the lesson of it all? Was it that Robert must not incite Elizabeth Barrett to disobedience and family quarrels, starting in the close-bound and loving Barrett household the sort of misery which had blighted the lives of his own parents?

Or was it not rather that he ought to encourage her to nerve herself to that very disobedience?

Had his father struck out on his own with his little income and made a life and a name for himself as an artist, he might have been a happier man. The rifts might have been healed when Robert's grandfather had found a new respect for his son. Even if he had not prospered, he would have led a life of fulfillment instead of frustration. He could hardly have earned less than he now did.

Besides, for Elizabeth Barrett the choice between submission and disobedience was more vital than it had ever been for his father. It might well make the difference between life and death.

As he brooded Robert stood more often than usual before his favourite picture, of Perseus rescuing a drooping, white-limbed maiden, bound to a rock, from a sea dragon—a reproduction of Caravaggio's *Andromeda.*

On his next visit he asked Elizabeth outright to disobey her father and go to Italy for her own sake.

All her remaining strength seemed gathered up in the one explosive *"No!"*

"Yet you cannot go to Italy if it rests with your father," he said as equably as he could. "That's clear."

"Then I cannot go."

He could not tell whether she spoke in resignation or despair. He pressed her harder and harder. He saw the panic grow in her eyes, and her hands fly to her face. He realized that she was almost breaking under the strain, torn intolerably between him and her father, and unable to give any reasons which would satisfy him.

In the end she simply sat with her head bowed, bearing it, but not replying. So he too sank into the silence of defeat.

At long last she raised her head and looked at him. "There's nothing for it," she said wearily. "I must tell you of the time when my heart was broken by that great stone that fell out of heaven. Then you will understand. Then you *must* understand why I cannot disobey Papa and go to Italy."

5

ROBERT HAD BROUGHT DOG ROSES FOR HER, AND
their scent at once filled the room. A week had limped by. Now
Elizabeth would keep her promise to explain why she would
not disobey her father.

He missed her smile. She did not even seem to notice when
Flush snarled as he approached their shared sofa. Her impetuous
nature was at war with the control she was exercising.

When Wilson had gone she made him draw his chair closer.

"Once you understand about the most important thing that
has ever happened to me you'll realize that what you're asking is
impossible."

She had written it all down in a letter, which he must read
at home. She gave it to him.

"I've never *spoken* of this to a living soul. You must give me
your promise never to mention it to me again."

"Another secret!"

She was not to be seduced into laughter. She was actually
trembling. "It's too painful to speak of. Just to write it down has
cost me—cost me . . ."

Suddenly he knew what he must do. "I think you should tell
me yourself." He spoke firmly, with authority.

"I *cannot* speak of it." It was a cry of horror. "Don't ask me."

He took her hands in his, those marmoset's hands which filled
him with love and pity. They never did more than handle pen
and paper, turn the leaves of a book, brush the golden curls of a
little pet dog and set down his water bowl.

"You must." Then, "Look at me."

For a moment Elizabeth raised her eyes. He felt the tension go out of her hands.

"Now tell me." He spoke in a whisper, knowing that this was a very important thing he was doing, for her, for him, for any future there might be for them both. He saw that she looked at him with trust.

And so she told him.

Seven years before, after the family had moved to Wimpole Street in the summer of 1838, soon after her thirty-second birthday, she had broken a blood vessel. Dr. Jago had called in Dr. Chambers, and he had warned her father that one of her lungs might be consumptive—a sentence of death. He made no attempt to tone down the starkness of the message. She would not survive another winter in London. She must go away at once, if possible to a sunnier climate, but at least to a warmer one.

All the family had had one reaction—all but Mr. Barrett. While her brothers and sisters were deciding that she must go to Torquay on the south Devon coast, where their mother's other sister, Aunt Hedley, lived and could keep an eye on her, they realized to their amazement that Mr. Barrett had set his face against it. He did not argue or explain. He simply shook his head.

Perhaps Mr. Barrett was remembering that when his wife had left Hope End for Cheltenham she had not returned; and she had hardly been ill. Elizabeth knew what he dreaded. He could not say it, of course, to her or anyone else. It was because he loved her that he would not let her go. Yet the only hope for her was that she should go. All that summer the battle between him and the family went on. At last he gave way.

Towards the end of August a miserable foursome—Elizabeth and Arabel, Edward and George, had sailed from London to Plymouth, and then reembarked on a packet boat for Torquay.

"The worst—what people call the worst—was feared for me," she whispered.

Only the fear of death would have driven the family to such extreme action. It was a cripplingly expensive undertaking to keep her so far away, with brothers and sisters ferrying to and fro in constant attendance. Torquay was a three-day land-and-sea journey from London. Then there was the heavy cost of doctors and medicines—just when Mr. Barrett had had to go bravely and uncomplainingly to live in London, which he hated, and work all day in the City, in order to make a little money, and help George become a barrister. Elizabeth might have to be away for years, too. That might be the best that could be hoped for.

The conflicts which had rent the family all summer had reduced her to extreme exhaustion. She found it unbearable that she was the cause of this disunity, and that there was nothing she could do about it except to die. As long as she remained at Torquay she, and she alone, would be the direct cause of dividing the family and putting a burden on them, and above all on her father. For how many years would she be there? Or for how many weeks?

It was bad enough to be so ill, and to know the truth, without such a weight of guilt. But she went as bravely as she could, fortified because her favourite brother, Edward, went with her. Elizabeth was sent with her sister Arabel to her Aunt and Uncle Hedley. Aunt Hedley was good-looking and rich and impulsive, and rather foolish; and she had two sons and three daughters of her own to care for. But she could not refuse to help her dead sister's dying child. Elizabeth's brother Edward was supposed to take his sisters to Torquay and return to London with George.

Edward—Bro to her—was her other self. She had been one year old when he had come into the world like a gift to her, his baby sister, his "Ba." The other brothers and sisters were different from her and from each other. But Bro and she were made of the same clay. They had ridden in the wind together, walked in the woods, read the same books, wept at the same sorrows, even shared the same lessons.

Her father was proud that she was such a clever girl and wrote poetry. But only with Bro could she talk about her poems, Bro alone understood everything.

Bro was charming, sensitive, alive. He was beautiful with his dark curls, and he laughed easily. His father loved him best of all his sons, as he loved her best of his daughters. He was his heir, the flower of his house, his favourite. Not as Elizabeth loved him, however. She loved her brother, she admitted, even more than she loved her father.

She was to be in Torquay for three long years. Her sisters Henrietta and Arabel lived with her nearly all the time, sometimes in turns, sometimes together. She longed for her father, and he for her. Whenever he could Mr. Barrett made the three-day journey to see her, and when he came he could not bear to go away. From day to day he stayed on, and often the days lengthened into months before suddenly, without a word, he disappeared to London and the City.

The other brothers came too, sometimes singly, sometimes in pairs, making it a holiday, bringing laughter to the sickroom, as if it was a game she was playing, this frightening them with her illness. But it was Bro she wanted, Bro she needed, and she wanted him with her all the time. He stayed on and on while the others came and went.

It was the summer of 1839 when Mr. Barrett decided that Bro must come home.

"And then the time came for him to leave me," Elizabeth said, her voice suddenly strained. "You cannot understand what that meant. I can only tell you that he was above us all, and kindest, and noblest, and dearest to me beyond any comparison. He was the only one of my family, who . . . Well, but I cannot speak of these things."

She paused for a long time, then went on: "When the time came for him to leave me I was so weak and ill that I could not drive back my tears. And my Aunt Hedley kissed my tears away instead of reproving me as she should have done."

She stared at the black silk lap of her dress.

"My Aunt Hedley is brave, not timid like my Aunt Bummy. So she sat down and wrote a letter to Papa to tell him that he would break my heart if he persisted in calling away my brother. I have thought bitterly since that my heart did not break for a good deal more than that."

She took a long shuddering breath.

"And Papa's answer was—it's burnt into me with fire—that in the circumstances he didn't refuse, but that he considered it to be *very wrong in me to exact such a thing*. I could keep my brother, but on pain of his severe displeasure."

In the silence Robert could hear the sparrows in the ivy, and the untroubled breathing of the sleeping Flush, where he lay warming himself like a cat in a narrow strip of sunlight on the floor. He had moved without their noticing him. Still holding her hands, Robert took the empty place beside her.

"So there was no separation *then*. And month after month

passed. And sometimes I was better and sometimes worse. And the medical men continued to say that they would not answer for my life if I were upset. So there was no more talk of separation from my Bro."

For two more years Elizabeth had kept her beloved brother by her bedside. Though he loved life and parties and was popular he seemed content to spend most of his time with the invalid.

Early in the autumn of 1838 Elizabeth and Henrietta and Elizabeth's maid had been moved by Bro to 3 Beacon Terrace, a house in the warmest part of Torquay, sheltered by a steep hill. It looked right out over the harbour; but Elizabeth did not appreciate the view. To her it seemed as if the house was in the sea, since she could see only water from her sofa, and whenever the steam packet arrived or departed her very bed was shaken by the vibrations.

Soon Aunt Bummy joined her sister, Aunt Hedley, to nurse her. At first Elizabeth's health had seemed to improve. Bro had taken her boating with him almost every day. Then in January, 1840, she had had a sudden relapse, and for two months hung by a thread between life and death.

With the coming of spring she had seemed to recover a little, and the improvement had gone on into summer. But that phase had lasted only a few months. From then on her condition had worsened rapidly. She was so weak that often she was unable to speak at all. She had very severe headaches. The doctors had reported a spot on the lung. She was spitting blood.

It was only when the warm weather had come to stay that she began to show any improvement. At last the doctors looked more cheerful and said she could leave her bed for the sofa again. Perhaps, she hoped, she might soon go out with Bro on the boating parties he loved.

It was at this time that Bro spoke tenderly to her in words that she would never forget. She could see him still, with the thick dark curls clustering about his forehead, looking so much younger than thirty-two. It was hard to believe there was only a year between them. He was quite serious, for once, when he took her hand.

"He told me he loved me better than anyone else, and would not leave me till I was well."

He never admitted to her that there was any possibility that she would not get well. Elizabeth knew that his real promise was that he would stay with her until the end, whatever that might be.

It was Saturday, July 11, 1840, ten days after Bro had held her hand and promised never to leave her. It was a beautiful day, calm and sunny. That morning her brother told her he was going out sailing. For once she spoke sharply to him; and for once he answered her in kind.

"He left me—with a pettish word."

Her voice was so low that Robert hardly caught what she said. He noticed that Elizabeth did not say exactly what it was that had passed between brother and sister. Had Bro rebelled against staying by a sickbed when the sun and the sea and his friends were all calling him to life outside? Clearly her brother had loved the sea, and as clearly she had not. It might have seemed to her to have been stealthily drawing him away from her, despite his promise.

Bro had gone out in *La Belle Sauvage,* which had been doing well in the regattas round the bay. With him were two others, Captain Clarke and Charles Vannek. The skipper was an experienced Devon seaman, William White. With a good "soldier's wind" and Bill White, and the *Belle* in her newly stretched summer canvas, the young men were sure they would have a good reach out to the Start and back again before sunset. Henrietta had run laughing down to the quayside to see them sail, the breeze whipping her flaming hair. They were all in high spirits as they cast off. Captain Clarke pinned a red carnation on his coat just before he disappeared down the little Jacob's ladder.

Elizabeth, unhappy at the sharp exchange, and anxious for Bro's return so she could make friends, waited impatiently. The afternoon turned to dusk. Bro and his friends must have been tempted by the glorious day into having a longer run.

The other yachts which had gone out that day came back one by one; but *La Belle Sauvage* did not return. All night the three sisters hoped against hope. Henrietta and Arabel kept coming into Elizabeth's room. They spoke of how calm the sea was, and how light the winds. They did not allow their uneasiness to creep into their voices; but they came more often as the hours went by.

Somehow the night passed. In the morning the sun shone on a sea so innocent it looked as though it was made only to mirror the blue sky. Elizabeth's sisters drew back the curtains in her room to show her what a lovely day it was.

Twice more the dawn broke in radiant loveliness. For two days more there was no wind and the sea was calm. Somehow the second day went by, and somehow they lived through the third day.

"For three days we waited, and I hoped while I could—oh, that awful agony! And the sun shone as it shines today, and there was no more wind than there is now. The sea under the windows was as smooth as paper. My sisters drew the curtains back every morning so that I could see for myself how calm it was, and how it could hurt nobody."

A rumour spread, and was brought to their back door, that a boat answering the *Belle*'s description had capsized in a squall in Babbacombe Bay. Two Exmouth seamen who had sighted her said there seemed to be four men aboard. Even then the sisters still hoped. But still Bro did not return.

They could wait no longer before telling their father. Mr. Barrett arrived, silent, stricken. He had nothing to say to them. He issued his orders to others. He sent out search parties all along the coast for miles, and offered a reward to anyone who brought him news of his son.

Elizabeth could think of nothing but how she and Bro had parted in anger.

She cried out to Robert as if her grief were new again. "He held my hand, and said he would never leave me. And ten days from that day the boat had left the shore which never returned, never—and he *had* left me."

Several days after Mr. Barrett arrived the *Belle* was sighted, overturned but afloat. Soon afterwards the body of young Captain Clarke was recovered, the remains of his carnation still in his buttonhole.

Three weeks after the *Belle* had left the shore another body was sighted, floating in the bay, and was brought ashore. Mr. Barrett identified it as his son's.

Bro was buried in Tor Churchyard on August 6, 1840.

Mr. Barrett's grief was the more awful because it was silent. His children did not recognize the man of loud laughter and sudden angers. His silence had a terrible effect on Elizabeth. She took it for an accusation. Bro, best beloved to her and to him, was dead, and she had killed him. If she had not wept at the thought of losing her brother, if her aunt had not written to implore her father to leave him with her, then Bro would still be alive! She felt she was as much to blame for his death as the squall which had blown up, the boat which had capsized and the crew which had not averted the disaster. Because of her selfish love for her brother her father's house was deprived of its cornerstone and she herself bereft of the affection that had filled her days. All day, every day, the words, "I killed him! I killed him!" beat into her brain. They came with every dash of the waves against the shore.

Edward had hardly been buried when the corpse of William White was washed ashore. Charles Vannek was never found.

Now Elizabeth almost longed for her father to accuse her openly, and now she flinched for fear that he might. "I lay for weeks and months half-unconscious. And all the while I thought to myself, *You have done this.*"

Robert could not suppress a small cry of protest. She did not seem to hear.

For more than three months she had been delirious. "I can remember visions of long dark spectral trains, and children's faces staring at me. It drove me almost to madness. I tell you, I could not pray, I could not weep. I have never wept."

Robert opened his arms, and, as if she did not know what she did, she came into them. But still her eyes were dry and her voice without hope.

Elizabeth had been astonished that she could not die. "I had —I must have had—an unnatural tenacity for life," she said, with anger. She had never recovered from the shock. She was weary of life, always longing for death. She could not bear to see anyone except her family and a very few close friends.

"I am evil, I have been the cause of unmitigated evil. I have killed Bro, the crown of our family. If I had not been selfish—if I had not begged him to stay with me—there—by the sea—"

"Hush." He held her closer, rocking her like a little child. He could only guess as yet at the extent of her sensitivity and her vulnerability. He knew, nonetheless, that she had taken him into the desolation of her heart, where no one else had been.

"I have killed my best beloved. All his life he gave me the tenderest affection. Never a harsh word—never an unkind look—until that pettish word. Oh, God, why *then?*"

66

She saw her father across a chasm of fear and guilt. They stood on opposite sides of Edward's grave, looking at each other. Conflicting emotions warred within her. Her father had loved Bro and been proud of him. But he had loved her too, and been proud of her—and jealous of her closer tie with Bro.

At first she had not known what to make of Mr. Barrett's behaviour. His other children had shrunk back from the silence and the rocklike hardness. Slowly Elizabeth had begun to realize that he did not mean to blame her. He stayed beside her through all her desperate illness, always kind, always tender.

"Not once, then or later, did Papa blame me. He was generous and forbearing in that hour of bitter trial. He never once said to me that if it had not been for *me* the crown of his house would not have fallen. And he might have said it, and more. I could have answered nothing except that I had paid my own price, and the price I paid was greater than his."

Somehow the grief they shared and her guilt had forged a stronger link between them. She had always loved her father, but now her heart bled for him too. She resolved to make up his loss by her own love—and she did love him more than anyone else left to her to love.

Fifteen months went by before Elizabeth returned to Wimpole Street, fifteen months during which she hated the sea more every day. At last she was allowed home, going against doctor's orders, by slow stages, in a specially sprung carriage.

Elizabeth returned to devote herself to her father, and he understood that. At night, late, before he went to bed, he would come to her room and kneel at her bedside to pray aloud. Soon she found she was listening for the sound of his footsteps on the stairs and looking forward to his visits all day. His prayers comforted her.

The doctors told her that she could only expect to live the life of an invalid. She still thought constantly of her own death. She would cling to her father, sobbing, "My best hope is to die under your eyes."

Now Robert tried to tell her that her guilt was wrong and that there was nothing for which to blame herself, but she swept him aside.

"You must see that I have strong reasons for being grateful."

"For what?"

"For the forbearance."

"It would have been cruel—wrong—to reproach you."

"Perhaps. Yet the kindness and patience of not reproaching me are positive things all the same."

This was what she had to tell him. To wound her father was out of the question. She had hurt him once, and he had not turned and rent her. There was to be no question of flouting his will, however unreasonable it was. What if her remaining in London instead of going to Italy should cost her her life? Her life had been forfeit and he had brought her back to it. It was a debt to him.

At last Robert understood what she was saying to him. He understood too all the things she was not saying and did not even know were there to be said. Her cry for help came to him through all her efforts to send him away and to sink back into the choking morass of her life. What he was looking at that afternoon in her quiet room, with the clock ticking and Flush breathing softly and the sparrows in the ivy making a false background of peace, was her slow destruction.

Silently he rose, and kissed both her hands. He tugged the bellpull by the fireplace, as he had learned to do, and waited for Wilson to show him out.

There was much to be thought over. Robert was not allowed even to tell her that he loved her and must still address her as Miss Barrett. Yet he must find a way to alter her whole life, from within. The charge was upon him to save this little creature whom he loved, infinitely wise and infinitely foolish, tenderly yielding and inflexibly stubborn, upheld by a great strength yet almost extinguished by a breath, most magical and most pitiful of women.

Grateful for his silence, she smiled at him as he went.

"Come soon again."

"Tomorrow," he said.

6

ROBERT DID NOT GO STRAIGHT HOME TO NEW
Cross.

His mother had asked him to call on the Silverthornes and see
her sister, his Aunt Christiana.

It was time he saw his cousins James and John Silverthorne.
They were more like brothers than cousins, especially big, lusty,
clumsy good-hearted James. They had run in and out of one another's houses as children, when the two sisters had lived near each
other.

Robert had seen Kean act in *Richard III* with James and
John, and made up his mind to be a playwright that night. He
had been to boxing bouts and cockfights with them too, and to
some other, stranger places—places more to their taste than his.
He did not care to spend his father's money on bawds and in
taverns. They had become men together, all the same, and he had
at least looked on strange women, as the Bible had it, in their
company.

Here he was at the house, with Aunt Chrissy hugging him in
her tight fat white arms and pressing him to stay for a plateful of
goose and a bottle of claret. Then it was for an hour of music, and
then for a game of cribbage. His uncle, in his red woollen waistcoat, went off to look at his brewery's accountbooks.

"Stay the night, Robert," his aunt urged.

"Now, Aunt, you know well I never sleep a night away from
home."

His mother would be expecting him, the door between her room and his ajar. Even after dancing the polka all night Robert would stump through the dawn so as not to disappoint her. Yet tonight he wanted to hurry home so as to be alone. For not a single moment of that noisy evening had his thoughts left the dark little figure in her silent room, enduring her private hell.

His cousin James Silverthorne went with him to the gate and along the road, clumping along in comfortable silence. They would never fail each other. When one called the other would answer, wherever he was. That was friendship, to be closer than brothers to the end of the day.

"How is it with you, James?" Robert asked.

"Still heart-whole and fancy-free, though there's a fair plump young lady who lives in a house in this very lane who's sick for love of me, and would marry me tomorrow. She has a comfortable income, too."

"You prefer to remain a bachelor?"

"I don't see myself as a husband."

"Doesn't one see oneself as a lover first? Then the other follows?"

"That's poetry, not life. But it's poets who should never marry. Look at Shelley! All ideals, yet his poor Harriet ended in the river. Take Byron! No ideals, and a trailing horror of a marriage, with Lady Byron a walking reproof to his memory and hints of incest wherever she goes. Marriage would clip *your* wings, Robert, and make the poor creature you married miserable. It wouldn't be fair to her. Not even if she was rich and could keep you."

"You're a cynic, James."

"Do you remember the romany queen at Gypsy Hill in Norwood?"

He would never forget her. He had described her in his *The Flight of the Duchess,* the pearl he was throwing to the swine in his next volume. It must have been ten years ago when he was —what? twenty-two?—that James and he had climbed up to the top of the hill a mile from where the romanies had lived for centuries when they were not on the road with their caravans doing tinkers' and cobblers' work, picking hops or cherries in season, selling wooden clothes pegs and stealing.

The gypsy was standing outside her brightly painted caravan, a tall woman, eagle-nosed and black-eyed. Two plaits of black hair, coarse as a horse's tail, fell over her shoulders. There were strings of gold sovereigns about her dirty neck. "Cross the gypsy's palm with silver, *giorgio!*" she had commanded him, and he had given her his half crown. Then she had grasped his hand in hers and chanted her low singsong.

"You are a singer of songs, and the world will be deaf to your songs for long and long, but you will sing on for the love of singing. It will be bitter for you, *giorgio* child."

She drew him closer.

"There is one waits for thee, a dark lady, as dark as thee, in suffering now. Wait for her. Keep for her the wisdom of a child and the strength of a man and she will be all to thee."

His eyes drawn deep into hers, he had known all she meant to say. He had tried to express it in the words of that other gypsy queen, persuading the Duchess to flee with her and join her tribe.

> How love is the only good in the world . . .
> If any two creatures grew into one,
> They would do more than the world has done;
> Though each apart were never so weak.

"You say you're not ready to marry, James," Robert said, "but you're talking like a husband!"

"Oh, I'll marry. I did go into Father's brewery, after all; and now I've buckled down to it! That's to grow up, to accept that a man must work for his bread, and take a wife and rear a family. You'll see me with my fat fair wife at my fireside with a babe at her breast, whether it's Kitty or another I marry, and you may dine at our table whenever you wish."

"I'll count on that, James."

At last, walking steadily home, his footsteps loud, he was able to let his mind dwell on all that Elizabeth Barrett had told him that afternoon.

The light from his father's study was still pouring its broad golden beam into the garden. He had probably fallen asleep making his painstaking notes in the margins of his books. Those books were the only things in the world about which he showed a grain of common sense. They said he had the scent of a bloodhound and the snap of a bulldog for a bargain there. Over six thousand old volumes lined his shelves and stood in heaps on the floor.

Robert leaned on the iron railing which surrounded the pond, dreaming over the beauty of the water lilies drained of colour in the moonlight, and the dark majesty of the horse chestnut tree beside it. An owl hooted and rose above him, its wings sweeping soundlessly by in long, slow strokes. Elizabeth Barrett would never see any of this unless he took her away. Her only life was in old, old memories.

He looked up again at his father's window.

Was his father selfish by James Silverthorne's standards? He followed his own tastes and cared nothing for making money. He never sold his books, only bought more. Did Robert's mother secretly envy her sister her solid brewer, and regret her marriage to a childlike man who would grow old but never grow up? Such thoughts might force their way out in the headaches which made her slip from the room and lie stretched on her bed for hours, her eyes glazed with pain.

His mother's father had come from Hamburg and settled in Dundee—a shipowner, a thrusting man. She and his sister Sarianna were the practical ones in the family. His mother even shaved his father, and cut his hair. Left to him, it would grow to his feet.

Did she bless the day she had come to Camberwell to stay with an uncle and meet the unhappy Mr. Robert Browning the second? The young man's father had taken the trouble to call on Miss Wiedemann's uncle and try to prevent the marriage. "She'll be thrown away on a man so clearly born to be hanged," he had declared. His own father. Miss Wiedemann had married her young man. And lived happily ever after?

Robert went into the house.

His mother was awake, sitting up in bed, reading the Scriptures. Her strong face was softened in the lamplight, the white in her hair lost. He remembered James Silverthorne saying she had the squarest head and forehead he had ever seen, putting him in mind of a tea caddy. James had been taken aback by Robert's anger.

As he gave her news of the Silverthornes, Robert wished that he could talk to her too of Elizabeth Barrett.

72

"Is something troubling you, Robert?" Her china-blue Wiedemann eyes were fixed on his.

"Tell me," he asked, "how much obedience does one owe to an unreasonable parent?"

"Honour thy father and thy mother that thy days may be long in the land which the Lord thy God giveth thee," she answered promptly.

"Wouldn't it have been better if my father had disobeyed his father from the start? He did, in the end, when he married you."

"*That* wasn't a father! He was a monster."

He kissed her. "You've answered me," he said soberly. "And now, I have something special for you, a poem I wrote when I was in Italy last year. Suddenly I was sick for England. I thought of all the things I loved most about her, especially the spring. They all seemed part of you and you part of them. So the poem is yours. Shall I read it to you?"

"Please."

He took a scroll of paper from his sleeve, a proof from his new volume, and began to read.

"Oh, to be in England
Now that April's there,
And whoever wakes in England
Sees, some morning, unaware,
That the lowest boughs and the brushwood sheaf
Round the elm-tree bole are in tiny leaf,
While the chaffinch sings on the orchard bough
In England—now!"

His mother heard the joy and passionate love in his voice ringing through the quiet room, and she said softly, "To think you once spoke of settling in Italy. You must never live out of England. It would break your heart."

She put the scroll under her pillow.

He kissed her again and said, "You smell of roses."

"It's only the potpourri." She gestured to a china bowl of shrivelled rose petals by her bedside. Every year she filled bowls with the fallen petals, mixing them with herbs and spices, and left them about the house.

He would show the poem about spring in England to Elizabeth too. But that was not the poem for her. The poem he had written for her was all about Italy, a poem to make her long to come and live with him there. It would not be for long. He would only lose an English spring or two.

Next day Elizabeth was sitting on her sofa waiting for him as if he had never gone away. Her eyes looked directly at him, as trustingly as on the day before. Nothing had been lost. Now he must risk everything again.

Robert took her hand as naturally as if he had never dropped it to leave her. Very simply he spoke of his gratitude to her for what she had told him. Then he told her again of his love for her. At least, he thought, she listened.

"I've obeyed you, haven't I?" he said. "For two months I've been silent. I don't think you realize what self-control I have, that I could sit, and speak, and listen and yet say nothing, as I've done. You don't know what I've suffered!"

He looked down once again on the white parting in the dark hair.

"Let me say now—and if you insist I'll never say it again— that I loved you from my soul, and I gave you my life from the beginning, and all that's done and can't be undone now."

She opened her lips but he swept on.

"Let me speak. My loving you had nothing to do with your loving me in return. I know you aren't like other women. I believe in you absolutely and utterly, the you who is like no one else in this whole wide world."

She looked at him.

"*You* do not need me to tell you what would be supreme happiness for me. If you ever . . . if you ever . . . oh, however far off that day may be, tell me that it will come!"

Suddenly he ended on a cry of anguish, breaking down into incoherence, holding her hand so tightly that he hurt her. After a moment he began to speak again, his voice hoarse.

"I'll never refer to this again. You won't see the least difference in my manner when I come to see you. We'll be just as we were before."

He waited, pain in his heart and in his throat.

At last she found something to say. And after all it was the

74

only thing which had to be said—that love between them was impossible.

"Won't you see what a miserable creature I am, and how wrong I am for you? From the beginning of our friendship I've been waiting for you to grow tired of me. I've watched for it on your face, and listened for it in your voice. Yes. If not today then tomorrow, if not tomorrow then some day, it must end. It's not natural for you to love me."

He looked hurt and impatient at once. She hastened on.

"If you felt as you say, then it's been hard for you. But it's been hard for me too."

He looked up, suddenly hopeful, and again she hurried on.

"I mean, it *is* easier for you, with your generous nature. It's easier for you to be noble than for me."

He saw with bitterness that now she was implying that his love was only pity. Still, he thought, she was confessing something very precious, something which had been carefully hidden from him before.

She laboured on. "What I've said I've always meant. And when I've said nothing there was a reason for my silence you couldn't understand. Of course I meant you to be silent. But what I really was asking for was for you to put away any idea of—you know very well what I mean."

She looked up then and saw his face.

"Oh, my friend! Don't look so hurt! I don't mean to wound you. But you must listen! It's for your own sake!"

She reminded him of what he had once written.

"You wrote in one of your letters that you'd been so lucky all your life that you would feel justified in taking any risk!" That was really what he was trying to do now, she said. "That would be to waste yourself, to empty your water gourds into the sand."

She repeated that. "I never could allow you to empty your water gourds into the sand. Your precious life! If you gave it to me and I put my whole heart into it, what should I bring you but anxiety and more sadness than you were born to? What could I give you that it wouldn't be cruelty to give?"

She had never changed her mind, no matter how fond she had grown of him.

"What I thought then I think now—just what any third person who knew you would think and feel. It is only common sense."

In the beginning she had not taken him seriously.

"I thought at first that the feeling on your part was a mere impulse, likely to wear out in a week or so. But now, I must say, it touches me more than I can say, that you should persist so."

Then she was saying that men were fickle.

"And if sometimes I have felt that after all you would give up, and that—being a man, you know—you might be mistaking the strength of your feelings, you oughtn't to mind."

Everything they had brought them happiness; and they had so much. Must he spoil it all by asking for more?

"Don't forget, Papa wouldn't forgive me at the end of ten years if he knew what has already passed between us. Remember, I *can* only receive you here alone if he believes me absolutely above suspicion. Oh, never let him know or guess!"

"Suspicion! As if what I ask of you is something to be ashamed of!"

She waved that away. "I shall remember today to my life's end, Mr. Browning, and be grateful. But what you ask must not be, because it cannot be."

She finished firmly, urgently. "Therefore we must abandon this subject without another word. If you're wise and want to be happy you must leave me—leave these thoughts of me, I mean. I hope we will always be friends."

So nothing had come of it all.

Yet every word she had spoken had cried out to him that she loved him and needed him and that her battle was with herself not to give herself to him. What had been a whisper in her letters was now a declaration. He had looked in her face and seen love there.

True, she had not acknowledged her love without reserve. She would not deny the truth; but she would not marry him either.

He would continue to make his secret visits and creep up the stairs to her room, and he would wait. What was wooing but waiting? Was not Elizabeth Barrett worth waiting for?

"I was made and meant to look for you and wait for you and become yours forever," he said to her, doggedly. "I will wait."

76

Yet he could not for the life of him understand this iron bar which she held up before their happiness. She would never say exactly what she meant. She came close, and closer, then shied away. He would not accept her health as a valid excuse, or that she was "unworthy"—she, the most wonderful of women! Her arguments were so frail. Her desire that things should be different, while she insisted that they could not, was so evident. Whatever it was that she was not telling him was of overwhelming importance to her. Yet she could not tell him what it was. Could not, or would not.

The thought that things might go on as they were forever filled him with gloom.

He could not know that only that morning Elizabeth had written out her heart.

We have met late—it is too late to meet,
    O friend, not more than friend!
Death's forecome shroud is tangled round my feet,
And if I step or stir, I touch the end.
    In this last jeopardy
Can I approach thee, I, who cannot move?
How shall I answer thy request for love?
    Look in my face and see.

I love thee not, I dare not love thee! Go
    In silence; drop my hand.
If thou seek roses, seek them where they blow
In garden alleys, not in desert sand.
    Can life and death agree,
That thou shouldst stoop thy song to my complaint?
I cannot love thee. If the word is faint,
    Look in my face and see. . . .

Meantime I bless thee. By these thoughts of mine
    I bless thee from all such!
I bless thy lamp to oil, thy cup to wine,
Thy hearth to joy, thy hand to an equal touch
    Of loyal troth. For me,
I love thee not, I love thee not!—Away!
Here's no more courage in my soul to say
    "Look in my face and see."

Now the summer of 1845 was almost over. Soon it would be too late for her to travel. For nearly four months Robert had been pleading with her, and every day it became more urgent for her to act.

Then Dr. Chambers took matters into his hands. The tall Scotsman dressed in black had been calling more often since her relapse. At the end of August he was visiting her every day. He increased his probings and pokings, listening to her heartbeats and taking her pulse and temperature.

"Oh, Dr. Chambers," she said listlessly. "Why do you bother? I'm as well as I'll ever be."

The morning came when he said, "May I have a word with you alone, Miss Arabel?"

It was September the second, 1845. Arabel left the room swiftly, and Elizabeth heard them going downstairs to the drawing room. When Arabel returned she began to plump the cushions behind her sister's head. There was a little pucker between her brows.

"Well? What is it, Arabel?"

"Oh, Ba. Don't concern yourself."

"I've a right to know. I'm not a child."

Arabel hesitated, standing with a pillow in her hands. She looked pityingly at her sister.

"Dr. Chambers says the left lung is affected."

"We've been waiting for that news all my life," Elizabeth said dully. "Now it has come."

"And—"

Elizabeth's eyes asked a frightened question.

"If you're sure you want to hear it," Arabel said, her voice tender.

Elizabeth nodded, unable to speak.

"He says your nervous system is absolutely shattered."

"That's exactly how I feel," Elizabeth said slowly. "And what cure does my physician propose for me, now? Bleeding? Blistering? Must I go through all that again?" Her voice shook.

"He says it's vital you should spend the winter in Pisa, and that if you'd gone to Italy years ago you'd be quite well now."

For a moment Elizabeth looked radiant.

"But Arabel, that's wonderful news. Why aren't you happy for me?"

"You know Papa would never hear of it."

78

"But now, Arabel, surely *now* he'll agree? Will you tell Papa tonight?"

"Wouldn't it be better to think it over for a little?"

"Tonight, Arabel. I beseech you!"

That night Arabel told her father what Dr. Chambers had said. She suggested that he should have a word with the physician himself.

"That won't be necessary. I'll give the matter thought."

Arabel's heart sank.

"Ba very much wants to go, Papa," she said hesitantly. "She feels she'll get well in the sunshine. Many people do, Dr. Chambers says."

"I'll give it thought," he repeated stiffly. "There's no more to be said."

She went away, meek as always before him.

When Elizabeth told Robert about the reception Arabel had had from Mr. Barrett he thought that Arabel must have misunderstood her father's reaction. Elizabeth had set her heart on going. Papa was the most loving of fathers. Of course he would let her go.

Yet, underneath, she was worrying. She had feverish bouts. Once when Robert raised her hand to his lips he was shocked by its heat.

While she waited for her father to speak Robert waited for her to decide. Now that Dr. Chambers had given his edict Mr. Barrett would have to accept her decision. Elizabeth must make up her mind to go—that was all there was to it.

Yet the whole household waited on, day by day, while Mr. Barrett thought things over. Robert felt as if he had been trapped in some macabre dance.

Suddenly there was reason to hope. George was home from circuit and came to her room after dinner to tell her that Mr. Barrett had enquired quite tenderly about her health.

"So, wish by wish, one gets one's wishes!" Robert dashed off an ebullient note. "You *will* go to Italy!" He set down for her the opening bars of Orfeo's aria from Gluck's opera.

Six months before Elizabeth would not have known what those bars meant. But Robert had wooed her in music, as in verse and in flowers. Now she knew the music was saying for him,

"What shall I do without my Eurydice? What shall I do without my darling?"

Two days later, Arabel ran upstairs to report with dancing eyes that Mr. Barrett had actually mentioned the plan.

"He spoke as if it was quite decided that you are to winter abroad, Ba. Only he said he preferred Malta to Pisa."

Two days after that it was Henrietta who came to her after dinner.

"Papa said—just out of the blue it was, as he helped himself to the roast fowl—that he liked Madeira better than Malta for Ba."

"Was that all?"

"Yes, George tried to go on with the subject, but Papa turned it aside."

For three more days Mr. Barrett played with the thought of the journey as he ate his mutton chop, his sirloin and his trout.

Then he dropped the subject completely. Her brothers and sisters visited her with doleful faces. There was nothing to report.

Watching Elizabeth's silent misery, almost out of his mind with anguish for her, Robert wrote for the first time words of open love.

"Dearest, my dearest, dearest, I kiss your hand *now*."

She did not rebuke him, and after that he wrote as he liked, caressing her in words.

7

WHEN THEY WERE TOGETHER THEY TRIED TO TALK about anything except Mr. Barrett and the trip to Pisa. Henrietta, Elizabeth's pretty copper-haired thirty-six-year-old second sister, whom Robert had once seen coming out of the drawing room as he was shown out, was a favourite topic. Bravely Elizabeth joked about the saga of Henrietta's courtship by her three suitors, nick-named by her brothers Perseverance, Hope and Despair. Suddenly Hope had abandoned hope, declaring, "I leave the field to Perseverance and Despair!" At once Despair had proposed, and been rejected, had appealed and been taken back. Then Captain Surtees Cook, living up to his nickname Perseverance, had spoken up for himself.

"He said to Henrietta," Elizabeth told Robert, " 'You love me! You love me, and if you don't you should.' "

Robert winced as he listened, hearing himself caricatured in the words of Henrietta's blunt and simple young soldier, who had elbowed Despair out and now reigned supreme.

Robert asked Elizabeth to marry him again and again. She met every proposal with an objection and stubbornly he opposed them all. There was always her health. The best that could be hoped for her, she insisted, was that she might be strong in ten years' time. When he swore to nurse her back to health again she said he had no idea what looking after her meant. How could he, whose mother packed his carpetbag for him, take on some-one who was a burden to her whole family?

She protested that she was not a fit wife for him, and had

not the strength or the heart for the ordinary duties of life. Did he know how old she was? she asked. "What has that got to do with it?" he replied. "You are you. As if a handful of years mattered, one way or the other. In any case, the first freshness of youth has gone for me too."

At last, one day he asked Elizabeth very seriously whether it was money that was worrying her.

"I've none now, of course I know that. I know too that we'll need money if you're to be looked after. I'm not such a fool as you think."

She made a little gesture of protest.

"Up till now I've never bothered about the future or cared a jot about money," Robert blundered on. "The only sacrifice I'll be making for you is my happy free bachelor's life."

"I don't want it."

At that Robert struck his palm with his fist. Ba was so obstinate, refusing to hear what was so simple and so clear!

"But my whole scheme of life was based on my not finding you. How could I expect *you*? I've obeyed the ten commandments. I've not coveted my neighbour's ox nor his ass. But because I renounced oxen and such-like that doesn't mean I'm going to turn away from the bright curved horn of my magic unicorn. And here you are, my love, my white unicorn!"

He paused, to see her listening.

"Do you see? At a word from you I'll turn my energies to getting whatever's to be got—not very much, surely? It won't be very difficult for me, either. Whenever I make up my mind to it I can be rich enough and to spare."

"I'm sure of that, but . . ."

"You think I'm a genius—well, perhaps not. But I can support us both whenever I choose."

Some of the very papers which had jeered at his *Paracelsus* had praised to the skies a little book on a new method of teaching elementary French grammar which he had written for his French master and published anonymously. The famous actor Charles Kean himself had offered him five hundred pounds for a play, and Mr. Colburn the publisher had asked him to write a novel set in Naples.

"If it comes to it I can groom a horse not too badly, and that's honest work."

She was suddenly angry, white-hot with it, trying impatiently to stop him. That he should even think of exchanging the noble work to which he had been called for low work which anyone could do.

"Do me the justice to believe that I couldn't bear—or dare— to do you *such* a wrong!"

"Well, then, no grooming of horses! Perhaps not even any more French textbooks! But writing a play for Kean wouldn't be low work; and we could live cheaply in Italy on a hundred pounds a year."

"As to that," she said steadily, her anger gone now that he had given in, "if I wanted to be very poor I couldn't be. I have three or four hundred pounds a year which no living human being can take away from me."

He was shocked into silence, not knowing what to think of this new fact which must alter everything. He sat for a long time absorbing it before he said wonderingly, "Then what prevents us marrying at once?"

"Oh, it was never *money* which was the obstacle for me! The obstacles are of quite another kind and all the stronger for that. The subject won't bear consideration. It breaks in our hands. You *must* give up this madness."

All the while Robert encouraged her to prepare for Pisa, and her brothers and sisters did the same.

Dr. Chambers was working for her. He asked Mr. Barrett's permission to get a second opinion. Dr. Thornley arrived, examined Elizabeth and was even more pessimistic about the condition of her lung, and even more emphatic that she must spend the winter in a warmer climate.

Yet the silence continued.

One night her father came up to see Elizabeth after dinner and walked about the room, stopping and staring at the pictures on the walls without apparently seeing them. He spoke pleasantly but in a staccato manner. He did not sit, and he did not speak to Flush.

At one moment she felt that she might almost dare to broach the subject herself.

"Papa?" she said.

He threw up his head and stared at her as if her voice had

warned him of some danger. Then he turned and went away without another word. He did not come to pray with her that night.

Next day he wrote her a letter. It was brought up to her by Wilson on a tray. She read, "You may go, but only with my strong disapproval and under my severe displeasure."

To write her a hard, cold letter instead of coming to see her. Then, to give her permission in such a way. Clearly, he expected her to abandon her plan; then he wouldn't be to blame. If it had not been for Mr. Browning's constant kindness, she thought, her father might not have seemed so heartless. She was on the verge of giving up the idea when George and Aunt Hedley came to strengthen her. Aunt Hedley was on her annual visit to London from Paris, where she and her family now lived.

They came together and sat by the sofa where she lay inert, unable even to lift the book which lay open on her breast.

"Pay no attention to that letter of so-called consent, my child," Aunt Hedley bade her boldly, cracking her knuckles with anger. "That's saying yes and no at once! Shame on Edward to be so cruel."

George agreed, his long face stern. "Papa must be brought to a clear yes or no. You must bring up the matter again." Aunt Hedley nodded vigorously.

"What can *I* do?"

"Couldn't you bring yourself to speak to him face to face, Ba?" George asked. "He's always loved you best of us all. Tell him how much it means to you for your health's sake. He cannot refuse to give you his reasons in the face of that."

"Can't he?"

"You must charm the dragon," George said. "Go tonight."

"If you insist."

"You're the bravest person in the household," Aunt Hedley applauded her, pink with excitement.

So that night when she heard her father go into his room to dress at seven o'clock Elizabeth made herself get up from her sofa and tap on the communicating door. Her heart was thudding when she went in.

He was sitting by the fire in his leather chair, simply staring into the coals. What was he thinking of? Of the City? Of his ships and cargoes? Of Jamaica, and the Barrett estates that were drawing Stormy out to them, as they had drawn poor dead Sam?

"What is it, Ba? I thought you were in bed, ill?" His tone was forbidding, and despite herself her heart sank.

"I've been thinking, Papa, and wanting very much to have a talk with you."

"It's not about this nonsense again, I hope."

"It's not nonsense, Papa. Dr. Chambers—and Dr. Thornley too—"

"Physicians!"

"Yes, Papa! The Queen's physician among them, that you chose for me out of the kindness of your heart. They say my life depends on my going to Pisa for the winter."

He frowned into the coals, his black brows meeting.

"Papa, do you care nothing for my life?"

She told him how much depended on her escaping the soot, the fogs, and the cold of London. She cried out, "Papa, do you *want* me to die?"

He was scowling at her. What, she wondered, had happened to the tousle-headed young father into whose ears she had whispered *"Embrasse-moi!"* Now they confronted each other like enemies. As if she were outside the scene she saw the bull-headed, burly man, still wonderfully young-looking, still handsome, but glaring at the sallow birdlike woman who was pleading with him for her life.

She must try to feel for him, never forgetting that it was she who had brought the worst of all his sufferings on him.

"Papa," she cried out, answering his silent rage with love. "George will go with me—or Alfred. There's no difficulty there." She limped to an end, stopped by the red spark in his eye which could ignite one of his rages in an instant.

"I will not allow any son of mine to take you on this—this selfish jaunt!"

She turned cold. That was refusal. It was impossible for her to travel alone.

"Oh, Papa!" she cried now, the tears pouring down her cheeks. "Why won't you let me go? Is it because you love me, and need me to be with you? If that's the reason I'll gladly stay, give up life itself—only tell me so!"

What did it matter if his love was misguided or selfish, so long as it was love?

"Oh, Papa! Tell me that you love me!"

She went to embrace him. Suddenly he was on his feet. She held out her arms to him and tried to twine them about his neck. He raised his hands, but it was only in order to seize her arms and jerk them away from him. In astonishment she looked down at those strong hands clasping the thinness of her arms, feeling the cruel pressure of his fingers, and saw a tear drop on them.

His voice rose to a shout. "To do such a thing! To want such a thing! For you to take a sister and a brother with you, just for the sake of going to Italy—it's impossible, clearly impossible. It is indecent."

"Oh, Papa!" she burst out, her anger rising to match his. "Now I know that you don't love me at all, that you don't care if I die!"

She put both her hands over her eyes and turned blindly towards the door. Somehow she found her way to it and stumbled into her room. She lay on her bed, in the deepest despair and bitterness she had felt since Torquay and the death of Bro.

She would not speak to George when he came to ask how she had fared, and she sent Wilson away when she came to help her to bed.

Next day, September 17, 1845, she wrote to Robert: "I send one word just to say that it's all over with Pisa."

With Elizabeth's letter in his hand, Robert decided that now there must be no more excuses. She must marry him and fly that house at once. He called that afternoon at Wimpole Street.

Nothing that he said had any effect. She would not marry him.

He pursued her hard, harassing her until, almost panting with exhaustion, she turned at last to meet her hunter.

"Very well. I will give you an answer."

"What is it? Tell me. Tell me now."

"Not now. At our next meeting."

That night staring out of his window at the large yellow moon, with his owl in the chestnut tree breaking the silence, Robert wrote to her.

"If I could marry you now, I would come when you let me, and go when you bade me. I would be no more than one of your brothers. No more? I should be with you for two hours for every one I am now. And when your head ached I should be with you. I choose it deliberately for my reality, the dream of simply sitting by you for an hour every day. I would rather have that than any dream I can imagine in this world—or any world I know—of which you were not a part."

It was only after he had posted his letter that he remembered he had not kissed his mother good night. As he walked quickly towards the stairs he met his sister Sarianna coming down in a dressing gown, her black hair in a thick plait.

"I was coming to call you, Robert," she said reproachfully. "Mama has been waiting for such a long time."

"I was just going up."

"I worry about her." Her plain face was troubled. "She doesn't complain, but—"

He hugged her firm, solid body.

"We *are* a close family, aren't we? I value you, you know, little sister."

"And I adore you, Robert." She pulled his nose, and turned towards her bedroom.

"You went to post a letter?" his mother greeted him.

"Yes."

Robert slipped away after a few minutes, to lie on his bed dreaming of his love and thinking how he might put it into poetry worthy of Elizabeth.

Elizabeth was moved to tears as she read his letter. She knew what that offer of platonic love must have cost him. She felt the flames in his blood every time his lips touched her hand. She saw them in his eyes as they rested on her face. His unselfishness was as much to be marvelled at as that Papa should threaten her life —for what?

She wrote, "How would any woman have felt who could feel at all, hearing such words, and from you?"

She chose her next words with care.

"You have touched me more profoundly than I thought even *you* could have touched me. Henceforward I am yours for everything but to do you harm. A promise goes to you with this that if

God should free me within a moderate time from this trailing chain of weakness and from the other obstacles he has put in our way I will then be to you whatever you want, friend or more than friend."

She paused for a long time before she added the last hard sentences.

"Only, in the meanwhile you are absolutely free—unentangled, as they call it. If I couldn't be sure that you considered yourself quite free I wouldn't see you any more, whatever it cost me."

Reading Elizabeth's letter in the morning sunshine by the glittering pond Robert could have sung aloud. So, it had been in the end as in the beginning. He had told her on paper of the fullness of his love, and on paper she had given her promise to him. Poet to poet, what could have been more perfect? The only better way would have been to have spoken poem to poem. He hardly noticed that the promise she had given him was a qualified one. Of course she would be free of that "trailing chain of weakness," and of course all her obstacles would melt like snow before his warm love.

So she would be to him what he wanted— "friend or more than friend"? He longed to leap up those stairs to her room and give her his answer to that. It would be three days before he saw her again, for still they dared not meet too often. Had there ever been a lover so frustrated since the world began? Back he must go to pen and paper to shout his joy and tell her things which could only be said with one's lips and arms, in silence.

"*My own, now*. Oh, do not fear I am 'entangled.' My crown is easy on my head, my pearl lies loose in my hand! My life is bound up with yours, my first and last love."

The three days went by like a year. At last Robert stood before his beloved and held open his arms, and she came to him. He bent his head, seeking her lips. She hid her face in his chest, and he kissed her hair. So she would not allow him her lips. Not yet. He held her body in his arms. That must be enough until she would give him more.

When he got home he wrote to ask her if he might call her by her pet name. "Aren't we betrothed, my dearest, and closer than all those who call you Ba?"

He asked it again in person, and she nodded her head dumbly. When he had gone she wrote down what she had not been able to say to him.

Yes, call me by my pet-name! Let me hear
The name I used to run at, when a child . . .
And catch the early love up in the late.
Yes, call me by that name, and I, in truth,
With the same heart, will answer and not wait.

It took a long time before he could persuade her to call him Robert, and then she had to write it before she could speak it.

At the end of September, when he had spent two whole days with her, if all the hours of his visits over those four months since their first meeting were added together, he asked for a ringlet.

"Give me just so much of you as may be given in a lock of hair. If you give me what I beg—shall I say next Tuesday?—when I leave you I will not speak a word. I promise what I know you will exact."

She was overcome with embarrassment. "I never gave away what you ask except to my nearest relatives and one or two women friends—never! Should you have it or not? Oh, *you,* who have your way in everything!"

It was a week before she gave him the silken curl coiled into a man's ring, and her gesture and look told him that she was plighting her troth. She had asked him for a lock of his own hair by then, writing, "You have come to me as a dream comes, dearest. I must have a sign, to show the difference between dream and reality."

She gave it to him in silence. Then he took from his waist-coat pocket a little packet. She spread the little parcel open to expose the curl of strong black hair which he had clipped so clumsily before his mirror. She kissed it, unfastened the little scent locket which she wore on a long chain, and slipped the curl inside. She snapped the locket shut, but kept her hand about it as if she could not bear to let it go.

"My Uncle Matthew Barrett gave me this when I was a child. 'Beware of ever loving,' he said to me. 'If you do, you won't do it by halves. It will be for life and death!' "

She watched Robert slip her ring on his finger. Then she added, almost fiercely, though she spoke in a whisper, "You're never to refer to this, never mention it to me!"

Hungrily, then, he took her in his arms and kissed her. He tasted the sweetness of her full, soft lips, warm and moist and yielding. He felt her respond to him, and held her closer and closer, not knowing that he was hurting her. Her hands clasped him to her. Elizabeth felt him trembling in her arms. It was all she could do to push him away.

"Ah, my sweet!" he groaned. "My sweet love! Marry me—now!"

That night he wrote to her, "I will live and die with your beautiful ring, your beloved hair, comforting me, blessing me." He put the ring on a cord round his neck. When he died her hair would be found there. If he kept no other oath in his life he would keep that one. He did not question the silence in which she had given it to him, or that which she had imposed on him.

But Elizabeth had not been quite silent. Before he came she had written a sonnet, working on it long and lovingly, saying to him all that she could not speak to his face.

I never gave a lock of hair away
To a man, Dearest, except this to thee,
Which now upon my fingers thoughtfully
I ring out to the full brown length and say
"Take it." My day of youth went yesterday;
My hair no longer bounds to my foot's glee . . .
     . . . It only may
Now shade on two pale cheeks the mark of tears,
Taught drooping from the head that hangs aside
Through sorrow's trick. I thought the funeral shears
Would take this first, but Love is justified—
Take it, thou—finding pure from all those years
The kiss my mother left here when she died.

There was something else she wanted to put into verse, and after he had gone she took a new quill and a new sheet of paper. It was midnight before she was satisfied with her second sonnet.

First time he kissed me, he but only kissed
The fingers of this hand wherewith I write;
And, ever since, it grew more clean and white,
Slow to world-greetings, quick with its "Oh, list,"
When the angels speak. A ring of amethyst
I could not wear here, plainer to my sight,
Than that first kiss. The second passed in height

The first, and sought the forehead, and half missed,
Half falling on the hair. O beyond meed!
That was the chrism of love, which love's own crown,
With sanctifying sweetness, did precede.
The third upon my lips was folded down
In perfect, purple state; since when, indeed,
I have been proud, and said, "My love, my own!"

Then, late as it was, Elizabeth copied both sonnets into a little white-covered notebook in her clear small writing.

She would show him her sonnets, and they would speak her love to him as perfectly as she could say it. Someday. But not yet.

Robert and Elizabeth watched the chestnuts nestle in the ruby coals, bursting with loud pops, and Robert moved his arm from her waist only to fish them out with the fire tongs and peel their charred husks so that she could nibble the nutty golden insides. Elizabeth seemed utterly content.

"He's sure someone's trying to shoot him," she murmured, as Flush leaped at a loud crack. "Probably you."

Suddenly Robert said, "We should be sitting by our own fireside, Ba, doing this, with a chubby little boy or girl to keep Flush company and share our chestnuts!"

She stirred uneasily.

"Don't you want that, Ba?"

"Yes, yes."

"Then why won't you marry me now? Don't you love me?"

"I do, Robert. With all my heart and with all my soul."

"And with all my body. Say it, Ba."

She was silent.

"Say it, Ba. What's wrong with the body? It's beautiful. It's natural. It's right."

He turned and took her into his arms. He kissed her lips, her eyes and her cheeks and felt her grow warmer. He put her hair back with one hand and kissed her ear and the cool skin behind it and drew his lips down her neck until it met the lace of her bodice. He thrust both hands into the showers of curls which fell on both sides of her face and took her mouth more fully to his. Something gave way under his fingers. A tortoise-shell comb slipped to her breast, and her hair fell loose.

He held her away, to look hungrily at her cheeks flushed red from his kisses and the fire, at her eyes languorous with love between their long delicate lashes and at the tumbled loveliness of her thick dark curls.

Suddenly she smiled in his face, her lips parting over her white teeth, and asked wickedly, "Do you want to twine my hair about my throat, like Porphyria's lover, and strangle me?"

"No," he said savagely. "I want to keep you alive, and make love to you all day—and all night—forever."

Her eyes fell again, but he took a hand from under the soft, warm hair and put it under her chin and held up her face to his.

"*Don't* you want that, Ba?"

"You shouldn't ask me that."

"Don't you want me, Ba, as I want you? Be honest, as you always are."

"Of course I do."

"Then why won't you marry me, Ba?"

She closed her eyes, and her face contracted with a little spasm of pain. He saw a tear well under one eyelid and brim over and find its way down the soft warm cheek he had kissed to rosiness.

"I can't. Now or ever."

"Tell me the real reason."

"Very well, then," she said despairingly. "I'll tell you. It's Papa. None of his children are allowed to marry."

He released her chin and took her hands in his. She let her head sink, and her tears continued to fall. He felt them drop, one by one, on their joined hands. After a while he released one hand and dried her cheeks with his handkerchief.

"You can't mean what you're saying, Ba," he said slowly.

"I wish to God I didn't."

"What has he got against marriage? He married, himself, didn't he? And he was happy in that marriage?"

"He loved my mother, I think, though he treated her very harshly. In every house we've lived in since she died he has set aside a room where all her things are kept, and he goes in alone to pray. If that is love, he loved her."

"Then why?" Was it because Mr. Barrett was one of those fathers who are jealous of their daughters? Robert asked. Elizabeth answered that her brothers were not allowed to marry either.

"And they submit to that?"

"Without Papa how could they live?"

"By their wits, I think the phrase is," he said drily. "George is a barrister. Setty too. Alfred works on the railways. Octavius will soon be an architect. Henry . . ."

Elizabeth cut him short. Once, she told him, a brother had rebelled—Edward, the eldest, her lost Bro. The reason why Mr. Barrett had summoned him from Torquay had been that he had fallen in love with a pretty young lady there and had asked his father's permission to marry her. Mr. Barrett had simply replied that Bro must return to London.

Bro, Robert calculated, must have been thirty-three, his own age, then.

Elizabeth was telling him that she had thought money might be the difficulty and had written to beg her father to make over to Bro the four thousand pounds which had been left to her by her Uncle Matthew Barrett. She would still have had the other four thousand pounds which her Granny Moulton had left her. "Enough and to spare for me."

"How did your father take that?"

"He seemed to consider the thought impure—obscene!"

She fell silent, unhappily remembering, while the sound of a muffinman's bell, advertising his hot cakes, came faintly up to them from the street. Robert recalled what John Kenyon had told him of that strange Jamaican night when the boy Edward had learned in a cruel way how ugly a marriage could be.

That was the first time Mr. Barrett had revealed his attitude to his sons' marrying; but he had never been able to bear the thought of any of his daughters taking a husband. Had he given reasons? Robert asked.

"Oh, Papa can always find objections when he condescends to do so. And how many couldn't he find now, Robert, to *my* marrying! But he deceives even himself when he tries to justify it. The real obstacle is in his own mind. It's his peculiarity."

But how, Robert asked again, had they all come to accept such a thing? Not suddenly, surely?

"Oh, no. My sisters and I all wanted to get married like everybody else. When I was a little girl I was going to have a husband called Dominic and be very happy. But we learned not to contravene Papa's system. That was what we called it. Like slaves we had to bear the whip. One even laughs under it until one's turn comes for weeping."

His peculiarity, she called it, and Papa's system. Robert marvelled at her determination always to use a gentle phrase for her father's most brutal action. Had not one of them ever tried to resist Mr. Barrett? he asked.

"Henrietta did try once."

"Was it for Perseverance or Despair?"

It had been long ago and for someone quite different. Henrietta had loved him. "She was so sweet, and warm with it, not at all as she is now."

He had been a very eligible suitor, and liked by everyone. Mr. Barrett should have been overjoyed for Henrietta. Yet when she had gone to her father he had exploded in a terrible rage. There was a look of horror on Elizabeth's face as she told Robert how Mr. Barrett had forced Henrietta to kneel before him and beg God's pardon.

"I can hear her knees ring on the floor now. She was carried out of the room in hysterics. I got up to follow her and fell down in a faint. Arabel thought I was dead. She shrieked and shrieked. Papa stood like a stone." She was staring straight ahead of her.

"And what did Miss Henrietta do?"

"At a word she gave everything up," Elizabeth said wonderingly. "No child ever submitted more meekly to a cancelled holiday. Yet how she was made to suffer. The dreadful scenes, even after she had given him up!"

"Well, she has other lovers now," Robert comforted her.

"She has Perseverance and Despair, yes, and one or two other gentlemen who visit her."

"And your father doesn't mind?"

"As long as she doesn't marry he doesn't mind."

"Even though they visit her alone?"

"He knows that she'll obey his wishes now. He trusts her."

"How does your sister feel about that?"

"She doesn't feel anything anymore. She likes to flirt, and play the pianoforte and dance the polka and go out to dinners, and above all she likes to be admired. She's entirely fickle, and now you can see why! For Henrietta, to love is to feel pain. So she merely suns herself in the admiration of men. Why not? It's innocent enough, God knows, and men are all faithless."

"You approve of such a way of life for your little sister, Ba?" he probed.

To his surprise she fired up. "Oh, no! How could I? What's to become of her, our pretty little Henrietta? She's made for love and kisses, and then for marriage and the dimpled arms of fat babies clutched about her neck. Arabel would be a good wife to a clergyman, but she doesn't need a husband and marriage as Henrietta does. Henrietta *must* love to be happy, and as things are to love is to be unhappy. So she's what she is, and it's Papa who has done it."

"Perhaps she'll fall in love again."

"I believe she won't even let herself know how much she cares for Captain Cook, since she knows it must be hopeless. Who could endure such suffering twice?"

"Has he ever spoken to you of his attitude to you, yourself, Ba, as distinct from your two sisters?" Robert ventured. "But, no, forget I said that. I've no right to ask."

She met his eyes frankly.

"You've the right to ask me anything. Papa believes me to be the purest among women. He idolizes me. Perhaps I should say he idolized me until recently. I was ill, you see, and had no time or need for anything but him and God. There's been no man in my life, or likelihood of one, since then."

Then she added shyly, "It wasn't always like that."

8

IT HADN'T ALWAYS BEEN LIKE THAT, ELIZABETH
told Robert. Mr. Barrett had been very resentful of her friendships with men when she was a girl.

First there had been Hugh Boyd, the handsome blind
scholar who lived in Malvern Wells, the little town near Hope
End, their home. Boyd had written to her after the publication
of her first serious book of poems when she was twenty and had
invited her to call on him at his Ruby Cottage. But although he
was blind and middle-aged and married, with a daughter as old
as Elizabeth, her father had forbidden the meeting. It was only
when Mr. Boyd had said he was leaving Malvern, and showed
how hurt he was, that Mr. Barrett had agreed to it.

The twenty-two-year-old Elizabeth had been strangely moved
by the slight pale man of forty-five with the unsmiling face, the
melancholy voice and the quenched, dead eyes. After meeting
her Mr. Boyd had not left the district after all, and she had
walked the seven miles between Hope End and Ruby Cottage
several times a week to read to the rather overbearing and caustic
man, take his dictation and correct his proofs. Sometimes she had
slept the night. Once she had stayed a week.

"Despite Papa's disapproval Hugh Boyd became my dearest
friend. He called me his Elibet. He said Ba lacked euphony."

Mrs. Boyd had grown very anxious to leave Malvern. Elizabeth spoke, Robert thought, as if the idea had never entered her
head that this wife might be jealous of the pretty, clever girl who

wrote her husband such warm letters and spent so many days alone with him.

When Elizabeth was twenty-six Hope End had been sold, and the Barretts had moved to Sidmouth in Devon, a hundred and thirty miles away.

Elizabeth had implored Hugh Boyd to write to her, weeping over her letters. Suddenly he had moved to Sidmouth to be near her again, although the lease of Ruby Cottage had not expired. She had seen him nearly every day, running all the way between her house and his so as not to lose a moment of his company.

Mrs. Boyd had played her last card. She had left her husband and gone back to Ruby Cottage. With no chaperone, Elizabeth's visits had had to stop. She was very angry with Mrs. Boyd, especially when she had to write to her on her husband's behalf, begging her to return to him. Eventually Mrs. Boyd had come back to Sidmouth on her own terms.

"She'd spoiled things. They were never quite the same after that," Elizabeth said.

Now, fourteen years later, Mrs. Boyd was dead, and Hugh Boyd, at sixty-four, lived in loneliness and apathy in London, an old man afraid to walk outside, brooding among his collection of striking and chiming clocks and sipping his Cyprus wine. His house was only a mile or so from Wimpole Street, but Elizabeth and he had not seen each other for years.

"Did he love you?" Robert asked bluntly, and saw her blush.

"He was like a father to me. Besides, he was blind."

"I loved you before I saw you, Ba."

One day, Elizabeth remembered, Hugh Boyd had taken her hand where it lay next to his on the table and held it while she read to him. When he had heard his wife's steps coming towards the door he had released it hastily. That had been all.

She had bewitched the dull, middle-aged, broken man into passion, Robert thought. She had torn his heart out of him, and then, seeing him for what he was, had let him go.

"Mr. Boyd hated Papa," she was saying. "He hates him still."

So that had been Hugh Boyd, the first man—limited, helpless and not particularly pleasant—on whom Ba had lavished her young ardour and sweetness.

"Then there was George Hunter," Elizabeth said.

The Reverend George Hunter, minister of the Marsh Independent Chapel in Sidmouth, was another tragic figure. He had no wife at the manse. A tired old woman slapped his food before him and his solemn-eyed six-year-old daughter Mary. Now and then he disappeared for a day or so, and came back looking even paler and more harassed. He had been visiting his mad wife in her asylum.

Mr. Barrett had been stirred by the clergyman's lurid descriptions of the pains of hellfire and had asked him to his table. Elizabeth was lonely, missing her dead mother, and Bro, who was away in Jamaica, and Hugh Boyd. By the time Boyd followed her to Sidmouth the new friendship was flourishing.

"What did George Hunter look like?" Robert asked.

"Not young, but a fine figure of a man." She sounded wistful.

She had written Boyd a hundred letters before they had parted. Now she wrote to Hunter. They had corresponded for twelve years.

"Until last year. We don't write to each other now," she said.

Hunter had been flattered, poor man, Robert thought, listening to this second tale of the entirely innocent but determined seduction by Elizabeth of a weak, middle-aged, essentially commonplace and rather disagreeable man. She must have been a very pretty girl, with her bright eyes and her red lips and her fine white teeth and her dark curls.

"We were close friends for more than two years. He taught me a great deal before the blow fell."

It had fallen in February of 1835, when she was twenty-eight, and George Hunter had left Marsh Chapel to become an itinerant preacher.

Frantic at losing him, Elizabeth had joined the little group of homely spinsters who travelled about with him. Once she had gone as far as Exmouth to hear him preach and had not got home until half-past one in the morning.

"It was a day of magic. We walked and talked together in the leafy Devonshire lanes, and by the sea. That night, after all that sweet, innocent day, Papa was waiting up for me like a thundercloud, and he said the most terrible things. Mr. Hunter had brought me home, and he was shocked—grey-faced with distress. He kept saying that he was a minister and a man of God, and Papa kept shouting at him that he was a man for all that, and married, even if he seemed to have forgotten it. Soon after that

Mr. Hunter left Sidmouth to live in Axminster. It was all because of Papa."

She had written to George Hunter telling him how desolate she was, and he had replied with passionate letters.

"I'm afraid his feeling for me went beyond the bounds of mere friendship," she said, so primly that Robert smiled.

Nothing had gone right for George Hunter after he had left Sidmouth. He was drafted from church to church, with a stipend which could hardly feed him and his child. "Papa ruined his life!"

He had grown bitter and violent. He forgot his mad wife, his child, everything but her. He had belaboured her for not admitting she was in love with him. He was cruel to her, even making unkind jests at her expense.

Six months after he had left Sidmouth the Barretts had moved to London. George Hunter had grasped at an opportunity to become minister at the Independent Chapel at Brighton and travelled up to visit her whenever he could. That ministry had soon come to an end, and then he had scratched a living in London by tutoring, leaving his daughter Mary in a boarding school in Brighton. He had only one pupil, and an income of forty guineas a year from which he had to pay rent. Now those ten years of grinding poverty and failure had changed him beyond recognition. He was white-haired, decrepit and full of complaints —a sour, mean man. He could not bear it that Elizabeth had grown famous while he was obscure and destitute.

"At least Papa knows now how little I care for him, so he doesn't in the least mind his visits. As for me, I'd prefer it if he didn't come at all. He still calls me the angel of his life and says he loves me, and he still has only harsh words for me!"

It was the same story all over again. The poor disappointed divine had been swept into the enchantment of the young Elizabeth, and then had been discarded. He was contemptible, no doubt about it, hysterical, self-centered and vicious. Yet Robert found it in his heart to pity George Hunter a little.

What a waste it had all been. Robert had been a boy mooning over Eliza Flower while she had been wasting her sweetness and her warmth on those two dried-up old maids of men. Mr. Barrett had a lot to answer for.

"You asked me whether Papa had always trusted me, and I've shown you the way it was. I wasn't allowed any life at all, even when all I wanted was a little help with Latin and Greek and poetry. But after my illness at Torquay he changed completely. When you came into my life, Robert, I was waiting for death, my only lover, and he knew that. I'll never be able to marry you and go to Italy."

"Gently, Ba, gently! I'll go to him—"

"No."

"Well, we'll marry, and he'll forgive us."

"No."

"Well, then, we'll marry, and he won't forgive us. It won't be the end of the world. We'll be happy together, and he'll be the loser."

She looked at him with her great eyes, without speaking.

You'll tire of me, she was thinking, my beloved one. It's a kind of madness, your loving me, and you've drawn me into the madness until I love you too, though I've tried not to. You're a poet, and I'm your moon maiden. But where will the poetry be, dear lover, after six months of life with me? Where will your hot kisses be then? There will be no house of solid brick to shelter me, no well-trained servants to wait on me, no loving family to bear with me, and no Papa to pray with me and forgive me for my sin. There will be only you and me, in a strange country, with not very much money, and always for me the terror of my falling ill. You would tire of me, and who could blame you? Not I. I would feel that I had wronged you in letting you load yourself with an intolerable burden, and the shame of not being able to carry it as well. And then, what would I do? How could I release you? Not by being able to steal home, for Papa wouldn't have me back. To choose death would be all that would be left to me when you had taken me up and loved me and then left me—in spirit if not in fact.

He could not tell what she was thinking as she looked at him so long without speaking, but he grew more and more uneasy.

"You'll have to trust me, Ba," he said.

"Yes, I would have to trust you, Robert."

He was despondent when he left her. He had beaten down all the "insurmountable obstacles" which she had raised up. Then, one by one, had come the greater difficulties to be overcome.

First there had been the Torquay business, wrenched from

her unwilling lips—he had comforted her, hadn't he, brought her back, joyfully, from death to life?

Then had come her father's refusal to let her go abroad to save her life. That had been surmounted too.

Now, suddenly, there was this great ugly plant, black and thorny and evil. Was this to be the really insurmountable obstacle?

It was not the madness of Mr. Barrett he feared, but Ba's attitude to it. Anything outside them both he could conquer. His Andromeda! If she wanted him to do so he could slay this last dragon and free her. But what if she did not want him to? What if she clung to her rock and drove him away?

He felt as if he were walking in a nightmare with her, and the worst of the nightmare was that she was his foe and struggling with him to prevent his saving her. But he would not let her go. He would not let her escape him. Never! He paused under a lamp-post to pull a piece of paper from his pocket and wrote down the words that had just leapt into his mind.

> Escape me?
> Never—
> Beloved!
> While I am I, and you are you,
>> So long as the world contains us both,
>> Me the loving and you the loth,
> While the one eludes, must the other pursue.

Was that a poem? It was an expression of his love, at any rate, born, as his poems so often were, almost of itself, leaping forth like a bird springing into flight from a hedge.

9

IT WAS NOVEMBER, AND ROBERT HAD KNOWN Elizabeth for six months, when she mentioned the opium. They were working on the final proofs of his new volume, and she had been searching them for his golden goddesses. Just as she had decided that only a small, black-eyed lady appeared in any of them she had found those lovely lines in the most haunting of all the poems.

> As for Venice and its people, merely born to bloom and drop,
> Here on earth they bore their fruitage, mirth and folly were
>   the crop:
> What of soul was left, I wonder, when the kissing had to stop?
> "Dust and Ashes!" So you creak it, and I want the heart to
>   scold.
> Dear dead women, with such hair, too—what's become of all
>   the gold
> Used to hang and brush their bosoms? I feel chilly and
>   grown old.

She would never let him know of the sharp splinter which pierced her heart.

However, she tried no less hard to purge his verses of the obscurity which hung like an albatross about his neck.

"For the rest, let them rave," she cheered him sweetly. "You'll live when they are all under the willows. But if people don't cry out about these poems, what are we to think of the world?"

It was then that she mentioned the opium. "There's one thing to be said for sleeplessness. I worked late on your poems before I took my draught of happiness. Then sleep came to me in its red hood of poppies."

It was only when he pressed her that she used its other name —morphine. But this was opium. Morphine and opium were one.

At his alarmed questionings she fluttered. "It's necessary. It keeps my pulse steady and gives the right balance to my nervous system."

"But surely you're the worse for it in the long run?"

"Oh, I don't suffer any ill effects at all, like most people. I don't even get an opium headache."

He was insistent. She confessed at last, twisting a ring on her finger, that she took forty drops of laudanum a day. She cried, "I *cannot* do with less!"

He jumped up and began to pace the room.

"The doctors themselves recommended it," she protested. "They must know what they're about."

He swung back. "But so *much!* And every day!"

It had begun, she told him, seven years before, in Torquay, when she had been so very ill, and Dr. Chambers had prescribed morphine and ether. Every year since then the dosage had been increased, with Dr. Jago's approval.

Robert shook his head at her. "I don't like it."

"Oh, Robert, here you are again, being so strong-minded about things you know nothing about. You're as annoying as Papa. I have to send Wilson out to the apothecary's secretly to buy it because he makes such scenes."

"And your brothers and sisters?"

"George keeps my secret. Arabel knows how I suffer. As for Henrietta, I don't think she gives it a thought." Robert could hear the sound of Henrietta's pianoforte coming up from the drawing room.

Elizabeth tried to laugh Robert out of his concern, crying, "Treppy says all the ladies in Jamaica carry bottles of laudanum and lumps of sugar in their pockets and dip and nibble whenever they feel like it." But he had studied the books on his father's shelves and knew what havoc opium had brought to the island. "I beg you to talk to Dr. Chambers or Dr. Jago," he implored her. "Ask them to help you give it up."

During those months in which he had tried to discover whether he had a vocation for medicine, he had attended Dr. Blundell's lectures on opiates at Guy's Hospital.

The large, grey-haired man on the dais had begun drily enough. "Opium is obtained from the milky exudate of the incised unripe seed capsules of the poppy plant, the *Papaver somniferum,* which is indigenous to Asia Minor. The milky juice is dried in the air and forms a gummy brownish mass. This mass is then dried and powdered to give opium."

Opium had reached Europe from the East, and opium eating had caught on at once. Opium eating—a strange name for the drinking of laudanum, that innocent-sounding tincture of opium in alcohol which women regarded as hardly more harmful than smelling salts. His Ba was an opium eater, like De Quincey, with her forty drops a day—an opium eater on a mammoth scale.

In 1803 the German pharmacist Serturner had isolated an opium alkaloid and named it morphine. "After Morpheus the Greek god of sleep," explained Dr. Blundell, "in order to emphasize its sleep-giving properties." The medical profession had welcomed this miraculous drug, which relieved anxiety as well as pain. However, they had found it necessary to increase the dosage constantly to produce the same results. (So over the years Ba's original three drops of laudanum had grown to a horrifying forty.)

The lecturer had rehearsed the dangers and benefits of the drug with a beautiful precision. But it was his concluding remarks which had caught Robert's startled attention.

Over many years Dr. Blundell had been able to watch the effects of opium and its sister morphine, and he had formed some definite reservations about them. He asked himself whether morphine should not be treated with greater caution than was normal. Again and again he had observed how rapidly dependence on the drug was formed and how difficult it was to abandon it. The agonies of patients deprived of it sometimes seemed greater than the pains it was prescribed to alleviate. They suffered from excruciating cramps, colic, perspiration, gooseflesh, vomiting, diarrhea—and an overwhelming desire for more. They would go to any lengths to obtain it.

Some well-balanced people of strong character were capable of giving it up. Others found it impossible. Though not a man given to flights of fancy, Dr. Blundell thought he had detected a common link in these patients. They were often spinsters and bachelors of strong, frustrated affections, frequently unmarried daughters devoted to harsh and demanding mothers or possessive, disciplinarian fathers. They tended to be highly strung, finding the ordinary strains of life almost unbearable. Every ache was torment, every unkind word laceration, every obstacle insurmountable. They had very low opinions of themselves. For such patients opium, he postulated, became a substitute for the love and life they were starved of.

One patient cured of the addiction had told him that the euphoria it brought felt like golden fire running through his veins. For such lonely, highly strung patients the prognosis was poor. They lost all interest in food, in the opposite sex, and in life, and were a prey to apathy and depression. Their lives were a constant seesawing between a pervasive longing for death and periodic brief periods of euphoria.

"The craving for morphine is intense, often intolerable. It asserts itself within a few hours after the last dose, reaches peak intensity in twenty-four to forty-eight hours, and subsides spontaneously. If morphine is *not* readministered the most severe symptoms usually disappear within ten days, though some may persist for much longer. If it *is* readministered a state of euphoria is restored at once. I've seen a patient in a state of abject filth and subhuman misery restored within thirty minutes to clean, laughing normality until the next dose was due."

Dr. Blundell gathered up his papers. "Gentlemen, the relief of pain is important, very important. But it is possible to buy it at too high a price."

He was gone from the dais. There was only a shaft of sunlight in which motes of dust danced, falling aslant from a high window onto the lectern at which he had stood.

Robert remained in his seat while the other students shuffled and banged their way out. Then he went home and questioned his mother. She had swallowed so many medicines in the hope of curing her headaches. Lately he had heard her speak of the relief which laudanum gave her. She had offered it to him when he had been tormented by his little hammer.

That day she gave up the laudanum. Calvinist as she was, she positively welcomed the thought of flailing out of her body anything which could be considered self-indulgence. Her headaches had continued, but he noticed that she ate more and slept better. She was less lethargic and more cheerful.

Now, strong in that experience, he asked Elizabeth to lessen the doses of laudanum gradually and give it up entirely.

"Perhaps in three months? Do you think you could do without it in three months—or less?"

She agreed to try, but almost playfully, still refusing to take him seriously.

Brooding at his window that night, he cursed the doctors who recommended the drug so freely. They had prescribed far too much and then encouraged her to go on with it. She did not even need a prescription. Wilson could run down to the apothecary's and get opium for the asking.

In how many other forms was she absorbing this poison, too? Her cupboards were bursting with bottles and boxes. Her cry rang in his ears, "I *cannot* do with less!"

He sat to write, begging her to listen to him. But he promised that he would not enquire into her efforts to give it up.

"Knowing you utterly as I do, I know you'll only take as much of it from now on as you absolutely must. So if you take more, it will only mean you are weaker, and if you take less that you are getting stronger. To think that you worry about my silly headaches. If a wet day at home causes one, an hour's walk cures it—that's all *I* have to worry about. Now, fancy me shut in a room for seven years! Oh, Ba, I understand. But, oh, Ba, do give it up—for me and for you."

"That you should care so much about the opium!" she replied. "Then *I* must care, and get to do with less, at least. But it would be dangerous to leave it off, Dr. Jago says, except very slowly and gradually."

He wrote back. "All the kind explaining about the opium makes me happier. Slowly and gradually what may not be done?"

She wrote and spoke bravely to him; but she had frightened herself by her promise. Robert was asking a great deal. Still, she had promised, and she would try.

That night when the time came Elizabeth unlocked her cupboard and took out the phial and the horn spoon before she remembered her promise. She frowned, and wavered. Then she put them back quickly and shut and locked the door. She removed the key and put it in the drawer of her sofa-table.

She decided to read for an hour before she slept. After half an hour she found she was not taking in what she read. She could think of nothing but the laudanum. She turned out her lamp.

There was no question of sleep. She turned from side to side, trying to find a comfortable position. An attack of yawning overcame her, but she was wide awake. A knee, an arm, began to pain her, then a whole leg. Soon she was one huge ache.

Elizabeth knew what was coming next. She could feel the wave of dry heat all over her body, rising and rising until it broke in a great sudden sweat. A vast anxiety and misery flooded her, and she longed to weep, to wail, to destroy herself. She buried her face in the pillow and flung her head from side to side. She bit her hand to keep from crying out.

The fever rose and rose, she breathed harder and suddenly a hand seemed to clench her stomach and twist it cruelly. She doubled up with the terrible cramp. It was then that the sickness overtook her.

Elizabeth half fell, half dragged herself out of bed, and blindly reached for the drawer of her sofa-table, fumbling for the key of her medicine cupboard.

When she had the laudanum she poured it out with a shaking hand and threw it down her throat. Then she stood, breathing deeply, waiting. Soon the glorious feeling came. All her pains had gone, all her grief and despair vanished. She felt well, happy and, best of all, sleepy.

Elizabeth walked across to her bed, erect and smiling. She was only deferring the trial. Next time it would be easier. She would tell Robert when she saw him that she had tried and failed but would try again.

In a few minutes she was deeply asleep.

"I tried for you, Robert," she told him. "I tried to give it up at one blow. But I was very ill. I had to get up and take it."

It was as he had feared.

"It can't be done like that," she said, gazing anxiously at him. "But I'll lessen the doses gradually, I promise."

They waited out the winter. She must remain shut up in that room for all the cold, dangerous months, the last two of 1845, and the first two of the new year. They could only pray she would not suffer too much. With the spring of 1846 they would begin to live again.

He began to realize how many others there were in her life.

Her father and her eight brothers and sisters, her Aunt Bummy and her Aunt and Uncle Hedley, and Miss Trepsack, formed a close ring about her. There was little Lizzie Barrett, a pretty, bright-eyed twelve-year-old cousin, who lived in the house. Her father, Captain Goodin Barrett, was in Jamaica, and her mother was insane.

There was an outer ring of the many people who corresponded with her. Even in Torquay, when she was too ill to be moved, she had written almost daily letters. She wrote regularly to her beloved Miss Mitford, of course, and to Hugh Boyd, her editor friend Mr. Horne, her American publisher and a score of others.

Then there were the callers—Miss Mitford and Mr. Kenyon frequently, Mrs. Anna Jameson very often, and George Hunter occasionally. Robert began to feel their eyes on him.

"Won't you release me from my promise to visit you only in secret?" he begged one day. "You have so many visitors."

"Oh, no. If Papa found out how often you came your letters would be opened and you would be forbidden the house."

He was toying with her fingers dejectedly. Now he put something in her palm.

She looked down at the silver heart studded with tiny diamonds, the crown above the heart, the plumes above the crown. There were diamonds in each plume and diamonds on the crown.

He turned her hand over, and slipped the ring on her third finger. The little diamonds glittered in the firelight.

"I won't be able to wear it!"

"Sometimes. When we are together. This damnable secrecy!"

Elizabeth was very nervous about whether her friends suspected anything. She dreaded Mr. Kenyon's sharp eyes behind his glittering spectacles and his relentless questions. "When did you last see Browning?" he asked unfailingly, and, "When are you going to see Browning next?" But George Hunter alarmed her most of all. He had suddenly decided to resume his visits and his scathing letters.

One Saturday, in a moment of madness, Elizabeth praised

Robert Browning to him. "He comes to see me all the way from New Cross. *He* doesn't abuse me. *He* is chivalrous."

Hunter pounced. "Hah! Your New Cross Knight!"

He wouldn't let it die. At last she said, "You'd better go."

Hunter burst into tears and flung his hat on the floor. For once Elizabeth did not react. He seized her hands and kissed them again and again. She looked down on the pink powdery scalp showing through the thinning locks, seeing the coarse white hairs sprouting from his nostrils and his ears. His cheeks were sunken, and his breath was stale. The hands holding hers were bony and veined and freckled with age.

Passion was for young men. Robert's skin was fresh and his breath sweet. His black hair was thick and strong. His body trembled only with its hunger for her. It wasn't her fault she didn't love this man, yet he could destroy them.

She wrote to Robert. "I begin to be afraid to see him alone, but I don't want you involved. I think I'll ask Arabel to stay in the room."

Her embarrassment was most acute with Anna Jameson. She had come into her life only the year before—forced her way into it, like Robert. Mr. Kenyon had begged her to receive the trenchant woman who had become famous with a book about her experiences on the continent as a governess. She was fifty, separated from her husband in Canada and struggling to supplement his allowance by writing guidebooks to art collections and galleries.

"Wherever there's a pioneer working for women's emancipation, there's Anna Jameson," Mr. Kenyon had declared, raising plump hands in admiration. "You will receive her, won't you?"

Elizabeth had ignored all Mrs. Jameson's calls and her cards. Then Mrs. Jameson had arrived next door to stay at number 51 Wimpole Street. Elizabeth had had to admit her, and so one wintry afternoon the strange fox-like Irish creature with very light red hair, a snowy skin, colourless lips, eyes like water and a paper-thin nose had come to her room. They had parted with an embrace and had become close friends. Now Elizabeth was ashamed of deceiving her.

It was John Kenyon who caused Robert most embarrassment. Robert had dedicated his last volume to him, to his voluble delight, and he asked, always, "How goes the book? Is it selling well?" No, it wasn't selling well, and people had not cried out about it. Once again Robert's father had paid for publication and lost by it.

For Robert the worst thing about the secrecy was that he was not allowed to tell his parents. He couldn't put his arms about his mother as he used to do, knowing that month after month was going by without a word to her about the most important thing that had ever happened to him. He tended to stay away from her and saw her reproachful eyes. When she was hurt she fell into a silence and drooped. It went to his heart and was far worse than any questions she might have put to him.

Then she fell ill. It was ridiculous, but he felt that he had caused it. For years she had had spells of staying in bed for a week or so. This time the week dragged into a fortnight and then over it.

Robert went to see her. "It's a cold winter. You're better in bed," he said. "Is there anything I can do for you?"

She smiled at him.

"Just don't change, Robert."

He knew what she meant, but he could not answer her.

That day he visited Elizabeth. At New Cross snow lay crisp and thick on the ground, but on the city streets it was slushy and foul. A group of urchins were blowing on the chilblains which showed an angry red through their ragged mittens and squealing round a snowman with battered top hat and pipe, scarlet muffler and lumps of charcoal for eyes and buttons.

It was the sort of London scene Dickens loved to describe. What a success the fellow had made, with his *Pickwick Papers* and his *Christmas Carol*. Yet he had started as a pauper. Robert and he were exactly of an age, yet Dickens had been famous for ten years.

Resolutely Robert shrugged off such depressing thoughts. He saw that the children's faces were pinched and green, their eyes red-rimmed. They were very thin, shivering in their rags. It struck him that they might be hungry, and he found a halfpenny for them. That started it up, of course, the endless train about the Corn Laws which absorbed every Englishman those days. Bread was dear. The poor were hungry. The Irish peasants were dying by thousands with dear bread and no potatoes, and those who could escape were crossing the Atlantic to America.

He turned into Wimpole Street and leapt up the stairs to Elizabeth's room.

"Don't you think," he asked her abruptly, "that my parents might be trusted?"

"It isn't that!" she cried, her eyes pleading. "I don't want them implicated in Papa's wrath. Let's keep our secret to ourselves, Robert."

He reminded himself that he had promised her, and himself, that whatever she wanted would be his law.

10

ONE DAY EARLY IN JANUARY ROBERT FOUND A troubled Elizabeth awaiting him. After much thought she had made up her mind to pass on some gossip to him.

Mr. Kenyon, she said, holding Robert's hand tight, had told her that Mrs. Procter, the wife of the Mr. Procter who wrote poetry and plays under the name of Barry Cornwall, had said before a roomful of people that it was a pity Robert Browning did not do seven or eight hours' work a day instead of living on his father, who was not by any means rich.

Robert lost his temper at once.

"It doesn't matter in the least," Elizabeth assured him. "I've only told you so there won't be any secrets between us."

"It does matter. The worst of it is, I can't do anything about it."

He told her about all the efforts he had been making to find some way of supporting her. He had asked his friend Dicky Monckton-Milnes to help him obtain a post in the foreign service. He was very influential, and the kindest man in the world—as good-hearted as he was ugly.

When Robert had heard nothing he had swallowed his pride and begged him for anything, however small, in the British Museum. It had all been in vain. Robert was badly shaken.

"I'm going to study for the Bar," he said now. "I can do it in Italy."

Elizabeth reminded him that he had once written, "I want

to be very rich and very important, but not in reading law gratis with dear old Basil Montagu, as he's always pestering me to do."

"But I'll have to work, if only so you won't be ashamed of me before others."

"I should never be ashamed of you unless you betrayed your star by taking some low post when there was no need."

"Not a penny of your money is going to enter into any of our plans for a life together," he said stubbornly. "When we marry—"

"*If* we marry!"

"Before we marry you must transfer it to your brothers and sisters and come penniless to me."

He wrote again to Monckton-Milnes that night. If only he could tell him about his love for Ba, it might help. Dicky had been hopelessly in love with Florence Nightingale for years. He would understand.

Mrs. Procter was not the only person whose gossip had troubled Elizabeth. One terrible afternoon her friend Miss Mitford came bustling in, a huge purple bonnet hiding the massive forehead.

She was very excited, for she had been held up by highwaymen and had lost her purse. She had been returning at night from Reading, and two masked robbers armed with bludgeons had attacked the gig in which she was travelling. She had escaped with a severe shaking, but the aftereffects had been upsetting. To her shame she had had a fit of hysterics.

Elizabeth persuaded her to accept a loan, and she relaxed into a gossiping mood, her small feet crossed on the shining brass fender.

That philanderer Mr. Horne had been pursuing yet another heiress. Mr. Wordsworth had refused to make his daughter Dora an allowance, though she was dreadfully poor since her marriage. The famous actress Fanny Kemble was on very bad terms with her American planter husband, and it might come to a bill of divorcement in Parliament. Dickens had gone to Switzerland for a year, and Mrs. Jameson was going to France and Italy for the autumn to work on a new book on sacred art.

Then she was saying disgraceful things about Robert. "He's a terrible snob and lies about his background. His grandfather kept a tavern on Hampstead Heath."

"His grandfather worked in the Bank of England," Elizabeth said stiffly.

"Not *that* one. His mother's father—Wiedemann. He was a German from Hamburg who settled in Scotland and married a Scotswoman."

"He was a shipowner."

Miss Mitford shot a bright, sharp glance at Elizabeth from under her massive brow.

"You won't find his name in the register of shipowners in Dundee, Ba. He was a mariner before he came south to keep a tavern. Mr. Robert Browning wears a signet ring with a crest to which he's not entitled."

Elizabeth said nothing.

"They're Jewish, of course, the Wiedemanns—German-Jewish. Mr. Browning gets his big nose and his music from that side."

Elizabeth was afraid of the anger in her. It would betray her if she spoke. Miss Mitford was rattling on, unaware.

"On the other side it's even more interesting! Did you know that Mr. Browning springs on his father's side of a Jamaican family called Tittle?"

"Yes."

"They were shoemakers—cordwainers—and coloured. That accounts for Mr. Browning's black hair and dark skin. When he was a young man his father was sent out to Saint Kitts to run his mother's sugar plantation. And *his* grandfather was the illegitimate son by a slave of a shoemaker in Port Royal in Jamaica who made shoes for the Barretts—"

"Miss Mitford, please—"

"Wait a minute, Ba, this will amuse you. Well, Mr. Browning's father went to church on his first Sunday, and the beadle came up to him and asked him to come away from where the white people were sitting and sit with the coloured part of the congregation. He was so upset he came right back to England."

It was the silence that made her glance up. Then she saw the look on Elizabeth's face.

"Would you think less of me if I had coloured blood?" Elizabeth asked coldly. "Look at my dark hair and black eyes."

"Oh, Ba," Miss Mitford quavered. "The Barretts are Cornish. They went out to Jamaica with Cromwell's armies."

"And the've been there for well over two hundred years since then. Can *you* swear that not one drop of the blood of a slave has found its way into my veins? *I* couldn't."

Miss Mitford's face was scarlet, and she was silent.

"And if there were, would you condemn me for it?"

"No, no, of course not, Ba."

"And as for the Jewish blood, don't you think it's a disgrace that we behave so badly to the Jews? That Mr. Disraeli can only sit in Parliament because he's a Christian by religion though a Jew by race?"

"Don't get so worked up, Ba," Miss Mitford pleaded. "I'm not talking politics, just passing on a little gossip about Mr. Browning. Let's leave it at that!"

Elizabeth had felt quite ill after Miss Mitford had gone. She had been about to write it all out to Robert, and then she had thought better of it.

It had been an old friendship. Miss Mitford had been kind, and had given her Flush. It would be better to hold her tongue.

Mr. Barrett had stopped his evening visits to Elizabeth. For over three months, ever since she had fled from his room in tears on the sixteenth of September, he had not been near her. She was angry and hurt. But one day Robert was glad to find her in high spirits.

"Henrietta's engaged!" she said, her eyes shining. "It's unofficial, of course. What else could it be, in this house?"

"To Captain Surtees Cook?"

"Who else? But he has no money—not a penny. They'll have to wait for years."

He almost said, "At least *we'll* be better off." Then he remembered Mrs. Procter.

"Will Captain Cook go to your father?"

"He'd be thrown into the street. Henrietta has explained Papa's system to him. But, perhaps I'll see him now in his scarlet coat."

At that moment the door was thrown open, and a thickset little bull of a man burst into the room. As Robert rose he had an impression of good dark cloth above fine checked trousers, and a fragrant whiff of cigar smoke. Then he took in the features of Ba's visitor, noting the frank face, the open smile, the candid eyes, and realized that this must be her father. "Why, I like him!" he thought, surprised. "He's charming!"

Then he saw a scowl cross the pleasant face and the smile vanish. Without a word Mr. Barrett turned and flung out of the room, not bothering to close the door. Robert was left holding out his hand to empty air. He dropped it to his side, went to the door and closed it.

"I'm sorry, Robert. He must have come home early." He could see that she was afraid. "He'll come back. I think you'd better go."

"You'll write at once and let me know what happens?"

"Yes, yes. Tonight."

So he left her, disliking Mr. Barrett and himself. In the eyes of the world Mr. Barrett would have every right to throw him out of the house if he suspected what was going on behind his back—that was how it would be put. He hardly cut a very fine figure, he, the penniless poet, acting the secret lover to his invalid daughter, and planning to run off with her, too.

Next morning the postman brought Robert two letters. He fell upon Elizabeth's, reading it in the hall. Her father had returned to her room, and there had been an explosion because she had not been free to talk to him.

Robert leapt up the stairs and poured out his anger and outrage on paper.

"After months of silence your father suddenly chooses to give *five minutes* to an invalid daughter who lives in a state which would drive any other human being mad. Then, when he finds her with a mere literary sympathizer who as far as he knows comes to chat with her for an hour or so once a month, he behaves like that! My Ba, it's SHOCKING!"

It was only when he had sealed the envelope that he opened the other letter. It was from Monckton-Milnes. He was now able to offer him the post of diplomatic attaché in Constantinople. Was he still interested?

Robert sat and stared at it. Mr. Barrett's churlish behaviour receded into the background. He was now facing the most important decision he might ever have to make.

He had got what he had asked for. Did he really want it? Well, he wanted Ba, and he wanted to hold his head up before

116

the Mrs. Procters of this world. Was the price too high? Would he end like his father, after all?

There would be politics involved in this job, too. With Peel as Prime Minister and Lord Aberdeen at the Foreign Office, all would be well. But what if Peel's party fell, and Lord Palmerston took over foreign affairs? To have to carry out the whims of that confounded trouble seeker would be a dog's life.

Stratford Canning was ambassador at Constantinople and had been there for forty years. He had the Sultan eating out of his hand, and flouted the Russians with devilish insolence. It would end in a bloody war with Russia, depend on it. Canning worked like ten men, half-killed his attachés, then packed them off home, demanding replacements. There'd be damnably little time for writing poetry—even for thinking about it!

Well, good-bye to his sweet independent way of life.

Robert risked calling again that afternoon. Proudfoot looked surprised, but disappeared and returned to admit him.

As soon as he entered Elizabeth began speaking about her father's outburst. "You really mustn't think that he was angry with *you*. It was just a sort of fury against seeing anyone here with me when he wanted me to himself."

"Well, we won't talk about it anymore. I came to see you about something much more important to us."

He told her about Monckton-Milnes's letter. "So I shall write the most beautiful lyrics in the intervals of bringing the Russians and the Turks to behave like Christians and brothers."

"No, Robert, you *must not* do it. It would shrivel your soul."

"It means I can take you away with me."

"Ill as I am, I mightn't even reach Constantinople. And supposing I did? An invalid wife isn't the best aid to promotion for a young diplomat, my love!"

"Sarianna would enjoy being hostess in your place."

"Don't try to take me there, Robert."

"Well, that's the end of it, then."

"I'll go to Italy with you, Robert, one day."

"This is the only offer I've had. It's Constantinople or nothing if I'm to support you."

"I don't care a fig whether you support me or not. It's of not the least importance to me whether the sixpence we live by comes from you or from me, so long as there's enough to live on."

117

He tried to interrupt her, but she held up her hand.

"No, listen to me. Let's be sensible, my darling, and make the most of what fate has given us through my Grandma Moulton and my Uncle Matthew. With my health, we'll need all the help that money can provide—for medicines, for physicians, for nurses, perhaps, if anything should go wrong."

"I would prefer you to make it over to your brothers and sisters."

"That's foolish pride, Robert. We can marry and live on what I have until you make your name and your fortune as a poet."

"The Mrs. Procters—"

"Will you let the Mrs. Procters rule our lives? When we're together what's mine will be yours and what's yours will be mine, in any case. I have more than enough for us both."

"Ba, here we are, almost quarrelling about how we're going to live," he wondered, "and you've never yet said when you will marry me, only that you *might* marry me one day. If I give up Constantinople and all hope of earning a living at once, will you promise to marry me soon and go to Italy with me?"

He took her in his arms and hid his face in her hair.

"Please, Ba."

She did not answer.

"Name the day, Ba. Say, at the summer's end. It can't be good for you, any more than for me, for this state of things to drag on. Let us go to Italy and live there for a year or two—yes, on your money, if that's the only way. Then we shall see. We can come back to England after that and make a life here."

He released her and looked into her eyes.

"Won't you, Ba? Won't you?"

She gave a great sigh.

"Very well, Robert. I promise. If when the fine weather comes I'm not ill—then, *not now*—you shall decide. What you decide I'll abide by. But *you* must decide. Such a step must be taken by you—never by me."

That night he wrote to Monckton-Milnes. Now it only remained to make Elizabeth really well and fit to travel by the time the warm weather came. It was January, 1846. How long would it be? By the end of June, perhaps, they could leave England.

11

NOW IT WAS THE END OF JUNE AND THERE WAS NO reason why they should not travel to Italy, no reason at all. Everything had gone miraculously well. They had known each other for a year and a month and they should be married before long.

Elizabeth had struggled to her feet, and staggered, then walked. She had gone out shopping, and returned with a plain little Quaker's bonnet—the height of fashion. In May she had picked a laburnum blossom in Regent's Park under the eyes of a keeper. Mr. Kenyon had taken her to see the train come into the Paddington terminus of the new Great Western Railway, and she had been more excited by the wonders of standing on grass again and of being rained on, than by the noisy iron monster. Best of all had been a carriage drive beside the Serpentine in Hyde Park.

"All the while," she wrote to Robert, "in the twilight which was lit only by the silvery water, I thought of one who is the whole world to me, and the stars besides, and as we came home the gas was in the shops—another strange sight for me."

By the beginning of June she had visited Treppy with Arabel, her first call on a friend in seven years. Then she had gone alone to see Hugh Boyd and sipped his Cyprus wine. Soon she went in the noisy streets by herself, walking to Hodgson's, the local booksellers, resting on a chair there, then going back home—enormous achievements for her.

She was well, and ready to travel.

*   *   *

To his horror Robert felt her slipping away from him. It was not that Elizabeth did not love him. She was not suffering from any prudishness when they were together. Once or twice he had thought as he held her that he could have taken her if he had wished. Yet she seemed to want to continue as they were forever, eternal lovers removed from the world and everyone else. Whenever he raised the subject of marriage she eluded him.

In June she had actually written, "Mightn't it be wiser to remain quietly as we are, you at New Cross and I here, until next summer or autumn?"

He had written back at once. "No, no, we mustn't waste another year. Every day is an unendurable irritation. Another year is altogether intolerable!"

For him, yes. But for her? Evidently not. "You must decide here, as in everything else," he insisted. "But *do* decide, Ba, my own only Ba, do think and decide. I love you, and I'm not a stock or a stone."

She had been eating better. She was sweetly, enchantingly rounded. She walked strongly. She was a different being. Still there was this total inability to act, even to emerge from her dreamlike state—this apathy. He remembered Dr. Blundell's words.

Could it be that she had not been very successful in giving up the opium, perhaps even in lessening the doses? Three months ago he had promised not to question her. She had not mentioned it since. That calmness, now—was it a morphine calmness? Well, if that was the trouble, it would have to wait until after they were married. He couldn't help her from afar. Yet that apathy would make it a thousand times more difficult to make her come away with him.

Or could it be her terror of the world's eyes on their marriage? "I shall be torn to pieces by most of my loving friends," she said. "There will be such stories. Lies, too. If I marry you we must leave England half an hour afterwards. Think. There's my father—and there's yours. Do you imagine I'm not afraid of your family?"

"Afraid of my family! Ba, I've told you—"

"I know a little about families, Robert. Oh, I must love you unspeakably to dare such things."

He held her and tried to comfort her, saying that when she met them it would all be different.

She could not even meet his sister Sarianna. For months Mr. Kenyon had been trying to bring them together. Flush gobbled up Sarianna's cakes but Elizabeth would not see her. She could not tell him that she feared his sister's contempt for the sick woman of forty in love with her charming and brilliant young brother.

Robert did not resent her brothers, he declared, even now that he was an object of ridicule. A young poet who paid regular visits to an invalid poetess was even better value than a stiff and persevering soldier. Only last Sunday, Elizabeth had told him, at her "levée," Alfred had thrown himself on the sofa moaning. "Oh, I'm going to be sick. Quick, someone, bring me a basin. Then perhaps some young lady will visit *me,* and come and talk sympathetically about the broad and narrow gauge of the railways!"

Little Lizzie Barrett had been in the room, and she had laughed louder than anyone. Alfred had pulled her long golden hair.

One day Robert had found Elizabeth thoughtful and uneasy.

"Papa brought me some flowers yesterday. They went a little to my heart as I took them."

The white roses were drooping. His own scarlet buds stood proudly on their stalks. She shook her head as she looked at them. "I wish he hadn't brought me these."

Then she burst out. "If he'd let me, I should have loved him with all my heart. It's not my fault that he wouldn't let me. And it's not my fault that I have to choose between you and him. Now it's too late. I'm not his anymore. I'm yours."

She saw that he was wounded, and she added: Ah, well. In any case I should have ended, probably, in giving everything up for you."

But still she made no move.

Elizabeth went shopping again with Arabel.

The carriage stopped outside Madame Paule's, the milliner and haberdasher, and Elizabeth and Arabel went in. Flush jumped down and bounced after them.

Elizabeth bought a pearl-embroidered spectacle case for

Treppy and a wide blue sash for Lizzie. Flush kept close to her as they left with their small packets swinging from their forefingers. Elizabeth sat back in the carriage and waited for him to leap in after her. After a while she looked out.

"Flush!" She cried in anguish. *"Flush!"*

There was no Flush. He had been snatched from under the wheels as she stepped up, kidnapped for the third time.

Arabel was alarmed at her sudden pallor. "Don't forget, Ba, the dog thieves promised to return him if you paid ten guineas next time. That's what they want, not Flush!"

At that moment a little boy ran up and thrust a piece of paper with an address on it at them through the window.

"Ten pounds for the little dog, miss. Mr. Taylor will call for it."

Legally a dog was not "property." Any man might steal Flush under the eyes of a policeman. All Elizabeth could do was pay up.

They trundled unhappily back to Wimpole Street to seek help, and found Elizabeth's fifth brother, Henry, asleep in a chair, his ginger head sunk on his chest. Henry drifted and was at home more often than at work.

"Henry, please go at once to this address in Shoreditch and get Flush back."

Henry threw on a cloak and went off grumbling in the cab.

An hour and a half later he was back.

"I could hardly bring myself to be civil to the brute. There he was, smoking a cigar, in a room hung with pictures, and silver everywhere. I advise you to let me put the police onto his tail at once for stealing silver."

"What good would that do Flush?"

"Well, he'll come tonight for his ten guineas or whatever I can beat him down to."

"Please don't haggle with him, Henry."

Henry did not tell her that Mr. Barrett had ordered him not to pay anything to the dog stealers, and had told him to say nothing to her about it. She sat in her room, waiting for Taylor, hour after hour.

"Perhaps he will come in the morning," she wrote to Robert, agonizing that a lady in the neighbourhood who refused to pay had had her dog's head sent back to her in a parcel.

Robert could not resist a dig at Flush.

"Poor fellow," he wrote back. "All that barking and brave show used up on such enemies as Mr. Kenyon and me, leaving only friendly tailwaggings for the man with the sack. I'm sure you're upset and frightened for our friend-and-follower-that-was-to-be at Pisa."

He tried hard to bring her back to a sense of urgency.

"I won't urge you anymore. You must arrange everything from now on without a word from me. But don't let our happiness be caught up and stolen from us like poor Flush. There may be no redeeming *that*."

She was deaf and blind to anything but Flush. "You think I shan't get him back at once. But I must and shall."

On the third night, Taylor rang at the bell and asked for Henry.

"The Society's got the dog, sure enough," he said in the hall, staring about him impudently. "Took him in Bond Street."

"Where is he now?" Henry asked.

"At headquarters in Whitechapel. The Society settles the ransom, and I'll return with the ultimatum."

"The *ultimatum?*" Henry could hardly contain his anger.

"Take it or leave it. Pay or say good-bye to the dog." He drew a grubby finger across his throat.

"Be damned to *you*," Henry began. Then he heard Elizabeth's voice in his ears, "Get Flush back, whatever you do." He heard his father's commands, too, "Don't pay a penny. And not a word to Ba, mind."

Henry was choking on this commission. Whatever he did was wrong. Papa and Ba were too much alike. Once they got their teeth into anything they never let go.

Like Henry, Robert was feeling that he could not do right. He was at odds with Elizabeth, and at a distance, and all because of Flush.

On that Thursday night he felt ill and went to bed early, but not before he had succeeded in doing a great deal more damage. Assuming that she had Flush safely home, he delivered a homily. He would not have given way to ruffians who victimized weak women through their pets—not *he*. He would have given the ten pounds to a beggar before their eyes, and threatened to hunt them down if they did not produce the dog at once.

"Do you think that I would be sent Flush's head? Perhaps. But all religion, right and justice are on my side. If you pay ten pounds promptly for a few minutes of villainy, then you'll be encouraging a hundred more such acts next month. And how are those poor owners going to manage who haven't got enough money to ransom their dogs?"

Elizabeth had not got Flush back, and his letter reached her like another blow. Taylor had turned up at Wimpole Street naming his price as six guineas and an extra half-guinea for him. She had asked Henry to go to Shoreditch at once to fetch Flush.

"Well, I'm very sorry, Ba, but I can't."

"Why not?"

"Papa has forbidden it. He said I wasn't to hand over any money. At least let me send him away now and tell him to come back with a lower price."

"Oh, no Henry, I don't like it."

"Try it, Ba. It's either that or a straight refusal to pay anything at all."

The waiting began again.

"I should have paid," she wrote to Robert. "If he doesn't come tonight, I shall go down tomorrow morning myself and bring Flush back. It may be very foolish—I don't say it isn't— but I cannot bear to run terrible risks about my poor Flush for the sake of a few pounds, or even for the sake of abstract principles of justice. You say that *you would,* but I know you better. Do you mean to say that if the *banditti* came down upon us in Italy and carried me off to the mountains and sent you one of my ears, to show you what was going to happen to me if you didn't let them have five or six *scudi* for me your answer would be 'Not a *crazie!'?* And would you wait, poised upon abstract principles, for the other ear and then my death? Would you, dearest? Because it's as well to know beforehand, perhaps!"

As she wrote she could hear the yelping and moaning of a dog shut up in the mews behind Wimpole Street. It had been going on for two days, as if it wanted to remind her of Flush.

Oh, but she did not need any reminders!

She remembered the fat sleek little puppy with bulging eyes and drooping ears which had been pulled out of the hamper in which he had travelled to Torquay all the way from Miss Mitford's cottage. For the first time after Bro's death she had smiled.

Everyone had loved Flush, even when he had torn up their letters and gnawed their slippers. She had spoiled him, sugaring his milk, salting his cheese, offering him coffee in his own coffee cup, and producing macaroons for special occasions. She had bought him a drinking bowl of royal purple and a succession of pretty collars.

He loved praise. He would hold his head still and his mouth half-open for minutes on end, until you could praise the beauty of his teeth no longer. He adored sympathy. He was the prince of cowards. The long list of Flush's cowardly retreats made one shudder.

Yet he was so vainglorious that he would only consent to go for walks in the park alongside Catiline and Resolute, a Cuban bloodhound and an alpine mastiff as big as horses and as fierce as tigers. Did he fancy that it made him their peer? And then, to be so lecherous as to father a litter of puppies when he was still only a puppy himself, and to leer at Catiline's wife Resolute through the window.

Oh, vain, greedy, spoiled, self-pitying, snobbish, lecherous, cowardly and jealous creature. Was there anything to be said for Flush at all? Yes, he loved greatly.

For he had come from the life of the fields and the brakes to which he had been bred to inhabit the dark, close, stale room of a weeping invalid and had given her all his love.

Other dogs in thymy dew
Tracked the hares and followed through
    Sunny moor or meadow;
This dog only crept and crept
Next a languid cheek that slept,
    Sharing in the shadow . . .

Blessings on thee, dog of mine,
Pretty collars make thee fine,
    Sugared milk make fat thee!
Pleasures wag on in thy tail,
Hands of gentle motion fail
    Nevermore to pat thee!

Downy pillow take thy head,
Silken coverlid be-stead,
    Sunshine help thy sleeping!
No fly's buzzing wake thee up,

No man break thy purple cup
   Set for drinking deep in.

Whiskered cats arointed flee,
Sturdy stoppers keep from thee
   Cologne distillations;
Nuts lie in thy path for stones,
And thy feast-day macaroons
   Turn to daily rations!

Mock I thee, in wishing weal?
Tears are in my eyes to feel
   Thou are made so straitly,
Blessing needs must straiten too—
Little canst thou joy or do,
   Thou who lovest *greatly*.

For that was it, that was what moved her so deeply about Flush, that with all his faults and follies, his affectations and his failings, with his greed, his vanity, his vaingloriousness, his jealousy, his lechery, and his abject, shaming cowardice, he loved so greatly. Like her with all her failings and unworthinesses, her weakness, her hidden pride, her jealousy and cowardice, the greatest of his capacities was love.

Was she now to betray this wretched little creature who loved her so and whose love she had vowed to return with something more than most human beings gave to their dogs? Not for all the abstract principles of justice in the world.

And, little though he seemed to realize it, writing in that peevish and bilious fashion from his sickbed, she would not be the woman that Robert Browning loved if she could, and did.

The next day Elizabeth went to see Taylor, taking a petrified Wilson with her.

"It's a very rough quarter as we're going to, Miss Elizabeth," Wilson pleaded, her small, periwinkle-blue eyes glittering with fright. "There's wicked men there as would think nothing of doing you a harm."

The four-wheeler drove them through streets of peeling houses with broken windows. Scabby children stared from the gutters. The cabman lost his way and had to ask for directions,

126

leaning down from his box and bawling into a dark doorway under a sign swinging on a broken hinge. A man with a black patch over one eye and a tooth jutting over his bluish lip came blinking out into the poor sunlight. "You'll be looking for Mr. Taylor!" he growled, and ran to show the way. He reached the house before the cab and dashed straight inside. Taylor was not at home, but an immense woman in a man's checked cap came out.

"Won't you step down, ma'am, and come inside?" she asked, grinning.

"Don't do it, Miss Elizabeth," Wilson begged in a terrified whisper, sitting bolt upright in her corner. "We'll have our throats cut, mark my words."

"Suppose Flush is there?"

"He's in Whitechapel, ma'am, at headquarters."

Elizabeth looked at the crowd of men and boys who had appeared from nowhere and were swarming about the cab. There was a leer on every face.

"We live but to oblige ye, ladies. Come down and come in. Are ye afeared?" Their voices were like the yelping of dogs, barking together, but each different.

"No thank you. It's about my dog. Will you please ask Mr. Taylor to come to Wimpole Street today and not delay any longer?"

The fat woman cocked her head to left and right. "I'm sure Mr. Taylor will give it his very best attention."

"The smell!" Wilson cried as they drove away, covering her face with a large handkerchief. "It's enough to give one the cholera."

All the way home Elizabeth saw the children, the women and the men, and heard their voices, and smelled the smells among which they lived.

These were people who existed on the fringes of her good, safe world, card sharpers, horse and dog stealers, promoters of cockfighting and prizefighting, the set which had flaunted itself under the name of The Fancy from Regency days, and had its own slang—dangerous men, who did not stop at murder.

The faces of those men. She would never forget them.

* * *

That evening Taylor appeared at the door for the third time.

"Are you prepared to hand over the six and a half guineas, or aren't you? I won't come again."

"But where's the dog?" Henry asked.

"I'm a man of honour. Give me the blunt. You'll have to trust me."

Elizabeth sent down the money by Wilson. Sniffing with outrage, Wilson took Henry aside and gave him his sister's message.

Henry was just about to pay over the money when Alfred came into the hall. Alfred took in the meaning of the scene at a glance.

"You scoundrel," he roared at Taylor. "Liar. Thief."

He flew at him, shaking his fist in his face.

Taylor drew himself up and glared at Alfred. Then he turned his back on him and addressed Henry, who was still holding out the money and gazing at Alfred with his mouth open.

"No gentleman can be expected to put up with this," Taylor blustered. "You'll never set eyes on your dog again."

He flung out of the house, swearing.

Wilson panted upstairs to report, and Elizabeth almost fell downstairs in her fury. The whole world was against her and Flush—Papa, Henry, Robert and now Alfred.

"*Alfred!*" she raged.

She took him by the shoulders and shook him with a strength she did not know she possessed.

Then she found her tongue. Alfred could not believe that it was the gentle Ba who was addressing him in such terms.

"How dare you! You've no business to risk Flush's life for the sake of abusing that man."

She lashed him until he flinched.

"All right. I'm sorry," he said sulkily. "What now? It's done."

"Now I'll go myself again to Mr. Taylor's in Shoreditch or wherever it is. I'll save my poor Flush from having his head cut off at any price. I'll pay him a hundred guineas if he asks me. And *that* is all you have achieved with your brave manly words."

"Oh no, Ba, you can't. You mustn't," Henrietta cried, for the hall was now full of the family. "It was bad enough going in daylight."

128

In the background Wilson was moaning, "Oh, *no* Miss Elizabeth! Oh *no*. Not again."

"You're obstinate," Henry cried. "It's not a thing a lady can do."

At last Elizabeth's seventh brother, Setty, managed to put in a quiet word. "Look, Ba, be calm. I'll go—yes, this minute, but only if you give up this storming and go up to your room again. Promise me, now."

"Very well, then. Take the money. And remember to speak politely to the man. What we want is to have Flush home again. Nothing else matters."

Elizabeth mounted slowly to her room again. Arabel put an arm about her waist and went with her.

"I'll wait with you, Ba, till he comes back—*with* Flush, never fear."

At eight o'clock Setty returned with Flush.

He carried him through the door and set him down in the hall. Flush at once leapt for the stairs and dashed up them. He struck against Elizabeth's door with his paw, she opened it and he hurled himself at her.

Wilson followed Flush upstairs, bearing a letter from Robert.

"Put it down, Wilson." She had no time for anything but this thin, dirty animal.

She filled his water bowl, and he drank all the water. She refilled it and he went on lapping. She filled it a third time, and he emptied it.

12

ROBERT HAD SEEN THE MUSICAL-BOX IN A SHOP window and had not been able to resist it. It was made of ivory and painted with little figures. The clear notes came, a little pause between each, with a golden sweetness. He had never been able to understand why the tune of a musical-box should have that particular quality of excruciating and slightly cynical sweetness.

He turned the handle, sure of Elizabeth's delight, and she listened expectantly. Then he was struck by the sadness on her face.

"I recognize it," she said, "the air."

"Yes, it's one of Shakespeare's songs."

She quoted it.

"Sigh no more, ladies, sigh no more,
Men were deceivers ever,
One foot on the sea and the other on shore,
To one thing constant never!

"Why did you choose that, Robert?"

"I never gave a thought to the words."

He would not rest until he had drawn from her what had caused that look on her face. As a child she had heard two women talking over the teacups. "The most painful part of marriage is the first year, when the lover changes into the husband," one had said, and the other had replied, "Surely. It's best to start with a little aversion."

Elizabeth had looked at her parents with new eyes. Yes, marriage, it seemed, killed love.

"I was very young then," she said, "and the world did, at the time, look ghastly."

Involuntarily Robert's hand jerked the handle of the musical-box, and he silenced it quickly.

"I do dread marriage, I admit it," Elizabeth said miserably. "What is there about it, Robert, to make all those people everywhere—who all began, I suppose, by talking of love—look at each other with hatred?" Then she added, "It never could be so with *us;* I know that."

But Robert thought there was a question in her voice.

He began gathering together the paper and string, and Elizabeth hastened to take it from him. She put her arms about his neck and whispered, "I'm sorry, my darling. How *could* I think you were like other men?" A little tear ran down her cheek, and he kissed her mouth, salty with it. "I will always cherish it," she said. "Let us play it together now."

They stood with their arms about each other and listened once more to the notes, so mechanical and yet so surprisingly sweet.

When the tune had ended he said to her, "Let us look at the horror of the world together, my Ba, and not use it to hurt each other. We are not like all those other people. When we are married we will be just the same as we are now, only better and happier. No one can hurt us except ourselves."

"No one but me, Robert. I am sorry, dearest. Look down on your Ba, and forgive her."

"I look *up* to my Ba, always *up.*"

What she had told him answered the question as to why she pinned her affections so determinedly on men she could never marry—men too old for her, too poor for her, married, and crippled by tragic afflictions. She was struggling hard to prevent anything coming of their own love, now.

Mr. Barrett's crazy disgust at the natural passions between man and woman was at least a knot which might be cut if it could not be unloosed. Far more dangerous were the emotions in her own heart which might make her join with her father to thrust away her lover for fear that he might turn into a husband.

In answer to all that she had told him he wrote his love to her.

"I desire more earnestly than I ever knew what desiring was to be yours and with you and, as far as may be in this life and this world, *you*. There is no hindrance to that, bar one, which causes me a moment's anxiety. That one is just your little hand. You have only to raise it and my happiness is sure. But now— what is to make you raise that hand?"

Elizabeth had not spoken to him about that other agony that racked her. She was consumed with jealousy—not of a real woman, simply of any woman he might see and love. The world was full of women who were younger and prettier than she was. One of them could steal him from her at any moment. She had tried to cast it out, this demon with its claws in her heart. Now and then she had said things to him she was ashamed to remember. When Robert had had to leave early she had accused him of going to meet another woman. Before his look of dumb disbelief she had wanted to die. At such times she felt she could never bear to look him in the face again. He had never blamed her, only waited patiently for her to recover.

She was writing out her love in her sonnets, but she never wrote of that poisonous flame which rose suddenly in her and made her mad. It might be better if she could exorcise it, but she could not. Even while she was most ashamed she asked herself, "Haven't I every reason to be afraid?"

It was at this most difficult of times for her that Miss Heaton called.

It was Mr. Kenyon, as usual, who had talked her into admitting his new friend. She came, a large square woman with a dark face and a mole on her chin. She was full of herself, with a knowing manner. She talked and talked.

Elizabeth never knew how they got onto the subject of Robert Browning. Suddenly she was listening to her giving out some very authoritative information about him.

"He was engaged to be married," Miss Heaton said, "and they were violently in love, but she broke off the engagement because of religious differences. He's an atheist, you know."

132

"I don't think that's true, that he was engaged," Elizabeth said faintly.

"Upon my oath, it's as true as I'm sitting here. But I'm telling you in the strictest confidence. You *will* keep the secret, won't you?"

"Yes," Elizabeth murmured, always weak before a forceful woman.

The claws closed about her heart and buried themselves deep in it, squeezing out her life's blood. Of course it's not true, she kept telling herself. He's certainly not an atheist now, and I know that well enough. Why can't I believe that the rest of it is just as false?

It did no good. The pain was there, impossible to bear, impossible to quell. Robert had put his arms about another woman, had called her by those tender, foolish names that he used to her. He had asked her to marry him, and she had consented. They had been happy before those "religious differences" had parted them. Why hadn't he told her, and spared her these thrusts from a stranger?

Elizabeth sat in such frigid silence, staring at Miss Heaton and saying nothing, that at last even she was put out of countenance and gathered up her gloves and took her leave. As soon as Miss Heaton had gone Elizabeth wrote to Robert and told him what she had said.

He had no inkling of what it had meant to her. He could see that she was jealous, but not how jealous. He treated it lightly.

"They used to get up better stories about Lord Byron," he wrote back. It was unfortunate identifying himself with Lord Byron, and it had not helped her at all.

Then worse followed. The very next afternoon Stormy came home from the Chelsea Flower Show and brought Elizabeth a sheaf of flame-coloured gladioli. He told her how wonderful the delphiniums and the roses had been.

In the midst he broke off. "Oh, by the way, B-ba. I met some friends of Mr. B-browning's, and they told me he's to be married immediately—to a Miss Campbell."

Elizabeth's world shattered. She knew how much gossip there was in the literary world. Miss Mitford had been bringing her false rumours for ten years. Yet she never dreamt of discounting this one. Of course it was true. There was a Miss Campbell. She could see her—plump, with blue eyes and golden hair and a fine big bosom. Tall, too, with marble limbs.

She had not known it was possible to suffer so, or that she had it in her to hate so much. She wished Miss Campbell dead. Robert understood the black passions in the hearts of men and women. The Duke in *My Last Duchess* had had his wife killed just because she smiled at others. Then there was the girl in *The Laboratory*, who went to buy poison for her rival.

> Soon, at the King's, a mere lozenge to give
> And Pauline should have just thirty minutes to live!
> But to light a pastille, and Elise, with her head
> And her breast and her arms and her hands, should drop dead!

Elizabeth felt exactly like that girl. When Robert called he saw at once that she had received a serious shock. She told him what Stormy had said. She meant to speak lightly, but her voice shook.

"I've never seen or heard of a Miss Campbell. It must be a straight falsehood—it can't even be a misunderstanding, or gossip."

If Robert had left it there, all might have been well, but from his very consciousness of complete innocence he blundered.

"I did mention, didn't I, the one person about whom such gossip *might* be spread—Miss Haworth?"

He had said in passing once that he corresponded with a Miss Haworth about literary matters. He had spoken so casually. That had been on purpose, of course.

"Miss Haworth," Elizabeth repeated, her face closing against him.

"Miss Euphrasia Fanny Haworth, to give her her full title. She's a poet, like you. Surely you've heard of her?"

"Have you known her long?"

"Ten years. She's very intelligent and—"

"Is she young?"

"She was thirty-five, I think, when I first knew her. She is unmarried but very susceptible to men—very!"

"And you were eleven years younger?"

"That is so." He told her how, when Macready had wanted him to write a tragedy, he had written to her, asking her for her ideas on wild and passionate love. "She being so interested in love, you know."

"And did Miss Haworth oblige?"

"She was very helpful, Ba."

He looked at her, knowing well enough what she was after, refusing to meet her on that level. He would give her nothing less than the truth, and she could make of it what she wanted to. There was nothing to it, and never had been.

"She wrote me sonnets," he said, deliberately laying his head on the block.

"Indeed."

"Yes. Two of them were published."

"When was all this?"

"They were addressed *To the Author of Paracelsus,* and they appeared ten years ago in the *New Monthly Magazine* in the autumn of the year we met, which would be 1836. They were kind. One described me and foretold a great future for me. The other asked for my friendship."

"How did she describe you? No poet could forget a poem about himself, surely!"

He quoted for her, obediently, but he had flushed at her tone.

"He hath the quiet calm and look of one
Who is assur'd in genius too intense
For doubt of its own power; yet with the sense
Of youth, not weakness—

"I don't remember any more. Something about rich autumn's promise, I believe."

"And how did she ask for your friendship, Robert? So publicly, too."

"I remember that better. Let me see."

He paused, rehearsing it in his mind, then quoted again.

". . . Then, poet, give to me
No splendour, but one feeling true and kind
That (if unskill'd wholly to comprehend
Thy scope of genius) I may call thee friend.

"And that, Ba, is all I gave her, and no more."

"And did you write poems to Miss Haworth, too?"

That, he thought, was unfortunate, but the question must be answered.

"Once I wrote her some lines. I didn't address her by her own name, precisely in order to avoid such a moment as I am now enduring."

"What name did you call her by?"

"Eyebright."

"You mean—Bright Eyes?"

He wriggled. "Something of that sort. I called her Eyebright since folks would know who Euphrasia or Fanny was."

Her silence chilled his bones.

"I never see her now. We write to each other now and then, solely on literary matters. You'll like her when you meet her. You *will*, Ba. Don't look so forbidding. I'm sure of it."

She was still silent.

"If there had been any more between us I would say so," he said. "But it was never on the cards."

"Have there been any other women—not young—of whom you have been specially fond?"

"Yes, two."

"Who were they?"

"Two sisters, Eliza and Sarah Flower."

"Will you tell me about them?"

"Of course."

So he told her, regretting that he must do so when she was in so unsympathetic a mood, but speaking frankly of his exact feelings towards the two kind, beautiful and talented women who had meant so much to him for so long.

"They're Benjamin Flower's daughters—Benjamin Flower, who was sent to Newgate for six months for daring to criticize Bishop Watson's politics in his paper. Eliza Gould, the pretty young schoolmistress, visited him in prison, and when he came out he married her. They went to live in Harlow in Essex, and that's where Eliza and Sarah were born."

She had heard of the Flower sisters of course. Both were taken seriously in the world of art and letters. Everyone agreed they were beautiful and talented.

"I was fourteen when I met them first."

His father had sent a copy of his first poem, in manuscript, to the well-known literary family. Robert had been invited to come and see them at once.

136

"They were orphans. Their mother died when they were very young, Eliza seven and Sarah five, I think. Their father looked after them, rather haphazardly. Eliza was a musical prodigy at two and a half; she had lessons on the organ now and then. But mostly they brought themselves up, except for intellectual conversation with their elders."

Robert glanced at Elizabeth, to see her listening attentively.

"In some ways they were like little savages, in others brilliant and cultivated. Someone once presented them with a pair of bonnets out of pity for two little girls who seemed to have no pretty clothes. Eliza got a silk bonnet, and she used it for a cradle for the kitten, and Sarah used hers as a basket to gather strawberries. It was made of straw, you see."

He remembered how he had journeyed out to Dalston, near Hackney, excited because the district was celebrated for highwaymen, and walked up the green lanes and past the nursery gardens to the small tree-shaded house.

At first he had been overawed by the skinny man with the fanatical eyes, the peaked bald dome of a head and the fall of silver locks, and overwhelmed by his lovely daughters. Eliza had been twenty-three and Sarah twenty-one. Eliza played the piano and the organ beautifully, and she set Sarah's poems to music. Sarah wanted to be an actress more than anything in the world. She had a beautiful voice and was extremely emotional.

Benjamin Flower had been kind. Eliza had called Robert "the poet boy" and said he was a genius. Sarah had stroked his long black hair.

It was to Eliza that he had sent poem after poem and letter after letter. He had caught her pasting them into an album and had been flattered.

"We met as equals," he said, "Eliza and I."

"Although you were only fourteen and she was nearly ten years older?"

"We met as equals," he insisted. He had liked Sarah too.

Their district was famous for dissenters as well as highwaymen, and the celebrated preacher Mr. Fox was a regular visitor. It was ten years or so after the South Place Unitarian Chapel had been specially built for him, and he still ministered there. More important for the boy gazing at him from a corner of the family circle was that he was also the editor of the *Monthly Repository*, and his literary articles carried great weight.

It had been a great day for Robert when Eliza had persuaded Mr. Fox to look at his poems. Mr. Fox was the most important person in Eliza's life. She looked at the little thickset pot-bellied man of forty-nine, with a head of bushy hair above his broad face and snuff on his waistcoat, as if he had descended from heaven in a cloud of fire.

"Eliza told told me I had great powers of conversation and that I was very original. But Sarah didn't think much of me. She said I would have looked very poetical if nature hadn't played me such a dirty trick and given me an ugly nose."

He felt it ruefully. "It is a large nose, I suppose, and must have looked even larger on a boy's face."

Elizabeth sprang to its defense, glad to oppose one of these insufferable young women.

"I think it's perfect."

"Perhaps she wanted to get her own back. You see, I was very hard on poor Sarah. I was an atheist then, as a disciple of Shelley, and I tried to convert her. I did, too."

"At only fourteen?"

"She was very religious. She wrote hymns. But she didn't know how to argue. It was all emotional. She was quite lost when I got her with her back to the wall."

Sarah had been tormented by a hell of doubt. She had written to Mr. Fox begging for his help as a preacher and family friend. She could no longer read her Bible and she dared not let her father know what had happened. It was all Robert Browning's fault.

"He showed me the letter, to make me sorry, and it did."

Sarah had returned to her faith, but she had never been as firmly and happily based on it as she had been before she met the terrible boy. Still, later on, she had composed that famous hymn, "Nearer, My God, to Thee."

"Poor Sarah. I behaved very badly," Robert laughed. After a pause, he said, "I don't know why, but I never teased Eliza like that."

"It was Eliza who was your real friend, wasn't she?"

"Yes. Eliza, who bears your name. I hadn't thought of that until this moment."

"Perhaps you began to like me a little because I too was called Elizabeth."

"Eliza was dark too, with black eyes and ringlets to her

shoulders. She wasn't at all well. It was her lungs. You've a great deal in common."

He could not win her to kindness to the other Elizabeth. Yet he would not deny the friendship which had meant everything to him.

When Robert was seventeen Benjamin Flower had died. Three years of visits to the house in Dalston had come to an end. The sisters had given it up, and he had lost touch with them.

Robert was a man of twenty-one before they met again. He had taken to whiskers and affected a velvet cloak swung about his shoulders on a chain. He found the sisters living at Stamford Grove West, in the home of their guardian, Mr. Fox. He might have known there would be trouble, and there was.

Fox was still a minister. He was unhappily married; everyone knew that, including his congregation. He had not wanted to marry his wife, and she had repaid that with sulkiness and laziness, neglecting him and resenting his work. They had two sons, Florance and Franklin, and a little girl called Tottie. Florance was a deaf-mute.

One might almost sympathize a little with the aging Mrs. Fox, confronted with Eliza's adoring presence in her home. Eliza had sat at the feet of her god at last, docile as a hind, tireless, worshipping. She had corrected his proof sheets, copied out his sermons and articles for him, looked up references, more beautiful at nearly thirty than she had been at twenty. How could he resist it, any more than Hugh Boyd and George Hunter had been able to resist the young Elizabeth Barrett? And how could his wife bear it?

It had come to a scandal, as of course it had to. Mrs. Fox had laid a complaint against her husband with his congregation. Terrible months had followed, some of his flock demanding his resignation, others insisting he stay on. Eliza had been fiercely attacked on all sides.

In the end Fox and his wife had decided to separate. Franklin had gone with his mother. Florance the deaf-mute and Tottie had stayed with their father and Eliza, whom they loved. Eliza and Fox had moved to a house together as unmarried—but only, it was understood, platonic—lovers.

Robert could see Mr. Fox's bright, sympathetic eyes in his thoughtful face, and watch him take snuff, in memory.

"It was Mr. Fox who praised my poem, *Pauline,* that was

published anonymously, in his magazine. You don't know what that meant to me in the midst of all the silence and contempt."

He did not tell her that he had read Shelley's lyrics to Eliza, that he had written her boyish poems, that he had fallen in love with her with the passionate love of a boy for an older woman, and that he had made the Pauline of his poem in her image. For what, after all, was a boy's love? Nothing.

It was thanks to Eliza that Fox had become his literary godfather, and thanks to Fox that he had had his *Paracelsus* considered by Moxon, and then by Saunders and Otley, and, at last, published by Effingham Wilson of the Royal Exchange, that other editors had looked at it with kindness, and that he had met Horne and Macready and Carlyle and Fanny Haworth and John Kenyon, and all the people he knew because of him. It was thanks to Fox, too, that he had met Anna Jameson, and even Elizabeth herself, indirectly. He owed everything, and any hope he had of anything more, to Fox, and through him to Eliza.

He could remember so well his visits to number 5 Craven Hill, Bayswater, where Eliza lived with Fox and Tottie and Florance.

The cottage faced Kensington Gardens. The days were past when one could buy a halfpenny mug of curds-and-whey at the gates, but it stood in the midst of emerald-green meadows where white cows grazed under the flowering limes in summertime. The house was tall and seemed hung high up in the boughs of the trees. It was filled with music all the hours there were in the day.

Robert could remember the squeak of the garden gate covered with ivy and set in the low ivy-covered wall as he pushed it open with difficulty. He knew every flagstone up to the porch, where the family sat in a bower of honeysuckle and sweetbrier. He could see Eliza playing at trapball with Florance in the long untidy back garden and Tottie in the cherry tree, lost in a book, and as deaf as her brother to shouts to come indoors. He could see Fox's protest against a neighbour who had used his shotgun on the birds, the placard he had nailed to the tree, "Blackbirds May Eat the Cherries Here."

He could remember the people who had come to that house too, scandal or no scandal, gods of the theater and the literary world, exciting to him.

He could see Richard Hengist Horne, determined to be picturesque, with his dead white face and his carefully curled coxcomb's whiskers, and hear him singing sea chanties to Sarah or telling Eliza long stories of his life in the Mexican navy—see him too, thrusting his head through the tangle of rambler roses at the window to engage in a whistling match with Jetty the tame blackbird. He could see Sarah, lovely in her veils, entering through the folding double doors to a round of applause, to act a scene from *Lord Ullin's Daughter*. He had read aloud his *Paracelsus* there, himself. And all to the lowing of the cows in the meadow.

Sarah had been married by then. Unable to face life without Eliza when she moved into a house with Fox, she had married the widower William Bridges Adams.

"Was Eliza lovely, Robert?" Elizabeth pulled him back from his dreams.

"Yes. She has a fine, strong face. The features are perfect, but it's sweet, not cold. Her lips are full and soft, and there's a smile in the corners. Haydon loves painting faces like hers."

"That was twenty years ago," Elizabeth pointed out, "and she's ten years older than you."

Eliza Flower, she thought, was only three years older than she was. But Robert did not know her age. It was he who had chosen to be ignorant, not she who had concealed it.

"Her kind of face doesn't age," he said. "Like you, she has large eyes and good bones and a firm, tight skin. Like you, she's finely made, yet warm as sunlight."

She did not want a compliment at second hand.

"In what respect were you closest to her, Robert?"

She had expected him to say, "In poetry." To her surprise he answered, "In music. She touched the very quick of my being with her playing."

Elizabeth could play nothing well—not even the Aeolian harp which hung in the window. Henrietta, with her polkas on the pianoforte, and Arabel, with her light airs on the guitar, were musicians compared with her. Even Papa could play the fiddle, and still did now and then.

Robert had known Eliza Flower for seven or eight years, she calculated, by the time his *Pauline* had been written. He was a man of nearly twenty-two by then, and Eliza in full bloom in her early thirties. Was Elizabeth to believe that this had been always and only a boy's love, a love of the imagination? Robert was a hot-blooded lover, and he would have been no less ardent ten years ago, in all the urgency of his young manhood. Had he been the lover of Eliza Flower, or had he merely wished that he were?

She remembered what he had written in *Pauline*.

"I am knit round/As with a charm by sin and lust and pride . . ."

It was he who had said it, not she. Now she could bear it in silence no longer. With a flushed face and flashing eyes she charged him with it. He had loved Eliza Flower and he still did, as he did not and could not love her, poor invalid as she was.

"She's beautiful, and full of music. She's well—oh, yes, well compared to me! She can walk beside you in the world wherever you go. Oh, Robert, don't torment me with this fine, healthy creature you adore. Go, and marry her."

Suddenly she broke down, and he was able to take her, sobbing, in his arms.

"Oh, Robert, I can't bear the thought of you and another woman—past, present or to come! It's such a *pang*—here." She pressed her hand against her breast. "I've tried to overcome it— I have tried! But it comes back again and again. It's easier to send you away, perhaps even to hate you, than to bear *that*."

"I understand."

"How could you understand? You, who haven't an ounce of jealousy in you? One of the things I love most about you is that you never seem to feel a spark of envy towards anyone. You love to praise, and you enjoy what other men do!"

"I'm not nearly as nice as all that. I'm very envious and very quarrelsome—very disagreeable altogether, make no mistake about it, little one. I understand. But you're not to be afraid. There's nothing to worry about. Nothing at all."

"Isn't there? Why did you love me when you might have chosen anyone in the world. The most perfect of women would have been glad to have been loved by you and would have loved you as you deserve to be loved. Why me, and not Eliza Flower?"

"Because I love you."

It was only then that he told her. He might have done it before, but, after all, their struggle was not about that.

"Eliza is dying," he said. "I've been trying to see her to say good-bye for weeks now."

142

She was dumb before that. Relief and shame warred in her.

"Soon," he said, "she'll be gone. It will be very painful. You've nothing to fear from that quarter, Elizabeth. Nor would you have done if she had lived another fifty years. All the same, I loved her, and I love her, and I'll always think of her with love. I am not ashamed of that."

Looking at her hard, he added: "I would never deny you, either, Elizabeth."

He felt the hand against his breast clench and unclench. He searched for it, drew it to his lips, opened the tight fingers and kissed them and then kissed the palm.

"You have nothing to be jealous of, nothing to fear," he repeated. "I don't know why you think so little of yourself, and why a look of terror comes into your face when I tell you that you are wonderful and beautiful—you who are all beauty and all wonder to me. But though you are beautiful and wonderful it's not because of that that I love you."

Speaking very slowly and emphatically, as if he were trying to teach a child, he said, "I love you because I *love* you, and because I love *you*. I see you once a week because I cannot see you all day long. I think of you all day long because I most certainly couldn't think of you once an hour less if I tried, or went to Pisa, or abroad, as you so continually beg me to do in order that I may be happy."

He held her face up to him by her chin, and with his other hand stroked her hair back from her forehead. She would not look at him. Those incredible lashes rested on her tear-stained cheeks.

"Do you really think," he said, "that before I found you I was going about the world seeking whom I might devour, that is, be devoured by, in the shape of a wife? Do you suppose I ever dreamed of marrying?"

The lashes trembled but did not lift.

"Just when I was congratulating myself that you'd given up accusing me of wanting to hurry away from you, or longing to exchange you for someone else—this! Tire of you? Life of my life, light of my soul, heart's joy of my heart, I never shall."

The face he looked at was still woebegone. He worked hard to bring a smile to it.

"See, love—just imagine that a year has gone. Am I weary of

you? Well, of course not. Now, let's pretend that many years have gone by, as that one did. We're married, my arms are around you and my face is touching yours—like *this!*—and I'm asking you whether in that dim, distant year of 1846 you weren't a joy beyond all joys to me. Believe in it *now* for *then,* dearest!"

Still the smile did not come, and the lashes did not lift.

"I am altogether your own, dearest. My love *is* a rock—not large enough to build a house on or small enough to make a mantelpiece from, much less a pedestal for a statue. But it *is* real rock."

The lashes lifted at last, and her eyes looked into his, not maidenly but trusting.

"At first, Ba, I only thought of being *happy* in you and with you. Now I mostly think of us in the dark hours that must come. I shall grow old with you and die with you. As far as I can see into the dark you are the only light I shall have with me. Will you deny me that? *Can* you *now* tell me, or yourself, that you could believe me happy with any other woman that ever breathed? *Now* kiss me, my best, dearest beloved!"

Then the smile came, and with the smile the kiss.

That night, for all women, Elizabeth wrote what she had felt in his arms.

> If thou must love me, let it be for nought
> Except for love's sake only. Do not say
> "I love her for her smile—her look—her way
> Of speaking gently—for a trick of thought
> That falls in well with mine, and certes brought
> A sense of pleasant ease on such a day"—
> For these things in themselves, Belovèd, may
> Be changed, or change for thee—and love, so wrought,
> May be unwrought so. Neither love me for
> Thine own dear pity's wiping my cheeks dry—
> A creature might forget to weep, who bore
> Thy comfort long, and lose thy love thereby!
> But love me for love's sake, that evermore
> Thou mayst love on, through love's eternity.

13

TWICE IN RAPID SUCCESSION DANGER CAME VERY close. One afternoon Robert had just entered the hall and was about to mount the stairs to Elizabeth's room when he saw George Hunter coming down. They had never met, but Hunter knew him at once. His wrinkled face grew white with passion, and he shook his fist in the air.

"The New Cross Knight!" he shouted. "The thief who climbs over the garden wall and steals the peaches!"

The butler was closing the door. Glancing round, Robert caught sight of his embarrassed face, then saw it wiped of expression.

Robert's temper had flared to meet Hunter's. Then he saw the broken glove Hunter was wearing, and the trembling of the upraised fist, and his anger died. He stood back and waited for the shrunken figure to pass him. The man must be out of his mind to be behaving like that in Mr. Barrett's house.

"Afraid of me, gallant knight?" Hunter sneered, passing him with an attempt at a swagger. Proudfoot opened the door for Hunter, holding out his hat. Ignoring the butler, he swung round and followed Robert upstairs.

Robert did not know what the unstable fellow might say or do. However, Hunter merely followed him into Elizabeth's room and sat in white-lipped and glaring-eyed silence, refusing to leave. Robert was in two minds as to whether it was better to stay and protect her or go away. At last he decided to leave.

He was immensely relieved to have Elizabeth's letter within a few hours. She wrote, "Afterwards there was an outburst and I told him that if he chose to make himself the laughingstock of the whole house, that was his affair, but I must insist on his not involving me in it." Hunter had apologized abjectly. He could see Elizabeth was in love with her New Cross Knight, he said, and that there was no hope for him anymore, so he would go away and live in a village. He begged for a last interview and promised to control himself.

"Oh, such stuff!" Elizabeth fumed. "Am I to hold a handkerchief to my eyes and sob a little? He has tired me out at last."

But they worried about the increased danger of discovery. Would Proudfoot mention what he had heard and, if so, to whom? The butler was very close to Rosie, the old housekeeper, and she had Mr. Barrett's ear. Then again, who else, in the drawing room perhaps, had heard Hunter's outbursts? They had sounded like gunshot to Robert.

Then Flush bit Robert, and Wilson took him downstairs and slapped him. What had *she* said to the other servants? Even that might be a danger!

On the second occasion, three days later, danger came very close to them indeed. It was a Saturday, a dull, leaden day, and a few heavy drops were beginning to fall from the sky as Robert arrived. He had hardly come into Elizabeth's room when there was a tremendous roll and crash, and a violent storm broke. The rain came beating down on the roof, drowning his words and lashing against the windowpanes.

"It might be Jamaica," she cried. "This is a hurricane."

Robert realized that she was afraid when she begged him not to leave her until it was over and clutched his hand. They sat close while she told him about the storm which she had watched as a child in the Malvern Hills. The local people had often warned the family that the metal spires and turrets which her father had put on the house were bound to attract lightning. The family had all stood at the windows watching. At one moment Mr. Barrett was sure that the house had been struck.

"It wasn't—but an oak was. It stood not two hundred yards from the window through which I was looking. The lightning flashed down in a great red and white zigzag, and the bark was

146

torn into long ribbons and hurled up in the air. I saw them, flying up and over the tops of the other trees. Then they fell, all twisted, and hung there in the branches."

She tried to make Robert see the stark, peeled white trunk of the tree, with the red scar running up it like the stamp of death and the branches still spreading their full summer foliage above it. "In the morning, three hours later, birds were singing in those leaves," she said. "Two girls on a holiday party were struck too. Each of their bodies had the mark on it. This"— she touched the seal which hung from his watch chain—"would cover it. But on them it was black, not red—as black as charred wood."

Since then Elizabeth had been afraid of lightning. Mr. Barrett was disgusted with her. "Disgraceful conduct in anyone who has ever learned her ABC," he growled.

She said again, simply, not apologizing, "Stay with me, Robert."

While he was with her she was not afraid. But the rain came down in vast sheets and went on and on, hour after hour. As the afternoon wore on Elizabeth began to feel very uneasy. She knew that her father had not gone to his office that Saturday as usual but had stayed at home to talk to Uncle and Aunt Hedley in the drawing room about the wedding of their daughter Charlotte to the brother of a rich brewer, Mr. James Bevan, which was to take place that month in London.

Elizabeth felt she could see her father sitting below her through the floor of her room. She grew terrified that he would suddenly appear and touch off the explosion which would put an end to all their hopes. Robert too was nervous. At last he asked if she did not feel he ought to leave, but she would not allow him to go out in the downpour. "I'm as strong as a horse," he smiled. But she would not hear of it.

At last the rain eased as suddenly as it had begun, and finally stopped. Robert found his way quietly downstairs and out of the front door.

Elizabeth was tired and oppressed. She summoned Wilson to undo her stays and help her into a dressing gown.

"Oh, it is good to get rid of the strings," she sighed.

Elizabeth lay on the sofa, scarcely able to breathe. The air was still heavy in spite of the storm's having broken. "I don't know whether I ought to say, Miss Elizabeth—" Wilson began hesitantly.

"What is it, Wilson?" Elizabeth asked without opening her eyes.

"It is just, Miss Elizabeth, that the master has been very put out about Mr. Browning being here. He asked how you were in the storm and Miss Henrietta told him that only Mr. Browning was with you."

"Thank you, Wilson." Her eyes were open now.

"Thank you, Miss Ba. I'll leave you now, Miss Ba." Wilson used her pet name to show her sympathy, Elizabeth thought. A strange, wooden creature, Wilson, but not without feeling. She lay motionless after Wilson had gone, not knowing what to do or even what to think, simply waiting for her doom. She hoped she would not faint when her father shouted at her.

Mr. Barrett found her still lying there, her light robe loose about her. She thought he looked as if the storm had moved into him. "Has *this* been your costume since the morning, pray?" he asked sternly. His voice shook her whole being.

"Oh, no, Papa! Only just now, because of the heat."

"Well, it appears that that man has spent the whole day with you."

Elizabeth spoke as quietly as she could, praying that her voice would not tremble. "He meant to leave several times, but the rain stopped him."

She waited for him to go on, but he said no more. Instead he asked her how she had borne up under the storm. He hoped she had been sensible and brave, especially with a stranger in the room. Perhaps, she hoped, he had only been afraid that she might have disgraced herself before an outsider.

"But think what a terrible day it was," she wrote to Robert next morning, "when the lightning was the least frightening thing about it!" And she wondered whether she dared let Robert pay his next visit.

He answered her at once. "See. *Now* talk of 'three or four months.' The thing to be wondered at is that this didn't happen until I'd paid my eighty-second visit!"

It was insane to go on as they were doing, with things getting worse every day.

* * *

At last Elizabeth had agreed that Robert should tell his parents of their marriage plans.

First he had gone to his mother in her rose garden and said, "Come and sit on this bench over here." Then, tenderly removing a withered rose leaf from her hair, he had said, "I love another woman."

Her blue eyes, so like his own, looked directly into his, and fear and joy fought for possession of them.

"You're serious, my son?"

"Never more so."

"Do I know her?"

"Miss Elizabeth Barrett, the poet."

"Mr. Kenyon's cousin? But surely she is—?"

"She has been imprisoned in her room for seven years, but she is well again and I mean to marry her if I can."

She did not say, You have no money and no occupation. Gratefully he thought, I knew she would not. She asked only, "It's not decided, then?"

"There are a thousand difficulties, the least of which is my lack of money."

Then he told her everything, and especially about Mr. Barrett's "system." What he had been waiting for and dreading came, of course. She said, smiling, "I should very much like to meet her." He could feel the blood rush to his face and cursed it silently.

"Her situation is very extraordinary," he said uneasily. "I can call as a mere literary gentleman of her acquaintance. But that the parents of that literary gentleman should call on her— that would be strange."

"Would it? She's well now, you say? She goes out?"

"For occasional drives, yes."

"Then she must call here on one of them. I must kiss your future wife, my boy, and welcome her. She'll want to see if she likes me, too."

"I will put it to her," he said, and she saw with surprise that he was not as certain as she was that that was the answer.

His father's delight was unshadowed when Robert went to him in his study. A broad beam spread over the childlike face, and he pounded his son on the back. "A poetess, eh? Or does she like to be called a poet? You'll have a genius for a son."

"There are problems," Robert tried to calm him. But Mr.

Browning was busy bringing out a bottle of wine and two rather dusty glasses with which to drink the health of the couple, and declaring, "Of course I'll do anything to help—anything!"

"Only lend me a hundred pounds, for the journey and so on. After that you can have it back and we shall be able to manage." Mr. Browning made no comment when Robert explained how they would manage.

When his mother joined them, and held a glass gingerly between her fingers, sipping as if she were having commerce with the devil, she said, "I'm not sure, Robert, you quite understand the responsibilities you're about to take on. But you're the one to decide."

"When do I meet my beautiful daughter-in-law-to-be?" his father interrupted. This time it was his mother who explained that there might be difficulties about that. Mr. Browning looked crestfallen.

Robert found Sarianna in the sitting room, waiting for the gong. When he had told her she flung her arms about him. "Oh, Robert! And she's clever and beautiful! I'm so happy for you. Will you take me to see her or bring her here?"

He had to explain it to her, too, and see the bewilderment and disappointment dawn in her eyes. It had seemed very extraordinary to all three of them.

He wrote to Elizabeth within the hour to tell her he had spoken to his parents, and to ask her again to receive his father and mother.

This time she replied, "No. I want to feel that they're quite safe from all the mud-splashing that's bound to come."

Again she found it impossible to tell him that she feared the critical eyes of the two women who adored him. They would blame her, and perhaps hate her, for being so unworthy of him, and so selfish as to burden him with her sick body. If she was to marry him, it must be in secret. She could not endure the humiliation of things going wrong. Robert saw the panic in her eyes, but he could not understand it.

At least, Robert thought, Elizabeth had given him something to say. It removed the dashed look from his parents' faces. They did not understand it, of course.

"We have no wish to be kept safe," his mother said. "It would be better if we could form a wall about you both with our ap-

proval and protection." Then she said, "It is good of her to consider us. But ask her to think again."

It was quite soon afterwards that Mrs. Browning fell ill.
Elizabeth sent her grapes and asked after her in the postscripts to
her letters. Mrs. Browning returned the compliment with flowers
from her garden.

Robert begged Elizabeth to think again. But in all the excur-
sions she made from 50 Wimpole Street not once did she drive
to New Cross, and she did not mention Sarianna again.

On Thursday, September 10, Robert awoke in a mood of
absolute despair, convinced that no matter what Elizabeth said
she would never come with him. There would always be some
excuse.

In that mood he wrote to her, taking no joy in the sun outside the window. He would never, he swore, force her to an
answer. "I will not add one word to what I've said already about
the extreme danger of delay. You *give* me yourself, or not. You
must come to me of your own free will." It all lay with her now.
He could and would do no more. "What a glorious dream it has
been, through nearly two years. I suppose I may say *that*, whatever befalls." He finished, "I am going to town this morning and
will leave off now."

He did not post the letter. He would do that when he came
back.

Two or three hours later Robert came in to find that a note
from Elizabeth, written the night before, had come while he had
been out. It told him that Mr. Barrett had decided that the house
in Wimpole Street was going to be shut up for painting and re-
pairs. George was being sent off to look for a suitable house at
Dover, Reigate or Tunbridge Wells. Papa had said that he did
not mind which, and that they could settle it amongst themselves,
but it must be taken for a month at least. As usual, once he had
taken a decision he was in a hurry to put it into action.

"Now, what *can* be done? Decide, after thinking it over. I am
completely at a loss as to what is the best thing to do. If we are
swept off on Monday, what then?"

On Monday. And it was Thursday already.

"It seems much too sudden and too soon for us to set out on
our Italian venture now, but you must think for both of us. It's

151

past twelve o'clock, midnight, and I'm just about to seal this and give it to Henrietta for the morning's post."

There was a postscript. "I will do as you wish—understand!"

So, she would never decide. In the end he must do it for her. He went down to the hall, recovered his own letter, broke the seal, and added a postscript.

"12 o'clock. On returning I find your note. You say 'I will do as you wish—understand!' Then I take it that you are in earnest. If you *do* go away on Monday our marriage will be put off for another year—the misery! You see what we have gained by waiting. Nothing. *We must be married directly* and go to Italy. I will call tomorrow at three and arrange everything with you. We can leave from Dover etc., *after* that—but, otherwise, impossible! Send me the ring or a substitute, to give me the size of your finger. I haven't a minute to spare for the post."

As Robert put his letter in the mailbox the postman arrived to empty it.

He felt as free as air. And yet—he had had to take the decision, after all.

14

NO SOONER HAD ROBERT CAUGIIT THE POST THAN he realized that it was four o'clock and too late to get a special license. The Bishop's office was probably already closed. He would have to wait until morning. He would call on his cousin James Silverthorne instead and ask him to be his best man on Saturday. James was his best friend. But before he left he wrote to Elizabeth more fully, comforting her by pointing out that there were advantages to the way things had turned out. After they were married she could choose her moment for leaving home. She would be able to pack under cover of the general upheaval, since everyone else would be doing the same.

He promised to come to see her next day, bringing all the information he could get hold of, and ended briskly, "Write short notes to those who ought to receive them, promising longer ones if necessary."

That letter, too, would reach her the same night. Thank God for England's wonderful penny post, with its frequent deliveries at all hours.

Elizabeth too was writing at that moment with fresh news. "We are not going to be taken away on Monday, after all, and probably not for several days afterwards. George has simply gone to look at suitable houses, starting with Reigate, in Surrey."

She rebuked him tenderly for not saying a word about how he was.

"I shall not fail you. I will abide by your decisions, and I want you to be the one to decide. I cannot write any more I'm so tired, having been out for a long time. But come tomorrow. Almost everybody is to be away at Richmond at a picnic by the river, and we shall be alone. I'll give you the ring then."

Only Wilson and Flush were in the house when Robert arrived. Wilson let him in, and he went up alone.

Elizabeth and he stood embracing for a long time, luxuriating in the knowledge that no one would open the door and walk in on them. Even Flush did not bark at him, though he was holding his mistress so closely and kissing her hair.

Elizabeth gave Robert the ring he had asked for, and he slipped it into the little inner fob pocket of his waistcoat. Then she told him how she planned to escape from the house next day for their wedding.

"I will say I am visiting someone. Treppy is too clever. Dear Mr. Boyd will provide a pretext, and I'll go to see him after the ceremony. He is blind and will never guess. If he does—well, he hates Papa."

"Nothing must go wrong," Robert said, kissing and kissing her.

As Robert slipped out of the house the carriage bringing the picnic party back from Richmond turned into Wimpole Street.

Arabel ran upstairs, warm and contented from her sunshine day, and washed her face in the flowered china basin in the corner before changing for dinner.

"I'd like an outing myself on Saturday," Elizabeth said casually, with her heart beating hard, "to pay a little visit to Mr. Boyd. I thought I would take Wilson to help me and then send her back in the cab. You and Henrietta could pick me up about noon, and then we might all go on for a drive."

"That sounds a good idea," Arabel said absently, fixing on a pearl earring at the looking glass, her golden hair an aureole about her face.

She buttoned on her pale green dress, smoothed her glinting hair and went down to join the family.

Elizabeth sat on in the quiet room, waiting for Wilson to bring up her supper tray. One hurdle had been leapt. Another lay before her.

When Wilson had put her tray beside her, she asked her to stay behind for a moment.

"I've something to say to you, Wilson."

Wilson adjusted her cap, folded her hands across her snowy apron and waited. "It's a secret."

"Yes, madam."

"I'm going to marry Mr. Browning." Wilson looked pleased but not surprised.

"Oh, ma'am. I hope you'll be very happy, ma'am, I'm sure."

"Thank you, Wilson. But it's to be a secret marriage. The master doesn't like his children to get married. I don't know if you knew that?"

"There's been talk of it belowstairs, madam. It's against nature, if I may make so bold as to say so, ma'am."

"You're quite right," Elizabeth said. "Now listen carefully. After the wedding we'll be going away to Italy."

Wilson's mouth fell open and she clasped her pink hands.

"How will you be managing, Miss Elizabeth? Do you think you can look after yourself in those terrible foreign parts? I mean, madam, not being well, and able to fend for yourself, like." She looked really worried.

"That's the point, Wilson. That's just it. Wilson, will you come with me and look after me?" There, it was out. Of course, Elizabeth thought, Wilson would not come.

There was a long pause, while Wilson considered it in her ponderous way. "How long would it be for, madam?" she asked at last.

"Oh, not for long. A year or so at the most. We'll come back as soon as things have blown over."

"I don't see how you could manage without me, Miss Ba, that I don't." There was a great struggle going on in solid little Wilson under the starched bosom.

"Nor do I. But if you won't come, I'll have to try. Mr. Browning and I are to be married tomorrow, you see."

"Tomorrow, Miss Ba!" Wilson's voice rose to a squeak of surprise.

Desperately Elizabeth outlined her plans. Then she looked up. She saw Wilson listening, unshrinking, dependable as a little tug.

"I'll come, Miss Ba. I'll go anywhere in the world with you. You've only to ask." It was totally unexpected. Wilson was telling her that she loved her. The tears rushed into Elizabeth's eyes. But Wilson had not finished.

"If I might ask, ma'am, just the one thing?"

"Yes, Wilson?"

"Flush, ma'am. Will he be coming, too?"

"Yes, Wilson. Flush is coming."

Elizabeth had never seen Wilson smile before. She held out her hand and drew down to her the plain face under the straight mousy hair and the crisp cap. She kissed her, saying, "I shall always remember, and I shall be grateful to you for the rest of my life."

Wilson bobbed a curtsy, overwhelmed, and went out.

Elizabeth wrote to Robert, telling him how very kind Wilson had been and what an affectionate person she was under her stolid exterior. Then at last she lifted the silver cover on her plate.

While the family were at dinner, and in the drawing room afterwards, she reread Robert's letters. They moved her as they always did. After tomorrow there would be no more letters, or hardly any. What there were, would be letters from Robert to his wife.

When she had looked through them again she let them lie on her lap and about her feet, and wrote.

My letters! all dead paper, mute and white!
And yet they seem alive and quivering
Against my tremulous hands which loose the string
And let them drop down on my knee tonight.
This said he wished to have me in his sight
Once, as a friend. *This* fixed a day in spring
To come and touch my hand—a simple thing
Yet I wept for it! *This*—the paper's light—
Said, "Dear, I love thee"; and I sank and quailed
As if God's future thundered on my past.
This said, "I am thine"—and so its ink has paled
With lying at my heart that beat too fast.
And *this*—O love, thy words have ill availed
If what *this* said I dared repeat at last!

In her tiny beautiful writing Elizabeth copied her sonnet into the little white notebook which contained all the others she had written during the past sixteen months—more than fourscore. Soon there would be no more. After all, these were love sonnets, and with her wedding day Robert's wooing of her would be over.

Elizabeth prepared herself for bed without summoning Wilson and poured out her dose of morphine herself. Life had been too disturbing of late for her to try any lessening of the dosage, but at least she had not increased it. It was important now for her to sleep, so as to be calm in the morning. It was an ordeal, with no one but Wilson to confide in.

She could not sleep. Hour after hour went by, and she lay with her eyes open, wide awake.

It was late when Arabel came to bed, but Elizabeth had not closed her eyes. She shut them then and lay very still. Arabel undressed on tiptoe, got into bed and blew out the candle she had brought up with her.

It was then that Elizabeth was tempted to get out of bed and take another dose of morphine. It was important that she should sleep. She wanted to look as well as she could, and as beautiful as possible, for Robert, on her wedding day.

And yet—she had promised him to lessen the doses and to try to give up the opium entirely. It would be a wedding gift to Robert not to take that second, much-needed dose.

He had been so good about it, even making a joke of it. When he had been prevented from seeing her, he had said, "How do you think I feel without my proper quantity of morphine? May I call you my morphine?" She had replied as lightly. "Can't you leave me off without risking your life? Or go on with me without danger?"

But she knew that he was deadly serious underneath. She was serious, too, dreadfully ashamed at the thought of his parents knowing that not only was she very ill, but that she had this dependence on the drug. She could not say so to him, and he could not see how his mother would feel, when he brought her such a bride for a daughter-in-law. If she could find the strength not to take another dose it would help him, and her, and be a good way to start their married life. So she did not take it and lay sleepless through the night.

At a little past ten o'clock next morning Elizabeth and Wilson left number 50 Wimpole Street. It was a beautiful crisp September morning. Elizabeth's black dress was hidden under a long black-braided grey woollen cape, and she wore her grey Quaker's bonnet. The only touch of colour about her was the blue ribbon which tied it in a crisp bow under her chin. Wilson had insisted on sewing that on, repeating the old rhyme which laid down what all brides must wear for their weddings for luck.

Something old, something new,
Something borrowed, and something blue.

"It's new, ma'am, and it's blue, and I'll lend it to you, so it's borrowed."

And everything else, Elizabeth thought, smiling, is old. She looked no more like a bride than Wilson in her black coat and bonnet.

As they walked towards the cab stand in Marylebone Road Elizabeth suddenly caught at the railings.

"Whatever's the matter, Miss Ba?" Wilson cried. "Are you going to faint?"

She took Elizabeth's arm, holding her strongly, hailed a cab and helped her into it. Elizabeth sat with her head back. She was as white as a sheet, Wilson thought.

"What would Mr. Browning say if you failed him now?" she asked almost severely, and Elizabeth opened her eyes on the blunt-featured face, its small blue eyes looking full at her, its mouth set in a firm line.

"I'm going to ask the cabbie to stop at a chemist's, ma'am, and get you some sal volatile."

Before long the cab stopped. Wilson helped Elizabeth down into the shop, asked for a chair and made her sit on it. Soon she brought a glass full of liquid to her.

Elizabeth swallowed the draught of medicinal spirit, which was so pungent that it made her gasp.

"I can go on now, Wilson," she said.

The cab rolled on again and stopped outside the church. Again Wilson helped her out, her hand very firm on her arm.

Robert was waiting on the pavement with a large young man, looking handsome and happy in a top hat and plum-coloured coat with a white carnation in his buttonhole and pearly pantaloons and gloves.

The large young man who stood squarely beside Robert, Elizabeth knew, must be his cousin James Silverthorne, come to be witness and best man. She saw Robert turn and say something to him and then saw him look at her with concern.

"By God, James," Robert was saying, "she looks more dead than alive. My poor Ba."

Robert strode to meet her and helped her struggle up the steps to the door of the church. They looked at each other and her eyes pierced his heart. She smiled and took Robert's arm. He hardly felt her weight, she was so light.

Stealing a glance at Robert as he paced slowly with her to the altar, Elizabeth saw that now his face was solemn above the snowy cravat and the plum-coloured coat. James Silverthorne walked at Robert's right hand. The clergyman looked taken aback to find this bride in her dark clothes rustling towards him on her bridegroom's arm with no father to give her away. When they stood before him he opened his prayer book and the marriage service began.

Robert gave his responses clearly, but Elizabeth's voice could hardly be heard. As Robert placed the ring on her finger he turned to her, willing her to look up into his eyes, and whispered, "It is all right, my Ba."

Her eyes on his, Elizabeth thought how different was this wedding of hers from that of Charlotte Hedley to her Mr. Bevan, with a church full of friends and flowers and music, and the bride in lace, with Lizzie as trainbearer—how different, in fact, from all the other weddings which had ever been held in that church.

Then suddenly they were all in the vestry. Three times Elizabeth tried to write her name, but her trembling hand could not form a letter. She heard someone say, "Let her wait a moment," and then someone else thrust a glass of water at her. She pulled off her glove and was able to sign at last. Robert was smiling and laughing and pressing pieces of gold on the clerk and the verger and even the pew opener, who had done nothing.

Then they were out on the pavement once more.

"Whenever I pass this door in future years," Robert said in her ear, "I will kneel and kiss the paving stones before it."

She smiled into his eyes, not taking him seriously, but he was not smiling. She climbed into the cab with Wilson, and they drove off to St. John's Wood, leaving Robert and James Silverthorne on the pavement, watching them out of sight under the astonished eyes of the verger.

Robert and James turned to each other. "Thank you, James. Keep the secret!"

"Trust me."

"With my life—and, what's more important, my love!"

"They're both safe with me. I'll always be there if you need me." James squeezed his shoulder and went off in a cab, back to the brewery.

Robert walked home, took out the letter of Elizabeth's which had been posted to him on their wedding eve and which had reached him that morning and wrote on it *Saturday, Septr. 12, 1846 ¼ 11—11¼ A.M. (91).*

It had been their ninety-first meeting. It had lasted from a quarter to eleven until a quarter past. It had been the first time that he had seen her outside her father's house.

He sat down at once to write to her.

"You will only expect a few words—what will those be? My heart is full. You asked me yesterday if I would ever repent. Yes, my own Ba, I could wish all the past over again, so that I could show more what I felt. What I have said (for I have done nothing) seems to have fallen so far short of what I have felt, even at the beginning—and when I think of what I feel *now!* In every word and gesture, every letter, every *silence,* you have been entirely perfect to me. You have given me the highest, completest proof of love that ever one human being gave another. I will write tomorrow, of course. Take every care of *my life,* which is in that dearest little hand. Try and be composed, my beloved. Remember to thank Wilson for me."

He had to add that his mother was sorry that she was not well enough to write personally, and must send her good wishes through him instead.

As he finished his letter, Elizabeth and Wilson were climbing down from their cab outside Hugh Boyd's house. They found that he was upstairs with his physician, so Wilson settled her mistress on a sofa, putting up her feet so that she might rest while she waited for her host. Then Wilson drove off back to Wimpole Street in the cab.

Elizabeth took off her glove and gazed at her ring and kissed it. After a while she removed it from her finger. She pulled out the chain with her locket on it and slipped the ring onto it too.

Eventually her blind old friend Hugh Boyd came hobbling down and felt his way to his chair and table while the doctor was being shown out. When he heard the door slam he summoned the maid to pour out Cyprus wine for them both.

"I think of your poem, *Wine of Cyprus,* every time I drink

it, Elibet. It is a wonderful memorial to our happy days together over our Greek and Latin poets."

Moving his fingers across the table before him as if it were a piano, just as he used to do twenty years before when he had recited his Greek verses to her, he quoted softly.

"If old Bacchus were the speaker,
　He would tell you with a sigh
Of the Cyprus in this beaker
　I am sipping like a fly—"

He broke off to urge her, "Come on! Say a verse with me!

"And I think of those long mornings
　Which my thought goes far to seek,
When, betwixt the folio's turnings,
　Solemn flowed the rhythmic Greek;
Past the pane the mountain spreading,
　Swept the sheep's-bell's tinkling noise,
While a girlish voice was reading,
　Somewhat low for ἀι's and ὀι's.

Then what golden hours were for us!
　While we sat together there—"

He broke off again.
"There's something wrong."

Her thoughts had not been with him. Those golden hours were from an existence long gone by, and she no longer lived in dreams of them. In the home of her old friend she felt as if she were in a tomb. He had chosen the right word—a memorial.

"There's nothing the matter," she said. "Arabel and Henrietta should have come to pick me up at noon, and all your clocks say it is past the quarter hour already. I'm afraid they may have forgotten all about it."

He gave her some bread and butter to eat to prevent her looking too pale, he said, and making people wonder what she had been doing. She was sure that he had guessed the truth.

At last Arabel and Henrietta arrived, explaining that Arabel had forgotten all about their arrangement and that they had had a fright when they had not been able to find her and Wilson. Flush's barking had upset them, since it was so unlike Elizabeth to go out without him. But Wilson had returned and had explained everything.

Elizabeth longed to go home and shut herself up alone in her room; but for an hour and a half she and her sisters drove round as planned, and she did not get home until half-past four.

"It all seems like a dream," she wrote to Robert then. "When we drove past the church there was a cloud before my eyes. Ask your mother to forgive me, Robert. If I had not been there, *she* would have been, perhaps. Please ask the indulgence of your father and mother for me, and ask your sister to love me. I feel as if I had slipped down over the wall into somebody's garden—I feel ashamed."

She was haunted, too, by that dark fear of hers, that she was cursed and might bring sorrow on him. "If either of us is to suffer for what happened in the church today, I pray that the misfortune may all fall upon *me*. That would not cause me the most pain, God knows."

She told him then too of her thoughts as she had stood before the altar, pouring out her love and her trust to her husband of five and a half hours.

"I thought that, of the many, many women who have stood where I stood, perhaps not a single one has had such good reason as I had for absolute trust and devotion in the man she was marrying. So it was only fair that those less happy women should have had the love and support of their nearest relations. None can put us asunder, now. I have the right to love you openly, and hear other people call it a *duty*, knowing that if it were a sin I should do it just the same!"

She ended, "I did hate so to have to take off the ring! You'll have to take the trouble to put it on again, someday."

She lay down on her bed and, for once, fell asleep immediately.

Robert, too, slept well and woke next morning to report to this bride in name only, "I have not woken feeling so well for perhaps two years. What have you been doing to me?"

Ba had put out a trembling, still distrustful hand towards his people at last, and he hastened to say, "My family all love you, dearest. I am full of hope that you will love them all. Last night I asked my father, who was absorbed in some old book, 'Won't you be glad to see your new daughter?' He started, and answered,

'Indeed, I *shall!*' with such fervour that it made my mother laugh. She laughed even more when he went on, 'And how glad I shall be when she sees Sis!' That's Sarianna, his *other* daughter."

Until they could leave together for Italy Robert and Elizabeth would communicate only by letter. Robert could not bring himself to call at the door of her father's house to ask for Miss Barrett when she was in fact Mrs. Robert Browning. There was no more embarrassment for him.

For Elizabeth, however, life was a continual embarrassment. Every hour of the day she was deceiving her family, every member of which she saw and spoke to daily. Only Wilson knew the truth, and Wilson knew that she was living a lie.

Then, Robert, her strength, could not be at her side, and his very absence was awkward for her. He had been such a regular visitor.

The day after her marriage was a Sunday; and all the family came up to her room before the midday meal. All the brothers trooped in, and sat or stood about discussing the business of leaving town for the country. Treppy was there as usual, perched on a straight-backed chair. Two ladies, old friends of Mr. Barrett's, had come up to town from Herefordshire, and were joining the family for dinner. The large crowd made an unbearable noise. In the midst of the loud talking and laughter the sound of church bells began.

"What are those bells?" asked one of the visiting ladies.

"Saint Marylebone Church bells," Henrietta answered from behind Elizabeth's chair, and suddenly Elizabeth felt faint.

At last the family went downstairs, and she sat down to write to Robert. Then Mr. Kenyon called in for a moment to see her. When was she going to see Browning again? he asked. "I don't know," she answered, flinching before those dreaded spectacles of his, and then was angry with herself. It was the first time she had told a lie.

Treppy returned after dinner to ask Elizabeth to come and see her next day for luncheon "and a long, long talk." Elizabeth agreed, knowing she would not go. She could not face an inquisition or be out of the house when at any moment there might be news to be rushed to Robert. Her heart missed a beat when Treppy squeezed her arm and laughed, "Secrets from Treppy!

What an idea!" What *did* she mean? Elizabeth asked herself.

Monday came and went. Elizabeth did not go to Treppy's and Mr. Barrett decided that he would take the house near Watford. Next day he changed his mind. Robert left it to Elizabeth to decide how and when she would leave. He was quite ready and had no problems. She was faced with a thousand difficulties.

Robert busied himself looking up times and routes.

"There is a packet from Brighton to Dieppe every day, but then we have to get to Rouen. The Le Havre boat leaves Southampton on Wednesdays and Saturdays, and Portsmouth on Mondays and Thursdays. The boat from London leaves on Thursdays and Saturdays at nine A.M."

He begged her to take the simplest possible wardrobe so as to reduce their luggage to the minimum. "We pay by the ounce. I shall only take a portmanteau and a carpetbag. No books."

"Wilson and I have a light box and a carpetbag between us," she replied, "and I'll be docile about the books, dearest. Remember we can't take the box and the carpetbag out of the house with us. We must send them the evening before we go. If they go direct to the railroad office they should have your name on them, shouldn't they?"

Robert was getting himself into a complete muddle with the boat and train times, which he sent enclosed with a rosebud in a letter.

"Nothing leaves Southampton, according to today's advertisement, till *Tuesday*. The days seem changed to *Tuesdays* and *Fridays*. Provoking! I will go to the railway office at once to enquire and get the timetable."

They could not travel by steamer direct from London, she explained, because the steamers all left in the morning. As Arabel slept in her room she could not leave without disturbing her, and thus involving her. They must take the five o'clock train from Nine Elms, Vauxhall, for Southampton, and embark on the night packet for Le Havre.

Robert undertook to get a passport, but begged her to estimate their expenses for the journey, if only roughly. "I will take about that much, and no more, and get Rothschild's letter of credit for Leghorn."

The luggage could be sent to his home at New Cross, he

said, and one cab could take him and her and Wilson and Flush and all their goods to the station.

Robert and Elizabeth were preparing the marriage announcement which was to appear in the press as soon as they left the country. The date was to be omitted, so as to spare their families embarrassment, for it would be published a week after their wedding had taken place.

"You might put 'Miss Barrett of Wimpole Street and Jamaica,' or 'of Cinnamon Hill, Jamaica,' " Elizabeth suggested.

After all, they were all Jamaicans. Her father wrote himself "Native of the Parish of Saint James, Jamaica."

But then she had added, "Perhaps it is best to put in as little about poor Papa as possible."

Robert cut the symbolic cord with a blow. "Jamaica sounds in the wrong direction, doesn't it?"

So now the announcement would read: "On Saturday, at St. Marylebone Church, by the Rev. Thomas Woods Goldhawk, M.A., Robert Browning, jun., Esq., of New Cross, Hatcham, to Elizabeth Barrett, eldest daughter of Edward Moulton Barrett, Esq., of Wimpole Street."

15

FIVE DAYS AFTER THEIR MARRIAGE, ON THURSDAY, September 17, Elizabeth wrote to Robert that at last the Barretts were to move. Mr. Barrett had ordered them to depart on Monday for a house at Little Bookham.

"I would much rather have waited, only it may be difficult to leave Bookham. The house is six miles from the nearest railroad and a mile and a half from Leatherhead, where a coach runs. Yet it might be possible. You must be the judge."

Something besides packing and wedding announcements was holding her back—the letters Robert had ordered her to write so commandingly, almost lightheartedly. As if they were so easily done.

"The letters. The letters. I am paralyzed when I think of having to write 'Papa, I'm married; I hope you won't be too displeased.' Ah, poor Papa. He will be appallingly angry with me, and cast me off utterly. How I felt tonight when I saw him at seven o'clock. He spoke kindly too and asked me how I was."

Robert replied merely, "The business of the letters will grow less difficult once you begin. And in the four or five days left to us epics might be written, let alone letters."

She returned to the subject of her father. "I'll put myself under his feet, begging to be forgiven a little. I love him. He's my father. I'll remind him of how obedient I've been to him all my life, and of all that I've suffered, and entreat him to pardon the happiness which has come for me at last."

She added despairingly, "And *he* will wish in return that I had died years ago. But in the end, perhaps, he will forgive us. That is my hope."

Then, at last, Robert ceased for a moment his bustling about luggage and passports and tickets and Wilson and money and answered her.

"Be sure, dearest, I will do my utmost to conciliate your father. Sometimes, it is true, I could not help speaking about him with impatience, but you don't need to remind me that he's your father—I'll be proud to call him *mine,* too. I love him for calling you the purest of women. It's what I think, too."

Even Robert did not understand.

Robert returned to his tangle of train and boat times, in note after note. On Thursday, at five o'clock, he wrote: "My own Ba—In the hurry I noted down the departures from *Le Havre* instead of Southampton. You must either be at Vauxhall Station by *four* o'clock, so as to arrive at Southampton three and a half hours later, that is, at half-past seven, and leave by a quarter past eight, or we must go by the Sunday boat, or wait until Tuesday. Dieppe is impossible, being too early. Let me know directly. To-morrow *is* too early, though *I* could manage."

By half-past seven that night he had written another note, which Wilson brought up to Elizabeth at nine o'clock, while the family were dining.

"My own Ba—Forgive my getting it wrong! I had not enough confidence in my having got it right. The advertisement about the Tuesday and Friday boats is one for the South of England Steam Company. The Wednesday and Saturday boats belong to the *South Western.* Perhaps you have seen my blunder already. In that case you can leave by one o'clock, for half-past two, whenever you like."

She wrote a note for Wilson to post at once.

"Dearest, only a word. I am so tired. Sunday and Friday are impossible. On Saturday I will go with you if you like—with everything only half done, in fact, scarcely anything done. Will you come for me to Hodgson's the booksellers? Or shall I meet you at the station? At what o'clock should I set out to be there at the time you say?"

The boxes were packed, or as good as packed. It was the letters which had not been written.

Now it was Friday morning, and they were going on Saturday. Elizabeth could not put off writing the letters a moment longer.

First she must write to Miss Mitford. As far back as July she had told Robert, "No one will be more utterly dumbfounded than Miss Mitford when she discovers what you are to me now—she'll be angry, perhaps."

Now she wrote: "When you read this letter I shall have given to one of the most gifted and admirable of men a wife unworthy of him. I shall be the wife of Robert Browning."

She had told no one, she said, not even Mr. Kenyon. "And now, oh, will you be hard on me? I tell you solemnly that nothing you can think of against this act of mine has not been put forward to *him* by *me*. He has loved me for nearly two years and said so from the beginning. I would not listen. I could not even believe it. How can I tell you on paper how he persevered and overcame me with such letters and such words that I would have been a stone if I had not given myself to him heart and soul?"

But she told her, as best she could, and at length, how it had been.

Now they were going to live a simple natural life, to write poems and read books. They would not be rich, but they would have enough to live as they liked and to allow them to escape from the winters, in Italy. "People will say that he is mad and I am *bad*—bad to marry him, because of my having suffered so long from all kinds of sickness. But I believe no woman with a heart could have done otherwise. You do not know *him*."

Next the letters to the family must be written. There must be a note for each brother and sister, with one long letter addressed to one of them, explaining everything. Who should that one be? Arabel and Henrietta already knew too much for their own safety. Stormy was a dear sweet fellow and the eldest son. It should be Stormy.

But George had been kind and valiant on her behalf. He had faced Papa again and again to plead for her. George was clever and discreet. He would choose the right moment to approach Papa, and put things wisely. Papa had very little respect for Stormy and his other sons. It must be George to whom she wrote the letter explaining her long deception.

"Dearest George, go to your room and read this letter. I beg

168

of you by all that we both cherish in this world still to hold me dear after what I am going to tell you, and I leave it to you to tell the others in whatever way seems best to you. And, oh, love me, George, while you are reading it—love me, that I may find pardon for me in your heart after you have read it."

She told him of how Robert had loved her from the beginning and of how she had been determined to refuse him. "I thought that a little more light on my sick, my ghastly, face would soon bring it to an end."

She took, she said, the whole blame for Robert's not having gone to her father, and for not telling their friends of their intentions. Mr. Browning himself had been only too anxious to make a formal approach and to reveal his intentions with pride and frankness. She emphasized that everyone in the house was completely ignorant of the whole affair, and absolutely innocent of any share in it. It had been her act, hers alone. She implored George, after reading the letter which she enclosed for her dearest Papa, to break the news to him gently before handing it to him. Perhaps her Papa would also deign to read the letter she had written to George. She begged for letters telling her of the forgiveness of the writers to be addressed to her at Orléans.

Then she wrote her short notes, seven of them, to all the other brothers and sisters. Then there was only the letter to her father.

She had worried for months over what she would say to him when the day came. It had haunted her since her marriage day. Whenever she had been alone she had fallen into a dream of love about Robert; and then, always, had followed the pain of anxiety about what she could say to her father when she left his home like a thief, stealing out to go to another life, and into the arms of another man, after her deliberate, long-drawn-out deceit.

He had been unreasonable and cruel to her. That could not be denied. Still, he was her father, and she loved him—and he was a fine man, apart from his aberration.

"Except for this," she wrote, "I have submitted to the least of your wishes all my life long. Set the life against the deed and forgive me for the sake of the daughter you once loved."

She wrote her love to him, for no one else's eyes, not even Robert's. Warming the stick of red sealing wax carefully over her candle flame, she dripped it on the envelope and sealed it. Then she put it with all the others into the envelope which was addressed to George. There was no more she could do. Only a few hours were left before she went to Robert.

Now she took a final look at his instructions. Hastily she wrote another note to him. "Dearest, Surely you are wrong about the time for tomorrow? Also there is an express train. Would that not be better? Your Ba."

He caught the post at half-past eleven that night. "My own best Ba, How thankful I am you noticed my blunder. I write now with the railway timetables and *today's* advertisement in *The Times* before me. The packet leaves tomorrow evening, from the Royal Pier, Southampton, at *nine*. We leave Nine Elms, Vauxhall, at *five,* to arrive at *eight.* Doors close five minutes before that. I will be at Hodgson's *from* half-past three to *four precisely.* I shall go to Vauxhall, let them know that some luggage is on its way (yours) and send *mine* there, so that we can both be unencumbered and can take a cab or a coach from Hodgson's. Depend on me."

On Friday night she wrote her last letter to him.

"At from half-past three to four, then. Four will not, I suppose, be too late. By tomorrow at this time I shall have only you to love me—my beloved! *Only you.* As if one said *only God.* I am taking your letters with me, expense about ounces or no. I *tried* to leave them behind, and I couldn't. It was not my fault, and I won't be scolded for it. Is this my last letter to you, ever dearest? Oh, if I loved you less, a little, little less!"

But the anguish at leaving was still there, and she must add, too, "It is dreadful, dreadful, to have to give pain here, intentionally, for the first time in my life."

At the very end she put a postscript. "Wilson has been perfect to me. And I, calling her 'timid'! I begin to think that none are so bold as the timid when they are fairly roused."

She laid down her pen for the last time in her father's house. She put out the letter she had written to George, together with all those to her other brothers and sisters, and the one to her father, all in their one envelope, to be posted next morning before she left home. They would arrive next evening, just when everyone was beginning to wonder where she and Wilson had got to. Then she rang for Wilson, and gave her instructions about the letters.

"Now the boxes, Wilson."

"Yes, ma'am. It has all been arranged. They'll be taken out this afternoon, ma'am, and put into a cab."

Who had Wilson persuaded to help her? Rosie the housekeeper? Proudfoot? No, not Proudfoot, she was sure of that. Perhaps the little kitchenmaid.

"I think it is best if I don't know, Wilson, who helps you. Then nobody can be blamed afterwards."

"I understand, ma'am, but there's no cause to concern yourself. Seeing as how the box is mine and your bag is nothing out of the ordinary, begging your pardon, ma'am, I let it be thought I was sending them both to my parents in Sheffield so as not to take them to the country with me, ma'am, or leave them here at the mercy of the workmen. They all know me to be very particular, and with all the packing that's going on, nothing was thought of it."

Saturday, September 19, 1846, broke fair and sunny. At New Cross Robert looked out of the window and thought it a delicious day.

In Wimpole Street the Barrett family were packing energetically all morning. It was the last opportunity they would have, though they were not leaving until Monday, for of course no work could be permitted on the Sabbath. No one thought anything of the fact that Elizabeth and Wilson were putting things into a couple of small bags.

Elizabeth forced herself to sit before the tray which Wilson brought up for her, and to eat a small cutlet and a slice of dry toast. She fed the syllabub to Flush, but swallowed a cup of coffee, staring at the little gilt coffee spoon as if she had never seen it before.

She grew increasingly uneasy as the hours ticked by towards the time when she must leave the house and drive across London with Robert and enter one of those monstrous trains. Now it seemed to her that they had chosen the worst possible time of day for her escape. At least Papa had gone to the City, as usual on a Saturday. It was like him to work six days a week and even to go on the day when everyone else was getting ready to leave the house. The others had sat down late to their meal, but they could hardly be expected to draw it out until half-past three.

She was wrong about that, however. Her brothers and sisters, in good conscience after their morning's packing and not anxious to hurry back to it, sat for a long time over their empty plates, cracking nuts and laughing and chatting in holiday mood.

Just before half-past three Wilson slipped upstairs to her door to remind her that it was time for her to get ready to leave. Elizabeth put on her Quaker bonnet, her gloves and the warm two-tiered cloak which Robert had given her and which she had hidden in a cupboard for this day.

Wilson was already bonnetted. She slipped out again, to lean over the banisters and peer and listen. The door of the dining room on the ground floor seemed firmly shut.

Wilson signalled to Elizabeth, and grasped the handles of the two small bags they had got ready. Elizabeth picked up Flush, who had begun to look expectant when she had put on her bonnet. She folded her arms tight about his warm body, rubbed her face against his silky ear, and whispered into it, "Oh, Flush, if you make a sound I am lost."

All the way down those two flights of stairs she expected him to bark, and her heart hammered so that she was sure he could feel it against his ribs. Flush was always so exited at going out; he yelped with joy at the prospect. But not a sound came from him.

Wilson opened the front door, stood back to let Elizabeth and Flush pass through it, followed them out onto the steps and closed the door softly behind her.

16

AT FIRST EVERYTHING WENT BEAUTIFULLY. ROBERT met Elizabeth and Wilson at Hodgson's with a cab, took them to Nine Elms Station at Vauxhall and collected their baggage. They caught the five o'clock train for Southampton and were aboard the Le Havre steamer by nine.

The Channel crossing was appallingly rough. Robert took a room at Le Havre where Elizabeth could rest before going on. Drained as she was, she insisted on writing to Treppy.

They would never forget that ride on the night diligence to Rouen. Elizabeth sat inside in the coupé staring at the horses as if in a trance. Robert watched them too, his face against hers, his arm about her shoulders. Now there were five, now seven, brown and white and black horses, plunging through the night in moonlight bright as day, their manes leaping wildly, the coachman's white reins dropping on their necks—a strange dream, and a far cry from the sofa in Wimpole Street.

At Rouen railway station Robert carried Elizabeth into the Travellers' Room and brought her coffee and rolls. For hours she lay there, wax-pale, before they could board the Paris express.

After two nights' travelling without sleep they reached their hotel with Elizabeth in a state of utter collapse. A frightened Robert ordered Wilson to put her to bed, and went round at once to leave a note for Elizabeth's friend, Mrs. Jameson, at the hotel in the Rue de la Ville l'Evêque where they knew she was staying, imploring her to come and see them that night.

Anna Jameson arrived in their suite still thunderstruck at their sudden appearance together in Paris. "Let me go to her," she begged Robert. "We can talk later."

In the bedroom a pale Wilson with dark rings under her eyes rose from a low chair, bobbed a feeble curtsy and left the room. Elizabeth was lying propped up on pillows in the vast bed, her face marble-white, her beautiful hands on the coverlet, her eyes closed.

Mrs. Jameson tiptoed to her and kissed her cold forehead. Elizabeth opened her eyes and gave her a smile of great sweetness and happiness but seemed too tired to speak.

"Oh, my dear," Mrs. Jameson cried, "I'm so very, very happy for you both." God forgive me, she thought, they need all the encouragement they can get.

"So you don't disapprove?" Elizabeth asked in a tremulous whisper. Mrs. Jameson realized with a shock that she was nervous and felt some sort of shame about her marriage. She has suffered much, she thought. She is frightened, ashamed, happy and miserable, all at once. She mopped her eyes. "Excuse me, we Irish are sentimental. No, he's a wise man, and you're a wise woman, let the world say what it likes."

Elizabeth flinched visibly. "It's not a suitable marriage, I know. I did everything I could to dissuade him."

"Two poets of genius! Both noble and charming! It's the most beautiful marriage since the world began."

"But Anna, you've often said that poets make unhappy marriages." The shadows of Lord Byron, of Shelley, of Landor, hung between them.

"You two will be the exception," Anna Jameson declared stoutly, and drawing a chair to the bed put her warm hand over the cold ones on the coverlet. "How long are you staying in Paris?" she asked at length.

"Just till the passport comes. It was taken away from Robert at Le Havre."

Mrs. Jameson doubted whether the other passengers had failed to reclaim their passports. There was this luxurious hotel, too, and this splendid suite, with separate rooms for husband and wife and the lady's maid. Yet everyone knew Mr. Browning was far from rich. A pretty pair to go through the world together! What did this spoiled son of doting parents know of life? Or this rich man's pampered daughter, secluded for years and almost help-less? But Elizabeth was asking her how her little niece Geddie Bate was getting on with her art studies.

"Wasting this golden opportunity I'm giving her to equip herself for life. She lies in bed late and hardly does any work at the Louvre."

"She's only seventeen," Elizabeth excused her.

Mrs. Jameson returned to find Robert with his arms resting on the mantelpiece and his head on them, staring into the flames. He straightened and turned at the sound of her voice.

"She looks frightfully ill," she said flatly, and saw the terror break into his face. "She's certainly not fit to go on to Italy yet."

"She wants to put as much distance between us and England as we can at once. But if anything happened—"

She heard his voice shake and understood.

"Would you travel with us to Italy?" Robert asked urgently. "I know you've done a great deal of nursing."

"That would mean a change of plan for me," she demurred. "I don't know whether Lady Byron is joining me or not. I'm waiting for her letter now."

Robert's face fell, and she added, "But Wilson is with you."

"She was dreadfully ill on the boat, and she's scared of the French," Robert said miserably. "She hasn't been able to fetch us a cup of coffee so far."

What a beginning to a honeymoon, with two sick women and a dog to look after, and a burden of guilt and fear, Mrs. Jameson thought, and at once her mind was made up.

"She must rest for at least a week. That's all she needs, rest and quiet and nursing. Why don't you come to my little *pension?* I could look after her there more easily. I'll go down the Rhone with you, and then perhaps on to Italy. I could stay for a while at Pisa before I go to Florence, and help there too."

Robert kissed her hand. "I won't forget."

Immediately he looked a different being—more like a bride-groom on a honeymoon, more like the brash young dandy of Lon-don days. He gave the fresh, young, loud laugh she remembered.

"I thought, you know—I thought—I was afraid—"

She pressed his hand with a rush of affection. "There's no need to explain, dear Mr. Browning."

* * *

175

To Mrs. Jameson's astonishment both the Brownings called on her at her hotel next morning.

"Isn't Ba amazing?" Robert crowed. "She frightened the life out of me yesterday, and now here she is, charging about Paris."

Mrs. Jameson introduced her chestnut-haired little niece. Geddie's peachlike face was pink with excitement, and she gazed at Robert and Elizabeth as if they had fallen from the skies. She's romantic, her aunt worried, I hope she won't get any silly ideas. Robert Browning was handsome enough to turn any girl's head. He looked very dapper in his blue coat and his plaid trousers, with his sleek black hair and his pretty young beard curling under his chin—as dapper as a cock blackbird in spring. Geddie could not stop looking at him, and her soft little wet red mouth was open with wonder.

"I like your earnest little niece," Robert said, trotting after Mrs. Jameson to inspect their new suite. "She adores Ba, that's obvious. Children always do."

Within half an hour Elizabeth was ensconced with her feet up, while Robert went off to superintend the packing by Wilson and to bring Flush from their former hotel.

"Isn't it romantic?" Geddie cried to her aunt when they were alone. "But she's older than he is, isn't she, Aunt Anna?"

"She's very ill, but they suit each other to perfection."

"Oh, *yes,*" Geddie breathed. "She's wonderful, too. But—"

"But what?"

"But . . . well, if she didn't wear *black*. It isn't very bridal, is it? And with a black veil, to

Elizabeth was still wearing the black velvet dress of Wimpole Street days, and she had not thrown up her thick dark veil until she was inside the kindly dimness of the hotel. Clearly, Anna Jameson reflected, she dreaded the harsh light of day. Yet her husband looked at her as if she were Venus herself.

Elizabeth had been in Paris before, over thirty years ago, four months after Wellington had won the battle of Waterloo in June, 1815. She had been nine, and Robert had been only three, not yet even wearing brown holland pinafores at his infant school. When Elizabeth had flung herself into Papa's arms, howling like an abandoned dog, he had swept her into the carriage which was about to drive off with him and Mama for the boat-train.

Papa, it had turned out, could not speak any more French than the *Embrasse-moi!* and *Couchez!* and *Venez!* of their language of love. Elizabeth had had a wonderful time, visiting the Louvre and the Opera Comique and Saint Cloud and Versailles and Malmaison and the curiosity shops. Now she longed to wander through Paris with Robert instead of lying on a sofa and begging him to go out without her. Still, she decided, there was no need to mention her old trip to him or anyone else. It was so very long ago.

Her only sortie was a visit to the Louvre with Robert and Mrs. Jameson. Robert took her on one arm and Mrs. Jameson on the other and said, bowing to their friend, "It's a wonderful thing, Ba, to be visiting the Louvre for the first time with the greatest living expert on early Italian paintings. As her new book will establish for all time."

"Rossetti told me," Anna said quietly, "that *your* knowledge of early Italian art is beyond that of anyone he ever met, Mr. Browning."

Back at their hotel Robert decided that to dine out would be tiring. He left Elizabeth, to arrange for their dinner to be brought up.

When he came back Robert found her asleep, her cheeks rosy, her hair covering the pillow, and one bare arm flung outside the bedclothes. The lace at her throat hardly hid the swell of her bosom. The locket which held his hair was half-concealed in its cleft. Her breath stirred a narrow blue ribbon running through the lace of her nightdress.

He stood looking down at her. She and her father were eternally young. It was something to do with the roundness of their faces and their high cheekbones. As she lay there she might have been a little, dewy, round-cheeked girl, younger than Geddie Bate. Yet she was all woman, too.

Robert watched her breathing softly for some time, then went to wait by the sitting room fire. He had been patient, and he would be patient as long as she wished. She must open her arms to him of her own accord. When it was dark he drew the curtains and lit the two tall candles on the chimneypiece.

At last there was a knock, and the waiter entered with a laden tray and set it down on a table. Then he brought a smaller table to the fire and flicked a white cloth over it. When the dishes were set out he uncorked the wine and stood it in the middle of the table. "I'll manage," Robert dismissed him.

He did not call Wilson, but woke Elizabeth gently. For a moment she did not seem to know where she was, then she smiled up at him. "Come," he said and went back to the fire to wait for her.

Elizabeth slid out of bed. There was no Wilson to help her. Where was her dressing gown? She opened the vast oaken wardrobe which towered to the high ceiling. She could not see the warm robe Wilson usually brought her. Only the light white summer one she had worn on that thundery day when Papa had thought she had received Mr. Browning in it was hanging there.

It was a mere cobweb, light and gauzy; but the rooms were warm, with a fire blazing in each one. Elizabeth slipped it on, leaving her hair loose, and went in to join Robert. He stood to meet her, and an expression almost of pain crossed his face, but he did not touch her.

"Has Flush been fed?" Elizabeth asked.

"Wilson is looking after him. I'm the only male creature here tonight." He filled her glass and toasted her gaily.

When she had been silent a long time, sitting over her empty plate and staring into the fire, he asked, "Are you tired, my Ba? Shall I carry you back to bed?" Elizabeth nodded, and he picked her up and took her into the bedroom. Tenderly he covered her with the bedclothes. She held her arms out to him and he knelt to kiss her. His hands wandered over her hair and under the lace. He drew away from her to look at her face and found it lost in dreams.

"I must go," he sighed. "I mustn't be selfish, my Ba."

"Don't leave me, Robert."

He blew out only one of the candles in the bedroom, saying, "I want to see your eyes."

As her passion flamed to meet his all the warm starry Jamaican nights which had lit such loves for men and women of his blood, and of hers, through the centuries, came together in that tall-ceilinged room in Paris dancing with firelight and candlelight. All the soaring music, all the high winds and seas, all the wild rides, all the sweet singing, that had ever swept him to delight that was almost pain, were there.

And she? As he worshipped her and praised her, and wooed

her and coerced her, and supplicated her and triumphed over her, she felt herself to be, at last, not the poor, plain, sick, unlucky woman of Wimpole Street, not the stone fit only to be cast away, but love itself, warm, young, happy—and beautiful. As she fell away, far, far down to the very bottom of some sea where sleep lay, she knew that there would never be any words, for him or for her, to describe this love without fear or awkwardness, this perfect coming together, this giving which was a gift of showers of shining gold.

All the way to Orléans in the diligence Elizabeth was silent, dreading what awaited her there, and when she arrived she said, "The time for my death warrant has come!"

Robert brought her a great packet of letters, and she sat in her room at the Hôtel de la Poste unable to open any of them, growing colder every moment with fear.

"Let me open them and read them first," he pleaded, "or let me read them to you."

"Never! I must meet it alone."

"At least, Ba, let me sit by you while you read them. Let me hold your hand."

"Please, my beloved, do as I say."

For a wild moment Robert thought of seizing them and opening them, crying, "See, there's nothing to be afraid of. Everything's all right while I'm with you." Instead he said, "Ten minutes, then. No more. I'll be close by." He went to stand just outside the door.

Elizabeth shut her eyes for a long moment, then thrust the string quickly from the packet. I'm always bravest alone, she said to herself, and I'd rather know the truth, however bad it is.

Hastily she sorted through the letters, searching for her father's and her brothers' writing. There was a letter from her father and one from George. The tears ran down her face as she read her father's letter, but she felt neither surprise nor anger, only grief. "Dearest Papa," she whispered, "dearest Papa."

"You have sold your soul for genius—mere genius!" she read. When she was eighteen at a word from Lord Byron she would have fled through the world with him. She still loved the idea of him enough to hate Lady Byron. She would never agree to meet her, whatever Anna Jameson said about her "dearest, wronged friend." But she had not sold her soul for "mere genius" in marrying Robert Browning. It was the tender lover, the honourable man, the man of truth and strength whom she had married.

Her father informed her in his letter that he had disinherited her and cast her off forever. For the rest of his life he would consider her as dead. "I don't deserve it," she whispered. "I'm not what he thinks me."

At least the worst was over. Her brothers would make everything all right. She opened George's letter. As she read she put her hand to her heart. George had written that letter? George, who only a year before had had high words with Papa on her behalf? George, to whom she had chosen to write rather than to Stormy, knowing that he was her stout friend? George's letter was more awful than all her father's threats and insults. "You've sacrificed all delicacy and honour," he wrote, as if she had run away without being married at all. "You've left the weight of sorrow and shame to be borne by your family."

Worst of all were the things George said about Robert. She had been right to send Robert from the room. She would never let Robert see those letters. If he read George's letter there could be no coming together with her family ever again.

But where were the letters from all her other brothers? She had written to each one—nine letters in all, with Papa's. Not one of them had taken the trouble to write her a line.

Elizabeth was holding letters from Henrietta and Arabel, crying and laughing over them, when Robert opened the door. The letters from her father and George were hidden. She put her sisters' letters in his hands, and Robert read them quickly and kissed them. "I love your sisters, Ba, for this," he cried. "I'll make it my life's work to justify their trust in me."

Then Elizabeth told him about the letters from her father and George, briefly, as steadily as possible, and only in general terms. "They were very hard letters I had from dearest Papa and dearest George," she said. "I must bow my head to Papa's, though I don't deserve it. But as for George, I thought it hard, I confess, that he should have written to me with a sword and half-broken my heart."

Robert held out his hand, looking savage.

"No, I won't show them to you, my darling Robert," Elizabeth said. "It's better not."

He drew his hand back as if she had struck it.

"It's not so as to hurt you," she cried. "It's the very opposite."

Robert gave her a searching look. Then he said, "Come, my love. Come."

He swept her up from where she sat, looking so forlorn and so brave under her load of letters, and carried her to her bed. "Whatever you say, we'll read the rest of them together," he said. "The worst's over."

"Yes. The worst *must* be over," she prayed.

"Don't fear, my Ba. I won't do anything to drive your family away; or tear you up by the roots. I'll love you more and more, to make up for the love you are losing, and I'll win it back for you if man can."

He said not a word about the false position in which she had put him by insisting on secrecy but sat beside her reading the other letters aloud. As he read, Robert told her stories and jokes from his old friendships with the writers. Suddenly Elizabeth found she was laughing and felt surrounded by friends. Watching, he saw that he had won her attention away from her family's letters and held it, as he had meant to. He chattered on, tempting her to smile whenever her thoughts seemed to be slipping away, forcing her attention back to him and the present, making her rejoice especially that John Kenyon had written full approval of their marriage, even if she had endangered her life, begging her to call on him for money if she needed it, and that Miss Mitford had wished them happiness.

At last Robert had talked himself to a standstill, and there was only one letter left, addressed to her. He opened it. It was from Dr. Jago, a prescription for morphine. So the opium had followed them like an unwelcome fellow traveller. He continued to sit beside her, silent now, until she closed her eyes and slept. It grew dark, but he sat on. When she woke at last he rang the bell and ordered supper to be sent up to their room. Then he came to her again and took her hand.

"I kissed your feet, my Ba, before I married you, but now I would kiss the ground under your feet, I love you with a so much greater love."

Looking at his sober face and his steady eyes, calmed as she was by the hours of tenderness and goodness he had poured out on her, she found the strength to tell him of how her father had received the news of her flight.

Her letters should have reached her family an hour after she had left Wimpole Street. For some reason they had not. Perhaps George had deliberately held them back; or perhaps he had been out when they came in the envelope addressed to him. At any rate her absence had been discovered long before it was explained. When George had finally opened his envelope he had refused to carry out her request to inform Mr. Barrett and give him her letter.

It was Henrietta who had taken that fearsome task on her shoulders. Mr. Barrett had been standing on the stairs, carrying the family Bible. He must have been looking up some date or other in it. Henrietta had not waited for a suitable moment. Running out onto the stairs from the drawing room, she had called out her message. Mr. Barrett had dropped the book. He had not hurled it, as all London said; it had simply fallen from his hands. But Henrietta, so used to violence from him, had been frightened. She had slipped. She and the book had fallen heavily downstairs, and Mr. Barrett's shouts had followed them.

Soon after Mr. Kenyon had called, asking to see his cousin Mr. Barrett. Robert's letter telling him of his marriage had reached him that evening. By the time Mr. Kenyon was shown up Mr. Barrett had regained an icy composure. He had said only, "My daughter should have been thinking of another world."

On Monday the family had left Wimpole Street for Little Bookham as arranged. That day the notice of Robert and Elizabeth's marriage had appeared in the newspapers. They would certainly be better away from a London buzzing with the elopement.

"That's all, Robert."

Looking at her haunted eyes, he was glad he had one more card to play. Without a word about what she had just told him he left the room and came back bearing a large parcel. "I've a present for you, I think, Ba," he said. "It's addressed by Sarianna."

"Oh, Robert, your family have written, too, and I haven't given them a thought. Forgive me; I'm so selfish."

"Not selfish—only harried, my dear love."

He unwrapped it. It was a travelling desk, with a note, "To EBB from her sister Sarianna." Robert noticed that Sarianna had not felt able to call Elizabeth by her first name in any form, though her own warm welcome to her came openly in her signature.

"My mother sends love, too, in her letter to me," he said. "And my father closed his, 'Give your wife a kiss for me.' And here it is." Elizabeth smiled as he kissed her.

"Now, Ba." He took her hands. "You're a part of my family now; and your life is here with me, not in Wimpole Street or Little Bookham or wherever your father and your brothers and sisters are living. They'll always be welcome in our home and loved by us both—not only by you—if they choose. But you mustn't allow them to spoil our happiness. You must live in the present with me, not in the past. I've love enough to make up for all of them, if need be. Will you give me your promise?"

She sighed. "Yes."

"Then give it to me now."

"I promise, Robert."

After luncheon at the hotel next day Mrs. Jameson caught Robert as he was about to follow Elizabeth upstairs. "I want to speak to you about something to do with your wife's health, Mr. Browning. I hope you won't think me impertinent."

He bowed and waited.

"What I'm going to say is only because of my deep affection for her," she continued, her eyes anxious.

"There was no need to say that." Robert's voice was warm.

Still she hesitated, then plunged. "I've noticed—it was impossible not to—the very large amount of morphine and other drugs she takes."

"She makes no secret of it," he sighed.

"But it's a *vast* amount, Mr. Browning. I'm horrified at how much. Never less than forty drops of laudanum, and brandy-and-ether too."

"It's those confounded physicians. They prescribe and prescribe. She'd only to write to Dr. Jago for him to send the prescription by the very next post with a letter positively urging her to keep on with it. She had it yesterday."

"She brought a stock with her from England, she tells me," Anna Jameson said.

"And now it's replenished. She can get it at any chemist's in Italy."

"But she must give it up. She really must!"

Robert told her of Elizabeth's promise to try to lessen the

dosage. "I think she has tried. But there's been a great deal of strain for her these last few months."

"Well, now that's all over, and you can help her to abandon it. I advise you to begin at once."

"Believe me, Mrs. Jameson, I'm heart and soul behind that, but I don't like to press her. Ba's a devilish private person. She'd resent it, I know."

At last she said, unwillingly, "What you want is for me to speak to her, then?"

Robert brightened. "Could you bear to?"

"No. But I will if it's the only way."

"There'd be two of us then."

"Three, as a matter of fact," Anna Jameson said. "Wilson is very disturbed, too. She spoke to me about it, regarding me as a nurse."

"Why not go to Ba now? She's alone," Robert begged.

At first Elizabeth tried to pooh-pooh Anna's fears as she had done Robert's.

"I don't believe it does any harm. Do you think I'd have tried to persuade dear Miss Mitford to use opium when she was upset after those highwaymen attacked her if I thought so? I don't know how I'd have managed without it since leaving England."

"It's a great worry to your husband," the Irish voice wheedled. "He suggested I should speak to you and told me you had promised to lessen the doses."

"I did promise, and I have tried—and I'll try again when life's easier."

"It will never be easy to give it up. Now, when you are together and so happy, is the time to make a serious effort. Will you lessen the dosage this very night?"

Mrs. Jameson could see that Elizabeth resented being pressed, but was struggling with herself. "Tonight is soon! But, yes, if Robert really wishes it and has sent you to me."

"Let him pour out your draughts, or give Wilson instructions to do so."

"I can be trusted to keep my word."

She looked on the verge of anger, and Mrs. Jameson left it there. She had achieved a great deal, after all.

17

THE PARTY OF FIVE TRAVELLED ON BY DILIGENCE
to Avignon and then to Marseilles by slow stages. There they
went on the French steamer *l'Océan* to Leghorn. As they were
rowed to shore the boat passed close to a jutting piece of rock on
which stood a tall man wrapped in a cloak.

"There's Father Prout!" Robert shouted, and told them
about the Jesuit priest, Father Mahony, who had been dismissed
from his order sixteen years before and was now Rome corre-
spondent for Dickens's paper *The Daily News* under the name of
"Father Prout." Over an inn breakfast ashore he introduced
them to the jovial man with soft hands and sardonic eyes. Father
Prout embraced Robert, exclaiming, "Married! And not only to a
poet but one more famous than yourself."

Then they took the train to Pisa, arriving in buckets of rain.
Elizabeth could only think that she was living through a miracle
wrought by the man who sat by her side. Was it a year ago that
she had written to Robert, "One word, just to say it's all over
with Pisa"?

Robert found lodgings within the hour—four rooms in the
Collegio di Fernandino, a great sixteenth-century palace in the
Piazza del Duomo, a few minutes' walk from the Cathedral and
the Leaning Tower for only one pound six shillings and nine-
pence a week, including pots and pans, china and cutlery. Tact-
fully, Anna Jameson and her niece refused to share them, and
took others nearby.

Soon Elizabeth leaned out of the window staring disbelievingly at the Leaning Tower with the Cathedral behind it and the Baptistery close by on the Campo Santo, and the streets bleached with light.

It was October but as hot as an English June.

Inside their palace (or rather, inside their four rooms on one corner of it) they were deliriously happy, leading their life of almost childish innocence and bliss.

They breakfasted on coffee and eggs and toasted rolls. Every day at two o'clock the nearby *trattoria* sent in a meal. It was usually thrushes and chianti and cost eightpence each. At five or six o'clock they had more coffee and rolls. At nine o'clock they had supper—always roast chestnuts and grapes and mulled wine. Elizabeth ate well, and Robert pressed her to drink the cheap light chianti by the tumblerful. At night he brought it to her in bed and continued to fill her glass.

They revelled in each other. Elizabeth was delighted with every new discovery she made about Robert. She loved to pass her hands through his rumpled black curls and to kiss his silky beard and his square blunt fingers, and she would make him bare his torso so that she could stroke the muscles on his arms and plunge her fingers into the mat of hair on his fine boxlike chest. When they had made love she slept soundly on their horribly uncomfortable bed stuffed with orange-tree shavings.

Robert insisted on celebrating their wedding anniversary every Saturday, and Elizabeth was allowed to do nothing except preside over their coffeepot, a present from Treppy. Elizabeth longed to show her overflowing love in extravagant presents, as she had always done to others, but there was not enough money for that. So she embroidered his monogram on fine cambric handkerchiefs, sending Wilson to buy her first thimble since her childhood. Robert bought the material for a pink dress for Wilson to make up for her and a fringed pink silk parasol, entering them in the household accounts which he kept meticulously.

Every day Elizabeth left the Collegio in her pink dress to walk in the sun with Robert and was amazed anew at the golden globes hanging from the orange trees behind the garden walls. When she grew tired they sat on a warm wall and watched the lizards. Then they walked slowly back through the narrow, quiet streets, hugging the shady side and crossing the bridges over the winding Arno. In their dark cool rooms there would be a bowl of fresh-gathered oranges left by the *padrone* to bring the sunshine indoors. Now and then they walked farther out between the vines heavily hung with purple grapes translucent in the light and bursting with sweetness.

"Now I know how far your lips are from mine as we walk," Robert boasted.

One day he took Elizabeth to the Palazzo Lanfranchi, where Byron had lived with his Countess Teresa Guiccioli, who had been only sixteen, a year younger than Geddie, when she had left her husband to live with him. In the little enclosed garden, where Teresa used to join Byron and the Shelleys after sleeping late in the mornings, Robert picked Elizabeth a bay leaf.

"Teresa's father was one of the Carbonari, the Italian resistance movement," he said almost idly as they strolled. "He got Byron quite involved in Italian revolutionary politics, you know."

"Byron? In Italian politics? I didn't realize that."

"Oh, this sleepy country's really very restless and bitter—against the Austrians here in Tuscany, and against the Bourbons in the south. There's always been a flame burning, ever since Napoleon."

"You mean—"

"I mean since his first campaign, when young Bonaparte beat the Austrians in Italy. The Italians had a brief dream of being one people and one free country. It all came to nothing, of course. But when Byron was here—"

"Byron," she interrupted, "for a free Italy! And I never knew."

The passion that fired her face gave him a shock of surprise. It was as though the revolutionary flame he had spoken of (with no great personal enthusiasm, if truth were told) had leapt like lightning into her blood. He remembered how she had dreamed as a girl of following Byron disguised as his page.

"Oh, yes," he said, slowly. "It might have been Italy, not Greece, for which Byron died. Teresa Guiccioli's father had been thrown out of Pisa, and Byron was packing his bags to follow when his friend Hobhouse turned up. Hobhouse was a Member of Parliament by then, and filled him full of Greece's troubles. Perhaps Byron was weary of Teresa, but at any rate he went off to Greece to die."

She wasn't listening. She could only repeat, *"Byron! Italy!"*

Robert could not know that at that moment he had lit the flame of a passion for Italy the nation, as opposed to Italy the enchanting country in which to live, which would consume Elizabeth until she drew her last breath. Byron had been the taper.

November came quickly, and they ate huddled close together over the fires lit in the rooms below, whispering and laughing like children or planning future travels. Sometimes hours went by before they left the table.

One morning over breakfast Robert said suddenly, "I wish your sisters could see us now!"

"Well, as long as they couldn't *hear* us!" Elizabeth giggled, and they laughed until she choked over a crumb.

Suddenly they heard it, the deep bell.

They loved the bells of Pisa, city of bells. Sometimes all the bells of all the churches rang together, and they found it charming. Now from the Cathedral came this strange bell, with its deep, sonorous, mournful note, a note of doom and dismay—of death. Their laughter died away, and they sat frozen in their chairs, suddenly unable to eat, filled with dread.

At that moment the landlord's daughter Maddalena came in with a message from her father, the *padrone*. "What's that bell, signorina?" Robert asked.

A shadow darkened her creamy face, and she crossed herself.

"It's the *Pasquareccia*, signor, the Duomo's fourth bell. It's tolled when there's an execution. Sometimes in the middle of the night—"

There were not many executions, fortunately.

Before Mrs. Jameson left with Geddie for Florence she tried to persuade them to go with her, pointing out how much cheaper life was there.

"For two hundred and fifty pounds a year you ought to have splendid apartments and keep your own carriage and horses and a manservant. These rooms will be cold later on."

The tradesmen, she hinted, too, were cheating them. It was clear that she thought Robert charming but impractical.

But Robert was afraid of the social life of Florence. There were so many English there, and they had endless parties and soirées and receptions. He did not want the world breaking in on their dreamlike life. Elizabeth wanted to visit the churches and climb the Leaning Tower before she left Pisa. They were not quite ready to go.

Suddenly the cold came like a blow, and their walks together stopped. The people of Pisa went about muffled in vast cloaks and carrying little earthenware pots full of live embers to keep their fingers warm. Yet at five o'clock in the afternoon Robert could still sit writing at an open window and look out at trees green with summery foliage.

Now for the first time they found life in Pisa a little boring. They began to miss their books. They had joined the local lending library, but Elizabeth complained that except for the Bible and Shakespeare they had not seen a real book since they had reached Pisa. Their rooms were very quiet. Elizabeth begged Robert to buy a piano.

"Why? Do you play?" he teased her.

"You know very well I don't. I want to listen to you."

"I won't spend your money on luxuries for myself, and I can't afford it."

"If I didn't owe so much money, I'd buy it for you!" she cried, exasperated.

"Owe money?" Robert was staggered.

She confessed that she had borrowed seventy pounds from Arabel and another thirty from Rosie the housekeeper not long before she had left home. "There were bills to be settled and things to be bought."

The morphine, no doubt, Robert thought. She had brought a great store, Mrs. Jameson had said. They would have to go to Florence and live more cheaply, he decided. They could not leave such large debts unpaid a moment longer than could be helped.

Elizabeth was sad when Anna Jameson left Pisa. She seemed to get all the news from England quickly. It was from her that Elizabeth had learned of the series of dinner parties Mr. Barrett had embarked on as soon as he and his family returned to London. He entertained with a grim-faced, determined gaiety. No one mentioned his eldest daughter, and his sons stood round him in a phalanx of dark disapproval. She had even heard before Elizabeth did that he had refused to act as her trustee any longer.

For her part, long before she brought herself to tell Robert, Elizabeth had wept to Anna Jameson because her father sent one of her letters back unopened. Elizabeth had confided in her friend too Henrietta's news that her father had ordered all Elizabeth's books to be packed in boxes and put into store and the bills sent to her. Until then she had felt that she had left her home. After that she knew she had been turned out.

In December frost came, and then snow, the first for five years. The sun continued bright and hot, yet it grew colder and colder. Through their windows Robert and Elizabeth could see women wrapped in furs but carrying parasols, and the snow heaped on the Duomo, glittering white between its yellow marble walls and the vivid blue sky.

The sun never touched their rooms. Elizabeth felt languid and blamed it on the cold. Robert worried and heaped sweet-scented pine logs on their fire. He would hardly leave her chair. Even Elizabeth grew nervous about her health. "If I were to fall ill after all," she wrote to her sisters, "I'd deserve to be stoned for having got married."

In England too the winter was unusually severe. Snow lay in the fields, and everywhere ponds were frozen week after week. If he had not brought her to Italy, Robert comforted himself, Elizabeth might not be alive.

On Christmas Eve Elizabeth seemed more her old self, declaring that she was determined to go to midnight mass in the Cathedral. Wilson wrapped her in her furs and a great coat, and they crossed quickly into a Duomo blazing with candles and filled with people chattering and walking about.

Next day there was a threat of the old discomfort in her throat, and she had pains. Robert wondered whether to send for Anna Jameson, but Elizabeth insisted that she felt very well. She still did nothing except write her long, long letters to her father and her sisters. She had broken her promise to Robert not to live in the past within twenty-four hours of making it.

"Please remember to tell me the colour of the drawing room

curtains and wallpaper etc. so that I can see it all as it really is after the redecorations," she begged her sisters. "Write, write, and at length and in detail. Half my heart is with you. *Speak of Papa always.*"

Was it safe, she asked them, to direct her letters to Wimpole Street? No, they answered, it was not safe, and after that her letters were sent care of Miss Trepsack at 5 Upper Montague Street, Montague Square, London.

Robert watched her, but did not ask her what she wrote. He said nothing, either, when she continued to go to the little shelf where the morphine was kept, though he counted her journeys— one, two, three, four a day, at least.

Now Pisa was really beginning to pall on them. They had taken their apartments until the seventeenth of April, in that new year of 1847, and that seemed a long way off. Robert had been into all the churches. He had gone for all the walks. The countryside was monotonously flat. The place was full of invalids waiting to die.

The bells had become a nightmare. They began at four o'clock in the morning, and now they wakened Elizabeth from the deepest sleep. What had been an enchantment was now only a clangour in their ears. Worst of all was the *Pasquareccia,* the execution bell. It had a ghastly effect on Elizabeth.

Then, if there were not many executions, there were a great many funerals, and they all seemed to pass the Collegio di Fernandino right under their windows. Monks of various orders, some in white robes, others in black, walked slowly past in a long procession chanting and carrying torches. One by one they filed by, one foot in front of the other, and then suddenly there was the bier and the corpse on it, its white face rigid and naked to the sky except for a veil.

At first Elizabeth and Robert had stood at the window to watch each funeral, but after a while her old horror of death had overwhelmed her and she had stayed in her corner. Robert felt something of her dislike, too, and sometimes he obeyed her when she begged, "Oh, *don't* go to the window!" But often he went in spite of her, crying, "I can't help it, Ba it *draws* me!"

"Oh, I don't know how you can look. Such horrible hoarse chanting it is, like the croaking of death itself."

Then sometimes she would fling herself into his arms in a storm of tears, crying, "Oh, never leave me!" He knew that the funeral bells reminded her of the loss of Bro and of how even more desolate and alone she would be if she lost him.

One day Robert came back with an Italian saying. *"Pisa pesa a chi posa.* Can you translate that?"

"Oh, yes," Elizabeth said, "Pisa depresses him who lives there. It does, doesn't it?" It was out in the open.

"Well, we'll move on, Ba, in April. Meanwhile—"

"Yes?"

"We must work. We really must. I'll get ready a collected edition."

"Good. And I'll work, too, but it's a secret."

They worked on through the winter months, huddled over the fire, she at improving her sonnets and he at revising *Pippa Passes.* Elizabeth seemed perfectly well once more; then in February she began to have pains at night. They came on suddenly and violently after she had gone to bed.

At first she did not mention them to Robert but rang for Wilson, who rubbed her down and gave her a few spoonsful of the brandy-and-ether mixture she demanded. Each time the pains went as suddenly as they had come, but they did not stop coming.

"Madam," Wilson said one night as she was rubbing her, "it's only right to tell you what I think."

"Yes, Wilson, of course," Elizabeth replied.

"I think you're with child, ma'am."

"Nonsense, Wilson! It's nothing but wishful thinking. I've seen that look in your eye from the start."

Wilson went on rubbing unsmilingly.

"Besides, pains in the night aren't a sign of being pregnant, are they?" Elizabeth prodded her.

"No, ma'am, not of a normal pregnancy. I think you're pregnant, ma'am, and in danger of a miscarriage. You should see a doctor, ma'am."

Really, Wilson was becoming too interfering, Elizabeth thought. First, making a fuss about the morphine, and now this.

"You're imagining things, Wilson," she said coldly.

"If I may make so bold, ma'am," Wilson said doggedly, "I think it's the morphine that's to blame. You're back to the heavy dosage again, and I'm dreadfully afraid it'll cause you to miscarry."

"It's the morphine that helps the pains, not the other way round."

"Yes, ma'am. If you say so, ma'am."

The next night Robert was beside her in bed when the pains came. Before she could stop herself she had been convulsed by a spasm of agony.

Robert leapt out of bed. "Ba! Ba! What's the matter?"

Holding her stomach with both hands, she gasped, "It's nothing. A little brandy— Oh, get Wilson."

When Wilson came she gave her the brandy-and-ether and said, "If you'll kindly leave, Mr. Browning, please. I know what to do."

When she came out Robert was waiting for her, and she told him what she had said to her mistress.

"Why didn't you tell me?" he demanded angrily.

"It wasn't suitable, sir."

Robert went back to Elizabeth and said with a stubborn face, "You must go to the English doctor, Dr. Wood. You must."

But she was more stubborn than he. "I'll do no such thing. You'll make a laughingstock of me."

"But I must know why you have these pains," he persisted.

"I may have caught an internal chill. I ran out barefoot into the passage one night when Wilson was unwell."

"Do you realize you are playing with my life?"

Elizabeth was a little frightened despite her bravado. She wasn't pregnant, she was sure. Of course not. She passed her hands over her body. She was fatter, yes, but she had been eating heartily ever since her marriage and drinking all that chianti. There were none of the usual symptoms. She wasn't half Wilson's size, and no one said *she* was pregnant. No, she would not see Dr. Wood.

When Robert next came to beseech her to do so she was obdurate. She was even rude; and though she repented and kissed him afterwards she would not change her mind.

Then the pains went away. They came back only once. It was a Friday, and she was sitting by the fire after their two o'clock meal, curled up with her feet under her. Suddenly she felt very ill. She could not move, and would not allow Robert to touch her so that he could carry her to bed.

Dr. Wood was with them almost immediately. He took one look at Elizabeth and burst out angrily, "What's this? The room at seventy degrees, a raging fire, and you crouched in that foolish position!" He took her wrist. "And a high pulse. I thought so."

He ordered her to be laid on the sofa and sent Wilson to bring her cold tea. "Just lie quietly, and we'll see. I'll come back on Sunday."

Everyone was now convinced that she was pregnant except Elizabeth. However, she did as she was told, and on Saturday morning she felt rather better.

Towards evening, however, regular pains came at five-minute intervals. Robert went himself to fetch Dr. Wood and returned with him. After he had examined Elizabeth he came out to Robert. "I'm sorry," he said. "This is a miscarriage. I'll do my best, but don't hope for too much."

He hesitated before Robert's stark misery. Then he gave a little gesture with both hands and said crossly, "If I'd been called in six weeks ago everything would have gone as well as could be. There was no need for this, no need at all. I would only have had to confine her to the sofa for a couple of months and apply leeches to her back and keep the temperature cool. I've delivered over a hundred babies and I know what I'm talking about. She's done everything wrong, baking herself by the fire, drinking hot coffee, twisting herself into such positions and refusing all advice." Then he went back in to Elizabeth.

Robert waited outside, cold as ice beside the fire. He stayed there all night, his head in his hands. When the doctor came out again it was four o'clock on Sunday morning.

"The child has miscarried," he said flatly. "A child of five months. I could do nothing."

He watched Robert absorbing it and put a hand on his shoulder. Then he said, "You may go in and see her now. She's surprisingly strong, you know—and brave. She *looks* so frail."

He said it with a sort of wonder, very telling from the cross self-centered man.

He added, angry again, "It was very foolish of her. Very."

Then, again, "If it's any comfort to you, it's excellent for her chest, this mishap. It'll do her nothing but good as far as her general health is concerned." He smiled abruptly, trying to make a joke between them. "I wish I could arrange something of the sort for mine. I'm here in Pisa for my lungs, too."

So he went away. When Robert went in Wilson was still in

the bedroom, shaking her head at Elizabeth behind the bed-curtains and weeping a little.

"I'm sorry," Elizabeth said, and looked it. "I was very stupid."

But Robert had thrown himself on the bed in a passion of tears and was sobbing like a child.

18

IT WAS THE AFTERNOON OF SEPTEMBER 12, 1847. Robert and Elizabeth had been married for exactly a year. They had been living in Florence for five months, and now on this shining day the city itself seemed to be rejoicing with them on their wedding anniversary. There was to be a grand procession of more than forty thousand Tuscans marching past their windows with rousing music and silken banners to the majestic Pitti Palace opposite where the local Grand Duke Leopoldo of Tuscany resided. There the province would express to him, representative of the Austrian oppressors, its profound gratitude for granting it a Civic Guard of its own. No longer would the Austrian whitecoats be the only soldiers allowed to bear arms in Tuscany.

Robert and Elizabeth were standing at the windows of their palatial apartment in the dark-looking fifteenth-century *palazzo* rather awkwardly placed on the corner where the Via Maggio and the Via Mazzetta met at an angle, which was known as the Casa Guidi because a certain Russian Prince Guidi had formerly lived there. Their suite of seven spacious rooms on the first floor was full of fine mirrors and carved marble and gilt consoles and armchairs covered with crimson and white satin, and the Guidi arms were emblazoned in mosaic on their bedroom floor. From the front the Casa Guidi looked onto the Piazza Pitti and a wing of the gigantic Pitti Palace, and from the back onto the ancient church of San Felice.

Every procession at *festa* time passed down the Via Maggio

and into the Piazza Pitti before the Grand Duke's palace. On her first visit to the Casa Guidi, Elizabeth had rejoiced, saying, "It'll make up for all those years when I saw nothing but chimneypots from my windows and for the funerals of Pisa." Then she had wandered out onto the small stone balcony at the back, onto which eight tall French windows opened, and gazed at the grey church opposite.

"Felice for happiness," she had murmured. "We'll be happy here, and we'll stroll here alone in the moonlight."

"There's just room for two to walk abreast," Robert had replied, his arm about her.

They had left Pisa in April, a month after Elizabeth's miscarriage, passing by train through vine-festooned plains and lush valleys full of pink asphodel, over hills and alongside lovely sweeps of river. Immediately they had fallen in love with Florence, that incomparable cluster of palaces and churches and noble piazzas threaded by its golden river, beautiful with its statues and gardens and fountains, lying beneath the parched blue Tuscan hills.

They were still living on the hundred pounds Robert had borrowed from his father, and must be economical until Elizabeth's money came through. John Kenyon, as her new trustee, would be sending an installment of the four hundred pounds a year income from her eight thousand pounds invested in government stock. There would be about two hundred pounds a year, too, coming in from her shares in her father's cargo ships, the *David Lyon* and the *Statira*—her "ship money," as she called it. Royalties from her 1844 volume of poems would swell their income.

Meanwhile, pinched though they had been, their magnificent apartment and the *trattoria* meals had been so cheap that Robert had consented to hire a grand piano and music and to take on a giggling, dumpy little maid called Annunziata to make the beds, clean the rooms and brush his clothes. Wilson, the superior lady's maid, had not cared for such work.

Wilson loved Florence, though it shocked her to find two Venuses on public display in the first art gallery she visited, one a marble statue just inside the door and another one a Titian painted on the ceiling.

"The marble one was nearly naked, ma'am, and the other one *stark* naked. I turned my back on them at once and came home. It wouldn't have been decent to stay."

"Oh, but Wilson, this is *art*," Elizabeth had laughed. "You have to leave such feelings behind you."

Wilson looked very doubtful. "Well, ma'am, if you say so. Perhaps I'll try again, ma'am, when there's no one else about."

Soon Elizabeth herself had been well enough to go out and fall under the spell of the Florentines. Graceful women walked on the streets in elegant dresses, flirting their glittering fans at handsome men with amber eyes. Every child on a doorstep had his slice of watermelon and his bunch of purple grapes. Rich and poor listened to the same music and admired the same Raphaels.

She and Robert had strolled out together in the cool evenings, walking as far as the Baptistery, over the Trinità Bridge where Dante had stood when he first saw Beatrice. Leaning over the parapet, they had gazed into the Arno in the sunset to see churches and houses and people reflected in it. Sometimes they had crossed the Ponte Vecchio to look at Ghiberti's bronze Doors of Paradise, or at Cellini's *Perseus* holding up Medusa's head in the Loggia dei Lanzi. Robert had led her close to it and traced with his finger the lovely relief of the rescue of Andromeda on the pedestal.

"You are my Andromeda."

"And you my Perseus."

But where was the dragon? she asked herself. And what was he doing at that hour? She dreamed at nights, more often as her father's birthday drew near, and woke crying, "Papa! Papa!"

As May departed they had taken long drives in a hired britska in the Cascine Park, or walked in the Boboli Gardens, strolling under the arbours and peeping through the lattices at vistas of the Apennines and Fiesole, magical Fiesole. In June they had gone to the grand *festa* of San Giovanni, the patron saint of Florence and had seen the chariot races in the Piazza Santa Maria Novella. People were massed close as bees in the seats raised in tiers against the houses and the church, the women shining like butterflies with their gay dresses and those moving, glittering fans. Every seat had been filled, every window alive with faces. Even monks stood two by two at the monastery windows.

Oh, it was like living in a poem, their life in Florence!

Elizabeth had blossomed there, laughing all day, warm and impetuous in their bed at night, growing ever younger and more seductive under Robert's eyes and being effortlessly, selflessly sweet to him, so that he found himself choking with love for her.

198

In England she had felt accursed, never anything but cold and ill and unhappy, a lonely prisoner haunted by death and disaster. Now she was well, radiantly happy, loved and, for the first time, free. She experienced a revulsion towards her own country, while her gratitude overflowed into a passion for the beautiful land which had given her so much and its charming, welcoming people.

Ironically it was that which had brought the only shadow on their perfect happiness. Elizabeth had never done anything by halves. Seeing this beloved country in chains, the hated Austrian soldiers everywhere and proud men hurled into prison for any show of independence, she had thrown herself so passionately into Italian politics that Robert was disturbed.

It was he who had lit the flame in that Byron-haunted garden of the Palazzo Lanfranchi in Pisa; but it was Anna Jameson who had heaped brushwood on it and blown it into a conflagration.

In May she and Geddie Bate had suddenly arrived in Florence from Rome, surprising Robert improvising on the piano and Elizabeth curled up on the sofa listening to him.

Over their *trattoria* banquet of vermicelli soup, sturgeon, turkey, beef casserole and cheesecakes, with green peas and asparagus (five courses for four people for four and sixpence) Anna had told them of recent happenings in Rome. Pale eyes suffused with emotion, she had rehearsed how only a few months after his accession to the papal throne the new Pope Pius IX had begun freeing political prisoners from his dungeons, educating artisans, building railways, installing gas lighting and even giving the press some freedom. He walked the streets by day dressed as a simple priest and rode a mule by night visiting the poor. Wild with love for him, the Italians knelt before him in the streets shouting *"Viva, Pio Nono!"* Here at last was a liberal Pope who might lead Italy against the Austrian tyrants.

"If he's a Pope," Robert had said drily, "he can't believe in freedom of thought, and in that case he's in a very awkward position."

But Elizabeth had been filled with love for the saintly man, seething with hatred for Austria's puppet kings and dukes, who dominated Italy. Then Anna had told them that Italy's only native ruler, the King of Sardinia, was ready to unite all the Italian states under him in rebellion against the Austrians.

"His armies are massing," Anna had declared, her voice sinking to a whisper as she glanced towards Geddie playing with Flush
on the hearthrug. "It won't be long now."

"Bloodshed!" Robert had said, and shuddered; but Elizabeth
had thrown up her chin, crying, "Man has always had to pay a
high price for liberty."

Robert himself was not unsympathetic towards the Pope's
humanitarian efforts. When he had heard there might be a British
embassy to the Vatican he had actually asked Dicky Monckton-
Milnes to propose him to the Foreign Office as its secretary. It was
not his fault there had not been a mission after all. He loved
Elizabeth for her hatred of oppression and her wish to do all she
could against it. Only these things needed to be taken soberly
and a little sceptically.

"I'm not at all happy about the position here in Florence,"
he told her after Anna had gone. "This Austrian Grand Duke
over in the Palazzo Pitti there, this great Leopoldo Secondo of
Tuscany, doesn't seem able to make up his mind whether he's
more frightened of his Austrian Emperor or of the Tuscan people
he's ruling. They call him the Grand Donkey. Anything might
happen, and remember we're foreigners here. Better not show
your hand, Ba."

Elizabeth had declared that the Austrian Duke was a liberal
and really on the side of a free Italy. The people loved him, and
he didn't tax them much.

So it had gone on ever since. That June Elizabeth had been
very excited when the Pope had granted the Romans the Civic
Guard they had been demanding and most incensed when the
Austrians had demonstrated their anger at such defiance by sending troops to Ferrara, near Venice, where they had garrison rights.
Then, when the Pope had protested against such open aggressive-
ness she had applauded him and praised the Italians for creating
disturbances in Genoa, Milan, Palermo, Naples, Lucca, Pisa—and
Florence.

Then Florence's Grand Duke Leopold (inspired by the Pope
according to Elizabeth, and frightened by the disturbances according to Robert) had allowed the Florentines to form their own
Civic Guard, like the Romans. Now they were celebrating this
benevolent concession with a great procession past the windows of

the Casa Guidi and up to the ducal Palazzo Pitti opposite on Robert and Elizabeth's first wedding anniversary.

Elizabeth *had* shown her hand. She had been up early draping their five front windows with great swags of crimson silk to let everyone in the Piazza Pitti know that they too wanted a Tuscany and an Italy freed from the Austrian tyrants.

Yes, Ba liked her own way, no doubt about it, Robert was thinking. He was eating large purple figs out of a blue dish as he looked out at the crowds massing in the piazza. How much did it matter? Would it lead to trouble? He remembered that business of their expedition to Vallombrosa only two months ago, in July.

They had not been able to afford to stay in the Casa Guidi during the summer, when the rent shot up from the guinea or so a week they paid in the dead season. They must leave Florence for somewhere cheaper or run out of money. The question was—where?

One day Elizabeth put down the book she was reading and said, "Vallombrosa's the place to spend the summer. It's cool and shady, and it'll cost hardly anything."

"Vallombrosa! That's out of the question!" Robert objected. "It's high up on a slope of the Pratomagno Mountains, and twenty miles of horribly rough travelling. Besides, where would we stay?"

"In the monastery of San Gualberto."

"Why, Ba, a monastery isn't a hostelry!"

"They take in travellers. Milton went there and used it for his description of paradise."

"Two hundred years ago."

"It would cost next to nothing, Robert. We could live on milk and eggs and bread-and-butter. The monks keep their own cows and hens and bake their bread. Do let us go. See how well I am!"

"Even if I said yes, I don't think we'd get permission."

"Do try, Robert."

He tried but was not at all surprised when permission was refused. It was a very austere monastery, he explained to her, where monks from proud patrician families mortified themselves by cleaning out the pigsties with their bare hands. They would have to think of something else.

Elizabeth, however, wanted to go to Vallombrosa and nowhere else. "I'm sorry to cry for the moon like a spoilt child, but I do want to go to Vallombrosa," she begged, standing on tiptoe to twine her arms about his neck. "Go and see the Minister Plenipotentiary and ask him for a letter. We'll go there with it and they won't be able to turn us away."

Only a few weeks before, Henrietta had teased Robert, asking him to say frankly whether Ba was always obedient. He recalled his reply. "This Ba, who is my wife, very *dis*obedient she is! Not all my commands or pleadings will make her eat a little more at dinner or supper or choose something she would like me to get her from this gay city of Florence. I don't believe she's capable of a selfish feeling. I solemnly declare that I've never been able to detect the slightest fault, failing or shortcoming in her—and remember we've lived together now for eight months. I never believed such a creature existed."

That had been in early May. By June Ba had thought of something she wanted him to get for her.

Robert went to see the Minister Plenipotentiary, Sir George Baillie Hamilton, and came away with a letter addressed to the Abbot at Vallombrosa, describing the Brownings as people of distinction and impeccable character and requesting him to allow them to stay at the monastery.

They left Florence at three o'clock in the morning. Elizabeth had never succeeded in paying a morning visit to the galleries yet she was up and dressed and ready to scale mountains before cockcrow. Robert had packed a dozen bottles of port in a carpetbag to support her on the way and keep up her strength later. That morning it seemed ludicrous.

They had a smooth carriage journey from Florence to the village of Pelago. There Elizabeth and Wilson and Flush and the luggage were loaded into wine baskets on sledges drawn by pairs of white bullocks. They left the road for a rough path and began the five-mile journey up the steep mountainside. Robert rode beside them on horseback, constantly reining in so as to keep the slow-paced oxen in sight. Their path wound up and up between pines and beeches and chestnuts. The soil was ink-black. Weirdly shaped rocks towered over them, and deep ravines fell away beside them, their blackness lit only by a distant silver shimmer of water. In the sky eagles glided, watching them. The silence was complete, as if unbroken since the beginning of time.

It took them four hours to cover the five hard miles to the monastery. Elizabeth was almost too tired to raise her eyes to the sprawling white buildings and the square tower. They walked into the House of Strangers and food was set before them. The black bread was coarse and smelled fetid. The tough, pale beef swam in a bath of rancid oil. She asked for an egg. There were no eggs. She sipped the glass of milk by her plate. It was blue and watery. She crumbled the bread and dropped it under the table. She took a forkful of the meat and laid down her fork.

Robert sat opposite her at the bare board, watching this small being who had been so passionately determined to enjoy this experience and was now so passionately hating it. He wondered at the strength of her feelings.

When Robert tried to get permission to stay the little red-faced Abbot was adamant. "This isn't a tourist resort," he insisted. "My monks are contemplatives and lead a life of deprivation. We offer a welcome to passing travellers in our House of Strangers, but by the rules of our order it must be brief. There's no question of your staying for two months, none whatever. No permit from any authority in Florence can override *me*. I'm Abbot here. You must go on the third day."

He stood, a small man made of steel, solid on his heels, a king in his kingdom. Robert argued and pleaded, trying to strike a spark of kindness from him, holding back his too quick temper. "My wife isn't strong. It's too much to ask her to go back at once."

"After five days, then. That's my last word."

Elizabeth raged with helpless fury. "They're throwing me out because I'm a woman. Up on this holy mountain a pigsty is cleaner than a woman's little finger."

"It's the same for me," Robert smiled.

Somehow they had enjoyed their short stay after all. The mountain air was good. Elizabeth found she was eating the beef and oil and drinking the wine with relish. She was enchanted when Robert sat at the organ on which Milton had played, making it peal out into the silence. Only Flush was frightened of the pinewoods when Wilson and he walked in them.

Robert had a suspicion that what Elizabeth was enjoying was the forbidden fruit. This Ba was a little closer to the one Henrietta knew than the one he had thought her. Could the quiet reasonable woman behave like a willful child, then? Was marriage, as they said, the discovery of the real woman beneath the ideal one with whom a man fell in love? If so, he was fortunate, for he loved the willful child, even when she embarrassed him.

Now, however, standing at his window on his wedding anniversary and remembering Vallombrosa, Robert found himself frightened of the passion Elizabeth was showing about Italy's politics. If the child who had gone to Vallombrosa took over from the rational woman there too—what then?

Anna Jameson arrived to watch the procession with them just as Elizabeth was climbing onto the great heap of cushions Wilson had piled on a chair for her so that she could see right across the square. Anna kissed Elizabeth, and at once embarked on a loud complaint.

"Geddie's made a perfect fool of herself," she cried. "What does she do in Rome but fall in love with a most unsuitable creature and go mad to marry him? A Scotsman. A bad artist. A coarse and quarrelsome fellow. A Roman Catholic convert. Without a farthing. *And* with a red beard. I blame you two for it. She never gave a thought to love and marriage before she met you."

Geddie stoutly defended her Scotsman, her baby face flushed and angry.

"Mr. Macpherson is *so* good and *so* generous and so handsome, Mrs. Browning. He'll probably be a fine artist when he tries and go back to being a Protestant if I ask him to. Why, he gave up smoking just to please Aunt Anna."

Robert smiled, but Elizabeth was not listening. At that moment there was a great rolling cry from the streets and the sound of loud lively music approaching.

For over three hours without a break the long procession filed by under the Casa Guidi windows, carrying flags and symbols into the piazza opposite. There the Grand Duke Leopold and his family received the marchers and accepted their thanks for their Civic Guard. They came in their thousands past windows bright with the silks and carpets hung from them: the magistrates, the priests, the lawyers, the artists, the guilds and the deputations from the different Tuscan cities. They carried their flowing banners and their ancient ensigns—Siena's she-wolf, Pisa's hare,

Massa's golden lion, Pienza's silver lion and Arezzo's prancing steed. Then came all the hundreds of foreign sympathizers. Pretty girls and lovely women leaned far out of the windows throwing flowers and waving handkerchiefs. Every inch of wall was alive. Clouds of flowers and a rain of laurel leaves fell continually on the endless procession, to the continuous noise of clapping and shouting and music. Men kissed each other, and richly dressed women ran out into the street to mix with the crowds. Elizabeth was particularly moved by the tiny children piping their *vivas*. Only the Austrians were missing. There were no white coats faced with purple anywhere, and no spurs jingling in the streets and cafés. Their drums were silent and the black and yellow flag was nowhere to be seen that day.

For over three hours Elizabeth watched, sometimes leaving her cushions and hanging over the crimson silk drapery, waving a handkerchief and shouting *"Viva! Viva!"* until her wrist ached and she was hoarse, while Anna looked on with approval.

It was growing dark when Elizabeth suddenly cried out, "Where's Flush?" He had been watching beside her, his paws hanging over the windowsill a moment before. Elizabeth rang the bell for Annunziata and questioned her *"Dov'è Flush?"*

Annunziata explained that Flush had asked to be taken for his walk, but as soon as they had set foot in the street a little dog with a turned-up tail had passed by and Flush had run after it. *"Oh, è niente,"* Annunziata giggled. *"Tornera presto, presto!* He'll come back very soon."

When Anna and Geddie had gone Robert and Elizabeth had a supper of roasted chestnuts and mulled wine in memory of their first meals in Italy.

Elizabeth was still excited. "It's hateful and loathsome of Austria to behave as she does to Italy," she exclaimed. "That snake Metternich, her chancellor, is the cause of it all."

Robert led her into the moon-washed bedroom. He was greedy for her, caressing her satiny skin, burying his face in her loosened hair, fiercely kissing every part of her and rousing her to the fiery sensuality to which she now gave rein without shame.

When at last Robert lay sprawled asleep across her breast Elizabeth picked up his hand and kissed it. How beautiful love was, she thought, between her and Robert. How especially beautiful it would be if he had given her a child that night. It would be the fruit of that glorious day, as if her love for Robert and her love for Italy had blossomed together, exactly one year after her marriage day.

As her lids were closing the thin voice of a child rose from the darkness outside, singing, *"O bella libertà! O bella!"*

Elizabeth opened her eyes, staring out through the open curtains at the great silver moon of Florence sailing across the star-dusted deep blue sky.

She would write a poem to bring Italy's wrongs to the eyes and ears of England. It would be quite different from anything she had ever done, no mere lyric but a work to be taken seriously. She would write it simply, speaking merely as a woman looking out of her windows and seeing the sort of things she saw from the Casa Guidi. She knew how it would begin.

> I heard last night a little child go singing
> 'Neath Casa Guidi windows, by the church,
> *"O bella libertà, O bella!"*

She would call it *Casa Guidi Windows*.

Robert stirred, and she put a naked arm about him and rubbed her hand against his cheek. Darling Robert. It was good to have a husband who believed in liberty.

19

WHEN THE LONG-AWAITED CHECK FOR SOME OF Elizabeth's government dividends arrived from Mr. Kenyon at the beginning of that October of 1847 Robert and Elizabeth decided to fulfill their dearest wish and winter in Rome.

As they were about to set out Elizabeth discovered without surprise that she was pregnant again. She said nothing. However, Robert came to her and said, "You must see the best *accoucheur* in Florence, Ba, at once." Wilson had spoken to him.

"I'm not sure, yet."

"Today, Ba."

A genial Dr. Harding smilingly confirmed their suspicions and forbade the journey to Rome.

"It's only three weeks on the way," Elizabeth rebelled. But Dr. Harding replied, "No. Longer than that by a good deal."

After he had gone Elizabeth said, "I *know* when this child was conceived, Robert, and it's perfectly all right to travel now."

Robert's face was set hard. "I don't think he can be wrong, Ba, and we mustn't take any risks."

So they sat together, disappointed but happy in each other, awaiting the birth of their baby. On the crimson velvet sofa in the splendid drawing room Elizabeth worked on her *Casa Guidi Windows.* Robert was writing in another room, since he could only work when alone and in absolute quiet. Sometimes he asked her opinion on alterations he had made for his proposed collected edition, but she never showed him her verses.

They saw hardly anyone. Anna Jameson and Geddie were back in Rome. Once Robert came in from an evening walk and said, "Ah-ha! I've been kissed since I last saw you." Elizabeth sprang to her feet crying joyously, "Henrietta's here!" But it was Father Prout, in Florence for an hour on his way to Rome, who had kissed him, to his horror, mouth to mouth in the street.

"Such a strange coarse man," Elizabeth mourned. "I can't believe he wrote that delicate poem, *The Bells of Shandon*." And Robert quoted,

"The bells of Shandon
That sound so grand on
The pleasant waters of the river Lee."

One morning Wilson came to Robert, twisting her hands in distress. "Madam's taking too much morphine again, sir. If you could do something?"

When Robert spoke to Elizabeth she objected. "Dr. Jago said that last time it did no harm at all."

"If there's the least little scintilla of doubt, then it must *stop*."

"You told me you'd never order me to do anything, Robert."

"You'll stop of your own accord. You can't want to murder all our babies with that poison, can you?"

"Very well. I don't agree, but I'll give it up. If I *must*."

Their dreamlike existence continued while outside their walls the world of the powerful shook and crashed. As 1848, that unforgettable year of destiny for Europe, dawned it brought more and more hope to those who worked to free Italy. January saw risings against the Austrians in Salerno and Naples. With February came revolution in Paris. The dynasty of the Bourbons fell for the last time, and the French King Louis Philippe departed for England to end his days as a quiet country gentleman. Independence was declared in Sicily. There were revolutions in the German states. In Vienna itself there was trouble, and the Emperor of Austria abdicated. In Florence Elizabeth's hopes soared for revolution in Italy.

The Grand Duke Leopold of Tuscany suffered torments, terrified of his masters at Vienna and mistrustful of the Florentines, who believed him liberal and might turn on him if he disillusioned them. In the end he granted them the constitution they demanded and they went mad with joy and love for him. One night Robert called Elizabeth to the window from her writing. Through the darkness below she saw what looked like a great mass of moving stars sweeping up the piazza. The people of Florence had recognized their Duke visiting the opera incognito and were bearing him home on their shoulders. The stars were hundreds of huge waxen torches, as large as trees. As they came up to the palace opposite the *vivas* were deafening. History was being made underneath the Casa Guidi's windows as she wrote her poem.

In early March there was an alarm. Elizabeth, drained of colour, announced that she had pains. The doctor came. He could do nothing. It was again a miscarriage.

This time Robert did not weep. But the strain for him was such that he came near to blaming her. "It's all those long, long letters you *would* write yesterday."

He looked at Wilson, standing silent. "Don't you think so, Wilson?" he demanded, but Wilson shook her head.

"Then, *what?*"

Wilson said nothing, but there was no need for her to speak.

While Elizabeth recovered from her miscarriage the trumpets of freedom sounded for Italy, and King Charles Albert of Sardinia marched forth at the head of his battalions. The Grand Duke Leopold of Tuscany made a stirring proclamation ("The Great Donkey is braying," Robert jibed) and sent off a contingent to join the King. The Florentines were quiet but hysterical with hope, and Elizabeth's heart beat with theirs. She celebrated with champagne when the King's troops defeated the Austrians and drove them back from Milan and Venice, and again as she and Robert watched crowds massing under their Casa Guidi windows, building a great bonfire outside the Pitti Palace and throwing on the blaze the wooden arms they had torn down from the Austrian Embassy. But Robert said, "I don't like this violence, Ba. All the English are going. Shall I take you home to England?"

"Oh, no, I'm not afraid," she answered proudly. "I want to see liberty burst like a flame over Italy It's a glorious time to be here."

Every morning when Robert went for the post and to read

the newspapers in the public newsroom Elizabeth called, "Bring me back news of a revolution!" Often he brought her news of several; but he reassured her sisters that if Florence were invaded by enemy troops they could reach Leghorn by train in a few hours and board a merchant vessel for England. Still, Elizabeth thought that Robert did not seem as happy as she was to stay, and at last he came out with it.

"I really believe all this excitement does you good, my little firebrand. I wouldn't suggest taking you away but for one thing. I think it's time I went home to see my mother. It's been two years since we left England, and we must go this year or she'll think I've quite forgotten her."

"There's no money."

There had been Dr. Harding's bill. The income from her shares in Papa's ships had been only a hundred pounds, half as much as usual. Worse still, they had been warned that it was likely to be even less in the future. Wilson was an expensive maid and cost sixteen pounds a year. Annunziata's wages were a strain now.

Enthusiastically Robert outlined the plan he had formed. If they took the Casa Guidi suite unfurnished, furnished it cheaply from secondhand shops and let it for ten pounds a month while they travelled, it would pay for their journey.

They concluded the business at once. Their landlord could not afford to lose tenants when so many apartments were empty because of the flight of the foreigners. For twenty-five guineas a year the palatial suite, the porter and a key to the Boboli Gardens were theirs.

Next day news came of the defeat of the Austrians, and all Florence was illuminated. To Robert's amusement even the Austrian Grand Duke's Pitti Palace was lit up, magically outlined against the sky by thousands of little oil lamps—the ancient *fiaccolata*.

Soon Elizabeth offered her own plan for saving money. "We can engage a manservant to cook for us, and save on the *trattoria* meals."

That was how Ferdinando came to them—small, fat, pompous and full of odious comparisons about his former employers, but efficient and punctual and a good chef at fricassées, bread-and-butter puddings and boiled apple dumplings. He promised them a "plum puddingo" for Christmas. His *tagliatelli* was superb, his ices better than those at the famous Doney's Café.

Ferdinando brought them news from the Florentines, and Wilson had surprised them all by producing a friend in the Civic Guard—the handsome six-foot-tall Signor Righi, resplendent in shining helmet and epaulettes—who brought news from the Palazzo Pitti. They were well informed.

All summer Robert was busy planning his visit to his mother and finding wonderful bargains in the secondhand shops. Furnishing wasn't so very cheap after all. It ate up as much money as Elizabeth had earned from her books in the past two years. But Robert was so happy, his dark face flushed with triumph at each find, that she could not begrudge it, and slowly the beautiful high rooms with their coved ceilings were filled with magnificent things.

There was one moment when all Count Guidi's luxurious furniture had been moved out and before anything had taken its place when Elizabeth felt as if Robert's mother had stripped her bare. But it was only for a moment. She left the furnishing to Robert, merely applauding as he brought home the tremendous bookcase carved with angels and cherubs and serpents which came from a convent; and the five paintings in massive dark frames he found in a grainshop and swore were a Cimabue, a Giottino, a Ghirlandaio, a Byzantine Virgin and Child, and a Giotto painted on linen; the mirror for the drawing room with a superb carved gilt frame which he bought from the French Chargé d'Affaires for five pounds; the enormous gilded bed for her bedroom and the dozens of black carved wooden chairs. When he had put up long mirrors and tapestries and hung his plaster cast of Keats's death mask, medallions of Carlyle and Tennyson and a pen-and-ink drawing of John Kenyon on the bright green-painted walls the drawing room looked like a room in a novel.

Robert asked her what she would like, but she could not think of anything. There was only one thing she wanted, and he could not give it to her. She had written to Henrietta asking for a picture of her father. When the courier arrived at their door with the parcel Robert watched her open it in silence. She hung the picture in her bedroom opposite her bed.

Robert bought her a green velvet sofa. They had eight sofas before he had finished, the rooms were so large. Last of all he furnished the balcony. Elizabeth had thought of festoons of vines and roses, but Robert decided on camellias and orange trees in pots.

That July in 1848 in Florence was so hot that Elizabeth lay all day on the sofa with her hair down and without a dress, shoes or stays, drinking fresh lemonade or eating Ferdinando's ices. Late in the month the dreadful news came that the Austrians had smashed the Italians at Custozza, the King of Sardinia was in full retreat, the Pope had fled in disguise from Rome and Tuscany was once again under Austria's heel. Elizabeth felt the cannon-shot like blows in her heart. Yet even in her disappointment, and in the heat, she was well.

"Your cheeks are round and rosy, and you are—dare I say it? —quite plump," Robert said.

She ran to one of his long gilded mirrors on the wall. Of course she was pregnant again. That ended all Robert's plans to go home that year. She could not travel in that state. They would have to take the baby to England next summer.

If there were a baby. Neither of them put the thought into words. But Robert's hopes for a living child flared again and with them a granite determination that this time there was to be no morphine.

Her suffering had begun, her lonely calvary. For, she told herself, Robert *could* not understand. How could he?

He controlled all her bottles and pillboxes and doled out her doses, making them smaller and smaller. When Elizabeth pleaded for more he held her to him until she fell silent, weeping from exhaustion. She had tried to give it up. It was only when the cramps came, and the drenching sweats, that she went to her secret store, furious with Robert for forcing her to deceive him —she who loved truth above everything. She could not tell him why she did it. It was not the physical torture; perhaps she could bear that. It was the degradation. Could love as fastidious as Robert's survive the sight of a woman in the throes of abandoning the drug?

So the day came that July when Elizabeth had used the last of her store and she said to herself, "Tomorrow there will be none." That was how she found herself in the Boboli Gardens that afternoon with Dr. Jago's prescription in her pocket, trying desperately to think of an excuse to shake off Wilson and Flush and escape to an apothecary's in the Via Tornabuoni across the Ponte Vecchio.

They had walked up to Giambologna's *Statue of Plenty,* into the Knight's Garden and on to the Falconing Lawn and were gazing down the stupendous avenue leading to the Island Piazzale. At last Elizabeth called to a Flush looking ridiculous because he had been shaved to rid him of the famous Florentine fleas, folded her parasol and summoned Wilson to sit beside her on a marble bench.

"And what does Signor Righi say about the situation?" she asked automatically.

Wilson plucked at her cotton gloves and stammered, "Signor Righi, ma'am? Oh, ma'am, I've something to say to you about Signor Righi." She was holding out a shiny red hand stripped of its glove. On the third finger was a pretty ring with three tiny pearls. She was telling Elizabeth that she and Signor Righi were going to be married, and saying, "I'll still go on working for you and Mr. Browning, madam."

Elizabeth's surprise even conquered the pain beating in her head. "But, Wilson, isn't Signor Righi a Catholic?" she asked.

"He's promised me I can do what I like about that, ma'am."

"Then I'm very happy for you, Wilson, and I'm sure Mr. Browning will be, too."

Suddenly the thought struck her that Wilson, of all people, had provided the miracle she needed. She pushed herself to her feet, saying, "Let us walk to the shops, and I'll buy you a betrothal present."

Elizabeth walked so briskly through the lemon grove that Wilson had to run after her, opening the parasol as she went and calling to Flush, who had fallen asleep under their bench. Elizabeth almost ran through the exit, into the sun-drenched Via Romana.

Elizabeth stood behind Wilson in the dark little shop. Wilson was choosing a leather sewing box, and could not decide whether it was to be scarlet or green.

"Take your time, Wilson. I'll be back directly."

Once outside Elizabeth ran across the street to the apothecary's and darted through the door. Trembling, she pulled Dr.

Jago's prescription from her pocket and held it out to the yawning young man behind the counter. He went into the back of the shop. It seemed a very long time before he returned with the little package. He handed it to her, and she paid for it and turned to leave.

There behind her was Wilson, her eyes on the packet. Had she suspected all along? Had Robert asked her to watch her? No, Robert was incapable of that!

Robert came to let them in, and Wilson went off to her quarters carrying her green sewing box.

Elizabeth kissed him and gave him the packet. "I bought this today, Robert, because I needed it. . . ." Then she handed him Dr. Jago's prescription. "You had better have this too. I'm not to be trusted. No, it's the truth. You cannot trust me and I cannot trust myself, no matter what I promise."

He took the slip of paper from her reluctantly. "Are you sure you want me to have this?"

"I *don't* want you to have it. But I must."

Then she broke down. When she was calmer he opened the packet and measured her a dose and watched her drink it. He put away the glass and took her hands.

"We won't give up, Ba, but we'll take it more slowly, and do it together."

"I want to explain why, Robert."

She told him how it would be, how it must be, if she gave it up entirely. She did not spare him any of the revolting details though she looked away as she spoke.

"Remember, Robert, that Dr. Jago says there's no need to stop, for the baby's sake or for mine."

"But it's not possible to be sure unless we give it up, my love."

"Well, now you know what it will be like."

He turned her to him. "But I knew that all along, Ba. I couldn't think why the symptoms were so long in coming."

Of course he had known. Twelve hours after the last dose, the uneasiness, the sense of weakness, the yawning, the shivering and the sweating, the hot watery discharge pouring from the eyes and inside the nose; twenty-four hours after the last dose the yawning grown so violent it threatened to dislocate the jaw, mucus flooding from the nose, tears streaming from eyes with dilated pupils, the skin clammy and covered with gooseflesh, the convulsive contractions of the intestines until the abdomen looked as if the muscles were knotted under it, the increasing cruel pain, the explosive vomiting of blood and bile, and the constant, the incessant purging; thirty-six hours after the last dose the icy chill which necessitated blanket upon blanket, the twitchings, the total lack of sleep, the complete inability to rest, the cramps, the screams of agony, the bedclothes drenched with sweat and filth, the rapid loss of weight and at last the quiet, deathly weakness frightening to the onlooker.

But he knew, too, that all would be over in ten days, the suffering wreck once more a normal human being ready to be restored to health with rest, good food and exercise. It was the only way, this brutal way.

"Trust me. Think of me as your doctor. It will be all right, my love. Nothing about you could ever repel me."

He put his arm about her shoulders and led her away.

In December, when Elizabeth was five months pregnant, Robert fell ill.

For some time he had seemed strung up and captious. He had grown waspish and had developed a twitch in his right eyelid. Then he had taken to his bed. For a month he had lain there refusing to get up or see the doctor.

It was the strain he had gone through with her, Elizabeth was sure. Those terrible nights and days had taken their toll of him. At the beginning he had not slept for a week. Only then had he given way to Wilson's pleas to take over for a few hours. Wilson sat and held Elizabeth's hands and massaged her and dabbed eau-de-cologne on her body. At the worst times she had held her while she screamed.

It was a pity that now Elizabeth was so well, eating and sleeping and going for walks, he should be struck down. There seemed to be nothing wrong with him except a sore throat and a high temperature. Perhaps, she wondered, he was disheartened at having written no poetry for six months.

As he lay in his room Robert was tormented by quite other problems.

Sarah Adams, sister of Eliza Flower, love of his youth, was

dead. The news had come from Richard Hengist Horne, who had sung sea-chanties at those enchanted evenings in the Flower home over twenty years ago.

Robert had never told Elizabeth of how he had gone from her to stand by the deathbed of Sarah's sister. Thin as a rail and racked with coughing, no longer the beautiful Eliza, she had held out her hand to him and he had taken it silently in a last farewell. When Eliza drew her last breath he was already on his way to Italy with Elizabeth. When Mr. Fox held her funeral service in that same South Place Chapel from which he had almost been expelled because of his love for her Robert and Elizabeth were as happy as runaway children in their first home in Pisa.

It was Horne who had written, too, to tell him about that service, where the organist had played Eliza's own music. When Mr. Fox rose the congregation stirred in expectation. There he had stood, struggling not to break down in the sight of everyone, and they had watched him, their breaths held, waiting to be rent by the famous orator in the most terrible moment of his life. No one could ever have called Fox handsome. Now he was sixty, his hair white, his eyes pouched and tired. He seemed broader and squatter than ever, his movements sluggish. It was said that he had heart trouble.

Suddenly he threw his arms out from his sides with a violent movement, and cried out one word in his harsh voice—*"God!"*

It was a long time before he went on. Then he made a brief address, very moving but very short, to the Almighty. "Not our will but Thine be done," he prayed. Through all he said his hearers heard only, echoing again and again that one angry cry, *"God!"* Horne had called it singularly effective. Perhaps there had been just a touch of the old artistry about it. Yet Fox had loved Eliza.

Soon, Horne wrote, Fox had given up the pulpit for politics. The very next year he had become Member of Parliament for Oldham, and gone back to his wife. Eliza's name was never mentioned between them.

All that had been painful enough. Then Robert had opened a newspaper to read that Sarah too had died. Horne's letter had followed soon after, to report a horrid raking up of all the correspondence anyone had ever written to her. Now that she was dead, where were all his letters to Eliza? He had seen Ba's face when they had spoken of Eliza Flower. It had only been a boy's love. Yet if those letters were published . . . It would kill her, his jealous and insecure darling.

He had written to Horne, telling him how Eliza had shown him the album into which she had copied all his poems and told him she had kept all his letters, and how he had not wanted to offend her but had meant to say something one day.

"Alas, the years have gone by, and Eliza has left us only her strange beautiful memory. And now comes poor Sarah's death, and who am I to deal with now? Do act for me, and try to rescue every scrap from the executors for me, Horne."

Then had come the most difficult part, for Horne and Ba had been friends for a very long time. Supposing Horne mentioned Robert's request to her, in all innocence?

"There, this is private, dear Horne, for the letters and so on are pure nonsense, written by a mere boy. I am simply nervous that some packet may be lost or given away, lie in unknown hands for a time, and then turn up to bother one's survivors and make them ashamed of one—and all for what? For having played at verses instead of cricket and trapball!"

But it was not of any descendants of his that he was thinking —not of the men and women who might grow from the child now big in Elizabeth's womb that December of 1848. It was of Elizabeth herself and the look on her face.

He had sat staring at the letter, hating to ask the favour of inquisitive little Horne, loathing himself for not being able to go to Elizabeth and tell her all he felt. At that moment he had heard her tap on the door and had found that he had shuffled the letter away swiftly as she came in. It was all damnable.

It was that night that the sore throat had come, and next morning he had not been able to rise from his bed.

Robert saw Elizabeth's distress at his refusal to see a doctor; but he knew that no doctor could cure him. Only let those letters of his be sent safe back to him to be put in the fire, and he would be well again.

When the knock came on the door Elizabeth answered it herself. Ferdinando was cooking, and Wilson was fetching the post. There on the threshold stood Father Prout. Behind him Wilson was climbing the stairs with the letters.

Father Prout listened while she described Robert's symptoms. "Nothing does him any good. He's absolutely wretched this morning."

"I'll soon have him on his feet again. Where's the kitchen?" He breezed his way in, calling for eggs and port. "I'll mix a potion, a jolly, jolly potion," he sang and, seizing a basin, broke four eggs into it, doused them liberally with port and beat them vigorously with one of her silver forks.

"I thought one should starve a fever?" Elizabeth ventured doubtfully; and Ferdinando raised eyes and hands to the ceiling behind Father Prout's dusty black back, muttering, "Oh, *Inglese! Inglese!* He goin' to kill the Signor Browning, this priest!"

"*Now* where's the patient?" Father Prout demanded. He swept through the door and made for Robert's room.

"Oh, Father, would you please hand him his post?" Elizabeth called after him. He took the letter and disappeared into the room. Within ten minutes he was out again, beaming. "He drank his potion and read his letter, and went off to sleep at once like a baby. He'll be better soon, you'll see."

That evening Robert was much better. He said nothing about the letter which Father Prout had brought in to him, and which, seeing Horne's writing on it, he had asked permission to read while he sipped his potion. All was well, Horne had said. Robert's letters had been recovered. Robert had smiled broadly at the old reprobate by his bed and downed the egg and port at a draught. In blessed relief he had fallen fast asleep. Let the old fellow take the credit.

By the end of December Elizabeth was past the sixth month of her pregnancy and the child was still with her. Robert and Wilson and the doctor were quietly optimistic. Elizabeth grew difficult and whimsical. She was impatient with Robert's slow making of their home and irritated with his determination not to spend before the money was earned. The dilatoriness of the Italians, who had undertaken to make white muslin curtains for her bedroom windows and the great gilded bed in preparation for the infant, sent her into little rages. Even the news that a production at Sadler's Wells of Robert's old failed play, *A Blot on the 'Scrutcheon,* had been a great success and would earn him something for each night it ran only made her fretful.

218

"How I wish I'd been there, sitting in a box, to see the author take his bow!"

"And I, Ba. But we've something better to do. And look, there are flowers about the house. White roses in December! It might be June."

"Forgive me, Robert. I'm weary. Three pregnancies in three years." She did not add, And I'm nearly forty-three, and not well, and have been through so much of late.

Wilson at least was happy all day, singing, looking forward to the *bambino,* and to marriage with her tall handsome *promesso sposo.* She seemed a different person, and almost pretty. Only Ferdinando clouded her days. "He thinks he knows everything, ma'am," she sniffed. "He's efficient—I'll grant him that—but he thinks he's perfect."

With January came revolution in Florence, and the Grand Duke Leopold fled to Gaeta, following the Pope.

"You're pleased, I suppose, Robert," Elizabeth said.

"I'm not pleased. I'm not surprised, that's all."

Strangers from Leghorn moved into the city, announcing that they were a republican party and that Florence was a republic. Not all Florentines welcomed them. Many longed to have their rich, kind oppressor back in the Pitti Palace, Grand Donkey or no, Austrian or no. But now it all seemed remote to Elizabeth, weighed down with child. She would never have believed that she could have witnessed the proclamation of a republic with so little enthusiasm. Besides she was sure it would not endure.

The last few English left in Florence packed their bags, ready for instant flight to the ships at Leghorn, and the British Plenipotentiary wrote threatening letters to the papers about the steps which would be taken if any of the subjects of Her Majesty Queen Victoria were insulted. But if they had wanted to go, Robert and Elizabeth could no longer do so. Elizabeth was in no condition to travel.

20

IN THE EARLY HOURS OF MARCH 9, 1849, THEIR child was born.

"It's a fine healthy boy," Dr. Harding announced to Robert. "I'll call you when your wife is ready to see you."

Light-headed and full of goodwill even to Miss Mitford, Robert wrote to that dragon on a tiny scrap of paper, a baby letter to announce the birth of a baby, male fruit of the marriage of which she disapproved. "Ba desires me to tell you that she gave birth at a quarter past two this morning to a fine strong boy with the voice of three—a fact we learned when he was about half born. Ba bore the twenty-one hours' pain without one cry or tear, as I know, for I held her hand whenever they would let me. Be joyful with her."

After Robert had signed he added an imaginary dramatic exchange between him and Flush to make the old lady laugh.

" 'And what message shall I send for you to Miss Mitford?' Here Flush, having licked his lips and made a sham swallow down his throat, says, 'Send her my love and be done with it! I could speak if I liked, but, you see, I am busy swallowing something and otherwise engaged.' "

To Ba's sisters Robert wrote in detail of the labour and of Wilson's goodness and Elizabeth's perfections. "How God has rewarded our dearest, most precious of creatures for her perfect goodness, patience and self-denial—and common sense. That resolution of leaving off the morphine, for instance. Is there one out of a thousand strong men who would have thrown himself on the mercy of an angel, as she did on me, who am quite another kind of being? For it was all my doing and against her judgment and Dr. Jago's."

At last he was summoned. As he entered the room Wilson touched his sleeve. "Miss Ba has refused to look at the babe, Mr. Browning, sir, until you can show him to her yourself."

He tore his eyes from those of the pale woman in the bed. Wilson led him across to the cradle by the window where his son lay. The Italian nurse followed, picked up the warm bundle and laid it in his arms. Robert looked down at the wizened red face, like an old man's, surmounted by a fuzz of soft dark hair, and was suffused by a surge of tenderness. He felt awkward and afraid of harming the infant, and they had to lead him, stumbling like a blind man, across the room to the bed. There he bent and held out the bundle to Elizabeth and saw her look at her child for the first time.

"Thank you, Ba," he whispered. "Thank you for my son."

Elizabeth hardly heard him. She was gazing at the creature in her arms as if she would never be able to look away again. "Wilson says his hands and fingers are wonderfully strong," she was murmuring, "and more delicate and beautiful than a boy's should be."

"How are *you*, Ba?" he asked, worshipping her.

"Look at him, Robert! Dr. Harding says he's fit to be a model for a Michelangelo angel!"

Now that he had seen his son, Robert could write to his mother. He went at once to do so, promising her a tuft of his soft fine hair and swearing that she would see him herself before long. He could not know that while he was writing and sealing his letter his mother lay gravely ill at her home in New Cross.

During the week that followed the child's birth life outside the windows of the Casa Guidi was noisy and tumultuous. The city was in a ferment. Shouts came up to them, now of *"Viva la Repubblica!"* and now of *"Viva Leopoldo!"* But when Robert went in to tell Elizabeth what was happening she would give him more news than he brought her.

"It's really a counterrevolution, this agitation for the return of the Grand Duke. And it's all because the men from Leghorn haven't paid their bills in the coffee shops. So Signor Righi says."

In fact the peasants were determined to have their Duke back, asking him only to promise to respect their constitution. He lay shivering in Gaeta, wondering whether an Austrian could trust the Florentines, renowned for treachery throughout the centuries.

Elizabeth could not feed her baby, and he bellowed until a wet nurse arrived, wearing her Tuscan nurse's costume, with its large rough straw hat with fluttering blue ribbons, white collar and muslin apron over a striped skirt. Then the baby fell to on her vast breast.

Elizabeth herself got out of bed at once, full of energy, and sat wearing coquettish little net caps made by Wilson, in blue and green, lilac and purple, on the front of her head, with her hair done up behind in a Grecian plait. With the morphine had always gone complete lack of interest in her appearance. Now she wore new dresses in the dark rich colours Robert loved, emerald and ruby and royal blue. He loved to look at her, so calm and fresh, with the baby in her lap, the picture of blissful motherhood.

The baby overate and had to be dieted. Robert chirruped at him and was overjoyed when he seized his nose. He boasted about the amount of hair on his head and his obvious intelligence. He sat by his crib, watching him sleep, and sang to him when he woke. He called him "Little Bacchus" because he was so rosy and round.

When they discovered that the wet nurse was trying to feed two babies at once they discharged her on the spot. Anguished hours of fear for a baby starving to death were only ended when a kind young mother living above them offered to feed him until a wet nurse could be brought from the country. The nurse arrived, and her milk dried up. A fourth *balia* had to be found hurriedly. She came, an enormous young woman with three chins and fat cheeks, so stupid she could not count, even on her fingers. But she had milk, fountains of it.

For weeks, racked by these devastating blows, Robert and Elizabeth had hardly a thought to spare for what was going on in Italy. Yet during that month of March the King of Sardinia had rallied his troops after the disaster at Custozza of the previous July, and had thrown everything against the enemy, only to be overwhelmingly defeated at Novara. The brokenhearted King had abdicated on the field of battle in favour of his son Victor Emmanuel. It was absolute cataclysmic disaster.

Congratulatory letters came from Henrietta and Arabel and Treppy. Only the letter from Robert's mother did not come. Instead, at last, came a careful one from Sarianna. Robert's mother had been taken ill with an ossification of the heart. There had been no warning. She was unconscious. Sarianna was keeping his letters and the curl of hair from the baby's head to show her later. She rejoiced at the birth of his son.

Robert's first instinct was to set out at once for England. Only a few months before, when Horne had written to ask him delicately whether the lady of the name of Browning whose death he had read of in the obituary columns was a relation of his, he had replied almost brutally. "The notice was only the death of my father's stepmother, thank God."

Florence, he had added, was only some ten days' and nights' journey from London. If there were ever any real need, like the merest hint of his mother's being ill, Horne might be sure that he would leave at a day's notice to hasten to her side. (It had been in the same letter in which Robert had asked him to try to recover his letters to Eliza Flower.)

Now here was more than a hint. But how could he leave Ba, newly delivered of his child? Besides, Sis had said that he must not do so on any account.

Sarianna's second letter came soon after her first. His mother was much worse. "I'll send you a telegraph message if you're needed," she promised.

Then the third letter came. Sarianna confessed that she had been trying to break the news gently to him. Their mother had been already dead when her first letter had been written.

At first Robert's grief was silent, stony. Elizabeth was frightened. She wrote to Sarianna how worried she was. "His only consolation would be if you and his father could come to him at once. Can you?"

Of course they could not. Mr. Browning had to earn his living at the bank. He was in a dreadful state of breakdown, Sarianna said, and could hardly summon the strength to go out each morning. He wept continually, and cried out that he could not live without his wife. Sarianna had to look after him like a child.

Robert broke silence at last. He blamed himself day and

night for those three years during which he had not once gone home.

"Let us go home now, Robert. You can comfort your father and Sarianna. The babe will bring joy into their lives."

"No!" he cried, as if she had suggested something obscene. "England is terrible to me now. It would break my heart to see her roses over the wall and the place where she used to put down her scissors and her gloves."

She was gentle with him, waiting for his grief to pass.

In April dreadful news came. On the twenty-fifth General Oudinot had landed at Civitavecchia with eight thousand men. With terrible irony he had been sent by Louis Napoleon in the name of the French Republic to obliterate all hope of republican freedom in Rome. The shock to the Italians was stunning.

Outside in Florence shooting broke out between the republicans and the Grand Duke's partisans. One day Robert ran into trouble coming home from the post office. He had to dodge into doorways to avoid the flying bullets and run through an alleyway to get home. The baby in the cradle stirred in his sleep. Noisy *festas,* shouts, the firing of guns and cannon—there was always something. Elizabeth had grown almost *blasée.*

At the beginning of May the Grand Duke finally decided to accept the invitation from his loving subjects to return to Florence. But he came wearing an Austrian uniform, and supported by Austrian bayonets.

That day Elizabeth and the wet nurse were sewing, with the baby sleeping in his cradle between them, when they heard the sound of clattering hooves. Elizabeth looked up eagerly, hope dawning, and the nurse ran to a window. Then the nurse cried out in dismay, *"Signora, signora, ecco i Tedeschi!* Madam, madam, it's the Austrians!"

"Don't wake the child!" Elizabeth warned. She joined the nurse at the windows to stare down at the Austrian soldiers. There must have been at least ten thousand of them, come to reinstate with their bayonets the man who had fled the revolution. Up the street they marched, close under their windows. The artillery and baggage wagons came by, with dusty soldiers sitting motionless on the cannon. The people on the streets shrank back in dead silence to let the hateful procession go by. The windows were crowded with faces, but not a sound came from them. The sight shocked Elizabeth like a blow and at that instant all her love for Italy and her hatred for the Austrians was reawakened tenfold. Silently she vowed the sleeping child to the country of his birth. He would be, she swore, an Italian, as graceful, as quick-witted, as beautiful and as charming as the proud people about him.

That evening she told Robert of what she had seen and of her vow, talking on against his heavy silence. After a time she said, "Are you listening, Robert?"

Robert was not listening. He was wrapped in his terrible grief. It seemed to grow worse, not better, and its manifestations were wounding to her.

She tried to understand. Perhaps it was because Robert had been spared the pain of bereavement until then. He seemed to feel a sense of self-horror because they had been so happy while his mother had been dying and because that close bond he had claimed between him and her had not brought any foreboding of her death.

Now, unbelievably, he shrank from the sight of his new-born son. He seemed almost to be blaming him. Elizabeth lay awake all one night, dreading the thought that Robert might never draw near her or her child again, wondering what she could do. Next day she sat on his knee and put her arms about his neck. He did not flinch, but it was not as it had been.

"Let us call the baby after your mother, Robert," she said. "Sarah? For a boy?"

"Wiedemann. Her maiden name."

He looked a little grateful and kissed her hands, but formally.

"He must be Robert, for you, as we planned, as his first name," Elizabeth pursued. "But let the next one be Wiedemann. And we'll call him that."

He considered it and nodded.

Papa, too, must be remembered, Elizabeth thought. The name Barrett, if not Edward, for him and Bro, must be commemorated. There would be time to say so later. Meanwhile Robert seemed a little happier for her gesture.

Yet his grief did not lighten. Month after month went by, and he hardly ate or slept. He grew pale and thin. If she left him alone for a little when she came back she found him with wet cheeks or with his head in his hands. He had always had three letters for every one of hers from England, and now he felt the absence of his mother's notes. When there was a letter from Sarianna or his father he was depressed for a whole day afterwards. He did not come to her bed, even to hold her in his arms.

She begged him to return to their life, holding their baby out to him. He did not even try. He said, "I can't help it. I'll never again feel as I used to."

By the end of July Robert began to look so worn and changed that panic overtook her. He must be persuaded to take a holiday. It was all she could think of.

"I don't want to," he said apathetically.

"Well, *I* need a change. The heat suffocates me."

"If it's for your sake . . ." He shrugged.

Elizabeth decided that they would go to the Baths of Lucca, where all Florence went sooner or later for the cool air. They rented a house until the end of October and left with Wilson, Ferdinando, the *balia* and the baby.

Their house was like an eagle's nest, the highest house in the highest of three villages in the heart of the mountains, beside a rushing mountain stream. The garden was full of pink oleanders. A few English people still clung on at the resort, but they avoided them. They did not go to hear lectures on Shakespeare or to the weekly balls at the casino.

Elizabeth insisted on Robert's walking in the woods and mountains with her every day and sitting by the waterfalls on starry nights. They never met anyone except a monk with a rope girdle, or a barefoot peasant. There was silence under the green shade of the chestnut forests except for the rushing of the river or the chirping of the cicadas. At night the fireflies were so thick they seemed to be living among the stars.

To Elizabeth the silence was full of joy and consolation. Not to Robert. He wrote to his sister, stubbornly, "Neither this place nor any other could do me any good. I'm tired of opening my eyes on the world now."

He watched his son kicking and crowing in bathwater whitened with bran to soften it and confessed to Sarianna that it meant nothing to him at all. "Everybody seems to think him remarkably flourishing. All of which ought to be unmixed pleasure to me, but is very far from it."

Elizabeth was well and vigorous. She walked for several hours at a time, climbed hills, explored the forests. Robert needed to work, and in these surroundings surely poetry must flow. He was still doing no work at all. In the three years since they had come to Italy he had written nothing new. Now he was not even working on his collected edition.

It was almost in desperation that Elizabeth took him on the expedition to the Prato Fiorito, the mountain famous for its beauty.

They set off at half-past eight in the morning with three guides. The women rode on donkeys, the men on mountain ponies. The baby came too, riding in turns with Wilson and the *balia*. There was no road. They climbed up steep slopes and down precipitous ones, even the donkeys stumbling and slipping. At some points one false move could have thrown horse and rider into a deep ravine. Sometimes they had to dismount and walk down.

When they reached the top they looked round on a world of mountain tops with the sea faint and far beyond them. They were alone except for a shepherd and his sheep and a goat or two. They turned the donkeys and the ponies loose to graze with them. Then they sat down, all eight of them, to picnic on cold pigeon pie and ham and a tart and lemonade. The *balia* suckled the baby at a discreet distance and then came to eat. Elizabeth spread her shawl and the *balia* put the baby on it. He rolled over and over, chuckling.

Elizabeth asked, her eyes pleading with Robert, "Could there be anything more beautiful? Aren't you glad we came? Aren't you happy?"

When they were back in their house she was not even tired or stiff, and the baby was still laughing and talking to himself though his delicate skin had caught the sun.

"Wasn't it daring of us to take the baby, Robert? Think of it. He never cried once all through the five hours' ride, three of them on donkeyback." He looked at the baby and at her, marvelling again at how she could do anything she wanted.

At last she fell silent, in despair. She could not shake him out of his brooding. She slept uneasily that night and dreamed horribly. She woke with a feeling of fear and oppression to their third wedding anniversary, September 12, 1849. After breakfast Wilson brought in the baby. He was six months and three days old that day.

Wilson had put a cap trimmed with pink ribbons on his head, and at sight of him Elizabeth laughed, thinking they matched his pink sunburned button of a nose. In one fist he was clutching a rose, and Wilson stretched out his arm so that his mother could take it from him. Then Wilson gave him another one to offer his father. The baby smiled happily, then cried to have them back.

Elizabeth took the baby in her arms and covered him with kisses, murmuring, *"Amore mio, mio caro, carissimo,"* into his fat neck until he gurgled. She almost dropped him as Robert turned on her sharply.

"I wish you wouldn't talk to him in Italian. I want my son to be an Englishman."

He had never spoken to her in that tone before. Dreadfully hurt, she answered, "The *balia* talks to him from morning till night in Italian, and even Wilson speaks Italian now to him, so he hears nothing else all day. It'll only do harm if we confuse him with another language. I heard of a little boy who stood stock-still between the two and couldn't get on with either."

"I shall hate it if he doesn't speak English," Robert persisted.

"Well, aren't we going to England next year? He'll learn English then, naturally."

Robert went over to the window. "I'm sorry. It annoyed me."

It was a dull day. The skies were leaden, and the rain was coming down in sheets. Elizabeth passed her hands over her eyes, suddenly feeling much older than her forty-three years, and as ill and tired as she had been before she had met Robert. Looking at him she thought that he too looked weary and much older than thirty-seven, and her heart was full of pity for him.

During the night she had made up her mind to speak out and try to make him face what he was doing to her by giving way to his depression. Their wedding anniversary was a good day for it perhaps.

"Robert," she said, with her heart thudding, "I blame myself for keeping you away from your mother for all these years."

"No, how can you?" he answered swiftly and generously. "You never wanted to marry me, did you, and come to Italy? It was all my doing."

"I should have made you go back. It was because of me that you never saw her again."

"Don't talk like that, Ba." His voice dragged but he was not shutting her out.

She called to him desperately, trying to keep him from going away from her again. "You must do something for her. It will bring you closer."

"Do you think I haven't thought of that? For three months I've been thinking of little else. But there's nothing I can do for her now. Nothing."

She clenched her hands in her nervousness, forgetting the rose she still held, and drove a thorn into her palm. Ignoring it, she went on. "A poem, Robert? In her memory? You would be giving her the best of yourself then."

His face was thunderous. "No—never. What a vulgarity, to give my sorrow to the world to snuffle over!"

She should have known. He had refused even to compose an epitaph for his mother's tombstone when his sister had asked it.

He turned and saw the hurt on her face. He was shocked out of himself into thinking of her. "I only meant that *I* couldn't do it, Ba. Some people may be able to speak out of their hearts and not debase their love—*you* might, I think, Ba—but I never could." He turned back to stare out of the window again at the tall mimosa tree under the downpour.

Now was the moment. She would lose him forever, or not. It must be done. She came up behind him and slid something into the pocket of his coat.

"Did you know I once wrote some poems to you, Robert? There they are, if you care to see them. No one else ever has."

He opened the little white book. In it there were forty-four sonnets, all written out in her tiny meticulous hand.

"Read the last one first," she said, and left the room.

The last sonnet began: "Belovèd, thou hast brought me many flowers . . ." It had been written in Wimpole Street during their courtship days. In it she offered him her poems as he had offered her his flowers.

So, in the like name of that love of ours,
Take back these thoughts which here unfolded too,
And which on warm and cold days I withdrew
From my heart's ground.

"Take back these thoughts." Those thoughts of love which she had thought in that terrible room, when he had come to her crying aloud of his love four years ago, and she had met it in silence, in shyness or in tears. Those thoughts which she had woven into poems during those magical sixteen months, and kept all these years to show him one day when the time was right.

It was he who had made her love him and give her whole self to him. He turned over the pages and stopped to read again.

How do I love thee? Let me count the ways.
I love thee to the depth and breadth and height
My soul can reach, when feeling out of sight
For the ends of being and ideal grace.
I love thee to the level of every day's
Most quiet need, by sun and candlelight.
I love thee freely, as men strive for right;
I love thee purely, as they turn from praise.
I love thee with the passion put to use
In my old griefs, and with my childhood's faith.
I love thee with a love I seemed to lose
With my lost saints—I love thee with the breath,
Smiles, tears, of all my life! And, if God choose,
I shall but love thee better after death.

Shame washed over him. He turned back to the beginning of the little book and, reading, found his way blindly to a chair. Two hours passed. Now and then he rested the book on his knee and dreamed before lifting it again.

Elizabeth did not return, and it was not until he had finished that he went to find her. When he took her in his arms she knew that he had come back to her. His eyes were clear and his lips were warm on hers.

" 'Not Death—but Love!' " she whispered.

"What was that?"

"Nothing, my love."

At the end of the month Elizabeth was able to write to Henrietta without a shadow on her spirits.

"Since our marriage we have lost some precious things—he his adored mother, and I some faith in loved ones whom I had counted on for my whole life long. But you may thank God for us that we have lost none of our love, none of our belief in one another. Indeed there is more love between us two at this moment than there ever has been—he is surer of me, I am surer of him; I am closer to him, and he to me. We live heart to heart all day long and every day the same."

21

NO SOONER WERE THEY BACK IN FLORENCE THAT
November than inspiration flowed for Robert. No longer was he
merely working over old verses for his collected edition. He was
writing a long poem in two parts, born of the conflict between
his grief for his mother and his longing to return to joy in life.
"How hard it is to be a Christian!" he cried in it again and again,
still repelled by his mother's narrow chapel religion yet yearning
to believe as she had done and to have faith in an afterlife where
he and she might meet again. As his sense of loss dimmed and
his old lust for life returned he was driven to try to hammer out
the truth about his real religious beliefs.

So Robert stood at his high desk in the small blue, stone-
flagged room he kept for himself, forging his *Christmas Eve and
Easter Day* in the furnace of his doubt. Elizabeth sat at her own
Pembroke table with turned legs on solid feet and a red leather
top which Robert had bought for her, underneath the glass and
gilt chandelier, choosing poems from her 1838 and 1844 collections, and from a heap of others published since then in periodicals, for her new edition. For hour after hour she worked,
patiently substituting modern words for antique affectations—
there would be no more words like *chrism* or *arointed*, no *ekes*
and *e'ens, ersts* and *enows*—and putting involved lines into clear
English. Her *Casa Guidi Windows* had gone off to London, and
such work was a pleasant change from creation.

Under this tranquil surface there was a new turbulence to

their lives. For the first time in eleven years Elizabeth had had a long period without morphine, sixteen months in all. With its cessation had come such a surging of physical passion as would have embarrassed her if Robert had not responded so ardently and gratefully. Both he and she had relished their hot love before. But now for the first time Elizabeth knew what a man's passion could really be, and a woman's. More, she knew to what she owed these new joys.

She remembered those exquisite shuddering transports, those climaxes of excruciating ecstasy, which she had undergone at the crisis of her sufferings when the drug had been withdrawn, and knew that some at least of her need for opium had been to quench those other deep desires she had hardly known existed in her deprived spinster's body. That euphoria, that golden fire running along the veins, she acknowledged, was as near as a pure woman could come to experiencing the sexual love of a man. Now in Robert's arms she found all the ecstasy, and more, that opium had brought, night after night. Their thirst for each other seemed insatiable.

Suddenly, in the spring of the new year 1850, while they were still copying out their poems for their publishers, Chapman and Hall, they found that the world was beating on their door. They fought against it, but it was a losing battle. When the Austrians had reestablished order the members of the English colony who had lain low during the troubles or had filtered back from abroad began to entertain again. An item in Father Prout's gossip columns had revealed that the famous Elizabeth Barrett Browning was living in Florence, and everyone wanted to meet her.

Mrs. Trollope, grandest of the Florence hostesses, already author of over a hundred novels and mother of two novelist sons —successful Thomas Adolphus in Florence and unsuccessful mole-like Anthony working at the Post Office in England—left her card and called again. Swearing and scowling, Robert took Elizabeth, on the day his poem was posted, to the Villino Trollope for a soirée.

A triumphant Mrs. Trollope introduced them to the other guests. First to her son Tom, who was bald, heavy-bearded, bespectacled and very deaf; then to a sleek, tiny woman with straight blue-black hair—the mysterious Miss Isa Blagden, who was said to be the illegitimate daughter of a rich Englishman and a high-caste Indian. "Dearest Isa," as she was always called, lived in the Villa Bricchieri on Bellosguardo, entertained everyone, nursed everyone and was loved by everyone. A charming, effete-looking young attaché from the British Legation called Robert Lytton gazed adoringly at the fine-boned little creature as delicate as an idol. Elizabeth and she loved each other at once, and chatted happily while Robert made friends with an American of thirty called Story, with a tawny beard and a curly mane. Story had abandoned a successful career as a lawyer in Boston to become a sculptor in Italy. Robert and he found they had every passion in common—versification, art, music, the theater, beloved wives—except cigars. Robert did not smoke.

Robert left William Story's side reluctantly even to meet the huge shaggy author of the world-famous novel *Vanity Fair,* Thackeray, and Alfred Tennyson's eccentric brother Frederick. But he liked Thackeray, and Tennyson even more when he found that the morose, odd-looking fellow hired whole orchestras to play to him alone in his villa. Everyone there was artistic or literary. Robert Lytton wrote poetry as "Owen Meredith." Even Dearest Isa had written one or two ladylike novels.

Expecting an affected and difficult genius, everyone was relieved and enchanted by Elizabeth's shyness and gentleness, and Robert's exuberance and good looks won all hearts. When Robert and Elizabeth walked home at last they knew that now they had friends, and were not sorry for it. No longer would they be alone together in their love. The petals of their tight-shut private life were opening under the warmth of their welcome. Their son would have a playmate, too, for the young Storys had a little girl called Edith who was also a year old.

It was April, a month later, and Elizabeth was about to wrap up her own poems for posting, when Robert said, "Ba, I hope you're going to put in your love sonnets. You can't deny them to the world."

"Everybody would know they were about you and me, Robert. Could you bear that?"

"No. But there must be a way." He thought, and said, "I've thought of one."

234

He led her across to the bookshelves and ran her finger across the gold lettering on a calf-bound volume.

"Pope's '*Odyssey*'?" she questioned, puzzled.

"Pope's *translation* from Homer's '*Odyssey*.'" Then, "Aren't you my little Portuguese?"

"My little Portuguese"—the love name he had given her because of the Portuguese girl who had loved a poet in her *Catarina to Camoens*. He used to recite it in company when he was away from her in those London days. As he saw memory dawn he said, "Let us call them *Sonnets from the Portuguese*. It's the absolute truth, yet our secret will be safe."

She leaned against him and laughed her high, light laugh. Joyful, he threw back his head and laughed his own great noisy laugh. They clung together like children excited by their secret.

Yet when their laughter was over and Robert turned to put the book back on the shelf his face was grave, and he sighed. He was happy that her poems should be given to the world and that it was he who had found the way. Yet it was a strange heavy crown, that wreath of sonnets she had put on him that morning when he had least expected it. He might never be famous as a poet himself, but now he knew beyond doubt that his name would be immortal, because she had loved him and had written of it in verse which could never die. To be known forever not as a poet but merely as the overpraised lover of a poet—that might prove a crown of thorns. He had placed it on his own head, but could he bear it? He must and with grace. She must never know what it cost him. If that day ever came.

The day after that everything seemed to happen at once.

Wilson was only just dressing Elizabeth's hair when Robert returned from the post and gave her Henrietta's letter. A moment later she ran into the drawing room, still in her negligée, in great excitement.

"Robert, Henrietta's married. She went to Papa herself, the brave thing, and asked for his formal consent. And do you know what he said, Robert? He said, 'You must either give up this engagement at once or leave this house!' And Henrietta said, "But, Papa, we've loved each other for five years, and I'm no longer a girl who doesn't know her mind, and Surtees can support

235

me, so why can't I marry him?' And Papa said, 'You heard what I said.' So Henrietta fled to Surtees's family and married him!"

"Well, that's a happy ending," Robert said, then interrupted himself. "By God, Ba, listen to this!"

He had continued to leaf idly through their new copy of the *Athenaeum,* most august of literary journals, which had arrived by the same post, as Elizabeth chattered on. "Ba," he continued, "Wordsworth's dead, and here's an article about who's to be the next Poet Laureate."

"How can *that* matter as compared to Henrietta's—" she began, but stopped before his serious eyes.

" 'To grant the laureateship to a woman,' " he read aloud, " 'would be an honourable tribute to her, a fitting recognition of the remarkable place the women of England have taken in the literature of the day, and a graceful compliment to the Sovereign herself. There is no living poet of either sex who can prefer a higher claim than Mrs. Elizabeth Barrett Browning.' "

Elizabeth's head reeled. She, a woman, to be crowned poet of poets, granted a pension and asked nothing of in return but the composition of an occasional poem for great occasions? Her face was flushed and her smile radiant. Even Henrietta was forgotten for a moment.

Then her smile faded. A sliver of ice had pierced her heart. It was Robert, as she had always said, who should be Laureate. She looked at him in fear. How could he, a man, and ambitious for the greatest heights in poetry, bear this?

"You deserve it, by God," he was crying, striding up and down, "and I'd like you to have it. Shall I ask John Kenyon and Dicky Monckton-Milnes to put in a word where it'll do most good?"

"No, no! I don't want it, and in any case I'm not likely to get it. It's only Miss Mitford's friend, the editor, wanting to pay me a compliment which can't be taken seriously."

Robert stared at her in disbelief. Ba *had* been pleased—delighted.

"Forget that nonsense," Elizabeth rushed on. "What I do want is to give a dinner party to celebrate Henrietta's marriage tonight. Yes, tonight, Robert. Please."

So Ferdinando was told, and Wilson was sent round with invitations to nine of their new friends—Mrs. Trollope and her son Tom and his wife Theodosia, William and Emelyn Story, Frederick Tennyson and his Italian wife Maria, Dearest Isa and young Robert Lytton. When at six o'clock Father Prout knocked unexpectedly at their door he was asked to make up the round dozen and partner old Mrs. Trollope.

It was all in order to divert Robert's mind from the wretched article. Unhappily literary Florence also took the *Athenaeum* and read it at once. Their guests entered the Casa Guidi congratulating Elizabeth as if she were already crowned and talked of nothing else all through dinner. At the end Father Prout rose and bibulously proposed a toast.

"To Robert Browning," he announced, "the poet who was brave enough to marry a poet—" He stumbled, and Elizabeth waited, her heart cold, for the words he had used at their first meeting in Leghorn. Worse was to come. Instead of "more famous than himself" Father Prout finished, "and a better one than himself."

Robert met Elizabeth's eyes calmly, almost gaily. He rose and replied gracefully and generously, praising her, speaking of his pride in her, and his happiness that she should be so far his superior in poetry as in all things.

Still she wondered if he could bear it. Was this truth or a fierce pride or his perfect manners? He would hate her for it; he must. It was cruel.

The disastrous evening ended at last, and the door shut even behind the lingering Father Prout. Elizabeth fled to the bedroom. When Robert opened the door he found the room in darkness. Not a candle burned and the curtains were drawn. As he tried to feel his way blindly with outstretched arms an Elizabeth naked except for her locket slipped between them and wound imploring arms about his neck.

"My moon maiden," he whispered, his hands enmeshed in the net of her hair, and she knew that all her fears were groundless.

Ferdinando smiled in the darkness of his own room as he heard Elizabeth's cry. *Per Bacco,* the signor was a man, even if he did spend too many daytime hours with his wife, and the signora was evidently passionate.

In the darkness, too, Wilson heard and wept. Her guardsman, Signor Righi, had not written to her at the Bagni di Lucca or visited her since her return to Florence. Now, when she too knew at last what it was to be loved by a hot-blooded man, she had lost him.

Towards the end of the year Robert's book, *Christmas Eve and Easter Day,* was published. The reviews were poor, and the reviewers even seemed divided as to what it was about. One called it "the most Christian poem of the century," but another damned it as "the sophisticated work of an atheist." Only two hundred copies were sold.

Two months later Elizabeth's *Casa Guidi Windows* came out and had a worse reception. The critics were not interested in Italy's war for freedom, or in Pio Nono or the Grand Duke in Florence; but they were angry that an Englishwoman should dare to criticize her country for not helping Italy. They advised her to stick to writing romantic lyrics. Robert was astounded at how calmly Elizabeth took their sneers. The poem had meant so much to her. Of course her collected edition had come out at the same time and was selling wonderfully well, though not a critic had mentioned the *Sonnets from the Portuguese.* "I can't believe it, Ba," he marvelled. "They're a bunch of donkeys."

They comforted each other, but with all their work done and published they were at a loose end. They longed to travel, but still there never seemed to be enough money. Mr. Kenyon insisted on making a gift of a hundred pounds a year to the baby, but it was quickly spent—on the *balia,* on baby clothes, on doctors' bills. Mr. Kenyon offered to pay for a tour for them, too, but Robert was adamant in refusal. "Never. The baby's one thing; it's his good fortune. But we'll manage by ourselves."

Then Dearest Isa brought them news of a good tenant who would pay a high rent for the Casa Guidi apartment, take care of their precious furniture and carpets and employ Ferdinando and Annunziata. Their problems were solved. They could leave in April of the new year 1851.

The last few months sped by. Long before the end of April they were packed and ready for their dreamed-of tour of northern Italy and Switzerland on their way to England. Wilson was to look after the two-year-old Wiedemann and, of course, Flush was coming.

The only drawback was that they had to leave before knowing how much ship money they could count on. It seemed to be less every year. Still, there was bound to be enough, Elizabeth assured Robert when he worried about it, and they would hear from the shipping agents at Venice or, at worst, at Lucerne.

Every night Robert and Elizabeth left Penini—as Wiedemann called himself now—asleep in their splendid rooms of their palazzo on the Grand Canal in Venice and went to the Piazza San Marco, to walk among the crowds of well-dressed people and children under the bright gas lamps. Robert listened to the musicians still playing that toccata of Galuppi's he loved as if they had never stopped since he had last been there eighteen years before. It ran across his nerve ends like a small, sweet torment, bringing again the same thoughts, the same grief for a Venice long dead, gone with all its beautiful gay women.

> As for Venice and its people, merely born to bloom and drop,
> Here on earth they bore their fruitage, mirth and folly
>   were the crop;
> What of soul was left, I wonder, when the kissing had to stop?
> "Dust and ashes!" So you creak it, and I want the heart to scold.
> Dear dead women, with such hair, too—what's become of all
>   the gold
> Used to hang and brush their bosoms? I feel chilly and grown
>   old.

Elizabeth ate vanilla ice creams and gazed unself-consciously about her, trying to guess which of her neighbours were the famous singers, actors or ex-kings who were there incognito. She seemed to bathe herself in the moonlight and the sunlight and the silences and the music of Venice. She loved the silver water by day and the inky water by night. She lived lazily, never going to see the churches or the pictures. She did not even go into the Accademia to look at the paintings of the great Venetian masters. Only once, idly, did she stroll into the Basilica of San Marco. Robert had never seen her so relaxed. She did not even write to her sisters.

Once they went to the Lido and came back in a gondola, having drunk too much wine. There were stars above their heads, and the gondolier sang in a throbbing baritone. They lay in the bottom of the gondola on the seat cushions, their arms about each other, watching the gondolier's rhythmic strokes as the prow cut through the treacly black water.

"Let's live here forever, Robert."

"Would you really give up Florence for Venice, Ba?"

"Yes. Venice is magical—sublime."

Robert smiled in the darkness. Ba, so fastidious in choosing the right word in poetry, had only two with which to express her ecstasy before art and architecture and the wonders of nature —*divine* and *sublime*. He would never tell her so—just as she would not correct the sweet baby errors of her child. It made him feel very tender towards her.

They were very late, and Wilson met them at the door, clutching a brown flannelette wrapper about her, her eyes under her nightcap red and swollen. "I was that frightened, sir, madam, as the time went by. I was sure you'd been drowned or stabbed. And then what would I have done?"

What, indeed, alone in Venice with a baby and a dog, and no money and very little Italian? Elizabeth sent her to bed. Watching Robert wolf the croissants and milk Wilson had left out, she said dreamily, "I'd forgotten I had a child."

So had he. In the gondola he had been again the young man of twenty-one of all those years ago who had listened to the toccata of Galuppi's in Venice. Suddenly with Wilson's face had come reality, and he had felt like a blow what it was to be a man married for five years with a child and responsibilities. This was what James Silverthorne had meant. And yet—

He saw Elizabeth struggling with the pins in her hair and shaking it down about her shoulders. Wilson had turned back the bed. "I'm not as tired as I thought. Come, Ba."

Next day Robert vomited after breakfast. The day after it was Wilson's turn. They both continued to feel queasy. It occurred to Elizabeth that the climate which suited her and her son to perfection was upsetting Robert and Wilson. She hoped she was wrong.

A month went by before she brought herself to accept it. It was one morning in Saint Mark's Square at the end of May.

They had walked to the Bridge of Sighs, and they were sitting in the sun in the miraculously clear morning light, waiting for the pigeons to be fed. On the stroke of the hour the Moors would come out of the clock tower to sound their big bell, and the maize would be scattered for the thousands of birds. During this Ascension week there was a special treat for Penini.

Elizabeth had made him wear a lace cap under his hat. Suddenly, as he darted after a strutting pigeon, Robert burst out: "I don't like that lace cap. It makes him look like a girl."

Taken aback, Elizabeth glanced at Penini, then back at Robert.

"People are always asking whether he's a boy or a girl," Robert went on. "It's all because of those damned lace caps and those ribbons you dress him in. I want my son to be a boy."

That stung her.

"That's because you're a man."

"Of course it is—and because he's a boy."

"The arrogance of men. *I* want him to be a baby as long as possible."

"It's not good for him."

"What's good? Is it good for him to force him into being something he isn't? The truth is, the child isn't *like* a boy, naturally. If you put him into a coat and waistcoat now he'll look ridiculous, like a little angel in a man's clothes." She spoke so passionately that he glanced about him in case anyone was listening.

"That's no reason to make him look like a girl," Robert persisted.

"He doesn't look like a girl. He looks like what he is—a strange, delicate creature, an elf with a scarlet rose leaf on each cheek. A fairy king of a child, born of a lily and a rose."

Robert grunted. Already he was ashamed of his outburst and yet not sorry he had spoken out. He hated the golden curls, the velvet dresses, the embroidered petticoats, the lace caps and collars and all the ribbons.

All the same, he had an uncomfortable feeling that there was something in what Elizabeth said. Penini was a strange child. He was such a small creature, healthy but not at all robust like Henrietta's boy, Altham, from all reports. In the past year he had lost all his baby flesh and turned into a frail thin child.

Yet again Penini seemed to have all the instincts of a normal boy. He was noisy, heaven knew. Robert had given him a toy gun, to Ba's horror, and he shot it off day and night, maddening everyone within earshot and shouting "Papa!" with every report.

241

Then, there had been that day when Robert had been playing a delicate piece of Chopin's, and there had been such a damnable din at the door he had stopped. In had come Penini and his mother, with Ba protesting, "How *could* you stop playing when Penini's brought three drums to accompany you with?"

They had all spoiled him. Robert, too. The day after his birth Robert had said, "I feel I could give my life for him already." Ba never let him forget that. What she didn't realize was that the child irritated him sometimes beyond bearing.

It wasn't only the fact that he screamed whenever he was refused anything, or even the clothes. There were other things Robert had noticed for the first time during the trip to Venice. There was the affected way in which he rolled his eyes whenever he saw anything he thought beautiful, and called out *"Lolli!"* *Lolli* was his way of saying *fiore*, it seemed, and *fiore* was flowers, and flowers were beautiful, and so *lolli* was beautiful. If things went on like that he'd have a language all his own which only Ba and Wilson could understand. Well, he must try to be patient. It was all because Ba adored the child, his child. But he wished she felt like Henrietta, who wanted her boy to be a real boy. Surtees had the say about that.

"You're ill, Robert. I've been noticing it. You can't eat without nausea, and you are cross at the least thing. But I understand. It's the climate. We'll have to go."

At that moment the bell on the corner of the Basilica rang to announce the hour. The two Moors, swivelling from the waist, struck the big bell in their deliberate way.

"Now, watch, Penini!" Elizabeth cried.

The shutters opened beside the old clock. A trumpeting angel came first, then the three Magi, rotating round the Madonna, bowing stiffly, shuffling as if their joints hurt. There was a whirring and grating of antique mechanisms, and they disappeared. The little doors closed jerkily behind them. The cogs ground creakily into silence. The crowd gave a sigh of pleasure.

"Dolls! Dolls!"

A loud wail rose into the air—appallingly loud. Penini was screaming for the Magi to reappear. Elizabeth took him in her arms, trying to quieten him against her shoulder.

Looking at Robert's face, she said, "We *must* go, or you'll get really ill. I've had a lovely stay. It's time to move on."

* * *

In the middle of June, 1851, they left by train for Milan. Bursting with energy, Elizabeth visited Da Vinci's *Last Supper* and insisted on climbing the three hundred and fifty steps up to the top of the Cathedral. At the top Robert held her hand and kissed it, remembering how six years before she had walked with difficulty from her sofa to her armchair.

From Milan they went to Como by diligence, then took a steamer down Lake Maggiore and back again to Menaggio. Then they went by carriage to Porlezza at the top of Lake Lugano, on by boat to Lugano, and then by carriage to Bellinzona in the foothills of the Alps.

They crossed into Switzerland over the great Saint Gotthard Pass to Flüelen. The snow was unusually heavy that year. A passage had been cut through it. Their carriage seemed tiny, a black fly, as it drove through the great walls of snow on either side of them, nodding over them as if about to fall. The cold was intense. Yet Elizabeth insisted on sitting outside so that she might have a view to remember. She was pink and shining-eyed with excitement. "It is like standing in the presence of God when he is terrible," she said.

They arrived at Lucerne by boat on June 24. When Robert tipped the coachman he found he had just ten francs left. He felt frightened, for no reason. The money would be there.

The letter from the shipping agents for the *David Lyon* and the *Statira* was waiting for them. It told them that they were to receive only fifty pounds ship money that year. Reading it in their hotel room, sitting beside each other on the bed, they knew that it was now impossible to visit the Swiss lakes and mountains and to make the trip by steamboat down the Rhine to Cologne. They would have to go straight to Paris in the cheapest possible way.

Robert fretted, but Elizabeth laughed at him. "If we can't live on bread and cheese, then we must live on bread alone. And *that's* better than nothing but cheese, isn't it? The whole journey of seven weeks including the month at Venice will cost exactly seventy-seven pounds. Why, it's nothing."

Only seventy-seven pounds, Robert thought. But when you had only two hundred pounds a year seventy-seven pounds on travel was beyond their means.

243

In the train to Paris Elizabeth said, "I had a letter from Mr. Kenyon in Lucerne today. He begs me not to write to Papa to let him know I am coming to England."

She was shivering as if with an ague. "Oh, if you knew how I dread going to England!" she cried.

I, too, he said, but only to himself. I too. He had thought himself ready, but he was not. He had lived and relived a hundred times the journey from London to New Cross, the train pulling up at the station, the walk up the little road, the opening of the gate and then the going into his mother's home, with his wife and child whom she had never seen.

It would not be so bad alone. But to descend on it like that, in a crowd, the child perhaps laughing or crying, was a desecration.

Yet the right and natural thing was for them to go straight to New Cross and stay there. Sarianna had taken it for granted. She was expecting them. How could he explain what he felt to Ba without wounding her beyond forgiveness?

22

IT WAS THE NIGHT OF THE FIRST OF DECEMBER. For seven months Robert and Elizabeth had been living in Paris in an apartment on the second floor of number 138 Avenue des Champs Elysées. In the darkness soldiers moved stealthily and secret agents slipped into dark doorways. At dawn Louis Napoleon's troops burst into the government printing offices and forced the printers at bayonet point to set up the proclamations concerning the President's coup d'état. Leading members of the Assembly were dragged from their beds and scores of radicals were taken prisoner.

Wilson took Penini out for his usual walk after breakfast and came panting back. "There's crowds down below, sir, and posters up on the trees. The President's coming by at any moment, and he's put all the deputies in prison and is going to be crowned Emperor!"

So, a few hours after the prisoners had been led off, Robert stood on the balcony with his son held high in his arms and Elizabeth on tiptoe by his side to see the Prince President riding along the Champs Elysées through a crowd which stretched from the Carrousel to the Arc de l'Étoile. Penini jigged in Robert's arms, excited by the white horses, the flashing helmets and the martial music.

"Isn't it wonderful?" Elizabeth was as excited as her child.

"This is the entry of the troops into Paris, Ba," Robert replied sternly. "Louis Napoleon is riding in with his soldiers.

He's broken the solemn oath he took to respect the constitution when he became President."

"Only the husk of an oath," Elizabeth disagreed. "He had the people behind him after all."

"So the end justifies the means?"

"I only know that I admire him for daring to do what he's done."

Not all the Parisians were as pleased as Elizabeth believed. The next day many of them threw up barricades and prepared to resist with their lives. Louis Napoleon gave orders that his troops were to fire on them. All day there was gunfire and the asphalt ran with blood. At night the dull sounds were still coming from the boulevards. Elizabeth could not make up her mind to go to bed. She put on her warmest dressing gown, wrapped a shawl about her shoulders and sat by the fire with a book, but she did not open it.

Robert sat opposite her, trying to think and to write. Moxon the publisher had commissioned him to prepare a preface to some newly discovered Shelley letters, and that night he had nearly finished it. He wrote the last sentence after midnight and dated it *"Paris, December 4th, 1851."*

Still the sound of gunfire came through their windows. Shelley, Robert thought, would have been in the darkness out there manning the barricades. A bad husband to his poor Harriet, whom he had driven to suicide, but a man nevertheless. At one o'clock Robert drew Elizabeth to her feet, put aside her book and led her to bed. "I'm going out on the balcony for a while," he said.

It was no better there. It was impossible to stay indoors while such things were happening. He slipped quietly out of the door, down the stairs and out into the darkness. He walked lightly but briskly towards the sound of the firing.

In another room in Paris that night George Sand sat writing in her journal. "Here am I, alone by my fire on this night of the 3rd and 4th of December. How bitter it is! Liberty is slain. What have I done to deserve to sit quietly by my fire?"

Next day the Brownings drove down to see the field of action—with Wilson and Penini, on Elizabeth's insistence. Their fiacre lumbered past the Madeleine and the Opera to the streets beyond the grand boulevards towards Montmartre. In the Rue Montmartre and the Rue Rambuteau and the Rue Saint-Martin Robert showed them the holes in the walls which the cannon had made and the dozens of smashed windows. "For *Liberté, égalité, fraternité* substitute *Infanterie, cavallerie, artillerie,*" he said bitterly. "There were more than twelve hundred people massacred last night, perhaps many more. It was carnage."

"That's absurd," Elizabeth protested. "It was nothing but a little popular scum, cleared off at once by the troops."

He had seen some of it, one or two gruesome things in the darkness. He started to tell her and stopped. She had not guessed that he had gone farther than the balcony.

Suddenly Penini, remembering his beloved puppet shows, began a thin wail of uttermost woe. "The soldiers are going to kill Punch. Oh, Punch!"

Elizabeth flew to his side and lifted him in her arms. His ridiculous feathered white hat fell off into the dust. She smoothed his forehead, kissing him, comforting him tenderly. "Punch is safe in the park. We're all going to say good morning to him."

As they clambered back into the carriage Robert said, "You seem to be two different people, Ba. You can't bear to see Pen cry, and yet—"

She laughed, quite untroubled. "Mr. Kenyon always said there was a tigress under the Ba-lamb."

"It's not fair to yourself. I wish you wouldn't—"

She put a hand on his arm. "Well, then, I won't do it any-more. I'll think what you think and say, 'Yes, Robert,' like a good wife."

For a moment he thought she was serious and he said, "Don't say such words to me, Ba. But I must try to scold you into the truth when you are in error."

Punch was in the park belabouring Judy, the same as ever. Penini was overjoyed. He began to laugh and could not stop. Robert picked him up and carried him to the park gates. All the way back in the cab Penini burst into little fits of laughter and cries of "Punch!"

"It's not that he's unhappy, sir," Wilson said, hushing him on her lap. "It's just that he's highly strung."

*   *   *

On the following Sunday afternoon Robert's father and his sister turned up without warning at the door.

Robert and Elizabeth sprang to their feet as Wilson showed them in.

"What's the matter? Is something wrong?" Robert asked before greeting them.

His father looked distressed and glanced at his daughter, who said, "Not now."

This was the meeting, Elizabeth thought, which she had been dreading for five years. She examined this very short, raven-haired, loquacious woman whose sharp eyes grew gentle when they rested on the old man, her father, and her brother. Robert had not told her that his sister was so small, that she lisped, that she had a habit of rising on tiptoe when she spoke, that she gestured freely with heavily beringed hands. Now she was troubled, perhaps frightened, and in need of help. With a profound sense of relief Elizabeth took her in her arms and then kissed old Mr. Browning. There had been nothing to be afraid of, after all. Sarianna was a friend.

After supper, during which Mr. Browning ate scarcely anything, Robert took his father to his writing room.

"Now, what is it, Father?"

Mr. Browning cracked his knuckles one after another. "Something that's been bothering me for months. I didn't like to mention it because of your mother." He paused, then said in a strangled voice, "I've been lonely, Robert."

The old man was very unhappy. For minutes he found it impossible to continue. Then he seemed to gather courage and plunged.

"There's a widow, a Mrs. von Müller. She used to live with her parents in a house not far away from ours. She's forty-five. She has three children."

His voice sank to a hoarse croak. "She picked acquaintance with me, and we became friends. Then I began to hear bad reports of her. She isn't a nice woman, Robert. She's done things—and I wrote to tell her so." He was hurrying now, his words tumbling over one another. "Don't fear for your mother's memory, Robert. It's sacred. I meant no harm by it! But now Mrs. von Müller is writing me letters full of threats. She says she'll expose me."

"Expose *what?*" Robert looked so thunderous his father quailed.

"Nothing—there's nothing to expose. But what's to prevent her lying? And then I'd be ruined—the bank—it would damage us all." He put his face in his hands and sobbed.

Robert patted his father's shoulder. "What do you want me to do?"

"Anything you like. Only get rid of her for me!"

Robert sat down at his writing table. "Madam," he began, "my father has informed me of the manner in which you have annoyed him and of the persecution he has undergone for some time. . . ."

"Will you read that?" he asked when he had finished.

His father read and looked frightened. He handed it back speechlessly.

"Don't you want to write to her yourself?" Robert asked.

"I've written too many letters to her already."

"She won't take her congé from me alone. You'll have to write too."

Mr. Browning moved to the table and reluctantly took up the pen, and standing over him Robert read his father's letter to Mrs. von Müller.

"That'll silence her," he said grimly. "Now, off to bed. There's nothing to worry about anymore."

He led Mr. Browning back to Sarianna, nodding towards the door of the room in which his father was to sleep. Sarianna rose, but caught Robert's arm. "I ought to tell you, Robert, Cousin James Silverthorne is far from well."

"What's the matter with him?"

"I don't know. He doesn't eat and is feverish."

"Poor James. I'll write at once."

Mr. Browning and Sarianna were both enchanted with Penini, and Mr. Browning decided that his grandson must call him Nonno, Italian for grandfather.

After breakfast Sarianna briskly brushed her father's hair for him and buttoned on his cloak, and they returned to London.

In February Elizabeth heard that George Sand was in Paris and tried to get an introduction to her, growing more impatient daily. At last she came to Robert waving a letter from Mr. Carlyle.

"How will you get the letter to her?" he asked. "She's in hiding as a friend of Louis Napoleon's enemies."

"Can't you help? If I miss this chance, we may never meet. You're not trying!"

Robert was not trying. He lounged in his chair, obstinately against her.

"I don't like your coming into contact with that shameless woman. She has led a terrible life. How many names has she had? Aurore Dupin—Mme. Dudevant—she's been Chopin's mistress and de Musset's."

"She's a woman who has refused to be bound by the rules set up by men. She's my heroine above all heroines. Don't sit there in your chair being proud. I won't die without seeing George Sand." She sat down and dashed off a note which was supposed to come from them both.

"Sign it, Robert. You won't refuse me the thing I want most in the world? You couldn't."

Was she pleading or insisting? He signed it.

At last all her questions and hints bore fruit. The letter was passed from hand to hand, and one day a reply was delivered to their door by a sinister-looking man who slipped away without giving his name. Would M. and Mme. Browning come on the following Sunday afternoon?

That Sunday afternoon in February was so bitterly cold that Robert tried to prevent Elizabeth from keeping her appointment with George Sand. But she ran across the boulevard and called out, *"Numero trois, Rue Racine!"* to the driver of a fiacre. Robert could only follow her.

As they were shown in they saw at least eight or nine young men in the room standing or lounging about and a woman sitting by the fire. After a long time the woman rose and came to meet them. Elizabeth realized with a shock that George Sand, who had been the mistress of Chopin and Mérimée and de Musset, was plain. The eyes in that tired face were fine and the wings of glossy black hair drawn up into a knot behind looked soft, but she was not beautiful or even pretty. Her chin receded a little, her teeth projected. Her eagle nose was a little forbidding. Her complexion was a deep olive.

Yet she wasn't the large mannish creature, badly dressed and smoking a cigar, everyone in England thought her. This tiny, rather plump woman was dressed with great elegance in a fashionable grey serge dress and jacket, fastened at the throat with a small white linen collar. She came up to Elizabeth, who stooped and kissed her hand. Elizabeth saw Robert's start of shocked disapproval, and George Sand withdrew her hand quickly, with a *"Mais non, je ne veux pas!"* Then she put her hands on Elizabeth's shoulders and kissed her on the lips.

As George Sand led them to chairs by the fire Elizabeth tried to compliment the Frenchwoman in carefully prepared phrases on her work for literature and for mankind. Mme. Sand waved it all aside.

"Mais c'est vous qui est illustre, madame."

"My husband's a much better poet than I am."

George Sand's eyes rested approvingly on Robert. She sat down, turned to her young men, and went on with her conversation as if she had not been interrupted. To Robert's horror she spoke quite freely about her activities for the release of her condemned friends.

As they were going Elizabeth begged her to return their visit, but she replied, "I don't know how long I'll be staying in Paris. That monster's coup d'état has changed all my plans."

Outside, Robert sniffed. "She's no idea of your politics, or she wouldn't have you near her. And what would your hero Napoleon think of your keeping quiet about her efforts to bring his would-be assassins back to Paris?"

"Did you notice how she kissed me?" Elizabeth replied.

"She's a Jezebel. I nearly walked out of the room. All those ill-bred men, that low theatrical riffraff and those gutter reds, down on their knees adoring that scornful woman between a puff of smoke and a spurt of saliva. And you, degrading yourself to kiss her hand."

"Don't be so English and so respectable, Robert."

All through supper Elizabeth talked about how she would receive George Sand. Mr. Kenyon might be coming to Paris and might like to meet her. She would not even listen to him when he pointed out that it would be ironical if a couple of English Francophiles were arrested by the secret police because they were parties to the plottings of the notorious Mme. Sand and her fellow conspirators. She was still making plans when Wilson answered a rat-a-tat on the door.

"There's a message come by electric telegraph for you, Mr. Browning."

Robert read it quickly and passed it to Elizabeth. It was from Sarianna and read, *"Please come. James is asking for you."*

In the morning Robert was packed and ready. He rose from the breakfast table, put on his warm shipboard cloak and held out his arms to kiss Elizabeth good-bye. At sight of her face he let them fall. She looked drained, ill, almost old.

"Don't stay for my sake. I could never forgive myself if you did that!" She was almost in a panic.

But he knew that he could not leave her. With a shock he had realized that her dependence on him, that terrible sense of her own worthlessness, was no less for five happy years of marriage. She really believed that he might not come back to her, and her face told him what his leaving her would do to her. The struggle between abandoning his cousin and best friend in his hour of need and failing her showed in his own face, and she cried out again in protest. He said, "How *can* I go when you—?"

He did not finish the sentence, but took his bag back to his room and asked Wilson to unpack it.

Two days later there was a knock on the door, and Robert said, "That's the telegraph boy again."

It was Sarianna's second telegram. James was dead.

23

IT WAS JUST BEFORE TEN O'CLOCK IN THE MORNING
when Robert slipped into the back bench of the public gallery
at the court of Queen's Bench at Guildhall in London.

When Sarianna's letter had arrived telling him that Mrs.
von Müller was bringing the action against his father it had been
a nasty surprise. But she was so confident that the action would
fail and so anxious that he should not come over for the trial,
that Robert had agreed not to put forward his family's summer
visit to England. The trial would be over before the end of June.
They would cross on the fifth of July, as planned, and arrive on
the sixth.

Suddenly Robert had rebelled. "I must be there, Ba. He's
an old man, and it probably worries him more than he says." But
something had kept him from telling his father and sister of his
change of plan.

So he had arrived at his father's trial on that morning of
June 30, 1852, his presence unknown to his father and sister. He
saw Sarianna and his father come in, Sarianna protective, his
father lost and rather frightened. Sarianna was very smart in a
white bonnet with a brave black plume.

There was a slight stir as a plump, good-looking woman ac-
companied by an older man was ushered to her seat. Mrs. von
Müller, of course. She did not look at all the vulgar hussy his
father had painted.

"Silence! Be upstanding in court!" the usher bellowed.

Lord Campbell, Chief Justice of the Queen's Bench Division, appeared, an ancient tortoise with sagging jowls, in his scarlet robe. He bowed to the court. The court bowed back. Everyone sat. The judge lowered himself into his high-backed chair and subsided into a scarlet heap on the table. His curled, full-bottomed wig stood out against the oak panelling, long where the barristers' wigs were short, drooping where theirs seemed impudent above their serious faces.

The special jury was sworn in, each man kissing the Bible.

"I appear for the plaintiff, my lord," said a dark, vivacious-looking counsel. Robert recognized Sir Alexander Cockburn. He was one of the highest fliers at the bar and a brilliant advocate. Until last February he had been Attorney-General. The von Müller clan were investing heavily in this case if they could afford to brief an ex-Attorney-General. His father's counsel, Mr. Willis, would have to be good. But, then, innocence was the best defense.

Cockburn began. "Gentlemen of the jury, this is an action to recover compensation in damages for a breach of promise of marriage. The plaintiff is a lady forty-five years old. The defendant is twenty years older. You, gentlemen of the jury, will judge how much wisdom, how much judgment, how much kindness, even, life has taught this elderly gentleman."

Now Cockburn hitched his gown over his shoulder. "The plaintiff is an English lady, the widow of an officer in the Austrian service. In early life she married a Mr. Meredith. Her husband proved to be a spendthrift and a libertine, and ruined his family. In the end he abandoned his wife and his son and daughter and went into the Spanish service. She could not know for certain whether she was a wife or a widow. Then fate was kinder. A Captain von Müller proposed marriage to her. She accepted on condition there would be no marriage until she had evidence that her husband was dead."

Sir Alexander paused for effect and continued. "In the year 1836 she received conclusive proof of her first husband's death. Then, and only then, did she marry Captain von Müller. Mrs. von Müller had a few brief years of happiness. Then once again she was left a widow. And now we come to the defendant."

He turned and glared in the direction of Robert's father, who seemed to quail under his eye. "The defendant resided near the house of Mrs. von Müller's parents. He was struck with the appearance of Mrs. von Müller, and he adopted an extraordinary method, one might think, for a man of his age, of showing his admiration of her. He used to pass the house waving his hand and looking up with great earnestness. This was in December, 1850."

December, 1850, Robert noted. His mother had died in March, 1849.

His father had forced himself on Mrs. von Müller in the street and had escorted her home, declaring his love for her. Mrs. von Müller, far from encouraging him, had left the district. Mr. Browning had pursued her with passionate letters, begging her again and again to marry him.

"At first his letters opened, 'My dear Mrs. von Müller,' but soon they grew warmer. I will now read the letters—upwards of fifty letters. Number one." It was then that the nightmare began for Robert. One after another, mercilessly, Sir Alexander read out those terrible letters. Most of them began, "My dearest, dearest, dearest, dearest, dearest, dearest, much-loved Minny." Robert heard the titters all about him. To him the worst thing about it all was that those letters seemed a crude, an awful caricature of his own love for Elizabeth.

At about letter number twelve a new note was introduced. Suddenly in the midst of the protestations of undying love would come charges that Mrs. von Müller was a loose woman. "But no sooner had those accusations been leveled at her than a letter would follow making the most abject apologies and assuring her that the hateful subject would never be mentioned again."

And so it went on, letter after letter written by an old man who had fallen in love and then taken fright.

"At last the defendant went to his son in Paris—"

Robert had not expected this. He waited, feeling that every eye was on him, nerving himself for his name to be mentioned. But no, Sir Alexander swept on. "Shortly afterwards a most extraordinary letter was received by Mrs. von Müller from the defendant's son stating that his father had informed him of the persecution he had undergone from her for some time, and saying that his father wanted nothing more to do with her."

Robert felt ashamed.

"What did she do? With dignity, she wrote a reply, expressing her extreme surprise. She had no further letters from the defendant's son."

Robert had thrown her letter on the fire, thinking her what his father had said she was.

"But she did receive a letter from the defendant. This time the defendant did not address her as 'My dearest, dearest, dearest, dearest, dearest, dearest much-loved Minny.' This time he began, simply, 'Mrs. von Müller.' And this time he gave as his reason for breaking off the match her misconduct since she had run away from the boarding school she had been sent to as a girl."

He had written: "I believe that when you married your second husband you knew your first husband was alive." That had not constituted defamation, since it was addressed to the lady herself. But he had concluded the letter by stating he intended to write to her brother, her son-in-law and her doctor and inform them of the disgraceful circumstances. The foolish old man, Robert thought, for it *would* be defamation if he had libelled her to others.

The three men had immediately gone to see him, and the action had followed.

Cockburn rose to his peroration, "I charge the defendant today with having been guilty of the most cruel and cold-blooded, the most malicious and cowardly villainy towards this lady to whom he had, so short a time before, and so warmly, professed his love." And again. "I repeat that charge, the charge of deliberate, calculated villainy! And I now call on the jury to award substantial damages."

Then came the witnesses. Mrs. von Müller's son-in-law, Samuel Sutor, an upstanding young man, gave evidence that he had gone with Dr. Collinson, her physician, and her brother to see Mr. Browning about the slanders.

"I asked the defendant if he knew the contents of his son's letter," Samuel Sutor said.

"And he said?" Cockburn asked.

"He replied that he did not, but that it was in his son's handwriting."

But Robert had shown his father the letter, and he had read it. Perhaps his father's shame at the lie accounted for his anxiety not to have him in the courtroom—that and other things.

256

When Dr. Collinson took the stand Robert prayed that he would not catch his eye. He was a decent man, and he had been a great friend of his mother's.

"Early this year," the physician was saying, "the defendant came to me, and told me about the action. He said that no person was ever loved as Mrs. von Müller had been loved at one time."

Robert felt stabbed to the heart. Not even his mother? His father might have spared him that.

The official return of Mr. Meredith's death was put in. Mrs. von Müller's first husband had died on the seventeenth of March, 1836, in Spain. The certificate of marriage of the plaintiff to her second husband, Captain von Müller, was put in. The marriage had taken place on the nineteenth of May, 1836.

Now, at last, something was going to be said for his father. Mr. Willis was addressing the jury for the defendant—deferentially, without fire.

"Gentlemen of the jury, I have no hesitation in designating this action as an idle and trumpery case. It should never have been brought, never come to this court today." That was right, Robert thought. "There is one case on the books which has some similarities to it—the great case of *Bardell versus Pickwick* by the famous Charles Dickens, a most comic description of a libel action brought by his landlady against the celebrated Mr. Pickwick."

Was that fair? Was ridicule the best weapon to help his father? Apparently Mr. Willis thought so. "The letters, members of the jury, are those of a besotted old man. They are the encores of dotage. My client is a poor old dotard in love."

If his own counsel felt that that was the best he could do for him, there was no hope.

"I submit, gentlemen of the jury, that the letters were not worth all learned counsel's art. They should have been dismissed for what they were. I call on the jury to give the smallest possible amount of damages."

So all *was* lost. The judge was already summing up. "It seems to me that this is not a case where the damages should be as large as in some that come before the court. On the other hand they should not be so small as to suggest that it was the court's opinion that the plaintiff has misconducted herself. I do not find anything to suggest that this lady held out any lure to this old gentleman. His folly was his own. He was smitten with her charms and he asked her to marry him. Mr. Browning is a clerk in the Bank of England, living in a very creditable manner. He is evidently a man of great intellectual prowess and of considerable attainments. He would have been a suitable, indeed a desirable, match for the lady. The plaintiff has been disappointed in her expectations, and she is entitled to damages. The defendant conducted himself, I must say, in a most cowardly manner. He made the most damaging and unjustified imputation against the plaintiff. It seems to me a very gross case."

It was over. Everyone was busy, now, about the damages. There would be no going back, no clearing his father's name, ever. Unless, of course, there was an appeal.

The foreman of the jury wanted to know what salary the defendant received. A clerk from the Bank of England was called, and he stated that the defendant got about three hundred and twenty pounds a year. His father could hardly have expected to keep the case secret from the bank, whatever he had hoped for with regard to his son and daughter-in-law. The jury seemed to be filing back into the jury box almost as soon as they had gone out of it. The verdict was given. For the plaintiff, of course. Damages, eight hundred pounds. His father would never be able to pay it—not without ruination.

Robert waited until Sarianna and his father had broken away from the black-gowned legal crows and were walking through the door. At that moment Robert saw the triumphant glance Mrs. von Müller gave his father. A sensible, respectable, insulted woman vindicated in the eyes of the world. His father's head was bent. He stumbled out holding Sarianna's arm.

Robert followed them out onto the pavement. They were trying to hail a hansom cab, alone. "Sarianna," he said in a low voice, trying not to startle her, touching her arm gently. "Sis."

She swung round. "Oh—*Wobert!*" she said. The lisp was very strong, the lisp of the little girl, his sister. He saw that though she held her head up there were tears in her eyes.

"Shall we go back to my lodgings?" he asked. "Ba will be glad to see you."

"No." She was firm. "I want to get him home."

They went by cab all the way to New Cross. Mr. Browning sat with his head in his hands, exclaiming, "My God! My God!" at intervals. Once in the house Sarianna helped him off with his coat and hung it up. She took off the hat with the brave black plume. She led him into the sitting room and went off to order tea.

"Robert," Mr. Browning said brokenly. "I am so sorry. Your mother."

Great tears ran down his cheeks. Robert held him against his shoulder, looking down on the grey head. Yet at that moment he almost hated his father for what he had done to him, and to his mother's memory and to Elizabeth.

"Don't worry about anything," he said. "I'll take care of it all."

When the storm had passed Robert settled the old man in his armchair, and Sarianna brought him tea and cakes.

Robert wandered out into the garden. There his mother's roses were, tumbling over the wall. Almost, he saw her, with her scissors in her hand, and heard her voice. He stood, the sun warm on his back, remembering, remembering.

> Here's the garden she walked across,
>   Arm in my arm, such a short while since;
> Hark, now I push its wicket, the moss
>   Hinders the hinges and makes them wince!

Sarianna found him there and put her arms about him. They stood like that for a long time, while he was shaken by harsh sobs.

Next morning there was a full report of the proceedings in *The Times* under the headline, "VON MÜLLER VS. BROWNING." Silently Robert handed Elizabeth the paper folded at the page and saw her reel under the blow.

"At least they don't mention *our* names," he said. "That's something."

"Is it, Robert? The general public won't connect the case with Robert Browning the poet, perhaps—"

"As if the general public has ever heard of Robert Browning the poet! Let's say Mrs. Browning the poetess."

"—but all our friends are sure to know who Mr. Browning of New Cross is. Mr. Kenyon. Miss Mitford. Mr. Carlyle. Anna Jameson."

"You aren't saying what's really hurting you, Ba."

"Very well. Papa and my brothers will know. They'll say, 'Ah, this is just what we expected of those Brownings.' That's what we both mind."

"Yes." His voice was bitter.

"It's unfair. The poor old man was the victim of a wicked, unscrupulous woman. I shall say so to everyone."

But was he? Robert had seen Mrs. von Müller and heard her son-in-law and Collinson giving evidence.

"Shall we appeal?" he asked abruptly.

"Oh, no." Her answer was swift. "There's been enough publicity! Besides—"

"Besides, it wouldn't be likely to succeed."

"So there's nothing for it but to pay the damages?" Now she was wistful.

"He's liable."

"Eight hundred pounds. It's a great deal of money."

"He says he can't pay."

"What else can he do?"

"He can go abroad. They can't follow him there. Florence is full of bankrupts who've fled from their debts—some of them living in style. Landor spent years avoiding his creditors."

"But if he goes abroad he can't work at the bank."

"And if he stays in England he must sell everything to pay up and still end in a debtors' prison. The bank *may* let him have his pension ahead of time, or some of it, to live on abroad. The house will have to be sold in any case, and Sarianna will have to go and look after him."

"In Florence?"

"In Paris."

"So it's all arranged. You didn't say so last night."

"It's this that has decided matters." He struck the table violently with the folded copy of *The Times*. "He can't live here anymore, poor and disgraced!"

"But won't he be more disgraced if he flees the country without giving this widow what the court has awarded?"

Mrs. von Müller would have Cockburn's fat fee and costs to pay, too, Robert thought. He said, "We've only a choice of evils."

Elizabeth thought about it, biting her thumb.

"We must decide quickly," Robert said. "He must be smuggled out of the country at once."

"How?"

"I'll take him."

"Robert!" It was a cry of pain. "We've not been separated since we married. Not for a single night in six years." Not even to

260

go and see his mother. Not even for James Silverthorne's death-bed. Not even for James Silverthorne's funeral.

"It's the only way. You can decide."

But Elizabeth knew that he had decided.

Robert returned at half-past six, three days after he had left her.

He seized her in his arms and pressed her to him as if there had been a war and years between them since their last meeting. As he held her he could feel Penini's thin arms clasped round his knees and hear his excited squeals of welcome. Then he took a piece of paper from his pocket, put it into her hand and folded her fingers over it.

"Don't read it now."

She smiled at him, undid the top button of her bodice and tucked it inside. As she rebuttoned it under his ardent eye and teasing smile she said, "Now tell me about your father."

"He can't be expected to be happy there in one room with nothing to do and not a soul to speak to. I'm tired and dis-heartened, that's the truth. Let's eat at once and go to bed."

At supper Elizabeth fed Penini a boiled egg, spooning it into his mouth. He ate with maddening slowness and talked all the time.

Afterwards she said, "I think you'd better sleep in Penini's room tonight."

Wilson had left for Sheffield on the morning Robert had gone to Paris. Since then, she told him, Penini had clung to her like a leech, refusing to let anyone else wash or dress or feed him, insisting on sleeping in her bed.

"He's three years of age, Ba. He must sleep in his own bed."

"He wept and wept! He followed me about asking 'Will Mama go away and leave Penini all alone?' Do you expect me to *beat* him?"

"Get him ready for bed, and I'll talk to him."

When she led in the minute figure in his long white night-dress Robert said, "Now, Pen, you're a brave boy, aren't you? A man who looks after his mama?"

Penini looked up at him distrustfully under his lashes.

"You aren't afraid of being alone?" Robert persisted.

"Yes," Penini said flatly.

"No. Boys aren't afraid."

"Yes. Penini's afraid."

At last Robert picked him up impatiently, carried him into his room and plumped him into bed. He left the night light burning. Elizabeth was in bed with her hair down. In a few minutes Robert was beside her. It was still light outside the windows. He turned to her.

There was a hammering of small fists on the door. "Let me in! I want to sleep with Mama!"

Robert got out of bed and led his son back to his room. He put him into bed again, covered him and shut the door. Once more he got into bed beside Elizabeh. A loud, unending wail rose.

Robert shouted to his son to be quiet. There was a pause. He turned to Elizabeth. The wail—high, thin, determined—rose again.

After half an hour, in which there was no sign that the crying would ever cease, Elizabeth said, "I think he'll have to come in."

Robert got out of bed, carried Penini in to her, went into Penini's room and threw himself on the bed. Penini snuggled up beside his mother, his cheeks wet, and fell asleep at once.

Elizabeth lay, looking out of the window at the late summer daylight. She remembered the piece of paper Robert had given her and which she had put on her bedside table when it had fallen out of her bodice as she undressed. She put out an arm, very quietly so as not to disturb her sleeping child, and picked it up. With one hand she unfolded it.

> So, I shall see her in three days
> And just one night, but nights are short,
> Then two long hours, and that is morn.
> See how I come, unchanged, unworn!
> Feel, where my life broke off from thine,
> How fresh the splinters keep and fine,—
> Only a touch and we combine! . . .
>
> O loaded curls, release your store
> Of warmth and scent as once before
> The tingling hair did, lights and darks
> Outbreaking into fairy sparks,
> When under curl and curl I pried
> After the warmth and scent inside,
> Thro' lights and darks how manifold—
> The dark inspired, the light controlled!
> As early art embrowned the gold . . .

. . . I shall see her in three days
And one night, now the nights are short,
Then just two hours, and that is morn.

She longed to have Robert beside her, to tell him how beautiful it was, and thank him. She looked down at Penini. She must not wake him. In the morning she would tell Robert.

Next morning Penini woke her with hugs and kisses, pulling her eyes open and prattling, *"O buona Mama!"* Robert came in, still looking angry, asking for breakfast at once. He was going out, he said, to put his father's house and furniture up for sale and to see the Bank of England about paying his pension.

After that Robert went out early every day and for days at a stretch returned late. He ate at home very seldom. When he came back he looked tired and worn. When letters began to arrive from Mr. Browning complaining that he was separated from Sarianna and all his friends and his books Elizabeth could see that Robert was afraid that the old man might do something desperate.

"Oh, Robert, I wish from the bottom of my heart that we were rich enough to pay the money and bring him back to his own country!" she cried.

It was the first time the need of money had been more than a nuisance, an irritation willingly borne. And she cried again, "Have you thought, Robert, that all our unhappiness now—and we *are* unhappy, both of us—is brought upon us by our families? Mine has laid a weight on me I can hardly bear, and your days are tormented by yours. Now we are biting at each other because of them."

He could not but agree. Perhaps it was true in all marriages. Yet it must be only a phase. Things would settle down, Wilson would return, Pen would grow into a boy, they would be happy again.

He said, "Remember what we have. You said yourself in one of your lovely sonnets that this is only 'A place to stand and love in for a day/With darkness and the death-hour rounding it.' "

"There are dark hours on the way to that darkness too," she sighed. "Let us share them, Robert."

24

NOW THAT THE TRIAL WAS OVER ROBERT AND
Elizabeth decided there was nothing to be lost by letting everyone
know that they were in London, just as they had planned.

Arabel came round at once and scooped up Penini, chortling,
"He's a Barrett, there's no doubt about that. He's just like—" and
stopped. Robert saw Elizabeth flinch and knew Arabel had been
about to say Bro's name. Perhaps that explained Elizabeth's almost
excessive tenderness to her child.

Treppy came hard on Arabel's heels, looking older and
frailer, but still treating Elizabeth like a recalcitrant child. Black
eyes snapping, she grasped Robert's arm with a skeletal hand and
said, "Ah, *you* may be able to control her. No one else ever could.
And she must be loved, she begins to die of it if she isn't. She's
so passionate, that Ba." They looked at each other, united in their
love for her.

Miss Mitford was on them within hours, too, bright eyes
asking questions under the slab of forehead, pudgy arms full of
flowers. "Don't you ever talk anything but Italian to that child?"
she asked brusquely. Anna Jameson brought a pale and suffering
Geddie, forbidden to marry her Macpherson, rapping out, "He
has a violent temper. She'd never be happy with him."

Next Henrietta and her Altham arrived from Taunton in
Somerset, where Surtees's regiment was stationed, to stay in rooms
nearby for a week. Altham was two years younger than Penini, but
he was nearly a head taller and his cheeks were scarlet with
country health. Beside him Penini looked even more of a sprite.

Yet Altham adored his cousin Pen and they gabbled happily together.

"Papa told Mr. Kenyon that he made a new will exactly a year after my marriage, and that neither you nor I are mentioned in it," Henrietta said bitterly.

"Oh, Henrietta, how different everything would have been if we'd married rich men," Elizabeth exclaimed. "Promise me you'll come and live near us in Florence or Paris."

"No, no. It's far too expensive, whatever you say, and there's the danger of revolution in France."

At five o'clock next day George's card was sent in.

George had grown solider, and his manner was even more magisterial.

"My dear fellow! It's been too long, hasn't it? I've come especially to see my nephew, little—Wiedemann!" Was there the slightest pause, as if the name stuck in his throat?

"We call him Pen," Robert said.

Penini advanced without shyness and took the painted tin top from his uncle. George knelt down and showed him how to spin it on a piece of uncarpeted floor. He too was disconcerted to find that his nephew did not understand a word of English.

Robert and George shared a glass of sherry affably, but when Elizabeth asked him when Papa was going to answer their letters he gave a slight shrug and rose to go away.

Mr. Kenyon himself called at six o'clock, making everything in their dingy parlour seem smaller and dingier.

"And your work, Robert?"

"Robert's been working very hard," Elizabeth defended him. "Only he's not ready to publish yet."

"Well, these things can't be hurried."

As he rose to go Mr. Kenyon asked, "You haven't written to your father, I hope, Ba?"

"No, since you asked me not to, but—"

"It wouldn't do any good." He sighed heavily. "I know."

When the door had closed behind him Elizabeth brought a quill and a sheet of paper to Robert.

"Now. The letter to Papa."

She sat watching him as he wrote with many pauses for thought. When he had finished he gave her the letter. Her face cleared as she read it.

"He couldn't resist that, Robert. It's manly and straight-forward. And now *I* shall write to Papa."

"After what Mr. Kenyon said?"

"A short letter. I can't be forbidden to write to my own father. Not by anyone."

She sent Wilson out at once to post the two letters.

After that every day was simply a number of hours during which Elizabeth waited for Mr. Barrett's answer, no matter what they did or where they went.

Determined to distract her, Robert took Elizabeth out daily. There were enough invitations to last them for six weeks. No one mentioned the trial, but she felt their friends' sympathy.

They went out in a hackney cab to see Thomas Carlyle and his caustic wife Jane, driving out between the hawthorn hedges to the riverside village in Chelsea, and pulled up at the front door of number five Great Cheyne Row with its bright brass knocker. Elizabeth sat beside plain Mrs. Carlyle on a gigantic sofa with a crocheted cover, sipping tea. But it was Robert who asked how the Sage of Chelsea's great work on Frederick the Great was progressing; and when the cross-faced old man clapped on his enormous black hat and led them into the garden to show them his neighbour's cocks, which drove him frantic with their crowing, it was Robert who advised him to soundproof his study. As they left Elizabeth realized that she had not even thanked Mr. Carlyle for arranging their introduction to George Sand.

It was the same when Dicky Monckton-Milnes entertained them to a dinner at his celebrated round table in Robert's honour. Elizabeth had so much to talk to him about—Dickens, Landor, his old love Florence Nightingale and all the famous people he knew. Yet it was Robert who talked about Florence and the past six years' doings in literary London. Elizabeth sat silent, gazing through the windows at the swans sailing down the river Thames.

Even when they journeyed out to see Miss Mitford in her garden it was Robert who gossiped with her about Flush and Penini and the orange trees and camellias on their Casa Guidi balcony.

After that Robert growled at Elizabeth, "You've wanted to meet all these people for years—and longed to talk to Miss Mitford above all. What *is* the matter, Ba?"

She turned her eyes to his, and he knew the answer. There

266

was only one house she wanted to go into and only one person she longed to see.

"But, Ba, you can't abandon all pleasure in life. You must make an effort." As Robert spoke he remembered Treppy's words, "And she must be loved—she begins to die of it if she isn't. She's so passionate, that Ba."

She made an effort for the next occasion. The summons from Mr. Kenyon had come. He never invited husbands and wives together, and she must go alone. How many years was it since she and Miss Mitford had dined with him? Fifteen? She had been thirty-one then.

Henrietta lent her a white satin dress with a flounced skirt and rosebuds outlining the heart-shaped neckline. She drew her ringlets over her shoulders to cover them, afraid of the women in décolleté, afraid of being alone without Robert. At the last moment she cried, "I can't go. I'm ill." Robert pulled her dress off her shoulders even more and kissed their plumpness and praised her bosom and pinned her Granny Moulton's diamond brooch among the rosebuds. He clasped Henrietta's evening cloak of shimmering Indian gauze round her, and said, "Leave it with the footman, remember." Then he took her in the brougham he had ordered from the livery stable and delivered her to the powdered lackey at Mr. Kenyon's mansion in Devonshire Place.

The chandeliers almost blinded her. The space between the door and her host seemed too far to cover in a lifetime. But when Mrs. Robert Browning's name was announced all the brilliant people in the bright dresses and the beautiful coats turned smilingly to face her, and Mr. Kenyon came over to kiss her hand and take care of her. Everyone had come to meet Mrs. Browning the poetess. No one mentioned *Casa Guidi Windows.* They praised the beauty of the *Sonnets from the Portuguese,* but no one had guessed her secret yet.

After dinner in the prettiest dining room in London, overlooking the green lawns of Regent's Park, Elizabeth met Fanny Haworth, Robert's Eyebright, of whom she had been foolishly jealous, long ago.

"Oh, Mrs. Browning," the large, good-looking woman gushed, "I wrote two sonnets to you once." She quoted from them. They were terrible—bad poetry and overblown compliments. Elizabeth smiled painfully.

Miss Haworth continued to chatter, unabashed. Suddenly Elizabeth found she was describing, most vividly, the new things which were happening in London, which proved beyond doubt that the living could communicate with the dead. Elizabeth leaned forward, holding Henrietta's painted fan across her bosom, to catch every word.

Afterwards Elizabeth said, "I quite enjoyed it, Robert, but I hope there won't be anything more like it for a long time."

She had only been able to go out that night because Robert had stayed with Penini. He had been growing more and more difficult, calling for his Lily, as he called Wilson, and screaming if Elizabeth left him for a moment. He insisted on being carried everywhere, standing before her, his legs apart, his arms stretched rigidly upwards, his face red, roaring in a voice of astonishing power.

One morning Arabel came in to find them in the middle of a scene. Robert was shouting at Penini, and Elizabeth had her hands over her ears. Her hair was escaping from its pins and she was still in her dressing gown. Penini was only half-dressed and bellowing to be lifted up.

"Come on, my rabbit," Arabel cooed at him. "Is that the way a man behaves? Look at your Papa! *He's* not crying like a baby, is he?"

Penini stared at her over tear-stained cheeks. He put his thumb in his mouth and sucked it noisily.

"It's a lucky thing he's so small for his age," Robert fumed. "He's heavy enough for Ba as it is, and he's already reduced her to a dreadful state of slavery. I for one can't wait for Wilson to come back."

Arabel put a finger to her lips. "I'll look after him till Wilson returns. I'll send my maid Bonser for him every day as soon as Papa leaves, and she can bring him back whenever you say. Isn't that a good idea, Pen, to come and play with your Aunt Arabel every day?"

Bonser arrived every morning to collect a Penini already watching at the window for her trim uniformed figure and her lively face, and life became possible again. Robert and Elizabeth could receive callers instead of not answering the bell for fear of a public scene from Penini.

Elizabeth at once relapsed into her previous state, merely

waiting. Even her Aunt Graham-Clarke's visit did not really reach her. Bummy came to sit rigidly on a chair, not letting go of her umbrella. Elizabeth was hardly able to believe her the same timid Bummy who had been so close to her at Hope End, so kind to her at Torquay. Her aunt asked her question after question, as of right, and Elizabeth answered them, as if acknowledging that right. Bummy left her without a kiss and went back to Torquay, then wrote a letter, asking Elizabeth to be reconciled to her father. Elizabeth read it and threw it away.

Now, against Robert's wishes, Elizabeth was going often to Wimpole Street, walking very fast along the pavements. The first time she and Penini had lunch in Arabel's room, waited on by Bonser; then Arabel took her over the house, room by room. The bright paint which had been put on after she left, and which had remained fresh in her mind, was now faded and old. The familiar rooms were smaller and darker than she remembered.

"The whole house needs to be thoroughly cleaned, Arabel," she said. "It seems bachelor-looking!"

"It's a house of bachelors. Seven of them."

Back in Arabel's room Elizabeth said, "I still owe you seventy pounds, Arabel." She had only been able to repay the housekeeper's loan of thirty pounds.

"If I need it, I'll ask you for it, Ba."

Elizabeth turned round.

"Arabel, George has been, but no one else. Aren't any of my other brothers coming to see me?"

"We must leave it to them, Ba. I daresay they're waiting to see what Papa's going to do."

"So am I. Waiting and waiting until my heart is sick. When is Papa going to answer?"

"Who can tell what Papa's doing or thinking?"

They did not realize it was late until they heard Mr. Barrett's footsteps coming upstairs.

"I must dress, Ba. Don't go now. You can't. Wait until we're at dinner, then slip out—on tiptoe, please. *Don't* be brave."

Elizabeth sat in the bed, watching Arabel as she dressed in her plain grey dress with the white collar of point lace and smoothed her shining fair hair into a small knob. Nothing had changed for Arabel in six years.

Elizabeth was slipping past the dining room door when she

rebelled at what she was doing. She stood outside it listening to their voices—the deep voices of her father and her brothers and the clear voice of her sister. They were laughing.

"I felt like a thief in my own home, Robert," she cried to him that night.

"It wasn't wise, Ba. It was a wild, foolish thing to do. *Please* don't do it again."

But she went back, day after day, all the same.

Mr. Barrett's answer came at last. It was very short and very violent. He asked them not to trouble him with their letters or their visits.

The postman brought two large packets with the letters. In them were all the letters Elizabeth had written to her father since she had left his house five years before. All the seals were unbroken. Not one had been opened.

Elizabeth stared at them in disbelief and horror. Her eyes fell on those envelopes which had thick black edgings and black seals. She had used them when Robert's mother had died. Papa was not to know that. He was not to know when the letters came to him that it was not Robert who had died—or perhaps a child of hers. Yet he had not opened them.

"So there's an end," she said brokenly.

Next morning Elizabeth went out with Dr. Jago's prescription and bought morphine at the first apothecary's she came to. When she came back she poured out a dose quite openly before Robert. He counted the drops one by one as she poured them out. At seven she stopped.

A fortnight later Robert and Elizabeth went back to Paris. Elizabeth's cough came back for the first time in six years, and the morphine helped her endure it.

They were back in Florence by the autumn.

270

25

TO ROBERT AND ELIZABETH THE THREE YEARS from 1852 to 1855 went like three months, though Elizabeth was never as strong again as before. She could no longer deny her father's rejection of her or her brothers' coolness. Her sisters refused to visit her. Sarianna and her father-in-law were pleasantly settled in Paris on two-thirds of the pension Nonno might have drawn on retirement, with Nonno sketching in the Louvre or hunting for old books on the left bank of the Seine. Robert and Elizabeth were in a sense truly alone for the first time, and they slid back into their quiet life as if Paris and London had never been. At first Robert found Florence dull, but soon he too took to comfortable old clothes again and preferred to sit alone with Elizabeth by their fireside.

> So grew my own small life complete
>   As nature obtained her best of me—
> One born to love you, Sweet!
> And to watch you sink by the fireside now
>   Back again, as you mutely sit
> Musing by firelight, that great brow
>   And the spirit-small hand propping it
> Yonder, my heart knows how!

So Robert put it, and to begin with months passed without either of them spending an evening away from home. Elizabeth's health, and then the *tramontana* whistling round the street corners, provided excuses.

Elizabeth's love for Robert blossomed in a thousand sweet and imaginative gestures, of the flesh and of the spirit, and most touching of all to him was her total dependence on him. Sometimes he would seek her out simply in order to push her heavy hair aside and kiss the downy nape of her neck or lift her chin to stare down at her face in silence.

They both worked hard and well, that winter of 1852. Elizabeth revised her collected edition for the second time and began a novel in blank verse which was to be her greatest work, expressing her outrage at men's attitude to women, especially to gifted ones. She was prepared to shock, to mention women's sexual needs as well as men's and to refer openly to the eighty thousand prostitutes who sold their bodies under London's gas lamps. She meant to be as fearless as George Sand. She had travelled a long way since Robert had rebuked her in Wimpole Street for prudery.

Her heroine Aurora Leigh—Aurora after George Sand's real name, Aurore—was like her a poet familiar with London and Paris, admiring Louis Napoleon and believing in spiritualism. Aurora's friend Marian, the innocent companion of streetwalkers of London's Oxford Street, was to be abducted, drugged and raped in a Paris brothel and bear an illegitimate baby. Most daring of all, Aurora's rival for the affections of her lover Romney would speak with brutal frankness of the carnal appetites of respectable women.

> "Am I coarse? . . .
> Well, love's coarse, nature's coarse—
> Ah, there's the rub!"

And again:

> "We have hearts within,
> Warm, live, improvident hearts,
> As ready for outrageous ends and acts,
> As any distressed sempstress of them all. . . .
> . . . We catch love
> And other fevers in the vulgar way."

Indecent hearts, like Elizabeth's. Outrageous acts, like Robert's love-making.

Into that verse novel, *Aurora Leigh,* too, would go everything Elizabeth was and had ever been and felt and done and thought; Papa and Mama, all her sweet childhood in the grounds and gardens of Hope End, and Bummy with her braided hair and down-turned lips. Paris, too, to the very dentists' advertisements of huge sets of false teeth grinning from the street corners; and London with its yellow fogs; the faces of those men and women she had seen in Shoreditch when she had gone to rescue Flush; and everything she loved about Italy—Vallombrosa, Isa's villa, the cypresses, the song of nightingales, the black figs, the purple grapes, the lightning lizards, the vanilla ices at Doney's Café, everything!

Robert, too, alone in his carpetless workroom at his high desk, was writing lyrics full of music and bright pictures, determined to catch the public's eye and ear. On New Year's Day of 1853 he came out to lay *Love Among the Ruins* smilingly before Elizabeth, his finger pointing to the last line, "Love is best!" On January the second he brought her *Women and Roses,* written, he said, because even in December in Florence their rooms were full of roses, and she read his man's passion for her flaming from it.

Deep as drops from a statue's plinth
The bee sucked in by the hyacinth,
So will I bury me while burning,
Quench like him at a plunge my yearning,
Eyes in your eyes, lips on your lips!
Fold me fast where the cincture slips,
Prison all my soul in eternities of pleasure!
Girdle me once!

Next day again he brought her a poem, the strange *Childe Roland to the Dark Tower Came.* Elizabeth did not understand its message, and Robert would only say that it had been a dream. But she sensed the resurgence of power and hope in him in the last, brave lines spoken defiantly by his knight after long failure in his unnamed quest.

And yet
Dauntless the slug-horn to my lips I set,
And blew. "Childe Roland to the Dark Tower came."

Robert, Elizabeth rejoiced, no longer feared his dark tower. He knew, as she did, that those three poems of genius written swiftly in three days would live forever.

To encourage him to keep on working Elizabeth said, "I'll lay you a wager, Robert, that I'll write more lines than you do by the time we leave for England."

"Done," he replied gaily. "And if the forfeit is paid in kisses, there can't be a loser whoever wins."

So Robert and Elizabeth worked on through a winter which proved mild even for Florence, both perfectly happy in their quiet life and in their four-year-old son.

It was true that Florence was dead, her people crushed and demoralized since that terrible day soon after Pen's birth when ten thousand Austrian soldiers had tramped down a Via Romana lined with silent onlookers to reinstate the Grand Duke Leopold in the Pitti Palace. The broken old King Charles Albert of Sardinia had died soon after his heart-cracking effort to create a free and united Italy had ended in defeat and humiliation on the battlefield, and no one knew whether his son Victor Emmanuel would someday try again. It was like a death to live there in Florence among the ancient houses in that sleepy climate, but it was a beautiful death.

When they were not working Robert and Elizabeth played with Pen or tried to teach him. He was now a startlingly beautiful and very affectionate child, with long silky hair of pale gold, a delicate lily-white skin, red lips, small widely spaced teeth, and his father's dark-blue eyes full of laughter—a creature straight out of one of Elizabeth's romantic ballads. She had his hair combed into ringlets by Wilson and clothed him in frilled silk and velvet dresses with embroidered collars and shoes of the softest leather. The Florentines admired him as he walked with Wilson along their cobbled streets, remarking to Elizabeth's delight that he was *molto elegante*.

Elizabeth was anxious that this dream child of hers should never be crossed or disciplined but should expand like a flower in an atmosphere of freedom, love, praise and beauty. Robert simply treated him as if he were a reincarnation of the boy he had been. But they both spoiled him, and so did a doting Wilson, a surprisingly tender-hearted Ferdinando and a gay little Annunziata. Even Flush let Pen pretend to ride him, though his ponderous fat body was creaking with arthritis, and almost hairless from mange.

Pen responded ungratefully to Elizabeth's permissiveness, wriggling down from her lap when she tried to teach him his tables or the alphabet. But he respected Robert's roars when he did not practice at the piano, and worked for him. "I'll make a musical prodigy of him inside two years," Robert boasted. Elizabeth disapproved of his being taught dull scales so young, and showed him how to dance with a tambourine hung with ribbons and how to draw music from a flute.

Everyone tried to spare Pen a moment's unhappiness. It was no one's fault that he ran into the dining room in his nightgown before anybody was up one cold morning in March and found Flush stiff and cold under the sideboard. His screams brought everyone running, in terror that he had fallen into the fire.

Elizabeth hugged the sobbing child. "Poor Flush was thirteen years old," she explained. "Very old for a dog."

Later, as they all stood in the cellar to bury the poor little corpse, she felt a pang of guilt. Once, she whispered to Robert, the plump glossy puppy had been everything to her, but since her marriage Flush had become only a dog.

"A happier dog," Robert consoled her, "and Pen's friend."

Ever since Edith Story's brother Joe had been born Pen had demanded a brother for himself. He was always begging Ferdinando to go out and catch a little boy for him. Now that Flush had gone he seemed lost, but his father and mother knew that there would be no brothers or sisters for him.

One day Robert came home from his walk with an owlet clasped tenderly in his hands. Pen was ecstatic, his grief for Flush assuaged, and before long he was trying to catch fireflies, dragonflies, lizards, bees and wasps on his walks in the Boboli Gardens and even wanting to make a pet of one of the scorpions which got in under the windowsill. He could never hear enough of Robert's tales of his own childhood pets, and soon Robert brought him a fieldmouse, and then a brown rabbit, and then a tortoise, and then a young green talking parrot. In no time there was a little zoo on the balcony among the camellias and orange trees. Father and son grew very close. They spent hours teaching the parrot to cry *"Per Bacco!"* in Robert's voice. Elizabeth said she was jealous, but she sang with joy because they loved each other.

It was Pen's lonely state which caused his parents to grasp at the opportunity of the children's party. The famous and beloved writer for children, Hans Christian Andersen, was visiting Florence, and William and Emelyn Story suggested that he should appear at little Edith's birthday party. Elizabeth offered the Casa Guidi apartment, since it was so much larger than the Storys', and Ferdinando would enjoy showing off his velvety ices and little cakes.

So that same afternoon, when the tall thin spidery man with immensely long arms and legs and gigantic feet rapped with his stick on their door, two dozen English and American children of all ages clustered like birds on the carved, high-backed settle, Pen's stool, the dark old chairs, and cushions on the carpet, waiting for him. Pen, dressed in silk the colour of the blue of the Della Robbia plaques on the Florentine houses, was most excited of all, looking adoringly up at the ugly face with the small pale sunken eyes half-hidden by huge eyelids, the enormous nose, and the unexpectedly beautiful mouth.

After the feasting in the tapestried dining room the children gathered in the drawing room again to hear the odd-looking man with the broken accent read *The Ugly Duckling*, the story of his life, gesturing all the time with one broad flat hand. Then Robert struck up with his *Pied Piper*. With the last line he seized Pen's flute from the piano and danced across the room piping. The children, high voices shrilling, lined up to dance after him. Through the vast rooms they went, round and round and in and out, and suddenly Robert was out of the door and the children were following him down the stone steps, and out into the baking street, and across the Piazza Pitti, with William and Emelyn Story and a laughing Hans Andersen bringing up the rear. Elizabeth snatched a cashmere shawl and ran after them, and Ferdinando, Wilson and Annunziata ran after her and they all streamed into the Boboli Gardens following Robert's merry fluting. Through the grottoes they went and into the old amphitheater, past Neptune's fishpond and the Belvedere, up to the *Statue of Plenty,* and into the enchanted Knight's Garden, down to the Falconing Lawn, and down again to the Ocean Fountain and back once more across the Piazza Pitti and up the cool stone steps and into the Casa Guidi.

"I'll carve a statue of the Pied Piper to mark the occasion," William Story swore, bearing off his children and the happy Hans Andersen.

After that party they could never be alone again as they had been. They saw all the friends they had left behind them when they had gone away for those drama-filled eighteen months in Paris and London and made new ones. People came to the Casa

Guidi, too, on three or four evenings a week to take tea and eat Wilson's knead cakes and slices of a watermelon that had been let down into the Casa Guidi's well to cool.

Extraordinary, wonderful things were happening in Florence, which drew Elizabeth with a shuddering fascination she had not experienced since the funerals of Pisa. The wave of spiritualism in America which had swept England and France now reached Florence. In the ghostly city Elizabeth's friends held séances in their beautiful ancient villas and whispered to each other tales of tables that rocked, spirit hands that rapped, pianos playing themselves, mediums floating to the ceiling, messages from the dead and a remarkable young clairvoyant called Daniel Dunglas Home.

It was Mrs. Trollope and her son Thomas Adolphus who drew Elizabeth and Robert into the new craze. Round tables in her villa sat Frederick Tennyson, eyes protruding even more than usual under his bald head, and his wife Maria, crying, *"Santa Lucia!"* under her breath, and William and Emelyn Story. The giant Thackeray clasped hands with tiny Isa Blagden, and young Robert Lytton was the most devout believer of all. Only Robert refused to take it seriously and teased Story for his naiveté, laughing at the most solemn moments—Robert and the obstreperous old cynic Landor, whom Robert had brought into their circle though everyone said he was too quarrelsome to be endured.

To Elizabeth this opening of the doors between the worlds of the living and the dead was the most important thing that had ever happened. Soon death would no longer be a horrible silence leaving questions unanswered and quarrels unhealed. Robert would believe; he must.

Then the day came in July at the Casa Guidi when the Italian Count Gennasi held a séance and asked Robert to lend him some personal possession. Holding Robert's cufflinks in his hand, the Count called out in bloodcurdling tones, "There's something here which cries out 'Murder! Murder!' " They were the cufflinks which had been taken from the murdered and mutilated corpse of Robert's great-uncle nearly sixty years before in the far-off island of Saint Kitts. Even Robert did not know what to say. Perhaps the Count had guessed from his face, he kept saying, stubbornly but unconvincingly.

Fanny Haworth arrived to settle in Florence in August— Robert's old admirer, his Eyebright, who had written him sonnets and made Elizabeth jealous seven years before in Wimpole Street, and who, in Mr. Kenyon's drawing room, had first told her of these strange things. Her handsome seal-smooth dark head and voluptuous figure joined the quiet ones round the tables. Before long Anna Jameson sat with them too. Her unloved husband had died in Canada and her allowance with him. Mr. Thackeray had pulled strings and got her a state pension, and now she too had come to live where the climate was kind and living cheap. But she was paler and bonier than ever, not at all well, and moping because Geddie had married her Scotsman and was already unhappy with him. He had given up art and set up in business as one of the first photographers in Rome; but that to Anna only made things worse.

It was September, 1853, by that time, and, like her friend Anna, Elizabeth was not at all well. She looked in the mirror anxiously, but Robert's eyes still caressed her. On the seventh of the month, as they watched the procession of the paper lanterns on the Vigil of the Virgin's Nativity winding its heart-catching way through the unlit streets of Florence, he said, "In five days' time, Ba, we will have been married seven years, and you look seven years younger than on our wedding day." How could she look only thirty-three when she was forty-seven? Still, the mirror did not distress her, and it was true that Robert Lytton, the poetical young attaché, who was only in his early twenties, looked at her as if he were dazzled and showed her his poems. Luckily Dearest Isa was not jealous.

Mr. Thackeray adored her too. He had kissed her hand and said that no two women could be further apart in spirit than his Becky Sharp, that dreadful girl in his *Vanity Fair,* and Elizabeth Barrett Browning and that she had restored his faith in human nature. His eyes had told her that it was not only her noble spirit which attracted him.

There was no disguising it, however. By the time 1854 had arrived the cough which had come back in Paris for the first time in six years was returning again and again, each time worse than before. Elizabeth felt tired too often and was losing interest in food and clothes. Ever since her father had returned her letters to him she had been taking morphine whenever she felt the need of it; but the doses had been small and infrequent. Without meaning to she began to increase them. (After all, for her there would be no more babies to be harmed, though lucky Henrietta had had her second child, a girl—she would yearn for a daughter to her dying day.) Never again would she take enough to muffle the passion of her Florentine nights of love. But, after all, for Robert's own sake it was right to take her elixir again. Twenty-four drops at bedtime meant that her cough would not keep him awake all night.

The opium helped her to write, too, and gave her the strength to teach Pen, who was surprisingly wearing. Besides, she must prepare a trousseau of clothes for him in readiness for their visit to London next year. Everyone must see him at his best, this miraculous child of theirs, perfect fruit of the love of two poets and of her passion for Italy.

So 1853 wore its way out and 1854 came in and slipped by, and nothing much happened in Florence except for the advent of Mrs. Eckley.

Sophie Eckley appeared at Mrs. Trollope's salon, a soft, pretty blond woman, very elegant and indolent, with blue eyes and side curls. She had published a novel or two at her own expense, and had a rich and adoring husband. Robert did not like her at all. He called her falsely sweet, sly and pretentious. Elizabeth took to her at once, and soon they were very close.

"She has fallen in love with me," Elizabeth laughed wickedly. "She worships me with a blind passion in all sorts of ways."

Mrs. Eckley had not had any experience of séances before, but she became an enthusiastic member of the circle, and before long her friends found that she had a real gift as a medium. At first she alone received the spirit messages, but soon she brought her maid Raffaele, a simple peasant girl of sixteen. To the awestruck excitement of the devotees Raffaele not only wrote down messages from the dead but spoke in languages she had never heard before. Elizabeth was so impressed she decided to try with Wilson.

In the autumn of 1854 news came from Henrietta that Mr. Barrett had been knocked down by a cab, and was lame, perhaps forever.

Elizabeth sat down at once to write to him, pouring out her sorrow and pity for him. Then she stood holding the letter, wondering what to do next, since her father would never open an envelope addressed in her writing. On an impulse she ran to get the solemn-eyed five-year-old Pen from the balcony and, lifting him up to the desk, thrust the quill into his hand. Bending over him, guiding the small fist, she traced his grandfather's name and address with it. Elizabeth sent the letter to Arabel to be posted in London. No answer came.

They were very poor during those three years. In 1854 they had no ship money at all, and Mr. Kenyon forgot to send the hundred pounds he had promised to give Pen every year. Robert refused to remind him, though he was growing more and more anxious to see his father and sister again. Even Elizabeth, who never worried about money, was depressed that year, wondering why no one ever proposed them for a state pension like Tennyson —who was now Poet Laureate as well—and Miss Mitford and Anna Jameson. She noticed their poverty more that year because Mrs. Eckley was always bringing her presents, and she disliked not being able to return them.

As their work neared completion they worried more. Robert had written enough poems for a volume already, and Elizabeth's *Aurora Leigh* was more than half done.

"How many lines have you written, Robert?" Elizabeth asked at last.

"Eight thousand."

"And I've written seven thousand. You've won because I had Pen's clothes to prepare as well."

"No excuses, Ba. I claim my forfeit."

She kissed him happily. "We're ready to go, Robert. I can finish *Aurora Leigh* in England while we're seeing your volume through the press. But—"

But there was no money. They might not be able to go after all.

Then, just at the right time, in March, 1855, the *Statira* and the *David Lyon* paid out a hundred and seventy-five pounds in ship money—a fortune. When Mr. Kenyon's hundred pounds came through they would be richer than ever before.

At last Robert and Elizabeth and Penini sat in the train, once again on their way to Paris and London. The precious manuscript of *Aurora Leigh* was in a suitcase with all Pen's new clothes, and Robert's eight thousand lines of poetry were in a case in the rack above his head. Ferdinando was coming as well as Wilson this time. Only Flush was missing. They were going to spend a few days in Marseilles and then a week in Paris in order to see Sarianna and Nonno and, astonishingly, to arrange Wilson's marriage to Ferdinando. Only a week before they had left, Ferdinando had come to them to explain that he wanted to marry Wilson, and no priest in Florence would unite a Catholic man to a Protestant bride unless she agreed to bring up the children as Catholics—which Wilson would not do. They were sure to find a more acquiescent priest in gay, free-thinking Paris, they thought.

They were all going to an England devastated by the terrible Crimean War, bleeding from the loss of her sons, and possessed by hatred—of the Russian enemy, of her own leaders, of her own generals, even of her own allies, the French. Everyone wore black, including those who had not lost relations at the front. Aunt Hedley, always so brave before, was terrified for her two sons Robin and Richard, but otherwise the family was untouched. At one time Surtees's regiment had been going to the Crimea, and then the sailing orders had been cancelled. Now Lord Aberdeen's coalition government was at an end, and Lord Palmerston was Prime Minister, a man of war to end a war.

Now, Elizabeth was thinking, it was 1855, and she and Robert had been married for nine years. There was no escaping it that she was nearly fifty, and Robert was six years younger.

She looked down at her hands—so thin they were, like the poor little feet of some bird. Nine years ago they had been beautiful. She knew that her face was drawn and that sometimes it had a parched look. The roses had gone, and all that transient plumpness he had enjoyed so much.

But Robert was as blind as ever. He still kissed her hands and her feet and called her beautiful.

At least her hair was still wonderfully thick and black and curled as resolutely as ever. Wilson still caught the comb in its tangles, making her cry out. When she let it down in a black bush about her shoulders Robert sighed with desire and buried his face in it. Her eyes, too. No illness could reduce their size or the length of their lashes. If nothing was left of her but her eyes and her hair Robert would still worship and kiss her with passion—and his passion would always light her own flame.

On the very steps of their Marseilles hotel they ran into

Alfred, Elizabeth's sixth brother who worked on the railways. He was staying there too. They had supper together, and, over a bottle of champagne Alfred insisted on providing, he revealed that he was planning to marry Lizzie Barrett, the little West Indian cousin who had lived at Wimpole Street because her mother was insane and her father Captain Barrett was in Jamaica. Elizabeth had a vivid memory of Alfred gawkishly pulling Lizzie's flaxen hair as he burlesqued Robert's visits to her.

"I can't believe Lizzie isn't still a little girl," Robert said, "but she must be twenty-one."

To his astonishment Elizabeth expressed her disapproval. Alfred was in debt and his job on the railways was poorly paid and without prospects.

"You're damned interfering, Ba," Alfred burst out. "As bad as Papa. I'm thirty-five and can decide for myself. Besides, who are *you* to talk?"

The silence was embarrassing. After nine years Robert still had neither paid occupation nor literary success. But Elizabeth answered unabashed, "I had a private income, Alfred, and we were not in debt."

She was not pleased either to learn that Stormy had set himself up with a coloured "housekeeper" in Jamaica and already had four children by her or that her seventh brother Septimus was drinking, gambling and spending money like water in the island.

In Paris it proved as difficult as in Florence to find a priest who would waive a Catholic husband's right to rear his children in his own faith. Every day Robert and Elizabeth visited two or three priests without success. Their money was disappearing fast with hotel and restaurant expenses. Robert complained that he hardly saw his father and sister though their apartment was directly over his rooms. A week went by, then two. The thing had become a nightmare.

Suddenly Wilson agreed to be married unconditionally after all. "Ferdinando feels there's been too much delay already, ma'am."

After the ceremony Robert and Elizabeth returned to their rooms to find a note from Alfred. He had been married to Lizzie at the Paris Embassy while Wilson was being made Signora Romagnoli. "Papa wrote that he would cut me out if I married," it read laconically. "Wish us luck."

"Wish them luck, Ba," Robert said to Elizabeth's disapproving face.

That night Robert overheard Elizabeth giving orders to Wilson to go to bed early with Penini as she herself was going out to a reception. "Then he won't notice my not being here."

Robert saw that Wilson looked upset, but she left the room obediently.

"Ba! Wilson won't be sleeping with Penini anymore," he said firmly.

"But Robert, you know Penini needs someone to sleep with him. Whenever he wakes at night he cries for attention."

"You can't separate husband and wife, Ba."

Elizabeth was unconvinced, but so excited at meeting Prosper Mérimée (as much because he was George Sand's ex-lover as because he was a famous novelist) at the reception that she forgot her worries about Penini. When they got home he was sleeping soundly, alone.

26

ROBERT AND ELIZABETH BOOKED NIGHT PASSAGES
from Marseilles to save money on hotel accommodation, and their
party arrived in London exhausted at three o'clock in the morning.

Robert woke next day in their rooms at number 13 Dorset
Street to hear Ferdinando exclaiming at the pouring rain, *"Povera
gente che deve vivere in questo posto!* Poor people who have to
live in such a country!"

When, later that day, Arabel took Penini home with her
and asked her to collect him, Elizabeth replied, "No, I won't go
creeping and sliding behind the doors of my old home as if I'd
stolen the teapot. What Papa's done to Henrietta is the last
straw."

It was five o'clock before Arabel brought Penini back. She
arrived red-faced and flustered, crying as soon as the door was
closed, "Oh, Ba, something terrible has happened. Papa saw
Penini."

"How did it happen?"

"George was playing with him in the hall, and he was in
fits of laughter—you know how he laughs and can't stop. Papa
heard him and he came out of the dining room and stood looking
—just looking—for two or three minutes. 'Whose child is that,
George?' he asked. 'Ba's child,' said George. 'And what's he doing
here, pray?' Then without waiting for an answer, Papa changed
the subject."

284

An hour later Mr. Barrett had called George and told him the whole family must pack up and go to the Isle of Wight as quickly as rooms could be taken there.

"But I won't go," Arabel declared. "I'm forty-two years old, and I won't be ordered about like a child. I'll go and live with Treppy and earn my living."

"But what could you do?"

"I could be a wood engraver or a companion."

"Would you do that for my sake, Arabel?"

"Yes, Ba."

Arabel seemed determined, yet there were tears in her eyes. Elizabeth's anger rose at sight of her tired, dutiful sister faced with an intolerable choice after years of devoted service to her father. Well, she could always give Arabel a home with her and Robert.

"Don't be upset, Arabel," Elizabeth comforted her. "Stay with us here, now. Mr. Tennyson is coming tonight to read his sensational new poem, *Maud*."

Thomas Carlyle was there, as uncouth and as dyspeptic as ever, with his plain Jane looking jealously about her. The exquisite Mr. Ruskin, the art critic, was there, suffering visibly because his pretty wife Effie had just had their seven-year-long marriage annulled and married the painter Millais. Everyone knew that Ruskin had not consummated his marriage because he had hitherto seen only beautiful naked statues of women and it had revolted him to find pubic hair on a woman's body. William Makepeace Thackeray was looming and booming in a corner at Anna Jameson, just as if they were still in Florence. The handsome young Dante Gabriel Rossetti, founder of the pre-Raphaelite school of painting and author of the poem everyone loved, *The Blessed Damozel*, was exercising his charm on nice ugly Dicky Monckton-Milnes and the pot-bellied Mr. Fox, Eliza Flower's old lover.

Tennyson was hurt that the critics had received his *Maud* badly and was defiantly enjoying his success with the public. "Five thousand copies sold," the Poet Laureate kept saying. "Five thousand."

Suddenly Tennyson's magnificent voice rose and silence fell.

"Come into the garden, Maud,
For the black bat, night, has flown.

Come into the garden, Maud,
I am here at the gate alone."

He sat, his left leg curled over his right, at the end of the sofa, smoking his pipe and reading in that voice like an organ, pausing every now and then to exclaim, "That's very tender," or "*There*'s a wonderful touch," or "How beautiful that is."

Dante Gabriel Rossetti made two sketches of him as he read and gave one to Elizabeth.

When Tennyson had finished Robert read his *Fra Lippo Lippi*. Elizabeth and he had chosen it from the poems he had brought over to be published under the general title of *Men and Women*. Elizabeth looked nervously about her as he began in his strong, resonant voice, not so much reading as dramatizing his poem. It was so different from the heavy, honeyed romanticism of *Maud*. The carnal monk's words shot like bullets into the quiet room—daring, racy, words, used by ordinary people. It was bold, unorthodox. Would these people be shocked by a monk seized at a brothel door?

"I am poor brother Lippo, by your leave!
You need not clap your torches to my face.
Zooks, what's to blame? You think you see a monk!
What, it's past midnight, and you go the rounds,
And here you catch me at an alley's end
Where sportive ladies leave their doors ajar?"

Elizabeth glanced at Arabel's blank face, then at Rossetti's radiant one. "Truly a night of the gods!" he whispered to Elizabeth. Yet everyone there, including Robert, thought Tennyson the king of poets. And he was Poet Laureate, though only three years older than Robert. Yet to her Robert was the genius, Tennyson the organ with only one stop.

The party did not break up until half-past two. Arabel had slipped away long before.

Next morning Arabel's maid Bonser brought a note. Arabel was going away with the family. All her brave words had come to nothing. She begged Elizabeth to follow her to Ventnor on the Channel side of the Isle of Wight. Mr. Barrett would only be coming down occasionally. Elizabeth could not afford it—or to go and see Henrietta. That extra ten days in Paris had eaten up too much money.

Another letter came that morning, however. Mr. Kenyon begged them to accept fifty pounds towards their lodgings, as he had not been able to keep an old promise about lending them his London house.

"At least that's one way of paying Penini's half-yearly fifty pounds," Elizabeth said ruefully. "Now we can follow the family and see Mr. Kenyon too."

When they told Wilson their plans she burst into tears and confessed that she was expecting a baby in a month or so.

Elizabeth was terribly shocked. Wilson *had* seemed to be growing plump, but such a thing had never entered her mind. "I'm disappointed in you, Wilson. I always thought you were virtuous and modest. I remember how shocked you were by the naked Venuses in Florence."

Wilson hid her face in her hands and howled. "Yes, m'm, and you told me it was natural, ma'am, and beautiful, and—" Sobs drowned the rest.

"You're very hard on poor Wilson, Ba—you who kissed the hand of George Sand," Robert said privately to Elizabeth later.

"She's going to her mother's for her confinement," she said, unrelentingly. "We'll have to do without her. I wish we could go back to Florence now!"

But they must prepare the proofs of Robert's *Men and Women.* Now at last his genius would be recognized. Soon the world would be able to read for the first time his *Fra Lippo Lippi, The Bishop Orders His Tomb at Saint Praxed's Church, Bishop Blougram's Apology* and *Andrea del Sarto,* with the two lines which proudly expressed Robert's own creed: "Ah, but a man's reach should exceed his grasp,/ Or what's a heaven for?"

This time he could not fail.

They packed up and went to join Arabel and her brothers in exile at Ventnor. For a fortnight they worked on the proofs and saw what they could of the family, always in dread of Mr. Barrett's sudden arrival. Then they went to stay with Mr. Kenyon at West Cowes on the other side of the island.

They did not know what to expect as they walked into the large silent house overlooking the parade and the Solent. Mr. Kenyon was standing to receive them, but he was leaning on a table. He was pallid and had lost a great deal of flesh. He drew breath with difficulty.

"Oh, dear Mr. Kenyon," Elizabeth cried, and ran to him.

He straightened. His face lit up, and he held out a hand to welcome Robert. Almost at once he crumpled, breathed stertorously again, and grasped at the table, groaning softly, "My God!"

"Are you sure you want us here?" Robert asked.

"Yes, yes. Plenty of servants. But if you'll forgive me, I'll go back to bed now. Take a glass of wine."

He walked out with a stick, in obvious pain.

"He hasn't got many months to live, Robert."

Robert nodded. Dicky Monckton-Milnes had told him that it was cancer.

They talked with their host when he was well enough, but for the most part they worked on at Robert's proof sheets, dispatching them by almost every post. It was particularly dull for Penini, who had to creep about like a mouse, with no other children, and no uncles to play with him on the sands and teach him how to put up his fists and show the "pluck" of an English boy.

Elizabeth said to Robert, "I'm ashamed that I've never dedicated any of my poems to Mr. Kenyon. I'd like to dedicate *Aurora Leigh* to him."

"Before it's finished?"

"I can write the dedication now."

On the morning they left she showed it to Mr. Kenyon.

"*Aurora Leigh* will be the best of all my works," she told him. "Everything I believe about life and art is going into it, as I've said here. I've worked for four years on it already."

The old man's hand shook as he took the piece of paper. He put on the spectacles which had filled her with terror ten years before and which roused only her pity now. She could see how moved he was.

From Mr. Kenyon's they went straight to Taunton to stay with Henrietta and Surtees. They found them living in a large pleasant house with four servants and a laburnum tree looking in at the window. Henrietta at forty-six was expecting her third child. Her coppery hair was fading, and she had thickened, but she looked happy. Pen and Altham and his little sister Mary played together on the grass. Robert and Surtees got on famously.

"What are you going to call the baby?" Elizabeth asked after supper on their first evening.

"If it's a girl, after you."

Elizabeth smiled with pleasure. "And if it's a boy?"

"Edward."

Elizabeth put her hand to the gold chain at her throat which held the lock of Robert's hair. "*Not* after Papa?"

"Not after Papa."

"Then—?"

"Yes, after Bro." Henrietta's eyes met her sister's without flinching.

"You *shouldn't!*"

"*Shouldn't?*"

"Even *I* didn't—I who was so close to him!"

"He was my brother, too."

Elizabeth said no more.

In her turn Henrietta was critical of Penini's education.

"He can't spell, Ba, and his writing is dreadful. Altham is two years younger and spells and writes much better."

"I don't think it matters."

"Oh, Ba, you're teaching him nothing suitable for his age and too much that isn't! To talk to him about history and politics for an hour and a half every day is too great a strain, but a quarter of an hour at his reading and writing would be useful to him later."

"The child is brilliant and can speak French and Italian fluently."

Henrietta did not care for Pen's "fantastic" clothes, either. But on the whole the visit was a great success, and Henrietta clung to Elizabeth when she left, saying, "It's been all too short."

"Yes, but we must go back to London to finish the proofs before the cold weather drives me from England. Robert's *Men and Women* is due out in November, and it's the end of September already."

"We've only seen each other twice in nine years, Ba."

"Come to Florence—" Elizabeth began and stopped. It was no use. She knew that Henrietta and Surtees would never leave England.

London was already shrouded in autumnal fog. Almost at

once Elizabeth developed a severe cough. It kept her awake night after night until she cried angrily, "There's always an east wind for me in England!" Yet she worked all day at Robert's proofs, swathed in cashmere shawls, not complaining of the toll it took of her.

Penini had a letter from Altham and sat down of his own accord to reply. He boasted, "I go out in the streets almost every day with my sword and my gun and frighten all the people." It was Robert who had to take him out for walks. Wilson's baby had just been born in the north. She wrote that he had great black Italian eyes and was to be christened Orestes.

Elizabeth was trying not only to help Robert with his proofs but to work on at *Aurora Leigh*. It was still only two-thirds written.

She wrote to Henrietta: "One thing which has put me out of sorts since I came back to London has been a mistake of Twin-berrow's, the chemist's near here. My morphine, which is indispensable, was made up weaker than usual. So I have had the feeling people often have in dreams—of being forced to run, for some important reason, and of not being able to move my legs. Now, however, Bell, the chemist I always used in the old days—and who told Robert he thought I was dead long ago!—has sent me the right mixture, and so I'm once again my old self, and comfortable. Really quite well."

She added: "Yes, Robert fetched it. He doesn't like me to take it, as you know, but he sees I need it, especially now."

27

HALF ASLEEP, ROBERT SEARCHED FOR THE CAUSES of the feeling of conflict and oppression. Ba's health? The war? Penini? The weather?

Then he remembered that Elizabeth and he were to drive out the ten miles down the Thames to Ealing that afternoon and attend a séance with the medium Daniel Dunglas Home at the house of some people called Rymer. "I cannot," he groaned aloud. "Not even for Ba."

He waited until breakfast had been cleared away and Penini had scampered out to play on the piano in the sitting room before he broached the subject to Elizabeth.

"Ba, I don't want to go to Ealing this afternoon."

"Oh, Robert, you gave me your promise!" She really minded, as he had known she would.

"What *is* the use of it, Ba? You know I think it's all complete humbug. I've been to so many of these affairs now. One more isn't going to alter anything."

"I *know* that once you have seen what Mr. Home can achieve your eyes will be opened," Elizabeth answered earnestly. "He was a sensation in America. All New York—all Boston, too—flocked to see him. The spirits talk through him."

"People believe what they want to believe."

"That is true, Robert."

He realized that Elizabeth was laughing at him, and he welcomed the momentary return to the everyday world of common sense and happy agreement. Elizabeth was not content to leave matters there, however.

"Remember the cufflinks! You've never been able to explain them away."

"There must be a reasonable explanation, Ba."

"The explanation is that you're deliberately shutting your mind to certain things just because you don't understand them."

Robert did not answer, and Elizabeth looked sad again.

"Think again, my Robert," she pleaded. "It was kind of Anna Jameson to arrange it for us with these friends of hers and so good of them to allow us to attend this very private meeting. Poor souls, they are praying Mr. Home will raise the spirit of Dotty, their baby girl who died three years ago."

"I knew there'd be something like that behind it."

Elizabeth would not release him, and she would not go without him. She always spoke and acted as if his coming round to her way of thinking was only a matter of time. She would not listen when he said he did not like to see her gulled and feared that she would pay a high price in the end.

She knew that he did not like her dwelling morbidly on Bro's death, and lived in dread of the return of that miasma of guilt and despair from which he had rescued her. She answered only, "And if it gives me hope, Robert?"

That was the crux of the matter, Robert thought. This was the unspoken thing between them, only half acknowledged. She hoped to have her beloved brother brought back from the dead. Elizabeth wanted to speak to her Bro so that those impatient words she and he had exchanged in their last moments together could be obliterated. Obviously she hoped to receive some precious message from him—of what? Forgiveness? Comfort? Confirmation of an afterlife, perhaps?

That was what lay behind her feverish attachment to this murky world of the occult, a world where reason was a stranger and sunlight was not allowed to enter. A world of drawn curtains and dark rooms, where strange doings were arranged for money. If there were anything behind these things, that was not the way it should be done. It was people like Ba who gave the impetus to this movement which was sweeping America and Europe like an epidemic and which allowed imposters to prey on the sorrowing weak, those who could not endure their grief without such aid.

292

"I can't refuse you, Ba. Even this," Robert said finally.

Elizabeth smiled then, that smile like a sunbeam. It made his heart ache that there should be such a smile lit by gratitude for such dark doings.

So that afternoon they drove out to the Rymers' house in Ealing, a substantial house in a garden full of flowers, where a little girl called Dotty had once played in the sun. Rymer was a prosperous solicitor.

There was already a small group of people in the large drawing room, and an excited buzz greeted Elizabeth's arrival. She was immediately led away from Robert's side and towards a tall, rather strange young man with a wreath of white clematis hanging from one hand, holding court beside a round table in the middle of the room.

Robert's host, a small quiet man, abandoned him almost at once. No one looked directly at Robert, but more than once he caught a cold eye on him. It was obvious that he was regarded as an enemy in the camp, and his distaste mounted. These were not people who sought the truth dispassionately but fanatics who demanded unquestioning conversion to a faith of their own creation.

Over the fireplace there was a picture in a round gilt frame of a cherubic child of about two years old, dimpled and smiling, in a blue dress, with a dove poised on her chubby fist. That would be little Dotty, no doubt.

The clairvoyant was gushing over Elizabeth's hand. "My dear Mrs. Browning, I've heard so much of the good work you and your circle have done in Florence."

Elizabeth was stammering with pleasure and embarrassment. "I've done nothing, Mr. Home."

"When someone of your intelligence—your eminence—your genius—helps our cause, it is beyond price." Robert felt sure he shot a glance at him as he spoke.

"I hope to visit Florence soon, Mrs. Browning," Home was continuing.

"That's wonderful news!" Again the smile like a sunbeam—but not for Robert this time.

Robert's heart sank. Here was a further reason for flattering Ba and fussing over her. The fellow would find a circle of ready-made devotees when he came, and Ba would be a feather in his cap. Her name carried weight in England and America.

Robert had heard that he had been born in Scotland but had grown up in America. He had a Scotsman's loose, bony frame and red hair; but his accent was American. Robert was surprised at how young he was—especially as he had been appearing in public for five years—not more than nineteen or twenty. Robert did not care for his large dull blue eyes or the slack mouth hanging between flat cheeks. His skin had a tubercular brightness. He was a bony and brightly coloured creature, yet there was something damp and flabby and pallid about him, too. He oozed unctuousness and insincerity.

Now Home was showing Elizabeth his wreath and gesturing towards two girls, younger and plumper replicas of Mrs. Rymer. They were like a hen and two chickens, Robert thought, trying to keep up his spirits. When she clucked they cheeped. A boy of about fourteen stood not far off. Master Rymer, the cockerel, presumably.

"Diana and Mary and I have been gathering these flowers as a humble tribute to your genius," Home was saying. "I am going to ask the spirits to place it on your brow." Elizabeth made a gesture of dissent, but Home smiled and placed the wreath on the table.

Very quickly after that, it seemed, Home was ushering everyone to the table, pulling chairs out and ordering people to them. Soon the host and hostess were at the windows drawing the curtains, then returning hastily to their own chairs. There was hardly any light in the room despite the bright July afternoon outside. Robert could distinguish nothing with any certainty, strain his eyes as he might. It was just as he had feared it would be.

He had seated Elizabeth and taken a chair beside her, across the table from Home. His uneasiness increased when Home asked Elizabeth to come and sit beside him. Robert put out a hand to prevent her leaving him, but she had already gone. Home placed her on his right.

There was an expectant silence while the little sounds around the table died away. Robert had no idea how long it lasted before that dreadful accordion music swelled from underneath the table. It was loud and crude. The spirits were squeezing the accordion, he supposed. Very bad musicians, they were.

Robert craned forward, cursing his shortsighted eye. Something white had appeared, solid enough in shape but hard to make out. It looked like a hand. It hovered above the table and seemed to catch hold of the wreath and pull it, or push it. It was a clumsy business anyway, for the wreath fell on the floor. The hand, if that was what it was, disappeared and swooped down—he could just see it, on his side—and picked up the wreath. Now it was floating it through the air, carrying it to Elizabeth, holding it above her head. He could swear that Elizabeth was shaking her head, obviously refusing it, and waving it towards him. He could see her leaning back, staring at it.

Something touched him on the nape of his neck and on his shoulder, making him jump. When he put up his hand to grasp whatever it was it had gone. All the while there was that dreadful music being churned out, covering up any other noise there might be.

To cap everything, the table suddenly rose at least a foot in the air and tilted over. It was all distracting—and meant to be, he was sure—and while everyone was scrambling to retain their seats anything might have been going on in the dark under that crazily tilting table, and with the loud music being pumped out.

Then the table righted itself, and all was still, and the music died away with a last tortured gasp. In the silence there was what he had expected before, the loud raps in answer to questions from the medium, the routine at all the sittings in Florence, and everywhere, now.

"Are you there, Dotty? Will you rap once if you are?"

One rap.

"Will you speak to us, Dotty? Please rap twice if you will!"

Two raps.

Then the medium was lolling sideways, in what was presumably a trance, gabbling in a new high-pitched voice, and Mrs. Rymer was moaning hysterically, "It's Dotty's voice. Oh, God, my child."

On and on Home went in his piping voice, calling for Mama and Papa, for a pet dog, lisping incredibly of dolls and swings. It was too much for Robert.

"I would like to see the spirit hand again," he called out in a strong voice. "I want to examine it! Will you please let me hold it, Mr. Home?"

There was a shocked chorus of shushings, but he tried again, determined to bring some sanity into the proceedings.

"Mr. Rymer, will you be so kind as to ask Mr. Home to let me hold the spirit hand?"

"Be quiet," Mr. Rymer hissed at him, with surprising vigour. "The medium mustn't be disturbed! Don't you know you can kill him in his present state?"

A wave of silent fury came at Robert across the soft moanings of Mrs. Rymer and the high pipings of Home about angels in heaven and dolls on earth—a strange duet from the two of them. When Home's voice finally died away everyone continued to sit in silence. Even Mrs. Rymer's sobbings subsided at last.

It was Mr. Rymer alone who tiptoed across to the curtains and drew them apart. The daylight struck into the room as into the scene of some shameful event. The medium still lolled dramatically in his chair, his eyes closed, his wiry hair rumpled, breathing stertorously. After a few minutes he came twitchingly back to life. He passed his veined hand across his eyes as if he were dazed, making it clear that he did not know what had passed in that room.

In the carriage Robert expressed himself forcibly to Elizabeth about Home. She was not to be moved.

"There's no doubt about it, Robert. There were the spirit hands, and I could see them as clearly as I see yours this minute. Mr. Home told them to place the garland on my head, and one of them approached me with it and did so."

"How do you know it was a spirit hand?"

"It was a hand, very large, as white as snow, and very beautiful. It was as near to me as mine is—like that!—and I saw it as clearly."

"It was Home's hand. Or a hand made out of rubber."

"I believe that Mr. Home had no more to do with organizing what happened than I did—or you."

"And I believe he's a fraud. Not even a very good one. You're as stubborn as a mule, my beloved Ba."

"You too, my beloved Robert."

Elizabeth had brought the wreath away with her. She carried it indoors and hung it on the mirror of her dressing table. It was a mistake. Every time Robert looked at it he remembered the afternoon at the Rymers, and his anger was renewed. Then as the days passed he made up his mind that something must be done.

Before a week had gone by he had written to ask Mrs. Rymer if she would arrange another séance with Home and allow him to be present once again. Almost at once he had a refusal. Mrs. Rymer wrote formally that her other engagements made it impossible. Robert was frustrated, insulted, angry and fearful of the thing which was getting such a hold on Ba.

Then Mrs. Rymer called with Home.

Robert would never understand why she had done so. Perhaps she regretted her abrupt rejection of his request, deciding that Elizabeth too might take offense. Or Home himself might have wished to preserve good relations with Elizabeth. They might well have hoped to find her in, and him out, in the afternoon.

At any rate there Mrs. Rymer was at their door in Dorset Street, asking if Mrs. Browning was in, with her son by her side, and Mr. Daniel Dunglas Home.

Penini had gone to Arabel's for one of his long spoiling days, and Robert had spent the afternoon correcting proofs beside Elizabeth. Wilson brought up the message, and before he could speak Elizabeth was on her feet, ordering, "Show them up at once, Wilson, and bring tea."

Robert could hardly believe that the fellow was there, in his own home, weeviling his way in without an invitation. He rose to his feet ominously as the three came chattering into the room, noting Home's nervous eye on him, and waited without speaking until Wilson had withdrawn. He put out a hand to stop Elizabeth in her happy rush towards them.

Home put out his pink freckled hand to him. Robert stared at it as if he did not quite know what it was. Then, pointedly, he flung his right hand across his left shoulder, turned his back and walked to the other side of the room. There he turned and stood waiting.

Elizabeth had remained where she was, distracted and distressed. Now she flew to Home. Putting both her hands in his, she pleaded, "Oh, dear Mr. Home, don't blame me! I am so sorry, but I'm not to blame."

Robert felt betrayed. His anger grew. He stalked back to the group, which seemed to huddle together against him. Looming over Mrs. Rymer, he said threateningly, "Why, madam, didn't you arrange for another séance, as I asked you? Is it because you're afraid of the truth?"

"Mr. Browning, I must protest—" Home began sanctimoniously.

"Be quiet," Robert roared at him.

"I've a right to speak in my own defense," Home shouted back.

"Yes, indeed," Mrs. Rymer clucked.

"Yes, indeed," her son chimed in.

Robert sprang forward. Home backed away, thinking he was being attacked. Then he tried to recover lost ground. "I cannot stay here in this house to be insulted," he piped, and rushed back to Elizabeth, who still stood not knowing what to do. Home took her hand and shook it.

"Oh, dear Mr. Home," Elizabeth stammered again, over and over. "I'm not to blame! Oh, dear. Oh, dear."

Home went with some dignity to the door and opened it. The two Rymers swept through it. Perhaps, Robert thought, watching them, swept was not the right word for Mrs. Rymer's plump and widespread departure. They went like a mother duck and her duckling rather than a hen and her cockerel. Quack-quack, not cluck-cluck! They passed Wilson on the stairs bringing up the tea tray.

"A *brawl*," Elizabeth said.

Robert hadn't finished, however. His anger was still hot in him and demanded action. Suddenly he thought of Home's garland, the symbol of all the trouble between him and Ba. He strode across the room and disappeared into the bedroom. He came out carrying it, now a withered object with dry brown leaves. In a moment he was at the window, throwing up the sash, hurling out the wreath in a triumphant arc and shouting a great "Cock-a-doodle-doo!"

Soon after Elizabeth heard the carriage wheels grinding off. "That was unseemly," she said coldly.

"And now, Elizabeth," Robert said, unrepentant, "I'm going for a long walk."

She heard him call her Elizabeth, not Ba. Yet it was Robert who was in the wrong. He had behaved outrageously. He had treated her like a child or a slave. He had been discourteous to guests who were welcome to her. For the first time in their marriage she was ashamed of him. He who could be so delicate in love—was this the tenderness he had offered her? Was this the respect he thought her due? That he must bully her into forced agreement with all his views and create scenes in public if she couldn't bring herself to obey him? Then their marriage was no better than anyone else's. What was the difference between him and Papa?

Robert had gone. She heard the front door slam. She walked across to the sofa and sank slowly down on it. She sat erect, the palms of her hands pressed tight together in front of her. She felt breathless.

After a while she remembered the morphine.

Robert strode fiercely for a long time before he was able to think, bringing down his heels hard, striking the pavement with the ferrule of his stick and paying no attention to anyone in his path. At last his pace slackened. It was in order to think that he had left the house, and think he must.

Things had reached a crisis in their lives which he had never thought to see. It must be resolved, and without a quarrel with Ba. Well, he supposed he *had* behaved in an unseemly way. Tongues would wag, and everything be exaggerated and distorted, and lies told, too, no doubt!

Throwing that accursed wreath after that snipe and seeing the look of surprise on his pink face before it was blotted out had done him good. He could see Home now, scrambling into the carriage, his knock-knees bumping in his hurry, and behind him the scared faces of Rymer mother and Rymer son staring up at him where he stood at the window. It still made him want to laugh.

He was damned if he regretted acting as he had done. Except for Ba. For the first time in their marriage she had left his side to go over to the enemy, and in a way that mattered to them both. Their differences about politics, about people, had not touched him in the same way. Even his unhappiness about her way with Penini, his only son, hadn't divided them. Why then had this brought them so close to a parting of minds and hearts? He must find the answer before he returned to her side.

He was past Marble Arch now. He turned into Hyde Park.

Was it only fear of Ba's being hurt that troubled him? Was there not something else which accounted for this violence and the feeling of loneliness? Slowly he wrested the answer from himself. It was like taking a rifle bullet from one's own shrinking flesh. It was painful, but it was better to have it out than leave it festering there.

He did not flinch from the truth when he saw it.

For nothing that Elizabeth had ever said or done had he ever felt anything but pride, or at least sympathy, except for this. Her political ideas were misguided, perhaps, but they sprang from a nobility of soul and a passion for heroes. The worst that could be said was that she had loved Italy and its people, who loved her, too hotly. As for Penini, again it was a question of loving too much. It was no great wickedness to pamper a highly strung child—to cherish him, even dress him like a Renaissance prince if she wished.

But this anger which burst from him now was, he knew, really directed at her because of what she was doing to him. He was deflecting it onto the medium because he must not, could not, be angry with her. He was angry to see her behaving like a foolish woman, degrading herself in his eyes. He was outraged because she was endangering his love for her, destroying the ideal by which he lived.

It was that against which he fought. His perfect Ba! Now she was making him wonder, deep within himself, whether he had not been mistaken in her after all. Had he exalted, not a goddess, but a ninny?

He paused, flinching now at the words that sprang to his mind, excoriating words, describing his own beloved. His tongue, his pen, had always been acid. But for others. He must not even think of her in those terms.

He had come to Apsley House. There the great Duke of Wellington had lived. He had married a silly woman. His Kitty had loved him, but had infuriated him with her extravagance and the way she had brought up his sons. She had driven him to Mrs. Arbuthnot's fireside.

What arrogance it was in him to think like that of his Ba. What right had he to demand Minerva as a wife? Did he even want Minerva? He thought of Mary Godwin, Shelley's wife. A wonderful woman, yes. Beautiful and clever, but comfortless. Ba had never been able to bear her. That marble calm, that cool brow, that brilliant mind, were all very well—but in a wife? Such women made chilly hearths. He preferred his Ba, warm and wrong-headed about politics, more disturbed that a lost trunk held

Penini's frills than that the manuscript of her *Aurora Leigh* was in it too.

Thoughts of Mary Godwin led naturally to Shelley's first wife, the poor, silly girl, so lost among his friends, who had ended her life in the river. Poor child. Of course, Ba would never do such a thing, never drown herself. But Ba was a harpstring for misery. Then, she need not drown herself, she might simply fade away from unhappiness. She had been well on the way to it when he had come into her life.

Down Constitution Hill, past Buckingham Palace, through Saint James's Park, and across Horse Guards Parade he thought of those days. In the park there was a young soldier in his red tunic sitting on a bench. There were crutches propped beside him.

The truth was, she needed him. He was the only person in the world who was responsible for her. If he walked away from her, in fact or in spirit, she would die. Her obstinacy, her pride, her arrogance in choosing her own way, were all nothing. They would be gone like a puff of wind. Her life was his. He held her in his hand, and he could kill her at his will. A great wave of tenderness came over him, and was followed by a humility strange to him. Who was he to wield such power?

What a small sacrifice it was, merely that he should hold his tongue. Yet must there be a silence between them? Always, before, they had thought aloud to each other.

He had walked down Whitehall and Parliament Street, past the entrance to Downing Street, into Parliament Square. There was Big Ben and the new Parliament Building. They said Disraeli had married a stupid woman for her money, but that she worshipped him. He walked on to Westminster Bridge. Halfway across he paused and leaned over the parapet, looking down at the ebb-tide swirling under the arches. A succession of mighty barges was heading downstream. As each one came to the bridge, at what seemed the very last instant before disaster, the towering mast and canvas sank backwards to the deck, and the vessel swept through beneath his feet.

Out of nowhere came a memory from those days which they had shared at 50 Wimpole Street. He remembered how often Elizabeth had insisted that he did not love the real woman but some creature of his own imagination, and that the day would come when he would be disappointed in her. That day had been a long time coming, ten years.

He remembered what he had said to Elizabeth in answer to her fears. He loved her for herself, as she was, whatever that was, and forever. He remembered too the joyous words into which she had put her thankfulness, words which would speak for women the world over.

If thou must love me let it be for nought
Except for love's sake only.

It was only because of his promise that Elizabeth had married him. Would he allow Home, or the spirits, or Elizabeth herself, to come between them? "Except for love's sake only"!

He turned round and walked home.

Elizabeth was still sitting on the sofa. How small she looked there, soft and calm again. He never ceased to be surprised at her minuteness. Everything about her was small, except those great eyes—and that great heart.

She smiled at him and he kissed her twice. First the soft curls and then the patient white face.

"I'm sorry to have made a brawl, Ba. I embarrassed you. That was unforgivable." He could not leave it there. Not in all honesty. "I'm afraid I can't be sorry to have spoken my mind."

"You have the right, Robert. Perhaps not quite so violently. But you'll never need to do it again. I've made up my mind to withdraw from—all that."

That took him by surprise. This was not a sacrifice he had expected from her.

"Not from conviction?"

"No, not from conviction. But if you feel so strongly—if it hurts you so much—"

"I cannot let you do this, Ba." Now he surprised himself with the vehemence of his cry. "You've a right to be your own self, too. We'll go on as we were, and I won't lose my temper again."

"Only if you want it so, Robert."

"Yes, I do."

"Very well. And we won't mention it again."

302

He couldn't help smiling. She had never changed. He remembered all the things he had been forbidden ever to speak of again in those early days. He had broken down each wall until there was nothing hidden, nothing between them that could not be spoken of freely at any hour. And now it was he who was setting up this wall between them, because he could not share this thing with her.

"How funny it must have been, Robert, that silly wreath hurtling through the air. Tell me how it looked!"

So the garland had not meant as much to Elizabeth as he had believed or that crafty fellow intended. It was like Home to think that such a crude piece of flattery would win her. She had not gone to the Rymers' house to be crowned with his pathetic substitute for laurel or bay, but to hear her brother's voice. Home had not known that. He had spoken in the voice of the Rymers' child. The wreath at least would not be between them.

So he told her how ludicrous it had been, the sight of them all looking up, and the garland so neatly catching the medium across his slack mouth and then plopping to the pavement.

Penini found them laughing together when he came back from his Aunt Arabel's and joined in without knowing why.

That night Elizabeth went early to bed. Robert remained for a long time in the darkening room.

He was thinking of Elizabeth's love and how she had expressed it to him that day and on so many other days. The supreme expression of that love had been in her gift of that wreath of sonnets, which she had slipped into his pocket at the Bagni di Lucca seven years before. What had he given her in return?

There, now, going through the presses, was his *Men and Women,* his crowning work of ten years, and so far he had not even written a line in dedication to her. He must write his own poem to Ba.

On the heels of that thought came another. Was not the best tribute a unique one? Had not Raphael the painter written sonnets to his mistress instead of painting a picture? Had not Dante the poet tried to paint a picture for Beatrice? Well, Robert Browning could paint, play the piano and model heads, but he could do nothing well enough to make a gift worthy of Elizabeth.

His offering would have to be a poem, after all. But for once in that work he would speak in his own voice and not through the lips of other men.

What would he say to her on this July night when his love had grown to maturity? He would write of the private nature of love between two people. He would remind her that every man had two sides to his soul, one to face the world with, and one to show the woman he loved. He would tell her, too, that he still worshipped her, his moon of poets, but more, even more, he loved the human being, with all her weaknesses, who was the wife of his private days and nights. That poem would be his dedication, the giving to her symbolically of all the work of all his married days, the fruit of all he was.

He lit the gas jets. He took a sheet of paper and wrote at the top of the page *"One Word More."* After a pause he added *"To E.B.B."*

When he had finished he knew that he had written perfectly of his love, as she had done of hers. Home's garland lay in the street, crushed by heavy carriage wheels and careless hooves. This one would not wither, but last, like their love, forever.

I shall never, in the years remaining,
Paint you pictures, no, nor carve you statues,
Make you music that should all-express me;
So it seems: I stand on my attainment.
This of verse alone, one life allows me;
Verse and nothing else have I to give you.
Other heights in other lives, God willing—
All the gifts from all the heights, your own, Love! . . .
Pray you, look on these my men and women,
Take and keep my fifty poems finished;
Where my heart lies, let my brain lie also! . . .
God be thanked, the meanest of His creatures
Boasts two soul-sides, one to face the world with,
One to show a woman when he loves her.
This I say of me, but think of you, Love!
This to you—yourself my moon of poets!
Ah, but that's the world's side, there's the wonder,
Thus they see you, praise you, think they know you.
There, in turn I stand with them and praise you,
Out of my own self, I dare to phrase it.
But the best is when I glide from out them,

Cross a step or two of dubious twilight,
Come out on the other side, the novel
Silent silver lights and darks undreamed of,
Where I hush and bless myself with silence.

So there was silence between them, but no quarrel, and no
compromise. Elizabeth saw to it that Robert was not irritated too
often or too much. To Sarianna she wrote, "Spirits are taboo in
this house." She implored Anna Jameson, "Never, never mention
Mr. Home's name. About him, Robert and I are like the lion and
the lamb, and Home is a bone in the lion's throat." It was not
quite fair to Robert. For that lion, bone or no bone, would never
willingly have harmed the lamb. However, it was true that he
was a lion and that the bone came near to choking him.

Events did not make things easier for Robert. Soon exaggerated reports of what had taken place at the Rymers' house
went the rounds. Excited friends innocently spoke of the spirit
hands of Dante which had crowned Elizabeth with a wreath of
orange blossom. As the story grew the details became more precise. Anna Jameson brought them a copy of the *Court Journal*.
Elizabeth did not show it to Robert, but he found it on a chair,
opened it and was faced with a story he did not recognize until he
was halfway through as referring to the incident. Mr. Browning, it
declared, was preserving the wreath "as a memorial of this honour."

He could not relieve his irritation to Elizabeth or to friends
for fear of embarrassing her again. But all his fury blazed out in
a poem of massive vituperation. He called it *Mr. Sludge, the
Medium*. That was one poem of his which Elizabeth would never
see, and for that too he would never forgive Home.

Many, many years in the future *Mr. Sludge, the Medium*
would be printed, and Daniel Dunglas Home would read it. Recog-
nizing himself in Sludge and knowing that everyone else would do
so as well, he would take his small, spiteful revenge. He would
give his version of the séance at Ealing, maintaining that Robert
had left his place at the table and gone to stand behind Elizabeth
in the hope that the spirit hand would place the garland on his
own head.

But by then it would not matter to Robert Browning what
arrows Home directed at him. He could no longer hurt Elizabeth.

28

BY OCTOBER THE TWO VOLUMES OF ROBERT'S *MEN and Women* had been set up in print. Robert and Elizabeth decided to return to Paris and await publication and the verdict of the critics there.

Robert was in no doubt about the quality of his poems. With their appearance the neglect of twenty years would be wiped out. His full stature would be acknowledged. Yet every now and then a cold hand seemed to close about his heart. Then Elizabeth held him steady with her faith in him and her certainty of the brilliant success which was bound to be his in only a matter of days. "I'm ready to die at the stake for them. They'll live forever."

Men and Women was published on November 10, 1855. They waited. A week later a letter came from the publishers Chapman and Hall. Robert opened it nervously, then gave a great crow of triumph. He flung his arms about Elizabeth and she felt his heart thudding with excitement and relief. "The orders from the bookstores were so large they paid the publisher's expenses within three days."

"We'll open a bottle of champagne tonight," Elizabeth exulted.

"Isn't that premature? We haven't seen any reviews yet!" But he had no fear, now.

The reviews were a long time appearing.

Every morning Robert went to Galignani's Reading Room where all the English papers could be seen and looked through them. Nothing. One day he came home more cheerful than usual. "There's a review in the *Oxford and Cambridge Magazine*—by an undergraduate called William Morris."

"Rossetti's friend," Elizabeth remembered.

"It's naive, but aflame with admiration. I'm afraid it'll cut no ice, though."

Then he began to find the reviews. One after another they came out, each one worse than the last. Most damning of all was the *Athenaeum*, since it was so influential. That landed on their doormat, and Robert tore it open, blanched and handed it to her. It began, "Who will not grieve over energy wasted, power misspent, and fancies overhung by the seven veils of obscurity?"

Elizabeth read in silence to the end, then burst out angrily, "Why didn't they give it to someone who could appreciate it? Say, Carlyle or Rossetti or Ruskin? *They* know how great your poetry is, and their voices carry weight."

Then Ruskin's review came out. He complained peevishly that he could not understand the poems, then delivered a patronizing lecture on what poetry should be.

"I expected better from *him*," Elizabeth cried.

Several reviewers charged Robert with advocating illicit love in *The Statue and the Bust,* the poem he had woven around Giovanni da Bologna's statue of Duke Ferdinand on horseback in the Annunziata Piazza in Florence. Had he not blamed the lovers for not consummating their love?

> And the sin I impute to each frustrate ghost
> Is the unlit lamp and the ungirt loin,
> Though the end in sight was a vice, I say.

Elizabeth tried to keep up Robert's spirits. Robert tried to put a brave face on it. His poems were too original, he said. But he was badly hurt, and because he refused to break he tried to fight back. He wrote to his publishers, "The reviews are mostly stupid and spiteful, and contradict each other." He wrote to Ruskin. "I look on my shortcomings sadly and modestly enough. But I shall only feel apprehensive when the public—critics and all—begins to understand and approve of me. A poet's business is with God. He answers only to Him." Worst of all, he wrote again to his publishers. "Don't take to heart the zoological utterances I have stopped my ears against at Galignani's of late. 'Whoo-oo-oo-

oo!' mouths the big monkey. 'Whee-ee-ee-ee!' squeaks the little monkey. I would give the brutes such a dig with my umbrella if I couldn't hold on to my temper and remember how they miss their nuts and gingerbread."

. He still went off every day to Galignani's, to search through all the journals and newspapers spread out on the table. When he came home he did nothing. He did not even read. He had no heart for anything.

Elizabeth wanted to be free to help and comfort him all day long in this most terrible of times for him. Yet she must finish her verse novel *Aurora Leigh*. It must be ready for publication that year, and the Americans had offered her a hundred pounds for simultaneous publication in England and America. They must have eleven thousand words, and there could be no delays. She was unbearably torn. It was not as if *Aurora Leigh* was a light lyric. It was dredged from her very depths. She must be able to give her whole self to it. She *could* not pause to give her days to healing Robert's wounds. If only he would work, himself.

"Won't you revise *Sordello?*" she begged, for she had never lost faith that he could make that poem, which had cost him ten years' work, acceptable to the public one day.

He agreed in a despondent, lackluster way. Soon he put it aside. She was in despair.

Then one morning Nonno turned up on the doorstep without warning. He had a portfolio under his arm and was beaming at her like a child with a present to give.

"I've come to take Robert to the Louvre. Not to see pictures. To draw them. He needs distraction. In the past I used to give him the money to go abroad—to Italy and all about. Twice I did that; and it did the trick. But now he *is* abroad."

Elizabeth was surprised at how willingly Robert went off with his father and amazed at how quickly the cure seemed to work. Robert returned from that first morning's sketching in a happier frame of mind, bearing a copy of the head of the Mona Lisa.

"It's quite startlingly good," she approved. "Bravo, my own!"

The evenings were still bad—long stretches of blankness for him. He was restless, looking for something to fill in the hours to bedtime. Then he called on the British Ambassador, and all at once, it seemed, he had a host of friends and was invited everywhere. The capital was full of interesting English visitors that spring.

She could not go, with her work to be done, and she had a bad cough.

But she was profoundly thankful to see him busy and ap-. parently happy. The worst was over. Soon Robert would work again.

But Robert's cure was neither as speedy nor as complete as Elizabeth imagined. Sometimes when she thought him at the Louvre he was trudging the streets of Paris, hardly raising his eyes, groaning aloud in his bitterness. Often he sat for hours at a café table over a cup of coffee or a glass of wine, his head sunk on his chest, determined not to distract Elizabeth from her work with his suffering. He had given his best and could give no more. Ten years of work were lost—twenty years since *Paracelsus*—and now his revulsion against any further effort at writing poetry was complete. He felt a failure and, worse, that he had betrayed Elizabeth's faith in him. His glorious future, in which he had believed all his life, was in ashes. Now her family could sneer at him with justice. When he thought of that, one of his old terrible headaches smote him.

Now did he give up and live on Ba's money forever? Thousands of Englishmen lived happily on their wives' incomes, which became theirs without restriction on marriage unless the lawyers had tied them up with marriage settlements—"hanging up one's hat," they called it. Precisely because there had been no settlement he had watched every penny, never even bought himself clothes unless she teased him to it, and insisted on Ba's making every major decision. But the male Barretts would never believe that, and now he would never escape the tag of idle fortune hunter. For what, at forty-three years of age, could a failed poet living in Florence with a wife who needed constant care do to earn money at last?

One day, unexpectedly, an answer to his question sprang to Robert's mind. Nonno had pointed the way, perhaps. He could try to become a painter or, better, a sculptor. Story had broken away from his legal chains to work in marble, and only the other day had turned down fifteen hundred pounds for his *Cleopatra*. People paid on the nail, too, for the marbles they commissioned.

He would begin a new career as a sculptor, and Story, good fellow, would help.

It was November, 1856, and the Crimean War was over. Poor Aunt Hedley had lost both Robin and Richard at Sevastopol, but Surtees—Major Cook—was safe for Henrietta. Elizabeth and Robert were back in Florence to await the publication of *Aurora Leigh,* due out almost exactly a year after Robert's *Men and Women.*

Coming back had been like dropping suddenly down a well out of the world; but Elizabeth was glad to be there, sitting in her own green velvet armchair, in her own special corner of the fireside, under Robert's gilt mirror, in her beloved Casa Guidi.

It was exceptionally cold. By the time the first *tramontana* swept the corner of the Via Maggio, Ferdinando had stacks of olivewood and pine logs in the cellar, where poor Flush was buried. The windows were shut close, the fires blazing day and night.

Already the advance payment for *Aurora Leigh* had come. Pen had a new bed. They were furnishing another bedroom and a second drawing room, so that they could raise the rent when letting. Elizabeth had a new wardrobe for her dresses. Best of all, Robert had been able to carpet and furnish his empty dressing room. Now he could work in it—if he ever wrote again.

In her own way Elizabeth was arming herself against what the world might say about the poem into which she had poured so much of herself. Of course she was fearful. Robert had been assailed for immorality because of a line or two in his *The Statue and the Bust,* and she had written a long, long poem, full of really bold and shocking things. Robert was confident for her; as confident as she had been for him. Five months before he had written on a corner of her manuscript the night he had first read it in Paris, "Read this Book, this divine Book—Wednesday night, July 9, 1856—R.B."

November 15, 1856, came at last, and Robert went out at noon, "just to go to the post," and came back all smiles.

"There's not a single copy left in a bookshop in Florence, Ba. They were all sold out as soon as they went on show this morning."

The sales went on and on, in London, in Florence, in America. The first edition sold out within two weeks. It went into a

310

second, then a third. The demand for it was so great that the lending libraries put a limit of two days on loans. It was a sensation. When a mighty post of letters and periodicals reached Florence, Elizabeth sat dazed by it all.

"Look, Robert. Mr. Ruskin has described *Aurora Leigh* as the greatest poem in the English language, unsurpassed by anything in Shakespeare, including the sonnets, and therefore the greatest poem in the language. Isn't that kind?"

"Only the truth, my Ba."

Then she remembered and spat like an angry little cat. "And worth *nothing* from a man who couldn't see any merit in your *Men and Women*."

"Here's something from Swinburne," Robert said. "He calls it a production worthy of the greatest poetess the world ever saw, and he says every reader is aware that he has never read, and will never read, anything comparable to that unique work of daringly feminine—"

"*Feminine!*"

"—daringly feminine and ambitiously impulsive genius. He says, 'It's one of the longest poems in the world, and there's not a dead line in it.' "

Landor had said, "I'm half drunk with it!" Rossetti had been "in a rapture" ever since reading it, unable to do more than exclaim, "Oh, the wonder of it!" In London, he wrote, the first question of the day was, "Have you read *Aurora Leigh?*" Even Queen Victoria had read it and had pronounced it extraordinary. Elizabeth's American publisher had shed tears over the proofs. The shocking passages had only helped, not harmed, the sales. The mothers of England found it shamefully immoral and its language coarse. But their daughters went out and bought it secretly. No woman would admit to a man that she had read it. A number of elderly women complained that they had never felt pure after doing so.

"It's too cruel, Robert that I should have all this, deserved or not, and you, *nothing*. And when you are worth so much more!"

He was gentle, unperturbed, unhurt. "I'm far, far happier than if it had all been for something of mine. Can't you see that? Haven't I always said that you were the genius and I merely the clever person in comparison?"

"Oh, my golden-hearted Robert! I don't know what to say

about the amazing stupidity of the English public. In America you're a power. It's only in England, your own country—oh, if I could tear what you deserve out of the very hearts of our countrymen, I swear I'd do it, Robert."

She flung her arms about his neck and wept with pity, with anger and with love.

At the very bottom of the pile was a large, official-looking letter. Robert slit it open with his ivory paperknife. A lock of white hair fell out of the envelope onto the carpet. The letter was from John Kenyon's executors. His only brother, Edward, had died a fortnight before him. As Edward's fortune was entailed on his brother, John Kenyon had died richer by eighty thousand pounds.

Robert put the letter down.

"It says here that he's left a fortune to us, Ba—five thousand pounds to you, and six and a half thousand to me. We'll never have to worry about money again as long as we live."

For the first time Robert knew what it was like to have money of his own and could spend without a struggle with his conscience. He blessed John Kenyon for his princely delicacy in leaving him the greater share. They would be able to count on more than seven hundred pounds a year from the legacy. Everything their books brought in would be extra, to say nothing of Ba's income.

Elizabeth was determined not to have their way of life changed, declaring, "Two servants, a man and a maid, are enough for us, and we don't need to save anything for Penini, since he'll be well off." But she tried hard to discover what little treats Robert had missed most from their poverty. For ten years he hadn't ridden a horse hard. For the first time he mentioned it, and from then on he rode regularly.

Robert bought presents now, too. On Twelfth Night Florence was always *en fête* for La Befana the Fairy. That year the seven-year-old Penini's stocking was fuller than ever before. There were the usual oranges and sugar rabbits, but there was also a powder flask and a box of tools and a carpenter's bench and a microscope for studying fleas and a knife with twelve blades from Robert, and an accordion to play at the carnival and *Robinson Crusoe* and a silver pencil-case from Elizabeth. One evening Robert took him out to see Stenterello the jester, and again to the opera of the monkeys. He bought new books for the Casa Guidi's library and a supply of gay cravats—even a sky-blue one—for himself. He ordered clothes of softer cloth and better cut and open waistcoats molded to his body.

News came from Henrietta that Mr. Kenyon had left her a hundred pounds and that Mr. Barrett had refused to give the executors her address. Papa, she said, was very angry that he had not been mentioned in the will.

Robert was happier and freed from financial anxiety, but still he was not working. The dressing room that had been turned into a workroom for a writer was now, he said, a studio. He sat and drew there occasionally. He wrote to his publishers for a book on the art of figure drawing. Elizabeth began to feel frightened and guilty. Perhaps if she had been able to devote herself to him in Paris instead of finishing *Aurora Leigh* Robert might not have fallen into such despair about his work.

Soon Robert took over the supervision of Penini's lessons as well as his music. Every morning he heard Penini recite French verbs.

For the rest, Robert strolled about Florence, visited the galleries, and rode. He rode hard and for hours in the hills, pressing on until his powerful chestnut Bravo was in a lather. Sometimes it was late before he mounted the stairs of the Casa Guidi again.

29

IT WAS THE MORNING AFTER CHRISTMAS DAY, 1856, and Elizabeth was in her drawing room arranging scarlet roses in a large bowl of dark green porcelain and thinking how well they looked with Robert's dark glowing furniture, the rich colours of his old pictures and the soft gleam of ancient gilt from chair backs, mirrors and the plaster moldings on the ceilings. A wood fire crackled under the handsome marble chimney piece, under the French gilt mirror and the Ghirlandaio triptych above it of the Eternal Father with one hand upraised in blessing, awaiting Robert's return from the Uffizi Gallery.

As Elizabeth set her bowl of roses on the piano Ferdinando returned with the post and handed her a letter from Henrietta. Elizabeth opened it, and then Penini came in, sat down under the roses and began to play his Beethoven Sonata in E flat. To escape the music Elizabeth went to her bedroom and, sinking on the bed, began to read, a smile on her lips. The smile died quickly, she let the letter fall and sank backwards. The sounds of Wilson shaking up pillows next door, of Ferdinando humming "La Donna e Mobile" in the kitchen, of Penini playing his sonata, came to her as from a great distance. Her eyes were open, fixed on the picture of her father opposite.

Twenty minutes later Robert returned and found her still lying there staring at the picture. The letter was on the floor.

"What is it, Ba? Shall I read this?" She did not answer, and he picked it up. It was a short letter. Mr. Barrett was dead. He had had only a brief illness which neither he nor his family had taken seriously, little more than a rash and a sudden feverishness. He had been within a month of his seventy-second birthday. They had taken him to the family vault at Hope End, his old home, and laid him beside his wife. Henrietta had written so as to spare her sister the shock of a telegraph, she said.

Robert knelt beside Elizabeth. Her eyes looked like a dying animal's. "I know what it is to grieve for a mother," he said softly.

She raised a hand and let it fall, hopelessly. "That was a different thing."

"Yes, a different thing. She loved me, and I blamed myself for not having gone to see her when I could have done so. I hated myself for being lost in my love for you and my happiness in our newborn son, forgetting her when she was ill and lonely. Even that was not a good sorrow, but this grief of yours is wrong. God knows, you've begged and entreated and buried your pride—even when he was cruellest to you and your heart most bitter. He has hurt you beyond bearing, even beyond forgiveness!"

She said, "Leave me. Please leave me."

She did not cry. He drew the curtains and covered her. He sat beside her, holding her hand. Eventually she slept. When she awoke it would be over, he told himself.

She did not get up for dinner or for supper. Wilson undressed her, and she slept alone. Next morning she did not stir from her bed. Next day it was the same, and the next. She lay in bed, day after day, staring at her father's portrait on the wall. She never asked for Penini. Now and then he came in with troubled eyes. For the first time she turned her face away from him.

Robert explained gently to the puzzled child that his Mama's father had died and that she was very sad. Penini remembered how one day he had said to her, "Mama, if you've done something very bad—if you've broken china—you should go to him and say, 'Papa, I'll be good,'" and how they had all laughed. Was she so sad for this angry grandfather of his? he asked, and Robert did not know what to say.

Robert hovered about her, trying to get her to eat, to allow them to open the curtains. After a week he led her into the drawing room, where it was light, and where the life of the household might rouse her. She subsided on the sofa and turned her head away from the light, unwilling to move or speak. She did not even answer Henrietta's letter—she who had scribbled to her sister on the verge of childbirth.

Robert saw her sinking before his eyes into the same morbid death-in-life which had followed her brother's drowning and from which he had rescued her. Her grief seemed to be getting worse. She seemed to want to drive even him away from her, to suffer her bereavement alone. He shook her into speaking to him of it.

For the first time he learned that both her friend Miss Mitford and her dauntless Aunt Hedley had made efforts only the summer before to persuade Mr. Barrett to "forgive" his three children who had dared to marry. They had urged him to treat the rebels in the same way as the others. Mr. Barrett's harsh reaction to his son Alfred's marriage had shocked Aunt Hedley out of her former sympathy for him, but she had come close to being forbidden the house by her brother-in-law. To Miss Mitford, Mr. Barrett had written that he had forgiven his three erring children and prayed that their families would behave well and be prosperous.

It was on the day Henrietta's second letter came that Elizabeth told Robert this. It said that she and Henrietta and Alfred had all three been cut out of Mr. Barrett's will.

This time Elizabeth replied to her sister. She got up from the sofa and went to the desk, and wrote swiftly, reminding Henrietta of her father's words to Miss Mitford: "He prayed for us. Let us hold that fast, beloved Henrietta. Our poor little children had *that* much from him." Then she gave Robert the letter.

"At least, Ba," Robert said, "let *us* be glad that our poor child doesn't need anything from your father, thanks to John Kenyon. Henrietta and Alfred are the real sufferers."

"He didn't *love* us!" she cried out. "I made up my mind long ago that there was no longer any hope on earth that he would give any sign of forgiveness. I tried to arm myself against it. But when it came it was as terrible as if I hadn't expected it. My heart goes walking up and down constantly through that house in Wimpole Street until it's tired, tired."

She went into her bedroom, walking listlessly, and he heard the bell ring in Wilson's room and then Wilson's footsteps approaching the bedroom door.

After a while Elizabeth came out again. She was dressed for

the first time since the news of her father's death had come six weeks before.

She was wearing black. The soft flounces fell to her feet. Her jewellery was jet. The cap on her head was of black net. She was wearing mourning for the man she had not spoken to since their marriage eleven years before. She felt the same love for him at fifty-one as she had done at forty, and at fourteen, and at four years of age. Robert saw her again in memory at Wimpole Street, always in black, like a widow, for her brother.

Anna Jameson came to offer her condolences. She was taken aback by her friend's passionate grieving for her cruel father. *She* did not grieve for her husband. At length, doubtfully, she said, "I wasn't going to tell you, but if that's how you feel—"

"What is it?"

"Fanny Haworth wants to see you. She says she's had a message for you from the spirit world."

"Oh, no." Elizabeth put both hands over her face.

"Will you see her?"

"Why not?"

So Fanny Haworth came and huddled by the fireside with her, talking earnestly and gesturing.

When she had gone, Elizabeth said fiercely, "It's all nonsense. I don't believe in this message."

She didn't tell Robert what it was, but he said, "I'm glad of that."

"Oh, it's not that I don't believe in the spirits, Robert. I do. But not in this message—this vulgarity!"

Yet Fanny Haworth returned, bringing Emelyn Story with her, and then again with Dearest Isa Blagden. Before long the women were coming twice a week, sitting round tables, looking in crystal balls and shuffling cards again. To Robert they seemed more menacing and dangerous than ever. He felt that they were taking advantage of Elizabeth in her vulnerable state.

He feared the women's gathering round her so regularly and so closely, jealously competing for her friendship. Fanny Haworth pouted if she smiled at Dearest Isa. Isa and Emelyn Story bickered with each other for her favours. Even dear sensible Anna Jameson was part of it all now. Ba had taken Lady Byron's place with her.

He particularly feared her new friend, Sophia Eckley. He didn't trust her, and they were growing far too close.

He set himself to woo Elizabeth back to life.

"Will you order one of the new crinolines? They'd suit you to perfection with your tiny waist. In rose colour, I think."

Elizabeth looked at him in astonishment. "I'm in mourning."

"It's time to come out of it. It's May, and five months since your father died."

"Where should I wear it?"

"Out! Your friends are waiting for you."

The crinoline was made, and he took her to Isa's Villa Bricchieri. Isa had invited Mrs. Harriet Beecher Stowe, the author of *Uncle Tom's Cabin,* who had come to settle in Florence. Elizabeth was charmed by the simple, gentle woman in her midforties, wearing a large cross round her neck, who had written the most famous book in the world. When she discovered that Mrs. Stowe had lost her eldest son, Henry, and was a spiritualist they whispered together for a long time. There would be another face at the tables, Robert could see.

Elizabeth even strolled back through the grand avenue of cypresses by the light of the moon, listening while Robert intoned: "Rounder 'twixt the cypresses and rounder,/Perfect till the nightingales applauded!"

But when Isa issued another invitation she said, "It'll be too much for me. You go, Robert. You can tell me all about it afterwards."

Reluctantly, he went, enjoyed the evening, and told her all about it, repeating the jokes, mimicking the visitors, making it all live for her. Then he went again, and to other villas. At least he could bring her amusement by proxy, and it helped him keep up his own spirits.

It became an understood thing in Florence that Mrs. Browning could not always be expected to accompany her husband on these occasions, especially if the weather was cold.

Before long there was the question of how all the hospitality Robert had enjoyed was to be reciprocated. They could not all be entertained at the Casa Guidi—not as Elizabeth felt.

The carnival provided the answer. At the close of the carnival season there was to be a grand ball at the opera house. Robert took a box. Their kind friends could come to supper and enjoy the ball.

All Florence was excited. The wearing of masks had been banned for years by the Austrians, always fearful of the faceless plotter and assassin. Now the ban was lifted. This carnival would be particularly gay.

Pen caught the prevailing excitement. He thought of nothing but the carnival, begging incessantly for a blue domino trimmed with pink. Robert was to have one in black silk so that Elizabeth could make it into a dress afterwards. When Pen asked her what colour hers would be she replied, "Oh, *I* shan't be going *en carnival*. Papa will be host in my place."

When Robert tried to persuade Elizabeth to have a domino made "just in case" she refused firmly, saying, "I should be quite exhausted."

On the day, Penini dressed up in his blue domino and satin mask and went out into the crowds. Wilson could hardly keep up with him as he danced about, hurling confetti and catching the bonbons that were thrown at him. With Orestes in tow, she had her hands full. The Florentines danced in the streets as if they hadn't a care in the world. Penini came home wearing a false nose, blowing a painted wooden whistle and carrying a little green grasshopper in a tiny cage. "The *grilli* brings luck for the whole year," he informed them.

Robert refused supper that evening.

"I'll be eating there, late. Besides Ferdinando's got enough to do, getting everything ready for tonight."

He came out dressed in his domino to show her.

"You look wonderfully handsome, Robert—so dark and sinister, and I like the touch of silver at your temples with the black."

He smiled, and her heart turned over. His teeth were so white against his dark skin. His eyes were so blue. He looked so young, even at forty-five and despite the frosting of his beard. She had always been afraid of what music could do to people, especially at a ball.

"It's a wonderfully warm evening, Ba," he said without hope. "Won't you change your mind?"

"Yes, I will!" She leapt to her feet.

"What will you wear?"

"I'll go out and hire a domino and a mask."

"*You'll* go?"

"Yes. *I'll* go! You can come with me if you want to. I know the very shop."

He threw off his domino and rushed out to hire a carriage.

She was ready, a light shawl about her shoulders, her eyes shining. "I feel happy!"

The shopkeeper was just locking the door, but he opened up again and produced a domino and a mask for her. The domino was a very special one, in silver tissue. It had not been hired because it was so expensive. The black silk mask was very pretty, sprinkled with tiny rhinestones.

"There's something very wicked about this mask, Robert!"

They arrived at the opera house at half-past ten. The Storys, Robert Lytton and Isa Blagden were already there.

"This is my first ball, Robert."

She hung over the edge of the box, gazing at the dancers below, surprised to see the Grand Duke go down among the crowd. The band was playing Chopin's waltzes. "It grows wilder later," Isa promised. "They're not angels, the Florentines."

Elizabeth thought, For once I must go down and dance among the dancers with Robert. She smiled at him and pointed downwards with her fan. He rose at once and took her arm. They had to elbow their way through the crowd, making for the farthest corner of the ballroom. As they went someone struck her on the shoulder and cried, "*Bella mascherina!*"

Bella mascherina. She felt beautiful—under her mask—and knew that Robert found her beautiful, too.

She laughed back into the face of her admirer, glad of her full lips, her fine teeth, her thick curls. Then Robert took her in his arms and they moved slowly around the floor. He guided her so surely that she seemed to float, as if she had been dancing all her life.

"We must do this more often, Ba," he breathed in her ear. "You are made for music."

She was proud of the eyes of her friends on them both.

At eleven o'clock Ferdinando served cold supper in the box, now crowded with their guests. With a flourish he produced his galantines, rolls, sandwiches, cakes, ices and champagne.

Elizabeth spooned her ice and sipped a little champagne from one of the glasses Robert had bought in Venice. She was growing tired. Under the mask her cheeks were warm. The domino suddenly seemed heavy. The next hour seemed like three.

When the Storys went down Robert too excused himself to dance with Isa. Soon the box was empty except for Elizabeth. Isa looked even tinier, down there, so far away, dancing with Robert, a little doll with ink-black hair in a crinoline of peacock blue. Sophie Eckley in a scarlet domino was in Robert Lytton's arms. A clock struck midnight somewhere, and the bells of the city pealed out, the music quickened, and the air was suddenly full of balloons and confetti and *coriandoli,* the tiny discs of coloured paste. The oppression in her chest was growing worse, and she felt terribly alone.

"Ferdinando," she called hoarsely, "get me a carriage, please, and help me to it. Don't say anything to anyone."

She scrawled a note for Robert. "I'm a little tired and have slipped away. You mustn't leave our guests. My love, Ba."

That was my first dance—and my last, she thought.

The carriage had just moved off when Elizabeth heard the noise like distant thunder approaching, and the coachman pulled aside to let the procession of Il Porco, King of Carnival, and his two wives, go by.

Wrapped in her silver domino, Elizabeth leaned forward to stare at the huge, unwieldy figure with the enormous protruding belly, his little legs in red shoes with rosettes astraddle a giant spotted pig, which was being dragged along on a float. Il Porco was dressed in a gorgeous cloak of purple velvet with huge gold stars and brandished a monster flask of chianti in one hand and a platter of food in the other. His gold crown, glittering with coloured glass, was topped by a clown's cap, which reached up to the first-floor windows of the houses. His great blotched red and white face, with its foolish grin, was obscene. His two fat wives came after him, each wearing tinsel crowns and riding on a pig. As they were dragged along the noise of whistles and tin trumpets, wooden rattles and drums, and the screaming and shouting, was deafening. The faces of the men and women were strange, white, elated, their eyes glazed. Most of them were already drunk.

"Il Porco is going to the marketplace to mount his throne, signora," the coachman said, his amber eyes flickering strangely under the flares that lit the scene, and drove off at last to the Casa Guidi.

Robert returned at four o'clock in the morning.

She heard him open her bedroom door and knew that he was standing looking down at her. She heard the rustling as he shed his domino and his clothes. She felt him slip into bed beside her. His hands were on her, his arms about her, his lips on hers. It was as if he had brought the music and the champagne to her again, as if she were still dancing with him, sweeping and turning, as light as air, there among the other happy dancers, in her glittering mask and her silver domino. Then the dancers and the music were gone, and suddenly there was Il Porco, King of Carnality, leering and beckoning to her obscenely, and she was running after him naked in the night in the streets and sobbing because she was afraid she could not keep up with the procession and join the saturnalia in the marketplace.

30

ROBERT WATCHED ELIZABETH'S EFFORTS FROM A distance to keep her family together in Wimpole Street. "I'm still the eldest, the head of the family," she insisted with that gentle obstinacy of hers. "I stand in Papa's place."

Her brothers and sister Arabel wanted to flee from their old home and from each other as far and as fast as they could. First the house was sold. Then Arabel bought one of her own facing London's Paddington Canal, Stormy settled in as a country squire in Shropshire near the Welsh border, Octavius leased a house in the Isle of Wight and George actually gave up his law practice and bought one in Devonshire. Even disinherited Alfred left his Lizzie in Cheltenham and went off on a government mission to China. None of them came to Florence.

Nowadays Robert haunted Story's studio, chipping away at the marble expertly in sculptor's cap, smock and slippers, or drew from the nude at art classes in the Via dei Ginori. Elizabeth had ceased to rebuke him, though he had not written a line since his *Men and Women* had been published two years before. She herself had done no work in the twelve months since *Aurora Leigh* had come out. She had not felt well enough. All through the winter of 1857 and up to the following spring, obeying Robert's urgent commands, she kept to the house, avoiding the *tramontana.*

In June Elizabeth felt a little better, and when she heard that the famous American author Nathaniel Hawthorne and his wife had arrived in Florence, she decided to give a party for them. She was fascinated by his novel on adultery, *The Scarlet Letter,* and Pen loved his *Tanglewood Tales,* which retold the Greek myths in language a child could understand.

She invited two dozen people. Fanny Haworth came, and David and Sophie Eckley, and Mrs. Trollope, and her son Thomas Adolphus and his wife, and William and Emelyn Story, and Mr. and Mrs. Frederick Tennyson and, of course, Isa Blagden.

Elizabeth sat on the sofa looking insubstantial, giving her slender fingers to each new arrival, while Penini, dressed in emerald-green silk with a lace collar over which his golden ringlets fell, moved about among the guests, joining in the conversation in his charming way. One or two of the women passed their hands over his silky hair. He looked more strange and ethereal and more like a boy from a pre-Raphaelite painting or poem than ever.

There was a bustling in the hall, and Ferdinando ushered in Mr. and Mrs. Hawthorne—a bald man in his fifties, with a walrus moustache, and his quiet wife. They had brought their son Julian, a big boy of about Penini's age. His hair was fair, too, but it was almost white, and straight, and cut short. He wore long trousers, a plain jacket and sturdy shoes. He was a raw-boned boy, not at all clever-looking, but likable. Robert could almost feel his boredom at being brought to a tea party where everyone was grownup and dull.

Penini came across the room swiftly and stood smiling before the boy, obviously welcoming him. The boy took a step backwards as if he could not help it. He stared at Penini's hair, his lace collar, his silk blouse. Then he drawled something. Penini blushed scarlet, turned away and went to stand by Dearest Isa.

"Mr. Browning, it's so kind of you to invite us here." Robert realized that Hawthorne was speaking to him and that he must attend to his guests.

Two dozen people were a great many even for the big drawing room in summer. The women had begun to use their fans. Mrs. Trollope, on the sofa beside Elizabeth, was fanning herself so energetically that Elizabeth's curls were being blown across her face.

Penini began to lead the visitors through the dim drawing room and out onto the balcony. They sighed with delight as they stepped onto the lozenge-shaped bricks, which Ferdinando had sluiced with water to cool the air, and smelled the fragrance of the orange trees. The first stars were already out.

"That's the Church of San Felice," Robert heard Penini saying. "Listen. The monks always do a special chant on midsummer's day."

Hawthorne had gone out, and the Eckleys had followed him. Mrs. Trollope's voice rose, destroying the peace.

Ferdinando put the silver tray in front of Elizabeth, then brought in the salvers loaded with the cakes he had made and great bowls of fat strawberries. He lit the candles in the chandelier with a long wax taper. Those on the balcony began to drift in at the sound of silver on china. Penini handed about the strawberries and cakes, avoiding the Hawthorne boy. Nearly everyone had come in, but Robert saw that Hawthorne was not in the room and went to fetch him.

As soon as he reached the balcony Robert saw Hawthorne's back. He was standing talking to Sophie Eckley, and now the chanting was coming full and strong from the glowing windows of the church. Robert waited for a suitable moment to break in.

"It's a very pretty face," Hawthorne was saying, "and he's most intelligent. But I never saw such a boy as that before. He seems at once less childlike and less manly than is right at nine years old."

"He's so like his dear mother, don't you think?" Mrs. Eckley answered swiftly. "As if he was not made of human flesh and blood."

"I wonder what's to become of him?" Hawthorne talked on as if he were thinking aloud. "I shouldn't quite like to be the father of such a boy."

"Poor little Penini! When women marry late in life they often worship their husbands and their children far too much and spoil them."

Robert flung back the window frame against the wall with a crash and came out talking in a loud voice.

When the party was over and they had all gone he called Penini. "What did that boy say to you?"

Penini flushed but answered unflinchingly. "He said, 'What a funny creature you look in those clothes. I bet I can lick you easily.'"

Suddenly Penini swung round to Elizabeth, bawling like a baby.

"Mama, can't I have proper clothes like a boy? I hate these pretty things. I hate them. I hate them. I want trousers and big thick shoes, like other boys."

"You want to look like that great, knobbly thing, Julian Hawthorne, is that it? Oh, Penini, no."

"All boys look like that. Even Italian boys."

Elizabeth knelt before him. "Coarse heavy clothing makes coarse heavy people, my darling. You would soon grow as coarse and crude as poor Julian if you dressed like him."

"I don't care. Besides, Papa wears coarse heavy clothing, and he isn't coarse and crude."

"As for shoes, you'll bless me for it one day. Your feet are perfect. They've never had a chilblain or a corn. I'll never let you wear anything but the beautiful soft leather made in this very city—it would be a crime. Now go to bed, my own, and don't be a foolish boy."

Penini blubbered his way to bed, unconsoled and unconsolable.

Next day Robert went for a ride after dinner.

He put on his corduroy riding breeches, thinking how happy Penini would be to be dressed like him.

"Have a good siesta, Ba. I'm going right up into the hills today. I may be back late."

An hour later he was high above Florence. He had galloped hard on every piece of level ground. He reined in, looking round at the panorama about him.

It was good to be able to ride again. How he had missed it. His poetry had always been full of the sound of hooves, whether in the sweet refrain of a love lyric or in the good galloping beat of *How They Brought the Good News from Ghent to Aix*.

Always, before he had married, he had been able to sweat out his troubles in a good gallop. Well, he had had his gallop, and his troubles were exorcised, for the time being at least. He had got the simpering face of Mrs. Eckley out of his mind, and the tear-stained cheeks of the poor boy, too, and he had beaten down his demon of despair about his own work, and his disappearing hopes of fame.

Well, what if he never wrote another verse as long as he lived? Did it matter?

He had said it all before, long ago, in *The Last Ride Together*. "Fail I alone, in words and deeds?/Why, all men strive, and who succeeds?" The world was full of men whose ambitions had never been realized. And what were the laurels worth to those who wore them?

> There's many a crown for who can reach.
> Ten lines, a statesman's life in each!
> The flag stuck on a heap of bones,
> A soldier's doing! What atones?
> They scratch his name on the Abbey-stones.
> My riding is better, by their leave.

Yes, his riding was better. Even in the far-off days before he had met Ba, when he had written that poem, he had seen what was best in life—not the sour rewards of fame, but the love of two people who were all in all to each other. Wasn't that heaven on earth?

> What if Heaven be that, fair and strong
> At life's best . . .
>   We, fixed so, ever should so abide?
> What if we still ride on, we two,
> With life for ever old yet new,
> Changed not in kind but in degree,
> The instant made eternity—
> And Heaven just prove that I and she
>   Ride, ride together, for ever ride?

So Ba and he, perfect in love, would ride together, through their life. It didn't matter about the spiritualists. It didn't matter about her obsessive grieving for her father. It didn't matter, even, about Penini. Who knew but that she might be right, even there? Perhaps the rest of the world *was* out of step. Perhaps children should be brought up on love, not discipline, should be seduced into learning, not condemned to drudgery, surrounded with beauty and softness and kept away from all things ugly and destructive and bellicose and coarse. Perhaps. Why should he care that his son couldn't lick Julian Hawthorne and that Julian exulted in that unworthy fact?

Ba had had the courage of her convictions, had dared an experiment with her child no other mother had tried. He must not lose heart and fail her. And yet she *was* out of step. The boy must live in the world as it was. It wasn't fair to him to make him into a laughingstock; especially when his boy's heart rebelled against it. He was nine years old. It was high time those ringlets were shorn, high time he dressed like a boy.

So the gallop had not cleared his troubles away, after all. He patted the horse's neck. It was good to own a horse of his own. Expensive but a good goer and stout-hearted—a horse like a friend.

How he loved the smell of leather in the sun and the creaking of the saddle. Pen should love them too. Stormy had given Pen's first cousin Altham a pony, and already he rode to hounds. A horse of his own—that would make Pen feel like a real boy.

He would put this old fellow to the gallop along the ridge-top track once again.

"Hup, Bravo!"

He pulled the horse's head up from the sparse tufts of grass he had found to crop and turned him onto the steep path leading up the hillside for the climb.

About halfway up, the slope on the valley side of the path became steeper. It ended in a sheer drop sixty feet down into the ravine below. It was very steep on the uphill side of the path, too. Stones and some sizable small boulders dislodged from above and falls of earth were strewn here and there across their way as they climbed. There had been a few small landslides here in the past.

It was the animal, with his quicker reactions, which first sensed danger. He was giving a great, high, chesty whinny of fear, rearing on his hind legs, turning sharply inwards, pawing the slippery hillside with his forefeet, before Robert heard, felt or saw anything to warn him. He saw the hillside move upwards past him before he realized what had happened. At the same instant he saw in his mind's eye a clear picture of the precipice behind him and the rocks at its bottom.

He would never know how he came to be clinging to the root, with his mouth and hair full of earth and grit. He could only think, as he spat, and gasped, and struggled blindly for a foothold, that he must somehow, instinctively, have shaken off those deadly stirrups. The old root was gnarled and as thick as a child's arm. It held, but it was just bending, creaking a little under his weight. He could feel that his feet were over the edge of the precipice. He turned his head carefully, first to the left, then to the right. His stomach lurched at the sight of the vertiginous edge.

Using his knees, his elbows, his nails, then his toes and chin, he inched himself from the edge of death upwards to safety. Every movement was a deadly risk, every minute an eternity. Time had stopped. Only life mattered. When at last he heaved himself onto the path, he was shaking with exhaustion, his muscles aching, the gash on his forehead throbbing. He could not stand upright but leant half crouched against a rock.

In the dusk, at last, he clambered down, the chill sweat drying on him. He was swept with the relief, the joy of being alive there on the sun-baked Tuscan hill instead of lying smashed down in the ravine. He wanted to cry aloud, to crack the skies with his laughter.

Then pain struck him as he thought of the terror and the agony at the foot of the cliff and the sweet strength of the horse he must now destroy.

It was after eight. Robert should have been back long ago.

Elizabeth had been growing more and more uneasy for the past two hours as she sat alone in the drawing room. The taste of waiting in dread for the return of a man she loved was in her mouth again. He had said that he would be late.

The sky darkened outside the windows, and the stars came out. Penini wandered in.

"Isn't Papa home yet?"

"Not yet."

"Shall I play to you?"

"No."

"Have you got a headache?"

"A little one."

He went out again, and Ferdinando came in.

"Would you like the curtains drawn, signora?"

"No—and no lights, Ferdinando." She sat on in the dark, thinking of life without Robert.

Suddenly there was a loud knocking on the door. She waited while Ferdinando answered it, unable to rise.

Robert came striding in. "I'm so sorry to be so late, Ba. Why are you sitting in the dark? Ferdinando, lights!"

She ran to him, and he held her while Ferdinando lit the lights over the mantelpiece.

"Robert! You're hurt—bloody!"

His clothes were smeared with mud and blood. There was a deep gash on his forehead and his shirt was torn. One hand was bandaged.

"I fell over a cliff—no, it was nothing. Bravo slipped. I'm quite all right, only my watch is smashed."

He told her how it had happened, matter-of-factly, as if there had been no moment of fear for him, and how he had found a peasant with a gun and gone down again in the dark to put Bravo out of his misery and then had been driven back in an ox cart.

"Papa!" Penini had come in, in his nightgown. He was all eyes and ears.

"Tomorrow I'll see about another mount," Robert said. Then, deliberately, "And about a pony for Pen. He's old enough. I'll make him a present of one."

Penini gave a cry of joy. "Oh, Papa! And we'll ride together?"

"Yes, boy."

He was watching Ba's face. Would she beg him not to ride now, or stop the boy from doing so? Would she? *She* had ridden once, all day, herself.

Her face was strained, but she said: "That will be good for him. He'll look beautiful, riding in the wind, with his golden hair streaming out behind him!"

He stood looking and looking at her.

Dear God. Dear God. Dear Ba. He loved her, and he always would.

31

IN THAT SUMMER AND AUTUMN OF 1858 ITALY BE-
gan stirring to revolution again. King Victor Emmanuel had
been growing impatient to seize a more glittering crown than the
one he wore as King of Sardinia—the crown of a new united Italy
liberated from the Austrians which his father had failed to win.
In Florence only Verdi's music was played in the theaters, with
frequent interruptions of *"Viva Verdi!"* Even Pen knew that the
V-E-R-D-I was made up of the initial letters of *Vittorio Emmanu-
ele Re d'Italia,* and that the King had already signed a "secret"
treaty of alliance with France against Austria.

By January of 1859—a bitter January which froze the fountains in Rome and loosed a cruel *tramontana* round the street
corners in Florence—Victor Emmanuel had told his parliament
that he could no longer be deaf to the cries of grief that were
reaching him from all over Italy.

"That can only mean one thing, Robert," Elizabeth triumphed. "War on Austria now. Louis Napoleon is the only man
on earth who can and will help Italy."

Elizabeth was disappointed with England for hanging back
and making excuses about her old alliance with Austria and
transported with joy for her adopted country. She told Penini
how she and Robert had lived through the Risorgimento of 1848
and 1849 in Florence when all the other foreigners were running
away and of the terrible shaming triumph of the Austrians just
after his birth. She told him, too, of how she had dedicated him

to Italy that day. Penini was afire with it all. "I don't want to be English," he proclaimed. *"Voglio essere Italiano,* I want to be Italian." Together he and his mother awaited the day of Italy's liberation, now that for the second time history was being made under the very windows of the Casa Guidi.

Amidst these mighty events eighty-three-year-old Landor arrived on their doorstep, blackening the air with curses on his wife and sons who had thrown him penniless out of his Fiesole villa. After a few days of him as a guest Elizabeth felt a sneaking sympathy with his family. Luckily Wilson and Ferdinando had just decided to set up a separate household in the Via Nunziatina and agreed to provide board and lodging for the old man. His brothers in England would pay thirty pounds a year for it and support Landor. Robert visited him often.

For the rest the spiritualists still sat round their tables, and Robert still disapproved of their activities and of Mrs. Eckley above all.

Sophie Eckley was growing more and more possessive of Elizabeth, taking her for drives in her carriage almost daily and heaping her with presents. When Elizabeth and Robert made plans to visit Nonno and Sarianna on the French coast Mrs. Eckley began to cry. "Do you mean I shan't see you for two or three months?" she wept, and every day after that brought Elizabeth a parting gift. First it was a ring, then a cameo brooch, then a leather travelling bag, then a pair of Damascus slippers and finally a rosary from the Holy Sepulcher. When in the end Elizabeth decided that she was not up to the journey Mrs. Eckley brought her a prettily wrapped box with the name of the most expensive furriers in Florence stamped on its lid in gold.

Elizabeth tugged at the golden ribbon. In the box was a pair of fur cuffs, dark and lustrous. Mrs. Eckley's adoring eyes were on her.

"It's a most expensive present. I can't accept these. They're beautiful—but no!"

Of course Elizabeth accepted them. Sophie Eckley, she explained to Robert, would have been brokenhearted if she had not. Not content with that, Mrs. Eckley commissioned a portrait of Elizabeth from the artist Gordigiani. She did not seem too pleased when he began one of Robert too.

Mrs. Eckley was claiming that the spirits were making signs

to her almost daily, too. Once when Robert returned from a day at Story's studio to find her sipping tea in the drawing room she drawled at him, "Do you know, Mr. Browning, the spirits told me you were going to have your accident that day you went over the precipice. If I hadn't fallen on my knees and prayed and prayed—for dear Mrs. Browning's sake—you'd be a dead man today."

Robert looked down at his muscular brown hands, which had saved him from death.

"So I owe my Robert to you," Elizabeth breathed.

Alone again with Elizabeth, Robert said, "She's a charlatan."

But Elizabeth declared, "She's the soul of truth. I know her."

They had reached an accommodation about the spiritualists on all other fronts. Robert no longer tore up the spiritualist papers when they arrived, and Elizabeth could even laugh with him when Daniel Dunglas Home the clairvoyant got married, joking, "Just think of the conjugal furniture floating about the room at night!" Complete honesty, together with tact, seemed possible about everything except Mrs. Eckley. Concerning her Elizabeth was deadly serious. She found it frustrating that nothing ever happened to her or to Wilson. There was Sophie Eckley's maid Raffaele spouting Latin and Greek and English and scribbling down wonderful messages from the dead. Not Wilson. Never Wilson. Elizabeth's greatest hope that the veil would be lifted for her remained with Sophie Eckley herself and her miraculous gift for communing with the other world, which seemed to increase with use. Only through her could the agony which had begun in Torquay be relieved.

They all waited impatiently for Italy to be liberated. Then, in April, came the incredible news that Louis Napoleon had agreed to England's proposal that France and Italy should disarm simultaneously and that a congress of five nations should dispose of a powerless and betrayed Italy.

Elizabeth was heartbroken, and retired, physically stricken, to bed. Almost at once, however, Austria sent an ultimatum that Italy must disarm in three days or she would attack. Then Louis Napoleon declared that any such action would be construed as an act of aggression against France. On April 29 Austria declared war on Victor Emmanuel and her troops crossed the Ticino River.

Elizabeth leapt out of bed again, full of joy. Her heart was high as Louis Napoleon began transporting the two hundred thousand Frenchmen he had promised his ally and went valiantly to the front himself to fight side by side with Victor Emmanuel.

On May 12 Louis Napoleon arrived at Genoa, ready to advance. Italian feeling was running high, and that very night the Austrian Grand Duke Leopold drove out of Florence through a large silent crowd. The Florentines still thought him a kind generous fellow. At the Casa Guidi windows Robert and Elizabeth stood beside Father Prout, who had come from Rome to see the end and report it for the *Daily News,* watching the Grand Duke start his journey from the Pitti Palace.

It was only after the Duke had gone that the Florentines learned that he had given orders that if they showed the slightest resistance both fortresses were to fire down on the city and the troops advance along the main thoroughfares in triple file with fixed bayonets, the soldiers nearest the pavements firing at the windows. There had been, in fact, a spurt of resistance, but the officers in the fortresses had refused to carry out their orders.

"He won't be coming back this time," Father Prout said grimly.

"It's all terrible," Elizabeth exploded. "But it's for a glorious end. Soon Italy will be free, thanks to Napoleon, my emperor."

Watching her anxiously, Robert thought that her reactions were too extreme, whether to defeat or victory. In 1848 and 1849 she had thrown herself into the Risorgimento, but she had enjoyed the successful revolutions and the blows had not struck her down. There came back to him from long ago an echo of Dr. Blundell's voice from the dais at Guy's Hospital, saying that with opium eaters every ache was a torment, every unkind word a laceration, every disappointment a disaster. Suddenly he was sure that the extremity of the emotions that racked Elizabeth's frail frame, now raising her to an unhealthy exhilaration and now casting her down into blackest dejection, was a direct result of all the morphine she was taking.

For some time he had noticed Elizabeth's increasing apathy and lack of appetite. Now she refused to go out in the evenings at all, urging him to go without her and bring her the news. He gave way once, and then again, and soon was going to soirées, concerts, receptions, dinners and even a dance at the British Legation, alone. "Do go to Isa's villa or I shall feel a drag on you," she begged, and he knew that to her that was the ultimate horror. So when Pen went to his bed with a candlestick and *The Count of Monte Cristo* translated into Italian she went to hers with *Jane Eyre*. She wrote to Sarianna, "Robert is up at the villa three or four times a week as a bachelor. The women adore him far too much for decency." When he came back he gave her all the news and fond messages from their friends, and she took her twenty-five or thirty drops of laudanum. There were times when, in one of her old moods of jealousy and depression, she berated herself for being too ill and too old to go with him and begged him to marry again when she was dead. But Robert swore such great oaths that he could never remarry that she had to put her hand over his mouth; and it all ended in laughter.

He was well and full of vigour, rising at six even after a late night to stride through the streets and fields, coming back to hack thick slices from the loaf and to gnaw a devilled leg of turkey. Little Annunziata had had to let out his waistband. He rode far up in the hills, too, with Pen thundering behind on the yellow Sardinian pony Robert had given him, growing brown and freckled as a boy should be.

It was a good life, Robert felt, except for his constant anxiety about Elizabeth's health—and the morphine shadow. The sculpting was going well. He was good at it, especially since he had bought a skeleton and begun to study anatomy. It was true that he did not enjoy it as he had done poetry. Yet he was not ready to go back to all that. Perhaps he never would. He had tried, more often than Ba knew, to write again, and turned away, heartsick.

For her part Elizabeth too was content, except for her wretched chest and that other blot. When she realized that three years barren of poetry had gone by for Robert she grew frightened and again rebuked him.

"There's plenty of distraction for you, Robert, but no *Men and Women*—men and women from the outside world instead. Don't get out of the habit of work entirely."

"Later!" he always answered. "Life is for living, too."

French troops came to camp under the elms in the Cascine Gardens. Three men controlled the city, and the name Ricasoli was on every tongue. He seemed to be a sort of dictator.

"Our hopes are about to be realized, Robert," Elizabeth exulted.

Men were pouring in from the unliberated states to join the forces. Funds were being collected for the prosecution of the war, and Robert and Elizabeth gave generously. Pen was told he could have half a paul a day—about threepence—to contribute if he did well with his lessons with his new tutor, the Abbé.

On the first of June, Penini and his mother hung two tri-colour flags over the balcony—one for France and one for the new Italy that was about to be born.

32

ELIZABETH SAT IN HER DRAWING ROOM STARING at the letter, unwilling to think about it. She had arrived only the day before from Rome to find it awaiting her.

She felt as if she was made of paper and that she tore if anyone so much as touched her. She was glad to be back in the Casa Guidi watching the patterns of slatted shadow the June sun cast on the Persian carpet through the half-closed shutters. Robert was out with her son, visiting Landor and Wilson. Landor was giving trouble, and Wilson was behaving in a very peculiar way.

Two years had gone by since the June day in 1859 when she and Pen had hung the two tricolour flags out of the Casa Guidi windows so hopefully. They had had to take them in again almost at once, when the news had come of Louis Napoleon's disgraceful betrayal of Italy, making peace with Austria at Villafranca. That had struck her down, literally, with angina pectoris, and made her ill for many months. Robert had nursed her selflessly, sitting up with her for three weeks, and then taken her to Rome for the winter.

They had not come back to Florence for a year, not until May of 1860. Ever since then she had watched Italy recovering, like herself, from Villafranca, gazing astounded at the heroic follies of Garibaldi, and marvelling at his foolish vow to march on Rome and crown Victor Emmanuel on the Campodoglio— impossible dream! Every day she had opened her eyes only to follow her beloved Italy's fortunes, and it had taken a heavy toll of her.

Everything else had been a weariness, even Pen's lessons. Henrietta had begged her to send Pen to school like her Altham, to be a boy among boys, and Robert wanted that, she knew. But she could not bear to part with their only child and see him broken in a school. Yet the Abbé set him heavy tasks, and now again she spent hours helping him with them. When the sun dropped she went down with it.

She was entirely pleased with her charming boy. True, Pen was small for a boy of twelve, and Robert recognized now that he would never be a musical prodigy or a genius. But he was strong and loving and lovable, golden-hearted and joyous like his father, and he enjoyed beauty in all its forms. He spoke Italian and French and English and had delightful manners. His startling baby beauty had gone, but his round boy's face with its snub nose and gap-toothed grin were so endearing it brought a catch to her heart whenever he smiled. What more could anyone ask? Were not kindness and happiness and understanding the best things in life? Pen was the fruit of love, reared in love to give love and shun coldness and cruelty. They were very close, Pen and she, and closest of all about Italy. He and she spoke of themselves as "we Italians," and it was not entirely in jest. Their hearts were Italian.

Miraculously, by July, 1860, Garibaldi had taken all Sicily. By September he had kept his oath and, incredibly, hailed Victor Emmanuel King of Italy. Then, refusing all reward, he had sailed home to his island. The great, the long-awaited day had come. War was over. Italy was liberated at last. Life would henceforth be all joy.

Then horror, totally unexpected and utterly devastating, had broken over Elizabeth. In August George had written that Henrietta was dying of cancer.

Robert had swept her off to Rome again, to make the waiting for the letter which would tell her that Henrietta was dead less insupportable. The news of her sister's death, after dreadful agony, had followed them to Rome, after being held up by the post office in Florence for a week.

Henrietta's death had been a blow from which she felt she would never recover. It had left an emptiness in her life which nothing else could fill. Before Elizabeth had married she had been closer to Arabel. Since then she and Henrietta had shared Papa's cruelty, their runaway marriages, and, above all, their children. Now Elizabeth would write no more long letters to her sister.

There was only Arabel left to write to. Miss Mitford and Hugh Boyd were dead, and her brothers did not want her letters. Only love, strong as that was, kept her and Arabel together. They were miles apart in politics, in religion, in ways of life, even in belief in the spirits. Everyone else had drifted away.

Stormy had gone back to his illegitimate family in Jamaica, and then had got himself into another scrape. Believing that he had made his children's coloured governess pregnant, he had married her. He was probably the first Jamaican planter to marry a coloured woman. Then when he had discovered that he had been deceived he had banished her to a bungalow on the plantation and never spoke to her.

Then Setty, grossly fat and self-indulgent, was spending like a madman, and more and more Barrett property was being sold to settle his debts. George called Stormy the family fool and Setty the family thief—Setty, the loving yellow-haired little boy who had stayed behind with Papa to comfort him when they had left Hope End, the kind young man who had brought Flush back from Shoreditch.

All her past life in Wimpole Street seemed to have disappeared into the clouds. Treppy alone, at ninety-two, went on the same, only complaining that her spectacles were not as strong as they used to be.

Nothing had gone right for Elizabeth of late. *Poems Before Congress,* her effort to tell the world about Italy's agonies, over which that unsympathetic congress of five powers was to have presided, had been published in the spring, and the critics had torn her to shreds. It had been *Casa Guidi Windows* all over again. Well, it did not matter a jot. *Aurora Leigh* was in its fifth edition, and she had spoken her mind on a serious subject—perhaps for the last time, she was so tired.

She had never cared what the public or the critics thought, or had any ambition for fame. It had always taken her by surprise. If Robert had been the same, he would be a happier man. Robert, her beloved, so determined to be happy and so deeply unhappy underneath it all because he was denying his genius. If only she could help him break into verse again.

In Rome Robert had modelled heads in clay in Story's studio

there during the days, and after a while he had gone out again to theaters, concerts, receptions, soirées, wrestling matches, moonlight drives to the Coliseum—anything! Often he had returned to their quiet apartment near the Spanish Steps at four o'clock in the morning. Of course she had been happy for his pleasure in life. But six years had gone by since the publication of his *Men and Women*.

Now she was afraid, sitting on the sofa there in the Casa Guidi, looking at the patterns the sun made through the green blinds, that the pattern of their lives was set and that Robert would never write again. He would be forever the handsome, popular husband of the famous Mrs. Browning who was seldom seen out in public. There was no longer even the need to earn money to drive him on. His body was strong, but his spirit was tired.

And she? She wondered if there was anything in the world she could find the strength to do, ever again, anything she wanted as passionately as she had always wanted everything before. The question answered itself at once. There was passion enough in her for one last thing. She wanted Robert to have what he deserved and what she was afraid that now he would never get, because the worm had entered into his soul and he could not or would not work anymore.

With her eyes closed she thought of all he was and all he had given to poetry and all that poetry had taken from him. She thought how cruelly a man must sacrifice himself to be a poet. Words and images began to flow into her mind. Automatically she went to sit at the dark little Pembroke table in the middle of the room, opened Sarianna's writing desk which stood on its red leather top, and with the sun touching her hair she wrote slowly and happily.

What was he doing, the great god Pan,
   Down in the reeds by the river?
Spreading ruin and scattering ban,
Splashing and paddling with hoofs of a goat,
And breaking the golden lilies afloat
   With the dragon-fly on the river.

He tore out a reed, the great god Pan,
   From the deep cool bed of the river:
The limpid water turbidly ran,

And the broken lilies a-dying lay,
And the dragon-fly had fled away,
  Ere he brought it out of the river.

High on the shore sat the great god Pan
  While turbidly flowed the river;
And hacked and hewed as a great god can,
With his hard bleak steel at the patient reed,
Till there was not a sign of the leaf indeed
  To prove it fresh from the river.

He cut it short, did the great god Pan,
  (How tall it stood in the river!)
Then drew the pith, like the heart of a man,
Steadily from the outside ring,
And notched the poor dry empty thing
  In holes, as he sat by the river.

"This is the way," laughed the great god Pan,
  (Laughed while he sat by the river),
"The only way, since gods began
To make sweet music, they could succeed."
Then, dropping his mouth to a hole in the reed,
  He blew in power by the river.

Sweet, sweet, sweet, O Pan!
  Piercing sweet by the river!
Blinding sweet, O great god Pan!
The sun on the hill forgot to die,
And the lilies revived, and the dragon-fly
  Came back to dream on the river.

Yet half a beast is the great god Pan,
  To laugh as he sits by the river,
Making a poet out of a man;
The true gods sigh for the cost and pain—
For the reed which grows nevermore again
  As a reed with the reeds in the river.

For two hours Elizabeth worked on her poem, and when she
had set down the last word she knew that she had written her last
lyric, but that it was worthy to be her last. For once thought and
expression had come together flawlessly. There was nothing to
mar this perfect piece.

The poem had been written, but the agony remained. Had it

all been wasted? After all the sacrifice, the dedication, was Robert to be at last no more than a pleasant party-goer, an idle popular fellow, a man frittering his life away?

As she put her poem aside Elizabeth saw the letter she had let fall by her sofa as she had risen—that strange letter from Dearest Isa and Anna Jameson and Fanny Haworth, signed by all three, asking if they might come and see her and Robert, as they had something of the greatest importance to tell them.

There could only be one subject which united those three, who were not as friendly to each other as they were to her, now. It must be to do with the spirits. But why did they want Robert there? She had written to tell them all to call the day after she got back to Florence from Rome, tomorrow morning.

The moment they came into the room she knew she had been right to be afraid. Their eyes did not meet hers, and their faces were strained. Anna Jameson looked particularly distressed, and Isa was biting her lower lip. They all refused coffee.

Robert stood by the hearth. He did not attempt to lighten the atmosphere. Fanny Haworth took the plunge. "It's about Mrs. Eckley. We've something dreadful to tell you."

Was there a fleeting look of triumph in those fine black eyes?

"In short, she's been deceiving you, and all of us, Ba." That was Dearest Isa, trying to get it over quickly.

No one seemed to know what to say next. After a while Anna Jameson gave a little cough. "I'll tell you what has happened." Her voice dragged. "You know Mrs. Eckley's servant girl?"

"Raffaele?"

"It was all a fraud, Ba," Anna soldiered on. "Sophie Eckley has been planting the spirit writings on her, and telling her what to say."

"I *can't* believe it."

"Raffaele told her father confessor what she'd been up to, and he ordered her to admit it all. So she came to us."

Coolly and clearly Anna gave the details of the sordid little cheatings. It was a long list, and to Robert it seemed as pathetic as it was distasteful.

Now, for the first time, he spoke. "What have you done about it, Anna, apart from writing to Ba?"

"We saw Mrs. Eckley," Anna replied.

"All of you?" Robert pursued.

"Yes, I—we thought it best. She broke down and confessed."

"Oh, no!" Elizabeth's last hope was gone.

"We asked her to write a letter to you, Ba, putting it all down, so you'd be in no doubt, and she couldn't withdraw later on," Anna said.

"She did that?" Robert put in.

"Here it is." Anna Jameson was taking one of Mrs. Eckley's small scented envelopes out of her pocket. Elizabeth could not bring herself to take it.

"There's no need to read it now," Robert said, determinedly cheerful. *"Now* let's have some coffee and kneadcakes."

After they had gone Elizabeth read Sophie Eckley's letter and then gave it to Robert. She had admitted it all. The imposture was as old as their friendship. Not only were all the "communications" she had claimed to have received from the spirits pure fabrications, she had been making up the "news" from other mediums with which she had bolstered Elizabeth's hopes. Little Raffaele was only one of her weapons of deceit.

Elizabeth was devastated. "Why do I always have to be the one who is taken in?" she asked bitterly.

"Because you always give the benefit of the doubt to everyone. In these matters that isn't a virtue."

"You warned me, and I didn't listen."

"I'd give my eyes to have been wrong." He meant it, every word of it, before that black unhappiness.

"The worst thing about it," Elizabeth said, "is the *reason* she gives for doing such a thing—to make me love her. Presents and lies! And it worked, I suppose."

Elizabeth's eyes travelled from the bronze inkstand of a lion at a well which Sophie Eckley had forced on Robert to the turquoise brooch she was wearing. She thought of all the toys Penini had been given, the travelling case, the Damascus slippers, the fur cuffs and the rosary from the Holy Sepulcher. For more than two years Sophie Eckley had been her almost daily companion.

"We must send them all back. I can't see her again," Elizabeth said.

"She begs for your forgiveness."

"She's not repentant. She seems to think the reason she gives is sufficient excuse."

"She promises she'll never practice as a medium again," Robert said.

"She hardly could, in Florence, after this, could she?"

Elizabeth was adamant against her, far more so than he, now that she was shown up.

"Look Ba, couldn't you see this experience as sent to show you the truth? Mrs. Eckley doesn't matter, only what you've learnt from her. May I speak cruelly?"

"Truthfully. You're never cruel."

"I'm going to be cruel now."

"Well, then." She straightened to meet it.

"I have, as you say, warned you again and again. She cheated you from the beginning, and I suspected she was telling you lies. I told you she was taking advantage of your innocence. But you wouldn't listen."

"No."

"Now I say, Ba, in the bitterness of this hour, that you deserve it for shutting your eyes and stopping your ears, as you so determinedly did."

"Yes."

"So won't you profit by it and give the whole thing up?"

"Don't ask me now, Robert. I feel broken, destroyed—as if life were not worth living anymore."

As bad as that! Robert did not know what to say. He held her and tried to comfort her. He reminded her of all they had to live for. He even quoted his verses to her.

"Grow old along with me!
The best is yet to be,
The last of life, for which the first was made."

He hoped he had helped her, but he felt far from certain of it. She had taken a bad blow, one of the worst of her life, and she had taken it hard.

To distract her Robert took her to see Wilson and Landor that afternoon.

Wilson was full of her woes. "He accuses the *contadini* of opening his desk, and if he doesn't like his food he dashes the plate on the floor. His mutton went out of the window yesterday."

"He's an old gentleman, Wilson. He's eighty-six years of age."

"The world's full of old gentlemen, sir, who don't behave like that."

Wilson was looking wasted, as if eaten away by an inner fire. Now a strange look came over her face. "I mayn't be able to look after him anymore, in any case. I'm leaving Ferdinando," she said.

"Aren't you happy?" Elizabeth exclaimed, shocked.

"We're too near in blood. These children are the first fruits of the Resurrection." Wilson leaned forward, her eyes blazing. "Last night I saw an angel take Orestes from his bed and carry him past the house."

Robert and Elizabeth slipped in to see the headstrong and quarrelsome old Landor. He was looking as handsome as ever, a black beret on his white hair, his frothy beard immaculate, but he was full of imprecations against Wilson. Listening to him, Robert smiled to recall the beautiful lines from his *Dying Speech of an Old Philosopher.*

I strove with none for none were worth my strife.
Nature I loved, and next to nature, art.
I warmed both hands before the fire of life.
It sinks, and I am ready to depart.

In the carriage Elizabeth could hardly speak of Landor for worrying about Wilson.

"It's religious mania, Ba."

"It's guilt. For her sin in conceiving Orestes out of wedlock. It's been festering all these years. But we must never abandon Wilson."

"Of course not. Or Landor. He was kind to me once when I needed it."

His plan had foundered, Robert thought. He would have to start all over again. What would happen to Wilson if she grew madder? Or to Landor, if she threw him out?

There were always questions about Pen worrying at him, too. He could never get used to the silks and satins Ba dressed him in, or his long hair. He still wanted his son to be an English boy. Pen was growing up with no knowledge of the mighty nation he belonged to, no stirring of the blood for her great heroes, her ancient traditions, her glorious history, no lifting of the heart at the sweet thought of an English spring. Then, too, the Abbé gave bad reports —he was indolent, incapable of self-discipline, could not concentrate, spelled atrociously and did not know a six from a nine in his sums. When Ba was stronger and had recovered from Henrietta's death he would break it to her that her son really must go home to England to school. Mothers, however tender, had to kiss their sons good-bye in the end. But he could not bring more sorrow to that tired little face with the great wounded eyes by tearing her beloved boy from her arms—not yet, and not even for Pen's sake. It must wait. Meanwhile he would continue to do all he could to help him lead the boy's life he craved. At least he was happy with his pony, riding all the hours they let him. Fearlessly, too.

Then there was the matter of the opium nagging at him. It made each blow life struck at her so great he feared the next one would kill her. Henrietta's death had driven her to taking more and more. She must be back to the old forty drops a day. He would cure his darling of that curse again, of course he would.

He took her hand. The tired face framed by the buttercup-yellow bonnet smiled at him—that smile like a sunbeam which the years had never changed—and courage came back to him. Life never stood still. There were always new problems to be faced. He had always been a fighter. He would fight on, for them all.

Robert saw Elizabeth to her room and waited until she fell asleep. Then he went out for his walk about the streets of Florence.

It was hot. He walked slowly, still thinking about Pen, about Wilson, about Landor, about Sophie Eckley. Those little troubles, like gnats, bit at him. Would he ever write again? Was it not time he set up in a studio of his own and sought commissions?

He turned into the Piazza San Lorenzo. He loved the stalls of Florence's markets. He paused by one, heaped with fire irons and dozens of tongs, shovels and skeleton bedsteads. On another were cheap wardrobes, some with their drawers removed and stacked on the ground. On a third were rows of tall slim brass lamps. The stall next to it was heaped with old clothes. That beating sun would make them sweet, no doubt, and from the look of them they needed it.

He stopped again by another stall, covered with a jumble of picture frames, carved angels' heads and bits of woven tapestry. There was a pile of prints and old volumes in the middle. How Nonno would enjoy that stall!

Lying on the top of the books was a square one bound in vellum yellowed with age. He picked it up and flipped it open. It was partly made up of printed pamphlets, and partly of sheets of ancient manuscript, all in Latin. The title page was in manuscript, and a manuscript index had been added. It seemed to be the court record of a triple murder that had shocked Rome in January of 1698—the Franceschini case.

He paid a lira for it—eightpence English money—and walked away, still reading. He paused by the fountain. It was cooler there. Drops of water touched his face as he read.

He turned back, past the fire irons and the toys, past the shovels and bedsteads, the wardrobes, the brass lamps and the cast-off clothing. He was still reading at the Strozzi, at the pillar, at the bridge. This was a story which should be put into verse—a story made for him.

He would create a great poem from what that old book had brought him—his greatest.

He hastened to Elizabeth and put it in her hands. She read it that night—or tried to read it. Sophie Eckley's face kept coming between her and the words. When she could keep her mind on it, the story seemed bizarre and disagreeable. For the first time she found herself unsympathetic towards something which had moved Robert deeply. She put the book on one side.

She could not know that she was turning away from the dawning of that poem of his which would fulfill all her hopes for him and bring him the fame for which he had waited so long.

33

IT WAS THE WORST JUNE ANYONE REMEMBERED, each day hotter than the last. All the foreigners except Isa had fled to the hills. Elizabeth was still languid. One evening Robert raised her from her sofa and led her to the balcony, saying, "We used to walk here so often in the past, Ba. Come and stroll up and down with me again just once."

The balcony was washed in moonlight. The sharp scent of the orange trees rose to her nostrils. Penini's brown rabbit gave a sudden thump with his hind legs, and the green parrot stirred in his sleep in his corner. Elizabeth took two steps, then went back and lay down on the sofa.

"Tomorrow, perhaps. I'm so tired."

The weather grew treacherous, now scorching, now icy cold. The Casa Guidi seemed all draughts. On the third Thursday of the month Isa came to tea at six o'clock. As she arrived Ferdinando threw open the windows, shut against the brazen heat, and the light breeze that awoke at twilight just lifted the muslin curtains. Elizabeth sighed with relief and pulled her chair into the cross draughts from doors and windows.

"Don't do that, Ba," Isa begged. "You'll catch cold."

"I'm stifling," Elizabeth replied. "I must."

Twenty minutes later Robert came in whistling and called, *"Porto subito il té, Ferdinando."* Ferdinando brought in the tea tray and a plate of *ciambellette,* the tiny sweet doughnuts he made so well. Isa noted fondly that Robert sat by Elizabeth on the sofa. Elizabeth poured, but did not fill the third cup. "You're not drinking, Ba?" Robert enquired.

"I think I've a sore throat," she answered.

"Ba, I *warned* you," Isa rebuked her.

After tea, as Robert went off, Isa said, "Robert's looking well."

"In my opinion," Elizabeth said lovingly, "he is infinitely handsomer than when I saw him first sixteen years ago. He's not worn and thin like me."

"You're still in love with him."

"We're one person. Nobody exactly understands him except me."

Isa kissed Elizabeth and slipped away.

Next day Elizabeth woke with a heavy cold. She got up but went back to bed before the morning was over.

"The Casa Guidi's too draughty and too hot and too noisy for you now," Robert said, stroking her hair back from her feverish face. "The Villa Niccolini outside Florence is to let. Shall we take it?"

"Oh, the poor Casa Guidi," Elizabeth smiled. "We've been happy here for fourteen years. Besides, I couldn't bear to leave Florence."

In her mind's eye she saw the sunlit piazzas with the *David* and the *Perseus* and the Neptune and Tacca's comic little bronze boar; the cathedral with its golden doors; the Ponte Vecchio with its load of little shops like treasure chests full of jewellery; the ancient palaces and houses; processions by lantern light and torchlight; dancers in the streets at carnival time; bright market stalls selling singing birds and crickets as well as fruit bursting with juice; slow soft-eyed oxen shouldering each other; young women with Botticelli faces carrying water jars on their heads; quick-smiling men with sensual lips and clever hands; beautiful barefoot children; tall cypresses and the sailing moon in the dark blue sky. She smelled the smell that was composed of centuries of wine lees and cheese, garlic and sawdust, paint and glue and woodsmoke and tobacco and candlegrease and incense. She heard the nightingales singing in the heart of the city which had been built on fields of lilies and named for them—Florence, the flowery city, the beloved place where she had been happy as never before and as nowhere else.

"No," she repeated. "I can't leave Florence. Somehow things have always gone best with me here."

"Well, sleep." Robert drew the curtains.

Elizabeth coughed most of that Friday night and sat up restlessly a good deal. On Saturday morning, as soon as she awoke, without telling Robert, she took a double dose of morphine to stave off the attack she felt was coming on. She seemed better that day, but at ten o'clock at night her chest felt so constricted that she woke Robert and begged him to go out and get her something to relieve the oppression.

Robert knocked at a chemist's and came back with a mustard plaster. Elizabeth bared one breast from the ruffle of her nightdress, and Robert applied it. As the caustic on the pad bit into her flesh Elizabeth drew in her breath sharply, and the locket containing Robert's hair swung against his hand. "I hate doing this," he protested, grimacing.

"It will draw out the evil fluids," Elizabeth said huskily.

Robert sat in a chair by the bed holding her hand, with the lamp turned low. She did not sleep and coughed a good deal, and when midnight struck she was no better. At one o'clock she suddenly sat up, her head back, clutching her chest and gasping for breath. Alarmed, Robert jumped up, called to Annunziata to stay with her mistress, threw on his clothes and ran out into the night. Dr. Griffiths was the best chest specialist in Florence. He would be able to help Ba.

Standing outside the doctor's close-shuttered house Robert felt a sudden intense loneliness, as if he were the only man left alive in Florence. His blows on the knocker echoed with shocking loudness down the dark silent street. At last a manservant unbarred the door, and soon afterwards the tall thin Dr. Griffiths, in frock coat and top hat and carrying his black bag, was striding silently beside him to the Casa Guidi.

They found Elizabeth still labouring for breath. Robert felt himself straining with her in sympathy. Dr. Griffiths examined her, and said, "The right lung is congested. I think there's an abscess on it. I recommend a sinapism."

He wrote out a prescription for the cruel blisters. As soon as the porter returned with them he applied one to Elizabeth's breast and another to her back and ordered Annunziata to bathe her feet in hot water.

By then it was half-past two. Dr. Griffiths sat with Robert in the drawing room, arms crossed, silently waiting. Now and then he went in to see Elizabeth. An hour and a half went by, with her distress unabated. Then at last she began to breathe a little more easily. At five o'clock in the morning she was so much better that the doctor sent Annunziata to bed and went home himself.

"The crisis is over," he said. "I'll come again later."

Robert could draw no more from him, and he was torn between relief and doubt. Two exhausting nights without a minute's sleep must have taxed Elizabeth's strength severely.

On Sunday morning Elizabeth was very tired, but she said, "None of the doctors have ever understood my case. Dr. Chambers said it was my left lung. Now Dr. Griffiths says it's the right one. It's only another of my old attacks. I was much worse after Villafranca."

She told Dr. Griffiths about her medical history and the feats she had performed with her damaged lungs, and he said, pinching his underlip, "Your wife may be a law unto herself, Mr. Browning. Still, it will take a long time for her to recover. Plenty of nourishment is the thing."

"She won't eat," Robert complained, and told him about the morphine.

"It will help her. And give her chicken broth at frequent intervals."

The doctor came every day, and each time he said Elizabeth was a little better. To Robert she seemed neither better nor worse. Every morning Annunziata dressed her in a fresh lacy nightdress and her little garnet-coloured satin slippers, and Robert carried her into the drawing room. There she sat on the crimson velvet sofa by the hearth, idly turning the pages of the newspapers. Now and then Pen came in to play for her on the piano or nuzzled into her lap, murmuring, "Get well, *piccola mama*." At about seven o'clock Robert carried her back to bed. He insisted on sitting up all night, only lying down beside her once or twice in the small hours.

By Wednesday, however, after four nights of anxiety, the strain was telling on him. He brought a small bed into the drawing room for her and stretched out on the sofa himself.

That night Robert noticed that Elizabeth was beginning to doze a good deal, but restlessly. Sometimes he thought that she was not quite aware of what was going on around her. When he reported this development, Dr. Griffiths began to call twice a day. But he still said only, "She's a little better."

On Thursday Elizabeth was as cheerful as ever, though her voice was almost inaudible as she insisted, "It's nothing." She still refused to take more than a sip or two of Ferdinando's chicken broth, so Dr. Griffiths recommended asses' milk. She drank it and had a better night. Robert noticed that her feet were a little swollen. But she seemed better, and when Wilson called Elizabeth talked to her about her two sons, Orestes and Pilades, and the truculent Mr. Landor.

"You're getting well, madam," Wilson beamed, then suddenly announced that the end of the world had been fixed for September.

"Not on our fifteenth wedding anniversary, please," Elizabeth joked, and Wilson answered, "I hope not, madam, but it's not for me to say."

Isa came that night, too, and watched Elizabeth drink her asses' milk.

"I've been a mere rag of a Ba," Elizabeth said, "but that's all over now."

Robert noticed as he poured her medicine that her great dark eyes seemed larger and blacker than ever, and her face smaller and whiter, and he pushed Isa out, whispering, "No more talking. Please go, Isa."

When Pen came in to say good night he asked his mother, "Are you really better, *mama mia?*" and she answered serenely, "Yes, truly, *mio amore.*"

Finally, Dr. Griffiths came in for his last visit of the day, and Robert asked him, "What's your opinion now, doctor?"

"Oh, decidedly better," he answered confidently.

For the first time Robert felt cheerful. He had been worrying unduly. Elizabeth had been seriously ill for a whole week, but at last the corner was turned and she was truly on the mend.

On Friday Robert was even happier. Elizabeth was much stronger, coughed very little, and at night she drank all her asses' milk, sipped chicken broth twice and even ate a little bread and butter. Dr. Griffiths ordered a strong chicken jelly to be put on ice for her.

Robert did not go to bed at all, but sat up beside her or dozed with his feet up on another chair. He was worried at her uneven sleep. Whenever he opened his eyes, in the dim golden glow of the candles he could see that she was awake or restless, but when he spoke to her she smiled and insisted that she was better.

At three o'clock in the morning Robert woke up from a short doze to see the bedclothes slipping to the floor, tossed aside by her movements. He rearranged them and found her hands as cold as ice. He slipped his hands down to feel her feet. They were icy, too. He shook her. She said, "You did right not to wait . . . what a fine ship . . . see its white sails . . ." He realized that her thoughts were wandering and felt frightened. He tiptoed to the door and left the flat to waken the porter and send him for Dr. Griffiths.

When he came back again he woke Annunziata and ordered her to bring a basin of hot water and warm up some chicken broth.

He raised Elizabeth very carefully and made her sit on the edge of the bed with her feet in the basin, holding her with his arm about her.

"Well, you *are* making a fuss about nothing!" She was almost laughing. He bathed her hands with the hot water and tried to make her drink the broth. She could not raise the cup to her lips, and he fed it to her teaspoonful by teaspoonful. He brought her a second cupful, and she took it all. He sponged her hands again, put the cup and spoon away and sat on the bed beside her, still holding her in his arms. She leaned against him, so light he hardly knew she was there—so light and so limp. Too limp, surely? She seemed about to fall asleep, and he asked her, anxiously, "Ba? Do you know me?"

She opened her eyes and, with an effort, reached up to put her arms about his neck and kissed him tenderly. In her ghost of a voice she said: "Know you? My Robert—my heaven, my beloved!"

Then she whispered, her arms still clasped about him, "God bless you."

He could not bear to let her go. But he laid her back gently on the pillows. She was still pursing her lips and making little kisses in the air.

"How do you feel?" he asked softly, looking down at her face.

She opened her eyes again and saw the love in his.

"Feel? Beautiful!" she sighed, and her lashes fell.

Suddenly terror invaded him. He felt she must be raised again and, grasping her in his arms once more, lifted her up. He felt her struggling to cough, the spasm shaking her, tearing her to pieces. Then she was still. There was no pain and no sigh. Her head fell quietly against his cheek. For a moment he thought she might have fainted. Then he saw a tremor pass across her face, the least knitting of the brows, and at that moment Annunziata cried from the doorway, *"Quest' anima benedetta é passata!* The blessed soul has gone to heaven!"

He laid her back on the pillows and stood gazing numbly down on her, unable to grasp what his mind told him was so. She lay there like a little child, slight and innocent, her face smoothed of every shadow—a face like a girl's.

"How perfectly beautiful she looks now," he whispered.

At that instant all the sixteen years they had shared seemed to pass across his mind like birds flying silently across a pure sky. Those years had been his real life. Nothing that had come before mattered at all; and the pain of living another hour was dreadful to him.

Yet from the beginning he had been aware of the fragile nature of their happiness. Ever since that summer's day when he and Elizabeth had looked into each other's eyes for the first time in that dark room in Wimpole Street he and she had been walking towards this moment when he stood alone beside his dead love.

Epilogue

ROBERT BROWNING LEFT FLORENCE IMMEDIATELY
after his wife's death, never to return. With a Penini shorn of his
curls and wearing long trousers he settled near Arabel's London
house.

Ironically, the success so long denied him came almost at
once. By 1863, two years after Elizabeth's death, he was writing
steadily again; by 1868 a six-volume edition of his works had
been published; and by 1869, with the appearance of the poem
based on the old manuscript he had found in Florence's marketplace, his fame was secure. The *Athenaeum,* which had snubbed
even his *Paracelsus* thirty-four years before, wrote: "We must record at once our conviction, not merely that *The Ring and the
Book* is beyond all parallel the supreme poetical achievement of
our time, but that it is the most precious and profound spiritual
treasure that England has produced since the days of Shakespeare."
The years that followed saw honours heaped on the poet and a
lionization which culminated in 1881 in the formation of the
Browning Society, which encouraged the reading of his poetry,
ended the legend of his unintelligibility and greatly increased his
sales.

Pen proved a sad disappointment to his father, growing into
an extravagant, lazy and pretentious youth. Before he was nineteen, it seems, he had fathered two illegitimate daughters by different peasant girls in Brittany, France, and he had to leave
Oxford University because he could not pass his examinations.

At twenty-five he decided to become a painter and achieved some success, whereupon his father made strenuous efforts to further the sales of his enormous canvases among his friends. Robert was delighted, too, when the rather unprepossessing Pen (by then thirty-eight and a short, bald, almost spherical, man) persuaded an American heiress, Fannie Coddington, to marry him. They bought one of the most imposing palaces in Italy, the Palazzo Rezzonico in Venice, and settled there with Ferdinando, Wilson and a large menagerie which included pythons, a monkey and a host of shrieking cockatoos. In it Penini restored a desecrated chapel in his mother's honour. The marriage proved childless and unhappy, and after four years Fannie left her husband to become a nun.

Long before then, in June, 1866, Nonno had died in Paris at the age of eighty-five, leaving Sarianna free to look after her brother and travel with him on holiday. On June 19, 1863, Arabel had had a dream, recorded in his diary by Robert, in which she had seen Elizabeth and asked her, "When shall I be with you?" Elizabeth had replied, "Dearest, in five years." When Arabel died in Robert's arms a month after the five years had expired, on July 21, 1868, Robert noted, "Only a coincidence, but noticeable."

Robert remained true to Elizabeth until his own death. In 1868 Lady Ashburton, an immensely rich and very beautiful widow, apparently proposed marriage to him. His blunt reply, that his heart was buried in Florence and that the only advantage the marriage could have for him would be the benefits Pen might gain from it, made the lady so angry that she vilified him everywhere and never forgave him. He was content to do his best by Elizabeth's son, living quietly in London with the beautiful bust of her which his friend Story made for him after her death, the painting of the salon at the Casa Guidi as it was in 1861, which he had commissioned George Mignaty to paint for him, the furniture he had bought in Florence, and all Nonno's books.

On December 12, 1889, twenty-eight years after Elizabeth's death, Robert died at the age of seventy-seven at the Palazzo Rezzonico. Sarianna was to outlive him by fourteen years and die at nearly ninety; and his son would die at only sixty-three in 1912, in Asolo, near Venice, in debt.

Long after Elizabeth's death Robert had written to her brother George that he would like his remains to lie beside hers in Florence if that caused no trouble to his survivors, though he regarded his body as only the old clothes of the soul. He added, "It is no matter, however," for he was convinced he would see his love again.

Fear death?—
. . . the element's rage, the fiend-voices that rave,
   Shall dwindle, shall blend,
Shall change, shall become first a peace, then a joy,
   Then a light, then thy breast,
O thou soul of my soul! I shall clasp thee again,
   And with God be the rest!

The cemetery in Florence had been closed, and an Act of Parliament would have been needed to allow Robert to lie beside his Ba. So he was buried on the last day of the year in Poet's Corner in Westminster Abbey, just below Chaucer's tomb and close to Spenser's. They had, after all, "scratched his name on the Abbey-stones."

Before his death Robert had handed his son an inlaid box containing all the love letters which had passed between him and Elizabeth during their Wimpole Street courtship, saying, "Do with them what you like." To his eternal honour, and the fury of his Barrett relations, Penini gave them to the world.

BIBLIOGRAPHY

BIOGRAPHIES AND GENERAL

Burdett, Osbert, *The Brownings*. Constable, 1928.
Griffin, W. Hall, and Minchin, H. C., *The Life of Robert Browning*. Methuen, 1910.
Hewlett, Dorothy, *Elizabeth Barrett Browning: A Life*. Cassell, 1953.
Marks, Jeannette, *The Family of the Barrett*. Macmillan, 1938.
Miller, Betty, *Robert Browning: A Portrait*. Murray, 1952.
Orr, Mrs. Sutherland, *Life and Letters of Robert Browning*, ed. by Frederic G. Kenyon. Murray, 1908.
Taplin, Gardner B., *The Life of Elizabeth Barrett Browning*. Murray, 1957.
Ward, Maisie, *Robert Browning and His World*, 2 vols. Cassell, 1967 & 1969.
Winwar, Frances, *The Immortal Lovers*. Hamish Hamilton, 1950.

LETTERS, ETC.

Dearest Isa: Robert Browning's Letters to Isabella Blagden, ed. by Edward C. McAleer. Nelson, 1952.
Elizabeth Barrett Browning: Letters to Her Sister, 1846–1859, ed. by Leonard Huxley. Murray, 1929.
Elizabeth Barrett Browning's Letters to Mrs. David Ogilvy, ed. by Peter N. Heydon and Philip Kelley. Murray, 1975.
Elizabeth Barrett to Miss Mitford, ed. by Betty Miller. Murray, 1954.
From Robert and Elizabeth Browning: A Further Selection of the Barrett-Browning Family Correspondence, ed. by William Rose Benet. Murray, 1936.

Letters of Robert Browning: Collected by Thomas J. Wise, ed. by Thurman L. Hood. Murray, 1933.
New Letters of Robert Browning, ed. by William Clyde de Vane and Kenneth Leslie Knickerbocker. Murray, 1951.
The Barretts at Hope End, ed. by Elizabeth Berridge. Murray, 1974.
The Letters of Elizabeth Barrett Browning, ed. with biographical additions by Frederic G. Kenyon. Smith Elder, 1897.
The Letters of Robert Browning and Elizabeth Barrett Barrett. Smith Elder, 1899.

MEMOIRS

Home, Daniel Dunglas, *Incidents in My Life.* Longmans, 1871.
MacPherson, Gerardine, *Memoirs of the Life of Anna Jameson.* Longmans Green, 1878.